YEN

GUY STANLEY

POCKET
BOOKS

LONDON · SYDNEY · NEW YORK · TOKYO · SINGAPORE · TORONTO

First published in Great Britain by Pocket Books, 1994
An imprint of Simon & Schuster Ltd
A Paramount Communications Company

Simon & Schuster Ltd
West Garden Place
Kendal Street
London W2 2AQ

Simon & Schuster of Australia Pty Ltd
Sydney

A CIP catalogue record for this book
is available from the British library.

ISBN 0–671–85288–4

Typeset in Sabon 10.5/12.5 by
Hewer Text Composition Services, Edinburgh
Printed in Great Britain by
Harper Collins Manufacturing, Glasgow

For My Sons
Gordon, Jeff and Adam

I wish to give my special thanks for
their valuable help and advice to
Phil Attwood, Sue Townrow and Mike Janes

PROLOGUE

16 September, 1992 – London

The Chancellor of the Exchequer stared lugubriously from the broad television screen. It hung in a steel frame above the two hundred and forty dealers arranged in rows at identical desks in Sternberg Chance's football field of a treasury department. He was brushing aside an insistent Press pack outside number eleven Downing Street, his official residence. He managed a weak smile before slipping gratefully into a car and speeding quickly away.

Then the Prime Minister came on the screen, a disarming smile masking the severity of his comments. The watching dealers, those who were not trading, turned away when they saw it was a week-old piece of file film. The Prime Minister was reaffirming his government's commitment to keeping the pound sterling within stipulated bands in the European Exchange Rate Mechanism. For months it had been the sick currency of Europe, bumping along a floor and threatening to crash through it, pushed by the power of the Deutschmark at the top.

'We'll take whatever measures necessary, bear whatever pain,' the Prime Minister intoned in his nasal whine. 'We are committed to Europe and the ERM.'

'Like the captain of the Titanic,' quipped someone in the dealing room.

'Does that mean higher interest rates?' a reporter's voice rose above the noise from the others.

'I said "any measure",' the Prime Minister repeated.

An intense woman spoke as the voices subsided. 'Britain's already in deep recession,' she reminded him. 'The reason the pound's weak is because German interest rates are moving up because they've had to borrow so much money to finance reunification. That strengthens the mark and pushes sterling down.'

'Is there a question in there somewhere?' the Prime Minister said irritably, as the journalists erupted again.

Nigel Simpson threw a 'what does he know?' glance at Kevin Nicholls who had half an eye on the flaying arms, the tense faces and the patches of sweat on ruffled shirts. 'I wonder what the PM'd say if he could see this today.'

Simpson was a short man with prematurely receding, mousey hair stretched over a dome of a head. He looked more like a harried bank clerk than the man responsible for a team which bought and sold twenty billion dollars worth of foreign currency every single business day. Nicholls was on home-leave from his job as Simpson's equivalent in Sternberg Chance's Hong Kong branch but now he was another hand at the pump on what was to be the most momentous day in financial history for the British currency. Tony Moore ambled in to join them, the pain in his hip and left side temporarily replaced by the exhilaration all dealers felt when they were in the midst of mega-dealing action.

'The world and his mother are short of sterling,' he said as an unreal stillness fell on the dealers. The two hours between seven and nine that morning had seen the most intense bout of concentrated trading they had ever known. They all knew the next move in the game belonged to the Chancellor.

A tall man in a City pinstripe walked behind the dealers and their built-in terminals where screens of multi-coloured charts and graphs constantly blipped and changed. Few of the dealers, had they had time to turn their heads from the telephones, would have identified Gervase Prideaux, board director of the bank and head of the global treasury division. Prideaux had been drawn from his office in the management suite by the crisis which was about to ram another nail into the coffin of European unity. The pound sterling was being crushed in the financial market as the players – the banks, multi-nationals, fund managers and individual, secretive speculators – bought every other currency against it.

'He's drained the country's foreign exchange reserves. He's going to have to raise interest rates now,' Prideaux said authoritatively as a shot of the Chancellor of the Exchequer appeared on the screen. The three senior dealers he joined, all barely thirty, were hardly aware of his comment. They were watching a television reporter standing in front of a mobile camera, flanked with high-powered lights, arranged near the edge of a line of desks. A slender woman in jeans dabbed his brow as the reporter checked a microphone attached to his tie. On a cue from a man with headphones and trailing cables, he straightened and, seconds after his image had appeared on the giant television, began to speak.

'Who is it today?' Prideaux asked, with a touch of annoyance.

'Independent,' Simpson said. 'The networks have been in every day for a week, either for a "live" transmission or for a few recorded news bytes.'

Sternberg Chance's senior economist Andrew Cole, an intense, bearded Yorkshireman, waited nervously while the reporter finished his breathless preamble and the camera panned around the trading floor.

His anxieties uncontrollable, Prideaux drew Simpson

aside, and said, 'If the Chancellor raises rates, what does that mean to us? Are we exposed?'

Hiding his impatience behind a comforting smile, Simpson led his chief to a console in his glass-panelled office and tapped the keyboard. In these tense times he was not disposed to remind Prideaux, who he believed lacked comprehension, perception and balls, that in the three years since Sternberg geared its personnel and technology to join the world's top ten foreign exchange trading banks he, Simpson, had delivered a hundred million pounds in net profit to the bottom line. There had been bad days, even whole months, when things did not go right, but the overall results had been exceptional. He answered calmly.

'I don't always run with the pack. I prefer to lead it. But there are fifty thousand players out there, and I mean the world, in the banks and every other institution with foreign currency holdings, and not one of them believes sterling can hold up.' He threw a hand towards the senior economist, now in full verbal flight on the trading floor and on the television screen. 'Andy's telling the world that the UK's got three million unemployed, falling sales, dead exports. We have a full-blown recession and the only people who don't recognize it are the Prime Minister and his Chancellor. Christ! We shouldn't even have interest rates where they are now at ten per cent base. They're six in the States and three in Japan. All we're doing is helping Germany keep its inflation down as it borrows like hell to finance reunification. Now it's payback. Where's Helmut and the Bundesbank with the support the ERM's supposed to give us? If we put interest rates up any more you can wave goodbye to economic recovery for a generation.'

'But the Chancellor has to act, doesn't he?' Prideaux insisted.

'Correct. Sterling's bouncing along the bottom of its permitted lower band at two marks seventy-eight pfennigs. It's already marginally out of the band, and according to the rules of the ERM the government has to intervene to keep its value within the effective range. The Germans are refusing to lower their rates so it's up to our Chancellor to prop the mark up from the bottom.'

'But this is ridiculous.' Prideaux said grimly. 'Are you saying everybody's short of sterling? Where does it leave Sternberg if he puts up interest rates?' He gave an ironic scoff and added. 'And our jobs?'

Simpson ran a finger down a column of figures on his position control screen. 'We're short of one and a half billion pounds, long of marks. That's in both my products, spot foreign exchange and options. If rates go up and sterling rises a couple of pfennigs it'll cost me ten, eleven million pounds to cover my short position.'

'Jesus!' Prideaux hissed, twisting away.

There was a shout, a sudden piercing outburst from a dealer clutching two telephones and listening to the commotion feeding through a voice box. 'Base rate's up,' he called. 'Two per cent.' Seconds later the message appeared on every Reuters, Knight Ridder and Telerate screen in the room.

Simpson joined Nicholls and Moore at vacant dealing desks as telephone lamps on the multi-line consoles blinked in unison.

'Where's sterling?' dealers bellowed at the brokers and each other.

'The sonofabitch did it,' Moore said, disbelief in the drawn out traces of a soft mid-Atlantic accent. 'He pulled the fucking pin.'

The economist interrupted his live interview and with astonishment announced the British Chancellor's dramatic move. The camera raked the room, where the scramble for information was being replaced by a curious puzzlement.

'What's happening?' Prideaux asked.

Simpson shook his head. He looked drained, his shadowed eyes betraying his thirty hours in the building broken only by a four-hour nap on an office couch. His shirt was damp, his trousers crumpled and uncomfortable.

'Sterling's not moved,' he muttered increduously. 'Look at the prices, the graph. It should've shot up. Nobody wants sterling.'

A voice came across the desks. 'Sterling mark in a hundred pounds.' He gave the name of a German bank and directed the request at Simpson. None of the dealers knew what to quote in these unprecedented, totally abnormal conditions, especially for a hundred million pound deal.

Simpson had seconds to analyse the variables.

'Tell me what's happening,' Prideaux demanded, but Kevin Nicholls restrained him gently with an arm.

The Chancellor's blown it. The thought raced through Simpson's mind and he jumped to his feet. Voices from the foreign exchange brokers' offices crackled through the voice amplifiers. 'Quote him,' he ordered. 'But mark sterling down. It's forty-fifty at the moment. That goes for all of you. Quote sterling lower.' He turned to Prideaux. 'It's unbelievable. Nobody rushed to buy sterling, even with base rates at twelve per cent.'

The interview finished, Andy Cole roamed the dealing room, looking for reasons why nobody wanted to invest in the British currency.

'The market's talking,' Simpson said. 'The government's ignored us before at their cost. If they do it now they're bigger fools than they appear.'

The foreign exchange market went on speaking, even more contemptuously, selling sterling in one, two million pounds lots until it nudged against the lower band again. Sternberg Chance bought it from customers but when it had built a twenty five million holding the dealers sold it through the brokers. The Bank of England was visibly active all morning, buying sterling, trying with grim, futile determination to hold its value up.

In the middle of the afternoon the government fired a last, desperate shot. It was a devastating move, but the shell was a blank.

'Another three per cent on base rate,' the dealers read, drained and inured to shock.

When Simpson's heartbeat slowed, he smiled in sad triumph. In a four-hour violent death rattle, the country's base interest rate changed more than it normally would in a decade. It was now fifteen per cent and should have sent the market into a frenzy of sterling buying as investors around the world scrambled to profit from the huge differential between British interest rates and those in Germany, the US and Japan. But the room was silent, even the brokers' voices muted. A few telephone lights flashed but the callers quickly gave up. Dealers stood and stretched, others looked bemused.

Suddenly the room erupted again in noise and gesticulations. Orders from Simpson sent traders back to their desks and brought others running from the toilet and drinks machine. Sterling had managed to blip up a fraction against the mark, as some short position holders were scared into covering them, but then it collapsed, first in tentative half mark clips, then in an avalanche, two, three marks on each new deal. The end of the trading day in Europe brought merciful relief but the selling continued in New York and into the following days, finally sinking sterling to a humiliating level fifteen per cent lower than the government had tried recklessly and expensively to defend.

The Exchange Rate Mechanism was dead. The British government admitted defeat by cutting the interest rates it had stubbornly believed was the weapon to crush the speculators. The dealers were drained, but elated. They had never earned so much in a single trading session. Simpson forbade his staff, on pain of dismissal, to speak to the Press who were searching the City's bars for loose-tongued dealers. The market participants had made billions from sterling's collapse, and buried in the 1992 accounts of Sternberg Chance would be the forty-five million pounds earned in a single day in September.

1

May 1993 – Tokyo

An attendant with a solemn, sallow face placed an opened urn beside the skull and withdrew a pace. The bones had cooled, but the moderated heat during incineration ensured that they had not pulverised completely but formed a brittle but distinct human skeleton.

'We should follow the proper custom,' the older Japanese said, his thick, purple lips opening into a wry smile. 'Even for him.' He handed his companion a single chopstick, and holding the other himself guided the pair into a pincer towards a piece of bone which had broken off the shoulder blade. Deftly they lifted the fragile fragment and placed it in the urn. The gaping mouth in the skull seemed to scream at them as they directed the chopsticks to the thread of vertibrae below it. Prominent and solid-looking among these gruesome remains lay the Adam's apple, the solemn objective of this timeless Buddhist ritual resembling, so the symbolism claimed, the squat image of the Buddha. A trail of powdery ash floated off their chopsticks as they eased it into the urn.

'Will that be all?' the attendant asked with a reverential hiss, a narrow, short-handled shovel hidden behind him, ready to scoop the remains into the urn and pummel them into powder.

The heavier of the two grunted a reply. He was sweating nervously, his glasses slipping on his greasy nose. They were about to leave and wait outside for the urn to be presented to them in its formal white linen wrapping when the older man noticed it. He dragged a chopstick

9

through the ridges of ash which formed a webbed hand. It had kept its shape in the fire but its natural burnish was now a dull, mottled grey. The man speared it and weighed it in his palm. 'It would have been regrettable to overlook the ring,' he said apologetically. 'His family must have it to remind them of their loved one.'

The air was stagnant and noisome beneath the cross pattern of overhead expressways in this densely built-up part of downtown Tokyo. They crossed a shadowed bridge over an oily black canal edged with garbage and rotting logs. The taller man rested his hands on the guardrail and swung his head casually sideways. When he was sure he was unobserved he took the ring from his pocket, looked at it once, and tossed it into the fetid water.

2

Kevin Nicholls walked stiffly to the window and stretched. Thirty levels below Exchange Square's towering twin office blocks, young Chinese couples sat close together on benches along the jetties which jabbed into the black waters of Victoria harbour. The deck lights on two Star Ferry boats merged as their paths crossed in the channel on their brief, monotonous voyages between Hong Kong island and the tip of the mainland at Tsim Sha Tsui. Red, yellow and white reflections from the Wanchai light show rolled and mixed on the swell in the clear May evening air. He still found the neon playgrounds invigorating, the thought of the pleasures along the shores arousing. Rubbing a rough, narrow chin he thought of Carole

Chai. It was Saturday tomorrow and they were going to take the bank's corporate junk to Clearwater Bay.

His air-conditioned dealing room was comfortable but Nicholls and his foreign exchange team had been there since seven that morning, fourteen hours earlier, and the explosions of activity, with tense moments between the extremes of fear and relief, had left his skin clammy, his shirt stained and sticky. Hours earlier he had dismissed the team which managed the assets and liabilities of his bank, the five young Cantonese who borrowed from the money markets to fund the bank's commercial loans and lent their surplus money back into it. Their's was the world of interest rates and they plotted the British pound, the yen, the mark, the US dollar and another dozen currencies and monitored the swings and blips in the bond, shares and futures markets: it was a less volatile, less stressful marketplace than foreign exchange, where money was bought and sold and changes in the prices were measured in fractions of a second.

Nicholls sensed a nervous mood, an uneasy calm waiting to explode at the slightest provocation. Traders in Japan were following the unstable, tense foreign exchange movements in Europe time and he had asked two of his best dealers and the keen, promising junior to stay late with him to track the markets from Hong Kong. A pair of graduate trainees in their first week in the bank, and attached for the day to the treasury, asked to stay, and they sat either side of Herman Cheung while the veteran dealer, all of twenty-seven, relieved his boredom with an idiot's guide to the business. Nicholls smiled. He spoke no Cantonese but he knew Cheung was enjoying having two young female listeners, hanging enraptured on his words.

'You start in the morning with nothing, no position,'

Cheung said, flourishing a blank dealing sheet from the middle of his pad. 'Nothing bought. Nothing sold. You're square. Then a bank asks you to quote, to buy or sell a currency expressed against another one. Like dollar yen, dollar mark, dollar swiss.'

'Always two way,' one of the women confirmed, remembering the afternoon session.

'That's right. You give him your bid and your offer. You don't know if he'll buy the dollars from you or sell them to you.' He raised a hand to anticipate the obvious question. 'That's right. I have nothing to sell because I started off completely square. So what do I do?'

The plain girl with the wire-rimmed glasses screwed her eyes in concentration.

'If he buys the dollars from you, you are now short of dollars and long of yen, or whatever he sells to you,' she said. 'You have to sell the yen you're going to get in the market in order to generate the dollars and give them to the first bank.'

'That's correct. And the difference between the price you sold the dollars at to your customer and the price you paid for them in the market when you sold the yen is your profit. Or your loss if the market's moved against you. The operation squares your book and brings you back where you started with no position. The deal is a formal agreement. Both parties must deliver the money in two days to the other bank. When we talk about a "spot" foreign exchange price we mean a deal which must be settled after two days.'

The second graduate touched at the heart of foreign exchange dealing when she said: 'And if you decide not to square the deal immediately, if you don't go into the market straight away to sell the currency you've been given and buy in the one you have to deliver to the other bank, then you have a position.'

'Correct again,' Cheung said, rubbing his hands. 'That's when we make money. And lose it.'

'Dollar up,' a staccato voice said.

Nicholls crossed the room swiftly to where his skeleton team watched its screens with intensity while toying with keyboards and powerful electronic calculators. Sternberg Chance was not alone in the currency market place, even in late evening. Banks in Sydney had as usual opened early to overlap with the close in New York the previous calendar day and they were joined by Tokyo, Singapore and Hong Kong to start the endless twenty-four hour chain from the East. Many banks like Sternberg Chance and powerful corporations throughout Asia worked their treasuries late, sometimes all night, to follow the capital flows into the European financial centres and then New York.

Danny Lam's message was urgent and by necessity brief. His Cantonese accent was thick and uncompromising.

'We're still long of twenty bucks?' Nicholls asked, more in praise than for confirmation. He had directed the Chinese to buy twenty million dollars against yen an hour ago and its value was creeping up.

Without looking round at his boss Lam said, 'Right. At forty.' He meant he had bought the dollars at a rate of one hundred and fourteen yen and forty sen to the US currency. The market traded the fraction, the sen, a unit too small to use in daily life in Japan.

Next to Lam, the sallow features of Herman Cheung creased into a broad, tired grin. '115.20's been paid,' he chortled. 'We almost a yen up.'

The two Chinese sat on one side of a desk divided by a raised bank of back-to-back monitors and screens, controlled from multi-functional keyboards which accessed eighteen separate systems. The key tool was the Reuters monitor with its rows of exchange rates which changed by the second in silent flashes. Across from Lam and Cheung, Maria Luk-Suarez, a Eurasian with dark Latin features around high, sharp Oriental cheekbones, jotted down the individual trade details, the bought and sold rates, the names of the counterparty banks and their agents. Before leaving tonight she would transcribe the deals on to tickets which the operations department would check and process into multi-million dollar money transfers.

Nicholls pressed one of the first keys on Herman Cheung's console and picked up a telephone receiver. Without a greeting he said, 'Who's buying dollars?'

A heavy, east London voice crackled through the amplified voice box perched on top of the screens. It was Gary Eastment, who headed the yen desk at a British firm running a twenty-four hour broking service out of Hong Kong. 'As soon as it bust through the chart resistance the Japs piled in. It's on its way to the figure.' Nicholls thanked him brusquely and pressed the button which connected him immediately to Sternberg Chance's Tokyo branch. Tony Moore was not in the dealing room but the night shift there, one hour ahead of Hong Kong, concurred with the broker's reading. Maria handed the Englishman a sheet of paper, a graph plotting on a trade by trade basis the movement of the dollar against the yen. He looked at the jagged lines and its peaks and troughs, more for confirmation than information. He knew by heart the high and low points on the graph which extrapolated the levels where the players in the multi-billion dollar foreign exchange market swung from being buyers to sellers and vice versa according to technical factors. You re-adjusted your speculative position according to the chart-points and when in doubt, when the market was uncertain,

14

you followed the pack on the grounds that the trend's your friend. The 'figure' the British broker mentioned was a clean, neat hundred and sixteen yen to the dollar, without the fractional sen.

Four letters, flashing luminously in the upper half of his split-screen monitor, caught Danny Lam's practised eyes. He activated direct contact with the caller by pressing a key which transferred this code to a space filling the lower third of the Reuters information screen. It was the visual telephone through which a dealer in Tokyo, New York, London or any financial centre made instant contact, 'speaking' to each other via a keyboard and agreeing the deals that made and lost fortunes. Conversations on the Reuters Dealing System were recorded automatically on hard copy at both ends, to be used as evidence in a dispute. Dealers had come to prefer screen dealing but were prepared to trade on the telephone whose calls were also recorded, just in case.

'Citi Tokyo,' Lam said calmly, his eyes on the succinct message on the screen. 'Dollar yen in fifty.' Citibank's Tokyo treasury were asking for a buy and sell price for fifty million dollars against the Japanese currency. It was a large single deal, the kind of amount traded among banks like Sternberg Chance which are market makers in foreign exchange.

'Get calls lined up,' Nicholls grunted to his small crew. He looked over Lam's shoulder at the columns of quotes on the Reuters. 'He should take the dollars,' he surmised aloud. 'Make him twenty-five thirty.' Nicholls's razor mind registered his own long dollar position and he was quoting around it.

Danny tapped the keys, and with almost immeasurable speed the green, fluorescent letters and numbers flashed back at him. 'At twenty-five, fifty yours.'

'Shit! He's given us,' Danny Lam said, and then typed noiselessly. 'Agreed. At 115.25 I buy dlrs 50 mio value 11 May. My dlrs Chase NY.' The no nonsense reply: 'Agreed. My yen Cititok.'*

Nicholls's mind raced, looking for logic. He had seconds to decide whether to sell the dollars he had just bought and buy in the yen he had to deliver to Citibank or hold them as a speculative position. Dollars might fall in value if the market in general was now selling, or it could appreciate so that the yen he had to buy to pay Citibank would be obtainable at a rate cheaper than the level contracted rate with the American bank in Tokyo. A major player had started to sell the dollar when he, and the brokers, thought it had some way to go before it peaked. Nicholls was already long of twenty million uncovered dollars at one hundred and fourteen yen and forty sen and now he had been given another fifty, at 115.25 when he expected to be taken. He was not comfortable with the risk he was carrying. It was time to sell.

'Get calls,' he rasped decisively, flinging himself into an empty dealing position.

Herman Cheung shouted a price quoted by Barclays Bank in London.

'Give him,' Nicholls ordered, earning twenty sen, two hundredths of a yen and happy for it.

'Twenty done,' Cheung reported casually, selling twenty millions dollars.

'Twenty-five to thirty. UBS Singapore.' It was Maria Luk-Suarez.

* My yen Cititok means 'deliver the yen I have bought from you to my account at Citibank in Tokyo. My dlrs Chase NY means 'deliver the dollars I have bought from you to my account with Chase Manhattan Bank in New York.'

'Give him.'

'Twenty,' Maria said without looking up. She sold the dollars at 115.25, the same rate as the dollars they had bought from Citibank, but she knew her chief was happy to get out of the deal at par if the dollar was falling. They were still thirty million dollars overbought but three calls later they were square, their sales equalling purchases after they had sold ten million each to banks in Zurich, Düsseldorf and Amsterdam.

The three Chinese slumped back in their chairs.

'Sell another fifty,' Nicholls said urgently, his instincts in control. Cheung's single, sceptical glance was too short to measure before he joined the others at the keyboards. They dealt in tranches of ten million dollars and to give the market the message that there were dollar sellers about, Nicholls sold ten million dollars through the broker Gary Eastment. In ninety seconds they had sold fifty million dollars at an average rate of 115.18 yen and the yen bought would be delivered to their account with the Bank of Tokyo's head-office in Japan in two days. The voices on the open broker lines were becoming more frenzied as banks scrambled for prices. The rates on the Reuters screen were changing rapidly, led by dollar yen, which was edging downwards. Everyone wanted yen, or more exactly did not want dollars. Danny Lam, full of tension, rubbed his knees with his knuckles. 'How long we wait?' he asked Nicholls.

'Five ten,' they heard through the chaos of static from the voice boxes. Herman Cheung held his arms aloft and waggled his shoulders. They were already eight sen in profit on this fifty million dollars, over thirty thousand US dollars.

'The buck could fall another half yen before a rebound,' Nicholls said.

Maria Luk-Suarez allowed herself a faint smile. Though her role was to note the deals, monitor the positions, make calls and fill dealing slips, she also shared the traders' successes and suffered when they lost.

The frenetic voices from the boxes testified to a minor collapse of the dollar. It was now falling in five sen blocks and went effortlessly below one hundred and fifteen yen. When Nicholls heard 114.80 yen being paid he was satisfied. 'Get the dollars back,' he rasped. Four pairs of hands went to work and in half a minute, in six deals, they had bought fifty million dollars and their book was square.

The dollar went even lower, but Nicholls never looked for the bottoms and tops. He believed in disciplined profit taking and prudent stop-loss dealing and the hundred and seventy thousand US dollars profit from this last position was ample reward for a tense, busy day which had yielded to him an even three hundred and fifty thousand dollars. He had made half the month's budget in fourteen hours.

The Chinese decided on a celebratory late meal and though Nicholls rarely drank with his staff he authorized them to charge the night to the bank. 'And take the trainees,' he said to a smiling Herman Cheung.

The telephone rang as he sat alone, in darkness but for the reflected light from a thousand harbour neons, a beer in his hand, his feet on a window sill, thinking about the call he would make soon to Carole Chai. It was Gervase Prideaux, Nicholls's boss and head of all treasury and capital markets business at Sternberg Chance, and a board director, three men removed from the chairman.

'Gerry! Where are you?' Nicholls asked cheerfully.

'God knows,' Prideaux said with silly, predictable indifference. After a silence he said, 'Taiwan, I suppose.'

Nicholls drew his watch close to his face and squinted, remembering. 'You're due here Monday.' It was Friday in Hong Kong.

'Sooner than that old boy. Look, I can't talk now. There are people from the central bank in the bar.' Prideaux's voice, usually jovial, often flippant, seemed tense, and clearer, as if the receiver was touching his lips. He reached the point of his call and drew Nicholls rigid in his chair.

'I'm sorry it's so late. I've been calling your flat all evening and then it occurred to me just now you might still be trading.' Nicholls was about to tell him how much he had contributed to his Asian junket but something in Prideaux's voice told him to hold it. 'The point is, Tony Moore's dead. No, don't interrupt. You must do exactly as I say. I'm flying in to Hong Kong from Taipei at nine thirty tomorrow morning. Buy yourself a ticket to Tokyo on the twelve fifteen Cathay. Take enough clothes for a long stay, have the rest sent on. Meet me in the Cathay lounge air-side at Kai Tak. I'll clear it with Peters tonight.'

Prideaux's conversation would have to wait, Nicholls thought. The head of Sternberg Chance's Hong Kong operations was at dinner with Beijing visitors.

'Morgan Trinkel is flying out from London to take over your dealing room. It's afternoon in Europe and he should have left by now. We may even see him at Kai Tak. I can't tell you a lot more until tomorrow.'

Nicholls was on his feet. 'Hold it, hold it,' he demanded, the veins in his head throbbing. 'Just tell me one thing. What happened to Tony? How did he die?'

There was a moment's pause as Nicholls's voice echoed on the line.

Prideaux's became distant, as if surprised by the question. 'Some accident or other,' he said, matter-of-factly. 'Apparently he'd been out on the piss and fell down some bloody steps.'

3

Kai Tak, Hong Kong's precariously located airport, was its usual multi-racial crossroads, noisy and comforting. Nicholls checked in without delay at a Cathay Pacific business desk and was invited to the Marco Polo executive lounge, which overlooked the crowded apron and runway. He guessed that one of the three-engined Tristars, liveried in Cathay's green and white and taxiing towards the terminal against a backdrop of weathered, laundry-draped tenements, ferried Gervase Prideaux.

He helped himself to a drink and for the first time since the sickening news hit him he felt at ease, if not cheerful. The passion and total commitment of a big day's trading, the urgency of the tragic summons, and the packing meant only a few hours of sleep, wracked with dreams he could not remember. Thoughts of Tony Moore had kept him awake long after Hong Kong entered that brief interlude of noiselessness before another relentless day.

He had not seen Moore for three months, although they had talked almost daily, the last time being Wednesday, two days earlier. He dredged a weary memory for any flimsy record of that last conversation.

It was around eleven fifteen and the Hong Kong money market had slowed to nothing as Tokyo, one hour ahead, took an official lunch break. Tony had been enthusiastic about a huge one-shot five hundred million dollar sell order which had torn a yen off its value in three minutes of frenzied dealing. He warned Nicholls forty seconds before the fall-out from the deal hit the market and his Hong Kong colleague had sold twenty million dollars himself, making a useful one hundred and thirty thousand dollars before his second cup of coffee of the morning. Later that morning Nicholls heard that the order had come from a Japanese insurance company for an investment in American treasury notes and was executed through a Japanese bank. He had then wondered how Moore knew about the deal if he had not been asked to discharge it. There was something else among the bravado and market trivia, something odd, different to Tony's normal patter, but consumed by fatigue and grief he could not generate enough concentration to arouse his recollections.

'You look awful,' Gervase Prideaux observed, easing himself with a forced sigh into a seat at right angles to the dealer.

'I had to pack, remember? And I was up late making enough to pay for your jolly round Asia.'

Nicholls had woken before dawn, an hour before the alarm, packed carelessly and scribbled notes for his maid and the managing agents of his apartment block. He called Carole Chai from the airport, imagining the hazy light flooding the snug bedroom in her compact apartment and the fine, smooth features of her face as she awoke, slightly confused by the the purring of the telephone. It was Saturday and they had planned to spend it together. Now he had no idea when he would see her again.

Prideaux was forty-eight and tall, with thick, well-groomed, hair swept-backed from a youngish, angular face. His double-breasted dark blue suit with thin chalk stripes gave him a distinguished look which he cherished. His handshake was firm but isolated and cold. He liked Nicholls, respected his talents, and trusted him, though both knew it was because the Essex boy was a big contributor to his bottom line. He preferred the company of the young aristocrats in asset management and the well-spoken decorative females who populated the bond sales department, even though Nicholls and his money market traders had more talent and intuitive brilliance in their feet than the yuppies had as a group.

Nicholls was twenty-nine, with dark, moody looks and driving ambition which he took from his Cypriot mother. His six-foot-two frame and withdrawn and suspicious temperament came from his English father, a trade union leader in the Ford car plant at Dagenham. A fine mathematics degree gave him access through a graduate entrant programme to Sternberg Chance. He was assigned to the dealing room, where his talents did not go unnoticed, and he progressed from the simplicities of the minor, so-called exotic currencies, to the majors: dollar-mark, dollar-yen, and sterling-dollar, still known as 'cable' from its early method of transmission. His skills both as a trader and as a strategist brought rapid promotion. He was known to be a contemplative person in private and a fierce competitor in the foreign exchange market. He gave Prideaux no aggravation as long as his annual bonus never fell below a hundred thousand pounds.

'Of course,' Prideaux offered lamely. 'I'm sorry to drag you away from the Wanchai.'

Nicholls sniffed and said, 'Tell me about Tony.'

Prideaux's faced creased with anguish. He could not tell whether it was grief for his dead employee or concern for the bank's reputation. 'Tony was found yesterday morning,' he said, 'Friday morning that would be, in some kind of Japanese church. A chap at the British consulate said they thought he died of heart failure brought on by shock when he fell down a flight of steps. They say he was drunk at the time.'

Nicholls's chin jerked. Prideaux's eyes followed a Malay ground hostess, her mottled maroon and gold chongsam moulded to her young, slender frame like a snake skin.

'No suggestion of foul play, thank goodness,' he continued.

'But the police think he was pissed at the time,' Nicholls said.

Prideaux gave a dismissive shake of his head, which made his cheeks wobble. 'You knew him better than most,' he admitted. 'But he did overdo it a few times. Remember when he was sick in the boardroom. Though I hear he had to calm down a lot after the accident.'

Nicholls ignored him. Yes, he knew Tony better. It was a friendship that lost nothing from separation. He had not seen him for months and then he was still fifty pounds overweight and his curled, wiry hair was more peppered with grey than a thirty year old man might expect. Tony's social life was relentless. He would dominate a drinks party or a pub crawl, chortling endlessly and pulling on his belt which lay hidden below folds of belly flab. In full flight, his English crossed the Atlantic, betraying in the distinct vowels his Canadian childhood. He was also an uncompromising foreign exchange dealer and his speciality was sterling against the German mark. When a quiet market bored him, or a heavy brokers' lunch inflamed his predatorial passions,

23

he would launch himself into the market, strategically selling or buying lots of ten million pounds against the German currency until the gullible masses thought the expectation of some as yet unannounced economic statistic was forcing a sell-off of sterling or a buying spree. But it was Tony Moore, or one of the handful of other dealers with the perceptiveness and the sheer balls who, by the time the market had wised up, had squared off at a fat profit and were watching the exchange rate return to its earlier level, with the toothless sharks that had tried to follow them now scrambling to escape the whiplash.

Prideaux was right, Tony had emerged a changed man, both physically and mentally, after his accident. He had been drunk at the wheel of a flame-red BMW with an American senator's daughter at his side after a party to celebrate the end of his three-year secondment to Sternberg Chance's New York branch. She had died when the car spun out of control on a wet road in New Jersey and he spent two months in hospital, a long list of charges awaiting his recovery. He was looking at a prison sentence and the wrath of the dead woman's father who was bringing his wealth and power to bear in a campaign of retribution, even before Tony had left hospital. He told Nicholls he paid a massive bill to discharge himself early and crossed the Canadian border quietly. It took the American Justice Department and the dead woman's family a year to prepare the legal assaults and Moore's lawyers had been repulsing them for almost two years. He rarely drove after the accident and was only comfortable walking with a stick. Nicholls's gift when Moore returned to his screens and keyboard in Sternberg Chance's head office in the City of London was a fine piece of natural blackthorn with a slightly arched handle which its proud owner would wave at moments of trading triumph. When the bank sent its best dealers abroad to track and intercept the big capital flows at their sources, Nicholls and Moore were sent to Hong Kong and Tokyo as the Asian links in Sternberg's twenty-four-hour global day.

'I've not heard of Tony drinking since the accident,' Nicholls said tersely. 'Are they sure it was booze?'

'We'll have to wait for the autopsy results. It could have been drugs.'

Nicholls head was shaking in disbelief before Prideaux had finished.

'Tony wasn't into drugs. We all popped a few things when we were young, but not Tony.'

Prideaux said with open distaste, 'The temptations of the exotic Orient must have got to him.'

'So what do you want me to do?' Nicholls asked, taking a deep pull on his wine and swift glance at his watch.

Prideaux made an arch with his hands. 'Make sure the dealing room ticks along,' he said, trying to sound professional and in command. 'Go through the books, see what positions Tony was running, square things out as it were.' He flapped a wrist as he struggled to generalize, the sign of man who understood little of the technical detail of dealing but wanted to appear as if he did. 'Just tidy the place up, get it ready for a permanent replacement.'

'Can't that Japanese guy cope? What's his name? Tony said he was competent, safe, not a big risk taker.'

'Mabuchi. He's very stuffy, hardly has anything to say when I'm there.'

Nicholls stifled a smirk. Even he knew that a Japanese dealer would have no comprehension of Prideaux's role in the bank and would care even less. Prideaux was saying, 'No I want someone who can communicate with us, fire-fight until we can re-group.' He measured the gap between him and a dozing Japanese businessman and leaned towards Nicholls. The dealer saw how his important visitor's eyes avoided his as he resorted to management jargon to hide his well-known dislike and mistrust of Orientals, and the Japanese in particular. Were it not for their possession of the keys to the world's most replete treasury and their insatiable appetite for the globe's resources and markets, Prideaux and the charmless bankers from Zurich, New York and London would have no need to pay homage to them at their court in Marunouchi. He said, 'We've got some serious plans for Tokyo and we don't want any bad publicity at this stage.'

'Can't Hanlon hold the rampaging Japs off?' Nicholls asked.

'He's on holiday,' Prideaux said defensively. 'Private safari, South Africa, somewhere hard to reach,' as if implying it was illegal and immoral to disturb the holiday of a merchant banker. 'We're trying to find him. Anyway, you've got to control the dealing. Hanlon couldn't do it.'

Of course he couldn't, Nicholls thought. Warron Hanlon's only interest was corporate finance, the sexy business of mergers and acquisitions, appropriate to a man of his upper-class but not quite aristocratic background. He was an attractive and articulate talker and a competent manipulator of clever people.

'Is that it?' he said, alert to the voice announcing the boarding of flight two six two to Tokyo. He bundled papers into a flight bag.

On the way to the gate, Prideaux said, 'Moore has no close family, apart from a sister we're trying to find. In the absence of instructions the British consul in Tokyo is co-ordinating things.'

'So what else do you want me to do?' Nicholls persisted. They were shuffling nearer the departure gate.

Prideaux sniffed a smile, surrendering. 'Be a good chap and sort out Tony's personal stuff. Move into his apartment, clear up his things, you know, do what you have to do, as tactfully as you can. It's much easier for a dealer to do this, don't you think?'

'Won't it be odd if I, a complete stranger, turn up in Tokyo and start posting bodies about?'

Prideaux invited a pair of Japanese businessman to pass them. 'Just cover the bank from embarrassment,' he urged. 'I've anticipated your co-operation. A chap from the consulate, Braithewaite or something, will meet you in the Palace Hotel tomorrow morning. Sorry, forgot to tell you. You're booked in there for couple of nights. He'll have the keys to Moore's flat and car, if the police have released them by then. You have my authority to do whatever necessary, Hanlon's number two in Japan, a local called Fujimori, has dealt with everything so far.' And he added without condescension. 'Fujimori's a good man. I suggest you get to know him. He'll introduce you to the people we're close to as a British bank in Japan. We have some very good friends there, especially on the treasury side.'

Nicholls handed over his boarding card. 'Right. How long do I have in Japan?' he said over a shoulder.

Prideaux showed him two open palms. 'As long as it takes.'

4

Low in its descent, the port wing of the Cathay 747 dipped and the plane lumbered into a steep turn as it crossed the Chiba coastline, filling Nicholls's window with a patch of rich greenery pitted with dark craters. His first view of Japan was a golf course. He had been warned about Narita, Tokyo's so-called international airport, and the forty-mile journey into the steel gridlock of the monster capital, but on this late Saturday afternoon the amber and white limousine bus made smooth progress. Avoid the taxis, the in-flight magazine had advised, and a two hundred dollar bill. The light was fading but a patchy moon lit the lush foliage and stalks of the rice plants in their small, flooded paddies. The bus was thirty minutes nearer Tokyo before Nicholls realized they were travelling on the left side of the road.

The city began suddenly at the Arakawa river, a broad, sluggish grey mass which would melt into Tokyo Bay. Grey, plain tenements, their balconies hung with washing, factories and warehouses fought for space with houses, garish, neon-lit hotels, shops and tiny precincts of temples and shrines. The only open land he saw was scrubby patches bordering the rivers the bus crossed, some of them cleared to make dusty baseball diamonds or driving school layouts. Despite the drabness of this stark urban landscape Nicholls sensed the economic wealth of the country, in the newness of the vehicles, the precision of the ticketing at Narita and the rigid orderliness of the functionaries. There was a purposeful, co-operative quality that was missing in self-centred Hong Kong.

He took a taxi from the City Air Terminal to the hotel in the heart of the Marunouchi business district and a short walk to the offices of Sternberg Chance in the Nichiban-kan building. There was no reaction from the driver when Nicholls kept the change from the five thousand yen note Prideaux had provided along with a packet of briefing documents.

His room overlooked the outer moat of the Imperial Palace where more papers awaited him and a message from Alistair Braithewaite, the British consul, to say he would be in the hotel lobby at eleven the next morning. Exhausted, he screwed the message into a bin, and toyed with a room service hamburger while flicking through half a dozen television channels, one of which was in English. The others were quiz shows or singing spectaculars featuring immature teenagers whining nasally and cavorting inexpertly to the music. He switched off and tried to look through the documents but gave up quickly. Instead he emptied two miniatures of gin and mixed a long drink, stretching on the couch and shuffling the hotel brochures, finally settling on a complimentary copy of the *Asahi Evening News*.

It was a colourless read, filled with tedious descriptions of deliberations in the Japanese parliament, the Diet, and routine items of international news from the wire services. On an inside page, among the local stories, a brief article, headlined 'Missing Scholar Sought', said an American post-graduate research student had not been seen for four weeks at the Japanese university where he was based. It triggered a reminder of Tony Moore and he made a mental note to see whether his death had been reported in the same dispassionate style.

He finished the drink and dozed uneasily as the weight of sorrow and fatigue overwhelmed him, but his mind refused to release him into sleep. His last talk with Tony, and the final deals they had put through together, would be his memorial and he had run them through his mind on the aeroplane and the airport bus. But as he summoned up these final images he saw something in them which did not fit. Tony had telephoned to warn about a big deal in the market, one which might move the prices, and it was the last time they had spoken. In the heat of the trading session he had missed it but in the morbid silence of his hotel room it began to eat into his confusion and sorrow.

<u>5</u>

Alistair Braithewaite had a soft north of England accent, worn down during eight years in three overseas postings. He was of Nicholls's age, with pallid, lightly freckled skin. A wave of light brown hair flopped over an eyebrow. He wore a blazer over a checkered, open-necked shirt, as if to remind the newcomer that Her Majesty's vice-consul did not normally turn out on Sundays and if he did he had the right to dress for leisure. Nicholls was impressed when he ordered drinks in unfaltering Japanese in the hotel's basement coffee shop cum simple restaurant. Few expatriates in Hong Kong bothered to learn Cantonese, even the simplest phrases.

After the opening pleasantries the consul announced, 'I knew Tony Moore. He came over for drinks, Saint George's day, Queen's birthday, that sort of thing.'

Nicholls reacted at once. 'Drinks? Did you see Tony drink alcohol or do you mean drinks in general?'

Braithewaite sounded almost disappointed when he said, 'I can't say I saw him tip the bottle personally, but he was a gregarious chap, really enjoyed it here. They called him Tony Tokyo.'

Nicholls detected a censorious, resentful edge but ignored it. He said, 'I've been sent here to replace him temporarily in the bank and sort out his belongings. I also want to know what really happened to Tony. For his sister.'

'We're still trying to contact her,' Braithewaite said. 'I don't think they were very close and there doesn't seem to be any other next of kin.'

'That's right. So I want to get the story right. Tell me how Tony died.'

The British consul withdrew some flimsy papers from his leather bureaucrat's briefcase. They were in Japanese: rows of vertical Chinese character letters signed off with a small round, orange stamp. 'This is the official police report,' he explained. 'We haven't had time to translate it yet but when we do it will be notarized and used as evidence at the English inquest. 'What it says is that Anthony Moore, chief treasury manager of the Tokyo branch of British bank Sternberg Chance, et cetera, et cetera, was found by . . . I can't read the man's name ideographs. Anyway, a chap walking his dog in the precincts of the Hie Shrine found your friend lying face downwards on an outdoor stairway. That was early Friday morning, about half past five. The autopsy conducted on Friday evening showed that Moore had consumed enough alcohol to poison him into unconsciousness and at some stage in the evening he had taken amphetamines in capsule form. He probably died within two hours of collapsing.'

Nicholls shook his head. 'Tony didn't take drugs,' he said forcefully, and then, 'Sorry. I interrupted you.'

Braithewaite had showed a refreshingly open approach for a government functionary. He was understanding and disarmingly frank, at least until he clamped on a pair of thick-rimmed glasses and cleared his throat officiously. Nicholls knew then that he had lost him; the consulate man had become a mouthpiece. Braithewaite coughed and continued. 'One point four microgrammes in his blood.'

'Would that be fatal in itself?' Nicholls asked.

'I understand fatalities have been recorded at nought point five microgrammes. The heart gets over-stimulated.'

'How was Tony identified?'

'On the basis of documents in his possession, the police went to your bank on Friday and met a Masaaki Fujimori, who declared himself to be your senior adviser. He agreed to see the body and identified it as Tony Moore.'

'Did any of the London staff see Tony? You know, after he died. Did you? In your official capacity.'

Waiters were laying tables for lunch. Braithewaite ordered more coffee and then scratched an imaginary itch on his nose.

'Have you been to Japan before Mr Nicholls?' he asked, in the manner of a suspicious policeman.

'First time,' Nicholls confessed, and waited for the lecture.

'The Japanese authorities are not comfortable when they deal with foreigners directly. It's not just the language, many of us speak Japanese fluently. It's more to do with the culture. I know it's become a cliché, and an army of Westerners earn a living telling the world how different the Japanese are, but most situations here are not legislated for and problems, or any conflicts, are resolved by compromise and consensus.'

Nicholls was about to challenge him when Braithe-waite held up a placatory hand. He said, 'The answer to your question is no. Your senior expatriate Mr Hanlon was away in any case, and the police were entirely comfortable to deal with your Japanese adviser in what is a simple case of a tragic accident. I was informed late on Friday by a liaison officer from the foreign ministry and by then the investigation was almost complete.'

Nicholls drained his coffee. 'So that's that,' he said resolutely. 'Would the police compromise and let me say my farewells to Tony?'

The British consul's chest heaved and sank. He brushed his jacket sleeve back and checked the time. 'Tony Moore was cremated two hours ago.'

Nicholls leaned across the table. 'What?'

'We had to give our approval,' Braithewaite insisted. 'There were no suspicious circumstances which might delay disposal and there was nobody here to authorize or pay for shipment of the body back to England.'

Nicholls cursed Hanlon silently. 'Where are the ashes?' he asked.

'I believe they'll be delivered to Mr Fujimori.'

'Was he at the funeral?'

'I don't know.' Braithewaite shuffled his papers uncomfortably. I understand how difficult it's been for you. Moore was your friend and you find yourself thrown into a strange city. Your Mr Prideaux has authorized us to consider you as Sternberg Chance's proxy and in this capacity Tony Moore's ashes and possessions will be handed over to you in due course.' The voice of the procedures manual, Nicholls thought. The official reached into his briefcase and extracted a sealed plastic bag and slid it and its rattling contents across the table.

'The police have released the keys to Moore's flat

and you are free to move in from tomorrow. They're on the ring with car keys and others not identified, presumably to his office. The police have searched the apartment in case there was something that might affect their investigation.'

'Like amphetamines, needles, crates of vodka,' Nicholls said facetiously.

'Yes, I suppose so,' Braithewaite said, slowly and with deliberate irritation, now even less sympathetic to the highly paid, loud representatives of the expatriate financial sector who passed through his city looking to Her Majesty's representatives to bail them out after bar brawls or the consequences of drunk driving charges. He gave Nicholls a card.

'It's on the other side of the Imperial Palace. Show this to the taxi driver and don't tip him.'

After Braithewaite's departure, Nicholls clutched a street map and ventured into the balmy May afternoon, joining the tourists, mostly elderly couples from the countryside, paying homage at the Sakurada bridge of the Imperial Palace. He stood on the wooden bridge, watching the carp snap at the surface of the brackish water of the moat and wondered what lay beyond the forbidden gate and its sentinels of thick, solid spruce and larch trees. There were no signs in English script and when he asked for directions people grinned and recoiled in embarrassment. He had travelled in seven other Asian countries but had never felt so illiterate, isolated and confused.

On Monday morning, as he followed the map through Marunouchi to his bank's office, he saw the Tokyo of the business briefing. A few solid, plain grey blocks of pre- and early post-war vintage remain but the economic heart of Japan forms a neat quadrant of architecturally functional, glass and tile structures with their height restricted in order not to overlook the inner reaches of the Imperial compounds. The area which a hundred years earlier was a mosquito infested swamp has clean, wide avenues bordered with struggling gingko and plane trees and travelled by lead-free executive saloons and multi-coloured taxi fleets. Not here the rattling, diesel-belching taxis of London or the furious choas of Hong Kong at all hours. Just the smooth flow of heavy traffic and the trampling of smartly dressed office workers, the men in dark blue suits and the women in colourful two-piece outfits which they would change for their bank and trading company uniforms. Massed, orderly ranks of office workers spread from the mouths of the underground; no children, no beggars, no meandering tourists and workers in overalls. It was a short, easy walk but the humidity was enough to remind him of Hong Kong and he was glad to reach the air-conditioned atrium of the Nichiban-kan building.

Sternberg Chance rented three floors of a modern earthquake-resistant building whose broad, dominant windows were rounded at the corners like an aeroplane's. A security guard, long in years, helped Nicholls identify Sternberg's reception desk on the ninth floor with gestures. There he was entrusted to Peter Stark, the bank's expatriate manager in charge of general administrative affairs, basically everything of a non-business nature. Every company has a Stark. With no executive role, he was the one you turned to when you wanted a difficult bar bill processed or a party organized for the regular parade of head-office visitors. A bachelor in his early forties, he had a round, pinched face, not enhanced by his loose, plastic glasses, and a head of greying hair which thinned to reveal his scalp at the crown. Nicholls told him about the reporters and cameramen in the lobby.

'Who's talking to them?' he asked, as they drifted between desks of computer terminals with their intense operators.

'Fujimori san. He's our senior Japanese adviser,' Stark replied.

'Yes, I've heard of him,' Nicholls said drily. 'This treasury operations?' He assumed the square of people, overseen by a severe looking woman with her back to the window, processed the deals which flowed from the room he could now see beyond a security door.

'That's correct,' Stark said precisely. 'Capital markets on the upper levels have their own settlements and reconciliations. This is for foreign exchange and money market dealing. Poor old Tony's support people.' He pressed a buzzer on a glass-fronted door and they were admitted by a tall young Japanese woman in a matching jacket and skirt and with a pair of red-rimmed designer glasses lodged in her glossy hair. The dealing room was spacious, offering a partial view of the Palace outbuildings through a gap between the modern sterile blocks across the Naka-dori road. Nicholls first sweep captured twenty, twenty-five people, all of them Orientals.

Seeing the visitors, a Japanese sitting at the desk

which headed two double-sided rows of screens, monitors and telephones with their attendant dealers rose wearily and put on his jacket. Without making eye contact, he introduced himself as Mabuchi and led Nicholls into a glass-panelled room which had obviously been Tony Moore's office, with its view of the dealing room and its own Reuters monitor and personal computer. Nicholls dismissed Stark and offered the Japanese the spare chair across the desk stacked with printouts and files. 'Please sit down. I didn't catch your first name.'

'Mabuchi is sufficient,' the other said icily. The business brief had told Nicholls that Mabuchi, the most senior Japanese in the dealing room, was thirty-seven and on permanent secondment from the Ohyama Bank, Japan's second largest commercial bank and Sternberg's 'sister' company. His speciality was the business he could weavil from those corporate sectors, manufacturers and trading conglomerates, which were employing their massive pool of financial resources in the volatile domestic and international money markets. Zaitech, the Japanese called it. Financial engineering in the speculative markets where the rewards were limitless. Like the potential losses. Insurance and trading giants, the trust banks with their pension funds, and oil and manufacturing firms were playing with their shareholders' funds in a dangerous gamble, and the banks competed ruthlessly to intermediate what they called corporate business. It was hard, you competed with a hundred other banks for a wedge of it, but the profit margin from the corporate client was much bigger than the spread you could expect when two banks traded with each other.

They spoke as dealers at first, Mabuchi summarizing the branch's exposed positions in clear but strongly accented staccato English. Eighty per cent of their balance sheet assets were one to twelve week yen loans to other banks and were funded on a day to day basis from the ocean of yen deposits left with banks in London and other financial centres or through the Tokyo money brokers. This mismatching of the bank's borrowing and lending periods was currently earning an average profit spread of forty basis points, against a budgeted target of a half per cent. Short date borrowing rates were temporarily rising on seasonal factors, Mabuchi said, to explain the ten point shortfall.

Nicholls glanced at his notes. 'That'll be Tomio Hashida, head of domestic money markets.'

Mabuchi nodded. 'That's correct. And he's assisted by Eto.'

Nicholls sensed a forced formality, a delicate, contrived barrier between him and this trusted manager he had only spoken to by telephone when Tony Moore was absent. Perhaps it was the shock, the grief which had not eased much over the weekend since Tony died.

Mabuchi was saying, 'They also manage the global interest rate swap book for London and there is a small portfolio of forward rate agreements. They use the Tokyo futures exchange for hedging.'

Nicholls studied his deputy, whose eyes were fixed at a point on the desk as he concentrated in a search for words which emerged in a rehearsed, precise pitch. Well-groomed hair shaved above the ears in the corporate style of Marunouchi glistened with cream. There was a suggestion of hardness in the thin lips of his small, compact face.

'Tell me about foreign exchange,' the Englishman said, his eyes flashing to the dealing room where two traders were on their feet, waiting with fierce concentration while a colleague nearby gripped a telephone in one hand and clenched the other, ready to make the familiar yours or mine sell/buy gesture.

'That's Kimura and Yamamoto,' Mabuchi said, following Nicholls's gaze. Spot FX traders. Seventy-five per cent of turnover is dollar yen and the yen crosses, mostly mark yen and sterling yen. We are market makers. Miss Sano keeps the positions. The man with the phone is Kawasaki. He assists me with the corporate customers. The woman is Miss Honda. She is our assistant.'

Nicholls saw it was Naomi Honda, with her oversized glasses, who had let him into the dealing room. 'And opposite Miss Sano?'

'Sawada. He manages the small dollar balance sheet and the forward FX.' Anticipating the question he said, 'Customer business only. The book is almost square. No large open positions.' He sucked in air noisily, a vocal expression Nicholls would struggle to interpret, and said, 'Our overall policy is to support customer business.' He was not convincing and Nicholls pounced.

'But Tony, Mr Moore, played the markets, didn't he? He took pretty big position.'

Mabuchi's lips tightened. 'Yes, of course,' he said. 'I assumed you already knew about his FX trading. He took all the proprietary positions, intra-day and overnight.'

Nicholls knew almost everything. He and Moore shared their knowledge, market information and rumours, but he doubted whether Mabuchi knew that Moore was allowed by a head-office mandate to run uncovered foreign exchange positions up to two hundred million dollars during the business day and fifty million dollars overnight.

He asked, 'How did he control his overnight positions?'

'He sometimes left stop-loss orders with London when he left the office.'

'Sometimes?'

'Moore san has a Reuters monitor in his apartment. Have you . . .?'

'I haven't moved in yet,' he said, warmed to hear that Tony had not changed his habits. He certainly transferred his open positions to London with instructions to close them out if specific price levels were reached but his predilection was to watch the rate movements through Tokyo's night, fortifying himself with coffee and cheese and the company of an insomniac girlfriend. He claimed his gammy hip throbbed when a price change somewhere on the globe sent him to the telephone for a short tense burst of dealing. All the trades done from home, after hours, were recorded and transferred to a control tape in the operations department of the Tokyo office. It had been five years since he and Nicholls had banned their dealers from making trades from bars or nightclubs. Nicholls stood and leaned against the glass partition, wondering whether this stern, unsmiling man, who had yet to express regret at the death of his boss, had told his staff to turn on the legendary Japanese efficiency for the new *gaijin*. 'I think you forgot someone,' he said.

Mabuchi squinted. 'The others are junior dealers. I'll introduce you later.'

'Who's that?' Nicholls said, indicating a short man with a large, square face and a shock of black hair sitting with Yamamoto on the spot foreign exchange desk. 'He doesn't look like a trainee.'

'I'm sorry,' Mabuchi said unconvincingly. 'That's Billy Soh. He assisted Mr Moore with the strategic positioning in FX and options.'

40

'Not a Japanese name, is it?' Nicholls asked innocently.

'He Korean. Korean-American actually. Mr Moore recruited him last year from Citibank Seoul. His Japanese is still poor.'

Did Mabuchi's immeasurable twist of the head imply disapproval at the American's role or his language ability? Nicholls was about to say something when there was a tap on the half-glass door which gave on to the outer office. Framed in the window was a tall, broad-shouldered Japanese with rich, dark silver hair and a well-cut, lightly checked double-breasted suit. He had a wide, easy smile which exposed his neat, generous teeth across an angular, deep olive face. Masaaki Fujimori, the most senior Japanese among Sternberg Chance's two hundred Tokyo staff, waited to be admitted.

'Mr Nicholls,' he effused, ignoring Mabuchi who opened the door. 'Welcome to Japan.' The face beamed, and just as suddenly straightened. 'Of course, it's such a sad occasion.' His English was delivered with a rich, sonorous fluency and a near perfect American accent. 'Please call me Masa.'

'I'll catch you later,' Nicholls called to Mabuchi as Fujimori led him through the open office to the lift hall and then to his rose-wood panelled executive office on the fabled eleventh floor. Glass on one side gave a prestigious view of the Imperial Palace moat and the trees rising above the outer wall. An austere, skeletal arrangement of twigs and their flowers complemented a shallow recess. They sunk into leather armchairs. The Japanese said, 'Mr Hanlon's office is next to this one and Mr Koda's beyond that. He is seconded from the Ohyama Bank. As I am.'

Nicholls appreciated the information. 'I know we're

partners in a number of joint ventures around the world but I didn't realize how close we were in Japan.'

'Very close,' Fujimori confided. 'And we plan to get closer.'

Nicholls had heard rumours of a joint project in Tokyo and was searching his memory when the Japanese leaned forward and tapped the glass-topped table. 'That's why Mr Moore's death might be embarrassing if our potential investors should be affected by what they read.'

'Why should the Press be interested?' Nicholls enquired, recalling the clutch of Pressmen in the lobby. 'It was an accident.'

Fujimori made an extravagant motion with his hand, a gesture he had learned on his countless trips to the Western business world. Then he hissed.

'The death of foreigner is quite unusual in Japan, from any cause, natural, accident or, dare I say, murder. We are a homogenous society Mr Nicholls, and if one of our non-Japanese residents expires here it's news.'

They were sitting at right angles on a sofa armchair combination, Nicholls occupying the guest position. Fujimori had entwined his fingers and let his uplifted chin rest on them. A young woman entered after knocking, bowed stiffly towards Fujimori, who ignored her, and placed two small, steaming bowls on to silver coasters on the table.

'*Ocha*. Japanese green tea,' Fujimori said, almost proudly.

'Did you know Tony well?' Nicholls asked, ignoring it.

'Not particularly well. Our roles were different. I advise on issues relating to mergers and acquisitions and my contacts are here, on the eleventh where we maintain a high degree of security. I don't go to the dealing room very often.'

'Yes, of course,' Nicholls said languidly as he summoned Alistair Braithewaite's reconstruction of the events following Tony Moore's death. 'But well enough to identify his corpse.'

Did that ruffle the shrewd Japanese adviser, Nicholls wondered in the silence.

Fujimori drank again from the bowl of *ocha*. 'To be frank,' he said finally and uncomfortably, his face losing its easy amiability. 'Mr Moore was a large person, physically. I mean, it's very difficult to mistake someone of that build and face, even if you didn't know them well.'

Nicholls pressed. 'I don't just mean recognition. Wouldn't it have been normal for an expatriate like Stark or one of the others to see him? People who socialized with him.'

'When the police called they were put through to me. You probably know that our chief executive Mr Hanlon was on extended vacation.' Fujimori drew deeply on a cigarette, constructing his reply in the roll of smoke he finally emitted. 'We are in Japan Mr Nicholls, not Hong Kong where the British determine the procedures and the police pursue their enquiries in English. Our laws are very specific and meticulous but they do not come over very well in translation, even if our police had the language skills to express them, which they don't. Are you suggesting I acted improperly?' Nicholls had stepped into the snare and now groped for an escape.

'No, of course not. I apologize if I gave that impression.' He raised the tea to his lips but stopped short of drinking. 'I heard Tony was injured. Did this make it difficult to recognize him?'

Fujimori made a conciliatory smile. He said, 'He was in poor condition. I'd like to think that the cuts and bruises were caused when he tripped and fell down the steps as he tried to find his way out of the shrine.'

'And what would you not like to think?'

He sucked noisily through his teeth, not noticing Nicholls's bemused smile. 'Your colleague had been drinking,' he said, as if quoting, 'and when he fell down the steps he was unable to get up.'

'My colleague,' Nicholls said through gritted teeth, 'pretended to be a drinker. He hasn't drunk for years. Is that what the police think? That he was a drunk?'

An impassive mask shielded Fujimori's sudden inner tension. 'Regrettably, yes,' he confided solemnly. The two men shared a moment's silence, then Fujimori said, 'Nicholls san, I see you are not satisfied with the procedures taken by the police, your embassy and, well, me.'

'Absolutely not,' Nicholls said. 'But his sister will want to know how he died and maybe why he was cremated so quickly.'

Fujimori arched his fingers again and thought about taking another cigarette from the ornate silver box. Instead he embarked on a controlled, flowing speech, laced with references to Japanese law and the country's customs, things often misunderstood by the foreign community. He excused himself and went behind his desk and reached beneath it. His hand appeared holding the knotted corners of a white silk cloth which wrapped a square box. 'Mr Moore's remains,' he announced solemnly. 'I entrust them to you.' He placed the bundle on the table.

Did Nicholls perceive, as the contents of the package fought to control his imagination, the corners of

Masaaki Fujimori's mouth turn down in a wry, barely perceptible scowl?

'I appreciate your leaving Hong Kong so hastily,' the Japanese said, signalling the end of the interview, 'although I have to say that Mabuchi and his team are very competent and motivated. I don't suppose you'll have to stay in Tokyo long.'

'There are other things to do,' Nicholls said as they walked the executive carpets to the lifts. Fujimori looked surprised.

'I'll pack Tony's things, clear up his affairs. I expect he left a few bills around. I ought to stay until Prideaux finds a replacement for him.'

Fujimori's smile faded before the lift doors had closed and he walked quickly back to his office. He opened a cabinet built into the wall behind his desk and lifted the receiver of a red telephone in the narrow space left in front of a safe. There was no dial and no buttons. They were not necessary. 'I hope there hasn't been a miscalculation. My first impression of Nicholls is not very favourable.'

7

Nicholls lunched with Mabuchi and Hashida, the squinting money market dealer with the serious face and delicate, long fingers who seemed to enjoy an unofficial role as Mabuchi's deputy. They fled the office promptly at twelve when the foreign exchange markets took a gentlemanly ninety-minute break and joined what appeared to Nicholls to be the entire population of Marunouchi in the maze of underground eateries, coffee houses and shops. Lunch came as a complete meal served on a tray within four minutes of ordering. Deep-fried, battered pork fillet on a bed of shredded cabbage, a bowl of rich, miso soup bubbling with tiny cubes of tofu bean curd and shreds of dark green seaweed, a bowl of glutinous rice and a cup of green tea. 'Tonkatsu,' Hashida explained helpfully. No one in the restaurant drank alcohol and his host did not offer it.

It was customary, Mabuchi said after their stiff, probing lunch, to take coffee and gossip but Nicholls excused himself for the genuine reason that an appointment had been made for him with the Tokyo metropolitan police in Tony Moore's apartment.

He collected Moore's ashes and checked out of the Palace Hotel, the staff bowing with closed eyes when they saw his pathetic burden. The green and yellow fleet taxi pulled sharply on to the outer palace moat road, forcing him to clutch the urn as they were both jolted forward.

So you got the taste back did you Tony? Nicholls mouthed, fingering the knot of the soft fabric which surrounded the precious package. He saw the young driver's eyes in the rear-view mirror, watching him. It's been three years since the accident left you crippled and with that weird but not unknown aversion to alcohol, unable to tolerate even a glass of diluted wine or half a pint of beer. Remember the lunches the brokers convened to welcome you back to the market after your convalescence when you tried to force a screwdriver and had to lurch to the toilet? We thought you were putting it on, especially when you cried. Was that it? The grief. Did drink remind you of the American girl who died in the crash? A psychological trigger? You gave up hard liquor for white wine but if you finished

46

the glass your food went undigested and we picked you out of the toilet bowl.

The doctors probed, the psychiatrists delved and the diagnosis was a compromise of the disciplines. The doctors found chemical imbalances resulting from organ damage which might irritate to the point of inducing vomiting. There were other recorded cases. The shrinks obviously zeroed in on the guilt complex. Your self-disgust and loathing at being drunk when you crashed the car and killed a lover took the form of revenge on yourself by rejecting the cause of the lethal event to the point where alcohol, even the smell of it, induced nausea.

Nicholls had not heard that Tony had beaten the curse in the last two and a half years or so but the British consul and the Japanese now knew him as a well-known pisshead who had died proving it.

The taxi left him outside a four-storey block of apartments, each with a bricked balcony, in a quiet street running parallel to the road which skirted the rear wall of the British Embassy in an area called Kojimachi. There was rich greenery and mellow, bright flowers everywhere; in the gaps between the ochre walls of the block and the low, token wall abutting the road, on the verandas and in the entrance porch where 'Palace Heights' was stencilled on the automatic sliding door. The lobby had its own clinical simplicity: a door announcing the entrance to the underground garage, a single lift and, in one corner, a raised miniature garden of finely raked white gravel with a mature bonsai red pine at its centre. The lift serviced two apartments on each floor and barely held Nicholls, two large suitcases and the remains of Tony Moore.

He fumbled with the ring of keys while struggling to keep a Cathay flight bag on his shoulder and dragged his luggage into a tiled entrance which gave on to a hall with doors on either side. The rooms of Moore's apartment were small by Hong Kong expatriate standards and were fitted with simple, functional furniture of the type which could be left without remorse after a three year secondment. The lounge, filled with light which pierced the mesh curtains and fanned across the space with dazzling clarity, was a pleasant contrast to his Hong Kong flat in a Mid-Levels high-rise, often shrouded in the damp, chilly clouds that seemed anchored to the Peak.

He found a rich supply of silver cans of Asahi Dry beer in the refrigerator and, glass in hand toured the dead man's apartment. Unsentimental, there were few reminders of his life, only some framed photographs of people Nicholls did not recognize and shelves with a short row of technical books and easy-on-the-brain novels. Some of the drawers were not closed and ornaments and photographs had been moved off line. The police, he assumed, had made a thorough search.

Nicholls knew that Tony's life-force flowed from wherever he kept the tools of his trade and when he entered the master bedroom he smiled at the screen and its keyboard on a trolley. He depressed a switch and sat on the bed to watch the rows of fluorescent green numbers emerge from the blackness of the Reuters monitor. He took in the early prices from continental Europe, London would be open in under an hour, and called Mabuchi from the bedroom for an update on actual real rates, ordering an immediate short dollar-yen position of twenty million dollars which he would manage through the night. He was engrossed in the figures when his first visitor arrived.

A frail woman in a white smock introduced herself in faltering English as the caretaker and handed Nicholls a sheaf of mail and several editions of *Japan Times* before retreating, bowing and struggling to express her sympathy. 'Mr Moore. I'm sorry, I'm sorry.' He reciprocated with his own clumsy attempt at a bow and made a mental note to learn how to position his feet and arms properly.

There were five bits of mail and he discarded three as junk before he reached the couch, and tore open the heaviest one. It was a long narrative from Moore's solicitor, the firm his bank had appointed to help him defend a ten million dollar liability claim from the lawyers representing the parents of the woman he had killed in the car crash. The US Justice Department had informed the British lawyers that a second request for Moore's extradition was being prepared but it would be deemed co-operative if he returned voluntarily to the jurisdiction of the American courts. His solicitors requested his presence in London at the earliest opportunity in order to address this most serious development. The other letter came from Sternberg Chance's personnel department, quoting someone called Ingham from Legal, to emphasize that the bank's ability to support Tony Moore under existing insurance cover could not exceed two hundred thousand pounds. A thirtieth of the American claim, he calculated easily.

Too late for all of you, Nicholls thought, relishing the image of empty-handed lawyers as he opened the Saturday edition of the *Japan Times* and found a generous half column on the accident in the Hie Shrine. Police sources were quoted: 'The caucasian banker had been drinking heavily and very likely had died of shock and exposure after falling drunk down a flight of steep steps in the shrine precinct.'

Nicholls had the newspaper open on his lap when

49

the two policemen arrived. One wore a sharp, slate-grey uniform with his cap under an arm, its peak touching the butt of a compact revolver carried high on the hip. The younger, in a loose dark-blue business suit and carrying a black, broad briefcase, could have been a Marunouchi salaryman and not an assistant police inspector with a degree in economics and the official interpreter. He introduced the other as Senior Police Superintendent Itoh of the Tokyo Metropolitan Police Department. A ritual calling card gave the interpreter's name as Mochizuki and he translated the other's words into stultified, practised English, apologizing first for poor ability and then for the tragic bereavement.

Nicholls beckoned them in and waited amused while they shuffled unnecessarily out of their shoes and looked incongruous in a carpeted apartment with its high ceiling and unused space. He noticed how the interpreter peered at the surroundings while the craggy veteran Itoh was at ease in a place he had obviously searched himself. They refused coffee or any drink.

When they were seated, Nicholls asked about the official cause of death.

'A regrettable accident,' Mochizuki interpreted. 'Mr Moore fell on stone steps and broke his face. Autopsy found more than one hundred milligrams of alcohol per hundred of blood. He was very drunk.' So that was it.

Flicking the briefcase locks, the interpreter policeman extracted a folded black vinyl bag and handed it ceremoniously to his chief, along with a sheaf of papers. 'Please check articles and sign,' he said in his colourless, economic style, as the pathetic remains of Tony's life were exposed on the coffee table. A wallet, which the manifest said contained six ten thousand yen notes, a five and four ones, a Japanese driving licence, a flight of credit cards and receipts, Tony's alien registration card and other bits of paper. In other pockets the police found a slender ball point pen, a calculator and a book of matches. Nicholls already had Tony's set of keys.

There was something comical in the scene and Nicholls had to suppress a smile as Itoh held up each article and solemnly named it in Japanese and his colleague put it into English. There was a handkerchief and some coins but no clothes because, the policemen claimed, they were very soiled and were still being examined.

Nicholls was no longer listening and only pretended to check each item. He scribbled his signature next to the tiny round orange stamps which gave the seals of authority to the columns of hieroglyphics.

'Is everything accounted for?' Mochizuki asked.

Nicholls neither knew nor cared. He nodded. The senior policeman rose and bowed fleetingly towards him, clearly relieved that the awkward but necessary meeting was over. He was turning towards the hallway when his interpreter nudged him weakly, indicating the white bundle high on a wall shelf. They placed themselves in front of the urn and with arms at their sides bowed deeply to the remains of Tony Moore.

Nicholls was guiding them to the door when a thought overtook him. He turned to the interpreter. 'Did you find Moore's stick?'

Mochizuki was struggling with his shoelaces and looked up from a crouch.

'Tony's walking stick. He was handicapped on his left side and needed help.'

'What does he want?' the uniformed officer growled. In Mochizuki's reply Nicholls heard '*wakarimasen*', I don't know, a rare stand-alone word he recognized. He took the long-handled shoe horn and mimicked a

51

hobble, which the policemen acknowledged and nodded their comprehension. Progress, Nicholls thought. 'It was bluey-black, a bit gnarled and knotted, with a smooth, curving handle.'

'Black,' the interpreter said, seizing on the only word he recognized.

'Right. He had to use it when he left hospital. It's a bit of a show but he needs it when the cold gets to him. He was never without it.' There was another interchange between the Japanese, which Nicholls interrupted. 'It's not important,' he said, 'but it was a gift from me and I'd like to keep it as a reminder.' The policemen conferred again and then Mochizuki turned to Nicholls. His chief was already half way out of the door. 'There was no walking stick. I'm sorry.'

The departure of the police gave Nicholls the relief he craved. They had tried their best to be dispassionate but even as they concluded the legal requirements and bowed to the shrouded urn of ashes Nicholls had detected something censorious in their tone, something condescending in their attitude, as if they were admonishing him for allowing his dog to stray and get run over by an innocent Japanese car. And why did Braithewaite of the consulate and Fujimori of his bank dismiss his dead friend as a hopeless drunk, a victim of his own excesses, and not someone the Japanese and international communities would mourn long over?

He made a more leisurely inventory of his temporary home, unpacking his clothes and hanging his suits and shirts alongside Tony's abundant wardrobe, and was looking for the solid piece of Victorian blackthorn he had bought for Tony from the specialist dealer in Kensington Church Street, a small, tangible memento at least, when he heard a faint metallic scratching. The doors to the kitchen and into the hallway were open, and the sound of a key engaging the front door lock carried easily through the compact, cheerless apartment. He sat motionless, intrigued as the entrance door closed with a gentle thump. The visitor, barely into the apartment, sensed that it was not unoccupied.

'Who's there?' a woman's voice said hesitantly, surprised.

'Hi,' he said, relieved at seeing the unthreatening face of a tall, young Japanese woman in a stretched tangerine sweater with coiled cable braiding which covered her hips over taut, black leggings. Raised heels on pointed shoes gave her a model's height and poise. Her pale, oval face and deep black tear-drop eyes formed an expression of relief and astonishment. He stood as she approached and offered a friendly hand.

'I'm Kevin Nicholls, a friend of Tony,' he said, holding the cold, limp hand of his attractive visitor and steering her to the lounge.

'Emi Mori,' she said, slowly and deliberately. She sank into the folds of the couch and Nicholls noticed that she had kept her shoes on.

'I'm sorry if I gave you a shock. I was also a friend of Tony's.'

'A good friend,' Nicholls suggested.

'Excuse me?'

'You have a key to his apartment. Tony must have trusted you.'

Nicholls saw no point in embarrassing her but his implication pierced her mask of Oriental calm. She smiled lamely. 'That's why I'm here. To pick up some things I kept here. Do you mind if I smoke?'

'Sure.' Nicholls lifted his glass. 'A drink?'

'No thank you.'

He watched her small, delicate hands emerge from the flared sleeves. They were tipped in tangerine to match her sweater and the colour of the pair of triangular earrings. She unclipped a pouch-like bag, flipped open a packet of American cigarettes with one hand and manipulated a gold lighter with the other. The performance reminded him of the dexterity of the hostess army in the Volvo Club in Hong Kong. She drew deeply on her cigarette and used a palm to flatten some errant wisps of hair. He was pondering her reason for being there when she seemed to read his mind. She reached into her handbag again and gave him a set of keys. 'I don't need these now,' she whispered. And when Nicholls was weighing them she added, 'Do I?'

She had darting, intelligent eyes and a finely contoured face with pale, near white skin. The trace of an overbite gave her a look of sensuous vulnerability. He had not come across any women's underwear or cosmetics in the flat which might suggest she was Tony's live-in lover. He drained his beer and said, 'Were you at the funeral, or the cremation ceremony, whatever it was?'

She seemed surprised by the question. 'No, of course not. It was arranged by the police and Tony's bank.' She had not noticed the urn.

Nicholls said, 'The police brought Tony's belongings this afternoon. Have they talked to you about him?'

She crooked her head. 'Yes, of course. I offered myself and talked to Itoh san.'

'Could you help them?'

'Help? How can I help?'

'You were his girlfriend, you had his doorkey. You might have been able to tell them why my non-drinking friend had suddenly turned into a drunk.'

Emi Mori sank into the couch and propelled a funnel of smoke at the ceiling. 'He drank with me and he sometimes came home to me drunk,' she said reluctantly. 'I think there was a lot of pressure recently. Some problems he wouldn't talk to me about. It must have been at his office.'

It wasn't, Nicholls told himself. Tony Moore ate pressure three times a day. Stuck with a two hundred million dollar position in a whip-sawing market, Tony didn't sweat. He'd seize his walking stick, becoming dominant, commanding and utterly cool, ticking off the covering deals with a chop of his hand, discarding the crappy prices with a dismissive flick of the head and taking on the whole fucking market if his gut told him he was right. If Tony had pressure which led him to drink it was from the threat of legal action and ruinous penalty from the lawsuit. Leave Emi Mori alone, an instinct said.

'I'm sorry to pry, but I want to tell Tony's sister, if I can find her, what happened to him. I don't want to tell her he was a drunk, just a victim of a freak accident.'

Emi Mori smiled for the first time, a weak defensive parting of the lips. 'I think Tony was in love with me,' she said, admiring her orange fingertips. 'I was very sad when he started to change and I saw him less and less.' Nicholls watched her impassively, coercing her to continue. 'I used to spend the weekend here. It was easy to tell my parents I was on a trip, or staying with friends on Saturdays and Sundays, but not during the week.'

'Do you work?' Nicholls asked.

'I'm still a student. I attend a design school.'

'Your English is perfect,' Nicholls said generously, recalling the struggles with Mabuchi and all the Japanese he had met so far, with the exception of the calculating Fujimori, and those structured, text-book sentence patterns.

'My father was sent to Los Angeles so I went to

high school there. But it's hard to keep up with the hearing.'

Nicholls guessed she meant she had spent her mid-teens in the States and was now struggling to hold her fluency in English. He said, 'You had Tony to speak to. Maybe someone before him.'

The slender Japanese woman thought about another cigarette but chose to fix her gaze at a spot near the television. Then she turned her clear eyes on her British interrogator.

'When you stay in Japan a little longer,' she said solemnly, 'and you know Japanese women better, you might understand why some of us are more comfortable in the company of Western men.'

She let Nicholls contemplate her meaning, crossing her tightly clad legs and twisting on to a hip while teasing an imaginary knot from the strands of silky hair around her neck. 'I have to go,' she said finally, brushing the sweater over her watch and then gathering her cigarettes and floppy shoulder bag.

Nicholls stood up. 'It was nice to meet a close friend of Tony's.' And he added casually. 'Please take what you want.'

'Excuse me?'

'You came to collect some things,' Nicholls said ingenuously.

'Of course,' Emi said. 'I really only wanted to collect some video tapes Tony had sent out from England. Soaps, films, that sort of thing. He said he'd take me there someday. I've never been. The videos were a kind of preview.' She smiled sadly. 'That's all gone now, but they'll remind me of him in a small way.'

She knelt before the row of tapes lodged in the television and video unit. Some were pre-recorded films but most bore a hand-written label which she studied with her head cocked to one side while her fingers played along the rim of the cassettes. She chose four, depositing them on the coffee table while she went in search of a bag. More out of curiosity than real interest Nicholls leaned across and looked at the labels. Under 'Football' someone had written 'Manchester U. v. Liverpool,' and on another 'Wildlife of the Amazon'. The other two were compilations of soap opera episodes dated February to April 1992. When she returned with a tartan carrier bag from the Isetan department store he said, 'Can you play English VHS tapes in Japan?'

Her answer was precise. 'I have an adaptor like Tony's over there,' she said, scooping the tapes into the bag.

'I hope you enjoy the football.'

For an instant he did not miss she looked nonplussed. Then she recovered. 'I will, and I'll be thinking of Tony whenever I watch the tapes.'

After she had left he paced his unfamiliar lodgings, still warm with her presence and fresh with her lingering flowery perfume. Fascinated by her vulnerable beauty, he was reminded of Carole Chai, the feline, intelligent Cantonese who was his first Oriental lover. He knew he wasn't the first Westerner to fall for the demure attentiveness of their company and the demanding tenderness of their lovemaking.

When he nudged the curtain aside to watch his visitor leave his apartment block, he found she had not been alone. Clutching the plastic carrier bag firmly against her, she looked both ways before recognizing a black saloon whose bonnet rippled into life on her approach. So much for the solitude of grief, Nicholls thought.

8

Araki jolted alive, reviving the pain which seared across his eyes. He was naked and clammy, and he wondered why until he felt his knees buried in the buttocks of a sleeping form. Then the images of the previous evening emerged reluctantly from the clouds of his memory. Her broad, creamy shoulders were bare above the thinly padded quilt and her hair covered her face, making identification impossible, even after he heaved himself on to an elbow. The tightly woven *tatami* reed matting covering the floor gave off a sour, musty smell.

He closed an eye and read his watch in the natural light which filtered from the kitchen through the panels of the fragile *shoji* walls. It was seven thirty. Without turning, the woman raised an arm and mumbled a farewell, presumably to mean that he had already paid the moonlighting divorcee whose name he had not asked.

Twelve-car, square-fronted yellow and orange trains glided smoothly in and out of the suburban station, three and a half minutes apart. Smartly uniformed railway staff clarified each departure with a wave of their lamp. Araki stood among the silent smooth-skinned commuters, conscious of his own shoddy appearance and the scars of physical excesses. The early daylight hours normally eluded him, but the call to be in the head-office of Japan's giant financial daily had reached him as he relaxed in a Nakano bar after attending the trial of a film star charged with importing cocaine. The court appearance was the reason he had been wearing a suit. A dozen platforms at Shinjuku seethed with placid office workers and students as railway lines converged like the spokes of a wheel at Tokyo's busiest interchange. He was pushed by an apologetic station worker into the carriage of an underground train which took him after one change to Nihonbashi in the heart of the old merchant quarter where mirror scenes of orderly white-collar chaos were taking place.

The *Japan Economic Press* building sparkled in glassy modernity, a monument to its flagship role as the monitor of the country's economic and financial life and daily required reading for three million subscribers. Like the multi-nationals it tracked and reported, the *JEP* was itself a publishing and information conglomerate of massive financial power and diversity. Each floor was a vast open-plan expanse of word processors, television screens and computer monitors, now quickly filling with operators and officious department chiefs who sat at the heads of the desks in splendid arrogance.

Special Projects Commission Editor Funada enjoyed the luxury of his own office enclave, a desk and some cabinets screened off from the general office and with a view across the fetid canals and low-slung expressways of downtown Tokyo. He was a decade older than Araki, five years from the company's statutory retirement age of fifty-five, and professionally expended. His last years were destined to be spent by the window, commissioning work which was not reputable enough for the prestigious daily newspaper but would fit the image of the popular downmarket magazines and news-sheets the *JEP* owned or had a major interest in. His eyes widened when he saw Araki's unembarrassed shabbiness and he greeted him with a smile of mock disapproval.

'How did you know where I was?' Araki asked, helping himself to a cigarette from the box on the stacked, untidy desk.

'I traced you to the Katsumoto trial and you told one of my people that you were going off to celebrate something. I tried the Roman in Shinjuku first and Mama Yoshida said you'd had your fill of sake and were heading, a little confused, in the direction of Nakano. She gave me the number of the bar you used to take me to and I left a message. You obviously stopped on the way. From the look of things you didn't find your way home.'

A uniformed office girl brought tepid green tea. It was a welcome relief to Araki's parched mouth. An unrepentant dropout from the corporate escalator which had consumed and emasculated his colleagues from Keio, the top-ranking university from which he graduated with a degree in economics, he had started in a prescribed and responsible way: a job with a prestigious daily newspaper, a wife he had married for love and not by arrangement and who gave him a son. In five years his patterned Japanese life was in ruins. At twenty-seven he was hustling bar girls for the secrets of their liaisons with politicians and actors and tracking drug financing scams for one of the hundreds of popular weekly magazines which the literate population of Japan consumed with open salacious hunger. His wife left him, returning to live with her parents, a prominent banking family, and his son barely acknowledged him. His peers said he failed as a Japanese, unable to re-adjust, to conform after a year spent at Berkeley and in London. He would say the experience opened his eyes, led him to look beyond the consuming culture in Japan for more than just the consensus mentality. He crusaded to prove that there were dangers in the mindless conformity at home, in the schools and work places. As a junior journalist he had ignored the tame political lobbies and in his enthusiasm bribed a government official to obtain a suppressed document exposing price-fixing by a cartel of powerful steel manufacturers. It was splendid work everyone agreed, and a handful of geriatric company chairmen had bowed deeply at the television cameras, their resignations conveying their heartfelt regret and sense of responsibility. Meanwhile, nothing, absolutely nothing changed, apart from the collapse of the good guy's life. The establishment regrouped and strangled him by exclusion.

'When did you last work for us?' Funada asked, sifting a folder out of the heap.

Araki eased his tie loose. 'Six, nine months ago. That story about the stock manipulation at the sewing machine firm. A case of greenmail I think we called it.'

Knowing the answer, Funada asked, 'Are you free for another assignment?'

Araki drew a slim diary from his pocket with a flourish and mimicked an overburdened executive, laboriously rubbing each page as he pondered his commitments. He had freelanced for a year, topping up earnings from English teaching with sporadic commissions from financial journals which could disassociate themselves from the author if his articles attracted controversy. His first fifty thousand yen a month paid for the ground floor of a ramshackle house on the edge of a construction site where he had gladly agreed to sit out the last months of its existence for the aged father of a friend. A month's research and a decent article for Funada would give him a cushion and breathing space to work on his own book. 'Who's it for?'

'Hirosawa.'

Araki forced a sardonic smile. Hirosawa was the editor of *One Point Finance*, a colourful weekly magazine which aimed to combine serious financial journalism with lurid sex tales and a batch of adult cartoons. It complemented the tedious economic output of the parent paper and was the preferred reading matter of the millions of white-collar salarymen who commuted on average three hours a day from the conurbations which turned Tokyo, Yokohama and Kawasaki and their suburbs into one immense, megalopolis of over thirty million media hungry people. *One Point Finance* sold three hundred thousand copies a week, leading its peer group in the fiercely competitive world of the popular weekly. 'And the story?' Araki said.

Funada opened a thick, buff folder and flipped the papers as he spoke. 'The Ohyama Bank is on the move again. They've been in the thick of all the financial scams since they started coming to light in January. They're the biggest maggot in the swelling tub of rotten, mouldy rice – Read: Japan's financial system. Of the ten big City banks, Ohyama took the heaviest criticism for inflating the stock market bubble with the money it lent to customers, taking their grossly overvalued land as security. Some of the borrowers were fronts for organized crime and the collateral was often worthless. The stock market crashed, the banks tried to get their money back from the speculators whose land value in the meantime had hit the floor. The result was chaos in the financial markets, bank managers in jail, including two of Ohyama's, and a ban by the ministry of finance on any further lending to the real estate sector.'

Araki interjected. 'The story's been well documented. Do you want me to revive it?'

Funada waved a hand. 'No, absolutely not. We have four cabinets of files on the wretched subject.' He picked a newspaper cutting and pushed it across the desk. 'Have you seen this?'

Araki ran his eyes up and down the columns and confessed he had not looked at a newspaper seriously for days.

'The man was British,' Funada explained. 'Worked as a foreign exchange dealer for a bank called Sternberg Chance, somewhere in Marunouchi. Got pissed last Thursday night and killed himself falling down the steps at the Hie Shrine of all places.

'Where does Ohyama come into it?' Araki asked, not seeing any mention of the bank in the article.

Funada's expression begged patience, not one of Araki's strengths. He said, 'The Englishman's death is not particularly important. They say those foreign exchange dealers are a reckless bunch, hardly live beyond thirty-five anyway. Our interest is in the connection between Sternberg Chance and Ohyama. They're close to some sort of financial tie-up. Ohyama have bought two per cent of the British bank's stock and have an informal joint venture in Tokyo which might lead to the setting up of a fully capitalized investment bank. That's a development my paper's watching. The death of the dealer is obviously of more interest to our friends at *One Point Finance*. Might be something readable behind it. The debauched lifestyle of the foreign banker, a Japanese mistress or two, distressed wife, that sort of thing.'

Araki nodded knowingly and helped himself to another cigarette.

'I spoke to Hirosawa yesterday,' Funada continued. 'He's happy for me to commission you and act as the go-between.'

'Why me?' Araki wondered. 'Hasn't he got enough sleuths with a liking for a bit of dirty reporting? What about Kobayashi, or that guy who got stabbed by the Kabuki actor? They can dig anything up.'

Funada hissed. 'It's a hard one,' he confessed. 'Sternberg are not talking to the press. They've drawn a tight curtain over Anthony Moore's death, beyond the usual expressions of regret. Hirosawa is not prepared to use his own resources on what will probably be nothing more than a frustrating waste of time. And, of course, your English is near perfect.

Araki smiled again. 'That sounds like Hirosawa. I think he invents most of his stories. Saves time. Are there any leads that stick out?'

Funada tapped the slim piece of newsprint. 'The bank spokesman it quotes is someone called Fujimori. He used to head the international division at Ohyama Bank and is now seconded to Sternberg as their senior adviser. You might try getting to him as well as the *gaijin* working in the Tokyo office.'

There was a pause while Araki reread the article.

'Well?' the older man said hopefully, adding, 'Hirosawa's generous with expenses if you can keep them under control.'

'I'll do it,' Araki said, trying to disguise his enthusiasm though the meagre contents of his wallet had already dictated the decision. 'I'd like an advance on expenses.'

'Of course,' Funada said gladly, returning the papers to the file, which he handed over. 'Please let me have a first background story by Thursday morning. That gives you two days. We have to get something in Friday's edition of *One Point Finance* in case the competition are looking at it.'

'I'll try,' Araki said, his thanks limited to a short bow from the shoulders.

Funada called after him. 'What were you celebrating last night anyway?'

Araki turned. 'My birthday. I was forty.'

9

Sorting through Tony Moore's things, Nicholls matched
a plastic card in his wallet with an invoice from the mail.
Tony had left a forty thousand yen bill at the Foreign
Correspondents Club. Nicholls agreed to settle it and
was allowed, in sympathy, to assume the dead man's
right to associate membership. The club, with its bar,
restaurants and library, sat atop a plain, modern twenty-
floor office block on a corner bordering the Ginza
and Marunouchi and served as a convivial office for
the world's foreign Press and an international setting
for Japanese and overseas businessmen. News service
printers thumped constantly and their scrolls adorned
the wall by the reception; journalists ate together in
their own corners while businessmen impressed their
guests with spectacular neon views from the main
dining room. The manager who showed Nicholls
around smiled sadly at Tony Moore's photograph.
The big, ebullient Englishman would meet friends in
the small, dark drinkers' bar once a week, perhaps less,
but didn't stay long. They were a young, well-dressed
rowdy crowd, using the club to meet before moving
to places where their energy and money could be
spent more vigorously. As far as the management
remembered, neither Tony nor his friends had ever
been cited for drunkenness. Tak, the barman with the
slicked-back hair and hang-dog jowls who prowled the
intimate bar, confirmed it. 'Ah, Tony Tokyo san,' he
lamented. 'A gentleman. No drink. Very noisy, but no
drink. What a waste.'

The bar was empty except for a party of four
Japanese in quiet conversation over a scattering of

papers at one of the half dozen tables. Nicholls sat on a bar stool drawing patterns in the condensation on his glass of draft Sapporo, his eyes moving instinctively every two minutes to the small machine, the size of a pocket calculator, propped against a bowl of nuts. The numbers on its liquid crystal display flickered and melted and were instantly replaced, reminding him that whether it was lunchtime or the cocktail hour in any dealing centre, a miniature monitor like Nicholls's would be rested on a bar counter or a bedside table when the trader was away from his desk.

Downing a second beer he thought gloomily of Tony, of the money they had made and lost, and the women they had enjoyed, and then shook off the creeping sentimentality with a thin smile. The drink was stimulating him to ask why some of the people he had met said Tony was drinking again and others said he wasn't. Tony drank tonic water, or other soft drinks, and within months of returning to London after the accident all the professional market knew it and it was no longer fun to tease or provoke him. He got high on atmosphere and soda and pretended it was alcohol. Nicholls's tiring mind returned to the silky hair and creamy, tear-drop eyes of Emi Mori when a husky American voice made him, and the Japanese barman, look round.

'How do you get a goddamn drink in this place?'

A woman, almost as tall as him, with naturally streaked, golden blonde hair teased into half curls over her slender shoulders, stood in the doorway. She had a narrow face with strong, sharp features and thin, uncoloured lips. A strained expression broke through her natural American confidence. Her shapeless cream dress hid what Nicholls guessed was a full figure on a model's legs. 'The guys out there, the journalists I was talking to, just upped and left. That says a lot for the power of my personality,' she said to the room in general.

'You must be a member,' Tak said, trying to be helpful, 'or with a member.'

The businessmen returned to their spread sheets. Nicholls smiled at the newcomer in the spirit of shared loneliness and fumbling in a pocket, produced a fantail of coloured tickets. 'You're welcome to these,' he said. 'They're chits for lapsed members passing through Tokyo.' He thought she hesitated without blinking, before stepping forward, a hand outstretched. A simple, dark mauve bag and the weight of her black, soft-leather briefcase dragged the lumpy corner of her loose jacket off her left shoulder.

'Jenny Collier,' she announced, and eased herself on to a bar stool.

'Nicholls. Kevin Nicholls.' There was a touch of hesitancy in his voice and looking into the striking face of the newcomer he sensed something oddly familiar.

'Well, are you going to get me that drink or should I start shouting again?' she said with mock annoyance. They exchanged smiles. Nicholls took another beer while Tak was pleased to show his skills when the American woman ordered a very dry vodka martini.

'I thought those things were forbidden in the States,' Nicholls quipped as she took a desperate swig at the nearly neat alcohol.

'Sorry Kevin. I needed that.'

They lowered a few barriers by sharing career details. Nicholls was not ready to confide the reasons for his hurried move to Tokyo, but Jenny said he might find it amusing to know she was a marketing executive for a baby food company. She admitted she had to test it. 'Vodka's the only thing that gets rid of the taste of the goddamn stuff,' she laughed. Then her broad Chicago drawl softened as she prepared to unburden herself of the serious reason for her trip to Japan.

'My younger brother's gone missing,' she said.

Then Nicholls remembered. 'Collier. That's right. I read about him in the papers. He was an academic or something wasn't he?'

Her ice-blue eyes misted. 'Can I have another drink?'

'Sure. Would you like to eat something? I'm going to fall off this stool if I have much more beer.'

Jenny accepted gratefully, and Tak produced a menu of bar snacks from which they ordered cheeseburgers and fries and a bottle of Napa Valley merlot. Then she continued in the same distracted, languid voice. 'He's got a scholarship to research financial systems in Japan for a year. He also writes serious stuff for newspapers and magazines in the States.'

'Have you talked to the police?'

'I've spent hours and hours with the police, embassy and university people. Now I'm trying to see if the journalists know what's happened to him. Everyone's very worried but there's no sign of Sam. He's not been seen or heard from for over three weeks. They all say he'll turn up. White males don't disappear easily in this country.'

Nicholls agreed. Even in his short time in Tokyo he had noticed that when he strayed from the main roads to the quiet streets he had the distinct feeling of being watched, if only out of curiosity.

'He left no message,' she was saying. 'His apartment's in good shape, there's money in his account. It's . . . it's . . .'

'It's not been that long,' Nicholls offered, laying a

68

hand over hers. The movement surprised her, and he saw her moist eyes soften.

They ate listlessly, talking as if by an unspoken accord about their homes. When she had finished and turned away to dab her lips with a paper napkin, Nicholls chose the moment to press a button on the tiny electronic device still propped against the nut bowl. The dollar was still falling in Europe, almost a yen and a half since the Tokyo close. The Bank of Japan was known to be interested at these levels. What were they waiting for? Were they plotting with the other central banks to smack the speculators in one giant orgy of dollar buying? It wouldn't be the first time.

'What the hell is that?' Jenny Collier had smoothed the dress over her knees and was reaching for her wine glass when she saw her companion playing with what she assumed was a computer game.

'Sorry Jenny. That was rude of me.' Nicholls made to pocket the machine, but then put the tiny television-like screen in front of her. 'It's a portable Reuters monitor,' he said. 'The figures on the screen are live foreign exchange rates. It's about noon in London. That's where the action is at present.

'Wow, that's fascinating,' she said genuinely. 'Sam, my brother, was researching the money markets here. He wrote to Mother a month ago, the last time we heard from him, saying his work was going well and he'd found out something that might really shake things up and earn him a fortune if he could get it published.'

Nicholls was interested. 'Do you know what it was? The research, what he'd found.'

She drained the rich, purple wine and waited for Nicholls to refill her glass. Her hair fell across one shoulder as she shook her head. 'No idea. The letter said he planned to tie up the last loose ends and head back to Illinois via South East Asia and the west coast. Said he'd got a special girl to introduce us to.'

'Has she come forward?' Nicholls asked.

'Not that I know.'

'He might have left Japan already. Taken his girl-friend with him.'

Again the bright, blonde strands of hair danced on her shoulders. 'No way. The ports and airports have been checked. His embarkation form has not been returned at any immigration desk. But we're going to keep trying. I paid to have that notice put in the English language newspaper. The police will have his picture all over the country and I want to get the Japanese press interested. I've spread round a selection of photos.' She reached down and across him, her hair brushing his knees, the movement releasing a misty, mellow fragrance of exotic herbs, and hoisted the leather briefcase.

'This is a pretty good likeness,' she said, extracting one, 'not too old. People change a lot when they're away from home. He might have shaved off his moustache because I hear they're unacceptable here.' The cut-off, enlarged section of the photograph showed a full-faced young man with neat, trimmed wispy hair against a background of coloured lights and hanging paper. 'He came home for Christmas.' She gave herself another pause but quickly found a rugged, defiant expression. 'I'll find him,' she said. 'Even if I have to give everyone in Japan a picture.'

Nicholls glanced at the numbers, then pocketed the miniature monitor. 'I'll keep an eye out for your brother,' he said sympathetically, 'but I've been in Japan less time than you.' To lift her spirits he added, 'If he was working in the finance sector there's a

70

chance I might come across him, or someone who knows of him.'

'You're very kind,' she said, with a kind of knowing hopelessness. 'You can keep this.' She slid the portrait of Sam Collier to him. 'I've made enough copies to bury Tokyo.'

What a distraction Jenny Collier could have been, Nicholls thought, as he wrote his office telephone number on a Hong Kong business card. But he wanted none until he had steadied Sternberg Chance's shaken Tokyo treasury and tidied Tony's affairs. 'You can get me here,' he said, 'if you're in a fix, though money's about the only thing I understand.'

She gave him a warm smile. 'I'm at the Dai Ichi Hotel in Ginza,' she said gratefully. 'If I don't find him soon I'll have to move somewhere cheaper. The yen rate's killing me, but I can't move into Sam's old place. It doesn't seem right.'

He carried her briefcase to the taxi rank.

'But I'll find him,' she said confidently. 'And then I'll buy *you* a drink.'

10

The dealing team were in their places when Nicholls reached the office at eight the next morning and activity was already building frantically. Tokyo is the first major market to open during the calendar day and it sets the trend for the other Asian centres and for London and New York as the sun drifts westward. New Zealand had already been quoting prices for three hours, its opening overlapping with the shut-down in

New York the previous day, but it was a dead zone with few trading counterparties and a killing ground for the professional sharks who moved two hundred million dollar chunks of money around the globe on a continual twenty-four hour patrol ready to pounce on any arbitrage opportunity in any time zone. Sydney had tried to become the continent's principal money centre, pulling in the world's banks in a frenzy of competition for the Asian capital flows, but the information and the customers who generated the funds were nine flying hours north in Tokyo and by December 1990 the Australian financial centre was dead.

Billy Soh on the foreign exchange desk was arguing on the telephone with his bank's New York dealing room, where it was early evening the previous day, and the late duty trader's fatigue fuelled his irritability. Naomi Honda, with her scarlet designer glasses, was holding a customer on her line while she waited for a price from the market traders. The brokers' voices crackled monotonously through the speakers and the numbers flickered and changed on the screens. Yamamoto's eyes bulged as he sprang to his feet.

'Fifty-seven sixty-two,' he barked. With Kimura, he was trying to quote around a modest long dollar position as a nervous market sensed a possible concerted central bank intervention to prop up the US currency by short, sharp punitive dollar buying aimed at forcing its value northwards. Honda repeated the numbers calmly into the handpiece, waited a second and then shook her head towards her dealer.

Nicholls greeted the staff with deliberate brevity. His first impression of the Tokyo dealing room gave him a reassuring confidence in their professionalism and abilities, and the clarity and comprehensiveness of the supporting operational reports convinced him that the back-office was also in competent hands. He closed his office door and called Charlie Farmer, who was on night standby at his home in London, and entrusted him with the rumours of central bank intervention in the foreign exchange market. 'The dollar's drifted down too far. Bank of Japan might be ready to buy. They could come in in your time.'

He called his replacement in Hong Kong, Morgan Trinkel, an irascible Swiss who had been flown from London with the same short notice as Nicholls had to Tokyo. 'Everything's fine,' the man from Zurich boomed. 'What are you worried about? My only problem is to stop your Chinese friends betting on everything that moves, let alone every bloody currency.'

Nicholls smiled. 'Morgan,' Nicholls asked, 'were you guys in London aware Tony was drinking again?'

There was a short pause while the Swiss dredged his memory and checked the rapidly changing prices on the screens. 'No my friend, but not because we didn't tempt him. No, Tony wouldn't touch it. He couldn't. Kevin, I have to . . .'

'Sorry Morgan. I know you're busy. Through the plate window the Japanese dealers mimed in violent gestures, scenes being repeated in a hundred foreign exchange trading rooms throughout Asia at that very instant. 'Tell me quickly,' Nicholls said urgently, 'when you last saw Tony was he still using a walking stick? That black one I gave him after the accident?' He heard the Swiss quoting away from the telephone before coming back.

'Of course he was. I've seen him take out two fucking dealing screens with it.'

'Thanks Morgan. Watch yourself out there today. Intervention rumours flying around.'

Peter Stark, fussy and precise, brought in another

stack of computer printouts and introduced Nicholls to Derek Lemon. The laconic, bearded financial controller talked him through the reports which showed every transaction of the day before and logged them among all other live, unsettled deals according to the maturity dates when principal amounts or differences had to be settled. Separate computer printouts evidenced the unmatched assets and liabilities, where the bank was at risk from interest rate changes, and the vital cash flows listing the cumulative daily inflows and outflows of money from today to the very last deal in the bank's books. After an hour they were studying a slim package of folded sheets which noted every deal in all products and then revalued the whole lot against current market rates to give a bottom line profit or loss in the event the whole portfolio was liquidated on that day. Nothing bothered Nicholls, except for some mismatches in the Australian dollar cash book. He would discuss them with Hashida. The vital customer limit printout was five centimetres thick. It listed the banks which Sternberg Chance's Tokyo branch was authorized by its head-office credit committee to deal with in a dozen categories of treasury business. He ran his practised eyes down the list, over the pages, instinctively switching his attention from the inviolable limit on the left to the deals outstanding under it on the right, noting the few where the alarm bells built into the computer system had rung and the stigma of EXCESS printed bluntly against the offending deal. A dealer would have to explain the transaction which may have been done accidently or approved exceptionally by a senior manager. Either way, a formal report would be submitted to London so that Sternberg Chance's global exposure to the counterparty bank could be measured, assessed and corrected.

At the midday market break, Nicholls sought relief in the dealing room, his eyes sore from peering at a stack of printouts. He shared a sandwich and green tea lunch with Kawasaki and the ever attentive Naomi Honda. The foreign exchange desk was subdued, the traders sitting close to their screens throughout lunch as the market remained wary of Bank of Japan intervention. Kimura's grey scalp shone with perspiration through his wire-brush cropped hair and he confessed that they were nursing a Deutschmark yen position which was twenty thousand dollars under water. When the running loss reached twenty-five thousand, Mabuchi said, patrolling unamused around the dealing desks, the internal dealing rules stated they must square the position, take the loss and start again.

Returning to Tony's office as the brokers' voices crackled into life at one thirty Nicholls found himself distracted by the appearance in his mind of pestering uncertainties. He flipped the printouts listlessly and let his doubts consume him. A superficial scan of the financial books and observation of the dealers had given him assurance that the bank's critical Tokyo treasury was operationally well-supported and controlled and his first impression of Mabuchi was positive. Now he had to concentrate on his second task. The bank's worldwide head of treasury had also asked him to tidy up Tony's affairs, a mission Nicholls thought could have been undertaken more effectively by Stark or Fujimori or anyone with local street knowledge. What could he contribute? So far he was left discontent with the degree of respect that Tony's death had aroused, not least in his British colleagues who, while dismissive of wild foreign exchange dealers, might have found the compassion to attend his funeral or lay a wreath on the spot where he died. Then there was his girlfriend, happy to mourn her lover over a couple of sporting videos. He looked without seeing at the columns of numbers. Was there a professional reason for his friend's relapse to drink? Was there a mega loss buried in the complex interplay of assets and liabilities, the consequences of whose discovery might be worth dying for? Dealers do crack, and some are tempted and mesmerized by the billions they trade every day. In Balls Brothers, the Green Man, Mithras and countless other City watering holes, dealers unwind at night by jokingly speculating not on the movements of the dollar and the Deutschmark but the amount of money which, if it could be diverted electronically, would break their resistance, cause them to give up a hundred thousand pound salary and a comfortable life in Essex or north Kent, and flee to South America or somewhere closer where extradition was difficult.

The thought of a tropical haven sprang his memory. He spoke into the intercom. 'Miss Ueda,' he said, calling the treasury secretary. 'I can't get into Mr Moore's desk drawer.'

Tomoko Ueda's pastel dress jogged over heavy hips and her full face smiled deferentially as she joined him, a brace of silver keys hooked on her little finger. There was an urgency he had not intended as he juggled the key into the lock. He brushed aside some papers, a desk diary issued by his bank, bits of stationery and a confidential report. Tony Moore's passport wasn't on his body, in his flat or at his workplace. Its location was one of the items he would have to clear up. He eased the drawer shut. His attention should have been on the ever changing prices on his personal Reuters monitor but the rolling, lively face of Tony Tokyo was still fresh in his mind's eye. He flipped open the scuffed pages of the leather-bound diary, embossed with Tony's initials

76

and the year, to that Thursday in May when Tony's personal chronicle ended. Seeing the crowded itinerary, with a meeting on computer systems, another on the April performance review and lunch with a Japanese broker, he knew that it was not the sort of day his friend would have chosen for his last on earth. At the foot of the page, in his precise, leaning capitals, he had written '9.00 M G'. A person? A company? Morgan Grenfell? There was no brokerage house with those initials but MG was probably the last place or human to witness Tony Moore's final hours. He moved forward to the present and found a gold-rimmed, embossed invitation to a cocktail party that evening at the Imperial Hotel, hosted by the Ohyama Bank. The secretary had helpfully written 'accepted' across the top. He slipped it into the inside pocket of his jacket.

11

A dozen eyes followed his hurried departure, unaware that he was racing the light which would fade ridiculously early in a Tokyo afternoon. His secretary had drawn four clear hieroglyphics on a piece of message paper and instructed him to buy white and yellow chrysanthemums: red and other gaudy colours were to be avoided, especially roses; their thorns were not appropriate symbols for the dead.

The taxi's automatic door swung open at the crown of a short incline where it had crested alongside two massive stone pillars topped with an overhanging crossbar which straddled a steep flight of broad steps. The giant *torii* gate awed the visitor with its solemnity. Hie Jinja, the Shinto shrine where Tony Moore's corpse was found. Nicholls climbed warily, hoping the place where Tony died was still marked with a police sign, imagining him in the dank undergrowth beneath the entangled canopies of cherry, paulownia and hisakaki trees or with his skull cracked against one of the the tall, splay-footed lanterns built from stacks of ancient stone. He stood under the ornate pillared gateway, hands on hips in frustration, and ran his gaze across the gravel courtyard to the main shrine. He had supposed he would find an isolated back-street temple littered with pedlars, like those in Hong Kong which clung to precipitous flights of cracked steps. They posed a serious danger after a long pub crawl and he was looking for a Japanese version which Tony somehow scaled and then tumbled down in his alleged drunken state. But there was nothing sinister, let alone dangerous about this peaceful place, sound-proofed by a girdle of imposing trees. The steps behind him were steep, but each was wide enough to have arrested Tony's fall.

He watched two old women pour water over their hands and stand before the hall of the shrine, their frail hands summoning the deities with three sharp claps. A *gaijin* couple admired a trained pine tree protected by a fence of criss-crossed bamboo staves before moving on to ponder the significance of the two statues of monkeys, swathed in red capes and sitting like humans beside the steps leading to the main hall. The precinct of the shrine was scrupulously clean and the wooden buildings on three sides glowed with modernity. His shoes crunched on the coarse gravel as he walked through a gap in the side buildings which housed a museum, shops and a utility area of storage sheds.

Nicholls's hopes grew when he saw another flight

78

of steps between the massive cedars, katsura and larches which surrounded the shrine and made it all but invisible from the road. He took the steps in turn, pausing to peer into the undergrowth which encroached over the edges. Once, he stepped over the rim of the stairway to separate the vegetation, the tip of a fallen branch suddenly reminding him of Tony's missing walking stick. The rotten dead wood crumpled in his hand as he tossed it away. Had Tony died here? And why hadn't the police found that damned piece of blackthorn? The steps bothered him. There must have been eighty, split into flights of ten by a platform break accommodating a bench. Like the main steps, these were ample and restraining and fell gently to the main Akasaka road. He was scratching among the weeds and failed to notice a man climbing laboriously from street level.

'Can I help you find it?' a voice said in lightly accented English. The characteristic tortured pronunciation, the way Japanese speak English by splitting words into distinct syllables, like their own language, was missing. Nicholls thought he was hearing the welcome voice of an Englishman or a New Englander, but it was a Japanese of indeterminable age who stood above him, a flabby frame hunched inside a drab, punished suit with a powerful camera dragging the jacket off his shoulder.

'I doubt it,' he said, eyeing the lens.

'My name's Araki,' the other said amiably.

'And you're a reporter. You don't look like a tourist.'

'You're right. Neither do you.'

Nicholls swiped at the dirt which specked his trousers. He was hot and uncomfortable but his charcoal-grey, Italian suit was sharp and his scarlet, patterned tie was tightly knotted against the collar of his hand-made shirt. He did not smile at the friendly quip but was curiously reassured. He had been feeling isolated and intimidated by the absurd mass oneness of Tokyo and the stranger's openness and self-deprecating tone blurred the cultural differences. He said, 'A friend of mine died in an accident here and I want to see exactly where it happened, for my own peace of mind.'

They sat on a bench, which was actually concrete moulded into the shapes of logs. Araki produced a note pad and read from it. '"Anthony Moore, British banker. Died in accidental fall in the Hie Shrine."' He slapped the covers shut and looked at the Englishman through weary eyes.

'We're on the same mission,' he said, with an enthusiasm the foreigner ignored. 'There's a major human interest element here,' Araki insisted, neglecting to explain the salacious detail he needed to attract and hold the fickle readership of *One Point Finance*. 'We're talking about a tragedy my readers will sympathize with.'

Nicholls stared ahead.

Araki lit a cigarette and pressed on. 'I only want a routine picture. It doesn't have to be controversial. A bit of background. You know; what a great guy he was, left a sad, young widow, girlfriend, devastated friends. It may help you to cope with his death if you talk about him.'

'I don't need any help from the Press,' Nicholls said forcefully and took to his feet. 'I could get disciplined just for talking to you.' The thought of a reprimand from the faceless non-producers of Sternberg Chance did not phase him. What he did not want at this time was the hassle from a misquote or a trumped up collection of half-truths attributed to him.

'That's fine,' Araki said, calling after him as he climbed briskly back up the stairs towards the shrine. 'But if you want to find where your friend died, it's on the other side of the shrine.'

Nicholls stopped in his tracks and looked towards the Japanese.

'It helps if you speak Japanese.'

The *gaijin* nodded in surrender. 'Nicholls,' he said, extending a hand. 'Call me Kevin.'

Nicholls let the Japanese lead him to the courtyard, where short, tough-skinned old men in baggy trousers and split-toed shoes, their heads wrapped in protective towelling, trimmed borders and pampered the shrubs and young trees. The man, who had given his name only as Araki, shuffled his feet and growled at the chickens scratching inside their own wire compound by the museum entrance.

'As Buddhist temples go this place is not very old,' Nicholls said, motioning at the fresh gold and ochre paint on the solid structures.

'It's not Buddhist and it's not a temple. It's a shrine for Shinto, our own nature worship religion. According to it we've all got the god in us, so have animals and plants. It was the national religion, with the emperor as the head god, until the Americans decided he wasn't after they won the war and abolished Shinto as the state religion. You're right, the buildings aren't old. The shrine was destroyed during a fire-bomb attack in the war but its origins go back to the Eighth Century. The generals who ruled Japan until the middle of the last century adopted it to protect them. It didn't help much but you can see some of their swords in

the museum back there. They are national treas-
ures.'

Araki stopped to find his bearings.

'What do people do here?' Nicholls asked as they
headed across the gravel to the narrow gateway which
split the line of low buildings on the opposite side of
the courtyard.

'Pure fertility traditions,' the other said. 'Naming
of babies, old-style weddings, new year celebrations,
spring and harvest festivals.'

'And Buddhism?'

'It came from India through China and Korea. China
was the biggest influence. Brought our writing system
and most of what we call our culture. Tea ceremony,
flower arrangement. Like most things we've imported,
if we find them useful we adopt and call them Japanese.
Buddhism is convenient for death. We have a Buddhist
funeral and bury our ashes in their temples.'

'And no place for Christianity?'

Araki stopped again. They were at the rear of the
shrine, a tarred driveway backed with storerooms, a
toilet shed among the trees and a small, private shrine
apparently under repair.

'Only as a Western novelty. It's too unreasonable.
It claims credit for the good in the world but not the
fault for the bad. In Japan we are guided by fate.
We could die now from an earthquake, tomorrow
from a typhoon and on Saturday from the liver
of the blowfish, or we can inherit a fortune. It's
all down to fate. But we like Christianity for the
weddings. The trendy thing to do is to dress up in
white in church. The missionaries have given up trying
to convert us and are making money like the rest of us.
Look over there.'

He pointed towards a clearing, darkened by the

overhang of the shrine's main building and the packed foliage, at a red *torii* gate barely the height of a man, a version in miniature of the stone monster which formed the shrine's main gate. 'It's the old, original entry. It reaches the road opposite the modern steps where I met you but hardly anyone uses it. You can see why.'

The cracked, slippery steps curled where they left the shrine and then fell abruptly. It was dark, like being in a tunnel, and the buzz of insects echoed in the damp sunless air. Taut vertical banners, painted with huge Chinese lettering, had central stems which formed a bamboo fence on both sides of the stairway and dozens of the red, miniature double-crossed *torii* gates, almost one for each step, decorated the desolate passage set deep in the rich greenery. 'There are seventy of them,' Araki said. 'I counted them out of curiosity. And eighty-seven steps. The *torii* and the banners are gifts from the supporters and patrons of the shrine.'

'What happened to my friend?' Nicholls said harshly, the mysteries of the Orient suddenly irrelevant.

'I asked one of the old gardeners,' Araki said, taking cautiously the steps which were slippery with age and insect slime. 'Moore stumbled from about the twentieth step. Most of the blood, the skin from his scalp and the vomit was on the twenty-seventh. Right here.' They stood in silence and looked at the clean, grey, freshly washed patch of concrete. 'Then the momentum carried him another ten steps before he rolled through the strips of bamboo and into the open bit of that drainage culvert.'

Nicholls winced, seeing in the moving shadows shaped by the filtering light the memory of his friend, grinning, full of life and waving his blackthorn walking stick like a sword. Araki was saying, 'His face was badly smashed and he was lying there for about eight hours before the gardeners found him.'

Nicholls broke in quickly: 'The *Japan Times* didn't have so much detail.'

'Neither did the Japanese Press,' Araki countered. 'I spoke to my contacts in the metropolitan police agency this morning and to the guy who found the body. They gave me enough factual details for my article.'

'Have you talked to my bank's spokesman?' Nicholls asked.

'Fujimori? He won't talk to the Press.'

Nicholls smiled sardonically. 'You can always invent the rest. I suppose the methods and standards of your papers can't be much different from those of the crap we pay for.' He was moving away from Araki, probing the gap opened by the falling body in the fragile bamboo barrier. 'There's nobody left to sue you. They all think Tony drank himself silly and fell over. I hear that's normal behaviour in this country.' He dropped to one knee and stood the flowers, still in their Cellophane wrapping, against the foot of the *torii* gate nearest the gap. He knelt motionless for a moment, then sprang up and plunged between two of the *torii* gates into a tangle of ground shrub and weed. There he squatted to twist some exposed tree roots and appeared with a blackened, straight shaft of wood, stripped where it curved at one end. He weighed it once and then hurled the deceptive piece of rotting branch against a tree, enjoying the vicious crack as it broke.

'What are you doing?' Araki said, his voice an inquisitive squeak.

'If you want something for your rag,' he hissed, 'try

this. Tony Moore hadn't touched a drop of alcohol for two years. The smell of it made him ill. There's no way he could have got boozed up last Thursday. The first drink would have been back on the bar. All over it. And this. Tony limped badly, not actually crippled, but enough to need a walking stick. The stick wasn't in the police report, it's not in the bank or his apartment. It's an old one I gave him after the accident that caused his limp and I'd like to have it as a memento.'

Araki nodded sympathetically and when Nicholls began his search with renewed vigour he pocketed his notebook, laid his camera on the ground and followed him through the gap into the packed bushes and trees. 'I'll do the culvert side,' he yelled commandingly, 'You work your way up from over there.'

They searched unnoticed, a pair of madmen playing in the undergrowth, save by a pair of American tourists, bemused at the strange miniature columns and crossbars and looking uncomfortable on the eerie stairway. Twenty minutes later they were sitting on the steps, empty handed.

'It doesn't make sense,' Nicholls said, as they re-traced their route through the shrine courtyard. 'I have to know what happened.' And in frustration he added, 'Nobody's interested. They say everything's been done properly, the questions answered and Tony properly cremated, ready to be sent home in a shoe-box. I'll have to see Tony's girlfriend again. She's the key.'

Araki was struggling to match Nicholls's pace, his breathing laboured, his steps unco-ordinated, but his practised hearing snared an inadvertent remark. 'Tony's girlfriend.' If he had heard correctly he had the whiff of an angle which would appeal to the readers of *One Point Finance*. He tossed a cigarette away.

Nicholls had propped himself sacrilegiously against a pillar of the giant *torii* and saw for the first time a sombre multi-tiered building with taxis parked under an awning. It blended so well into the depth of the greenery that he had not noticed it when he had first reached the shrine.

Araki sensed the other's weakness and stalked him slowly. 'The police theory is that Moore walked out of there.' He gestured to the building. 'That's the Capitol Tokyu Hotel. It used to be the Hilton. For some reason he ignored the taxis and the underground station near the hotel's back entrance and decided to cut through the shrine, probably heading for Akasaka. It is vaguely on the way to his apartment in Kojimachi. Having managed to climb to head of this flight of steps into the courtyard he had the choice of turning left and taking the safe, wide stairway or right, round the back to the steep, uneven steps. He chose wrongly.'

'How do you know all this?' Nicholls demanded.

'I've been a street writer for fifteen years. The cops I knew when I started are now well placed in the service. We value continuity here. That's how I know where your friend was last Thursday night.'

Nicholls remembered the entry in Tony Moore's diary. MG. Was it a person or a place? It was not something he needed to share with a hack of suspect motives. He said, 'How can I find out where he was before the hotel?'

Araki cupped a reluctant flame and drew it to his cigarette. 'The police won't give you anything. You're not an official. It's easier for me to get around them. Let's check things out together.' They moved off again, towards the road.

86

'No thanks. You were a big help in the shrine. There are only a few loose ends I'd like to clear up for the sake of his family. His sister. I can manage that on my own.'

You don't understand, do you?' Araki said desperately. 'You won't get far. Tokyo's not Hong Kong. Hardly anybody speaks English here. You can't get by with gestures and pidgin language.'

Nicholls stopped.

The Japanese circled him. 'Let's have a drink in the hotel. Talk to the staff. See if they remember something they didn't tell the police.'

Nicholls liked the scruffy Japanese journalist whose English was effortless and strewn with British and American idioms. He found him humorous and straight-talking but wondered what his real motives were. He liked him because he was the first person he had met in Japan to tell him how tough and different the local scene was and then offer to help him face it. 'I'd like to,' he said honestly, tapping his jacket pocket. 'I have to be at a party in an hour at the Imperial Hotel. But I'll think about your offer and if there's anything I need I'll call you. Give me a telephone number.' Moving away from the Japanese, he said: 'You look like you could do with an early night yourself.'

12

Under the brilliant chandeliers, orbited by filmy clouds of cigarette smoke, the vast ballroom was a sea of black hair from a thousand Japanese men and women. An army of young hostesses in exquisite, fiercely bright and intricately patterned kimonos passed among the guests with trays of champagne, whisky and orange juice. Nicholls joined guests to be received by a line of beaming, sombrely dressed, late middle-aged men, each with a closed, blood-red rose on his lapel. They bowed deeply to the Japanese guests, not head-to-head Nicholls noted but marginally aside, their hands brushing their thighs. The foreigners were seized absurdly with both hands. 'Congratulations,' he said to the elderly, slightly stooped figure he assumed was Ryusuke Sakamoto, the chairman, and host at what the invitation trumpeted as the one hundredth anniversary of the founding of the Ohyama Bank.

Nicholls was pleased to see Peter Stark emerging from the crowd to rescue him from his anonymity. He would appreciate his company, and be grateful for the identifications and the prompts on etiquette that the more experienced expatriate could give. Stark's face was already flushed as he stopped a smiling hostess and replaced his empty champagne glass. 'They're all out-of-work actresses and models,' he said knowingly, watching with appreciation as she moved away, seeming to glide effortlessly in spite of the tightly bound folds of the kimono. 'Not drinking?'

Nicholls held a glass out of convention: he hardly noticed the juice in it. He said, 'I'm going back to the office to go over some papers when it's quiet. It's not a problem is it?'

Stark drained his glass. 'Not at all. You've got Tony's key. The security people downstairs will ask you to sign in if you arrive after nine. Do you remember the door codes?'

Nicholls nodded and the two men drifted into the throng, towards the centre where tables groaned under heaps of shellfish, smoked salmon, and skewers of barbecued chicken. They were nudged aside by the men jostling for the attention of a chef who was shaving slices off a side of pink marbled beef, a pompous, unsmiling expression on his pale face.

'The only chance they get to eat it,' Stark explained. 'Costs fifty pounds a pound.'

'Is there any Japanese food?' Nicholls asked ingenuously.

'No. That's what they come for,' Stark laughed as they passed another dark-suited guest struggling to cradle his drink and support his plate of roast beef. The meat had been helpfully cut into strips to accommodate chopsticks.

Employees of the host bank, distinguished by the red rose in their lapels, circulated with a soft drink or an empty glass. Catching sight of Masaaki Fujimori, who stood a head above most of his countrymen, Nicholls saw that he too boasted a rose and reminded himself that Sternberg Chance's senior adviser was only seconded to his bank. His pension and probably his loyalty were with Ohyama.

He also began to notice scattered groups of outsiders, foreigners, mostly young white men with the clean, buttoned-down look of American investment bankers, and their older professional expatriate managers.

'Kev, Kev!' A high voice pleaded above the din and

a man with short, blond hi-lighted hair and a grey, checked suit broke through and seized his hand. 'I heard you were in town. Why haven't you dealt through us?'

Nicholls grinned. 'Hi Pat. Give me time. I've only been in Tokyo a day.'

The other man's smiled faded. 'I'm sorry about Tony,' he said, remembering. 'We all are.' And then, 'There are more of your mates in the corner. They've trained one of the butterflies to bring them food and keep the champagne coming.'

Patrick Regan was thirty-two but looked fifty and was frighteningly thin inside his expensively tailored suit. Always animated and forceful, the desperate pallor of his face was testimony to a decade of excess in the fast, all-consuming life of foreign exchange trading. Fired from a German bank in London for tearing out a telephone when drunk and hurling it at a colleague who had accidently dealt on the buy side instead of sell, he took the natural route, becoming broker middleman with Carsworth, where the ability to entertain lavishly was a job requirement and the rewards limitless. He now intermediated deals from the offices of their Japanese partner, which traded under the name of Carsworth Tanaka Tokyo.

Bumping shoulders as they sidled through the crowd, Nicholls said, 'Pat. Had Tony started drinking again?'

Regan waved a cigarette dismissively. 'No way. He couldn't be tempted.' His sallow, abused face broke into a broad smile, showing a row of stained teeth. 'We tried it once. Spiked his tonic water with vodka at a Christmas party last year. Threw up over the *maître d'* at the Tokyo Prince.' Nicholls pretended to find the anecdote amusing.

'Something must have happened to force him off the

90

wagon,' Nicholls said in frustration. 'He drank himself out of control according to the police.'

'He seemed OK last week,' a broker said. 'At Romy's. You were there Pat.'

Pat scratched his sparse hair. 'We were all a bit pissed,' he laughed. 'The memory's gone cloudy.'

'Tony as well?' Nicholls asked.

Marcus Levy, another broker with Carsworth said, 'I wouldn't normally remember, but me and Tony are the only non-drinkers in Tokyo. We were in Romy's early Thursday, the night he died. Tony was a bit down, probably lost a few grand on the yen. I got the impression he was shipping in the vodka tonics. I might be wrong. There was a lot of booze on the counter.'

'Was he ill afterwards?' Nicholls demanded.

Levy looked at Regan and the others. They agreed that Tony Moore was quieter than usual but they could not swear he had taken alcohol in the hour or so he was with them before he went off on another date.

'I thought he was slurring a bit but then they all were by that time,' Levy said laughing. 'Apart from that he seemed normal.'

Nicholls addressed the group. 'Do you guys know a bank, a person, a club maybe, something that fits the initials M G? Tony marked his diary last Thursday, the night he died. Probably the date he left you for.'

The chief dealer from the Chartered Bank, Mike Green, said it was not him; Morgan Grenfell, the British merchant bank, had a Tokyo office which Nicholls said he would check. A dollar-mark broker called Roy assumed it was a woman, though none of them could think of a Japanese surname beginning with G. Another tray of drinks revived them, all that is except Hugh Carter from Austins, a sloppy sweating giant. The rolls of his neck covered his open collar and the knot of his tie was spotted with dripped soya sauce. 'What about Mama Gimbasha's?' he bawled. 'It's a bar in Roppongi. We just call it Gimbasha's. Some guy, a dealer with one of the Jap banks, opened it in March or April.'

'Where's Roppongi?'

'You haven't been here long, have you?' a broker called Painton said. 'It's a mass of lights, a great big neon playground, not far from Tony's old flat.'

'Mama Gimbasha's is one of our locals,' Regan guffawed. 'With Deja Vu and a couple of others. The fact is we're banned from the best bars in Roppongi.'

Nicholls felt a tug on his sleeve.

'How are you Nicholls san? How good to see you here.' Masaaki Fujimori's voice was mellow and conciliatory, influenced by the contents of the tumbler he clutched to his chest.

'I came with Tony Moore's invitation,' the Englishman said.

Sternberg Chance's adviser grasped the inference. 'I do apologize for not inviting you personally this morning. We did, of course, have other things on our minds. But please let me introduce you to some Ohyama people.'

Nicholls looked at his watch. 'I was about to go back to the office,' he said, missing, as he turned to thank the brokers, the faint change which dimmed for an instant Fujimori's cheery expression. Looking for the moment to leave, he edged nearer the grand doorway when a man with a Ohyama rose and a smug expression appeared from the crowd and bade farewell to a guest.

'And that's our head of treasury,' Fujimori said,

92

steering Nicholls between the knots of partygoers. 'He would like to meet you.'

'I already know him,' Nicholls remarked coldly. 'Very well.' And so does the whole dealing world.

Katsuro Koga was a feared man, even among the dealers for whom the predatorial instincts of the shark are a requirement of the job. In a business where trust and credibility permitted money to move across the world at a word on the telephone, he was mistrusted. Opportunism was Koga's ruthless obsession. He took advantage of temporary market imperfections, perhaps a currency overvalued against economic forecasts, or another bank's quotations a shade out of line with the market. And he promoted himself as the world's most important trader of the Japanese currency.

Nicholls coveted his access to Japan's capital flows, to the pension funds and cash surpluses of his customers and grudgingly envied his contacts and the scope and depth of his information, the key to staying ahead of the competition. When Koga decided it was his moment, he moved a barrage of money to drive the market his way, billions of dollars unleashed by Ohyama dealers in a concerted assault. Koga's tool was money and he used it like a pile-driver. You either stayed with him or dropped out. You did not ignore him. When Koga's bank called for a two-way price Nicholls would alert his dealers, warning them against a man who seemed to know which way the rates were going or intended to move them where he wanted. Yes, Kevin Nicholls knew Katsuro Koga.

In person, Koga was short and slender and wore his customary London-made double-breasted suit and the tie of an elite association of worldwide foreign exchange dealers. 'Nice to see you again, Nicholls san,' Koga said amiably, as Fujimori drifted away.

93

'When was the last time? The Sydney forex meeting I think. Let's get a drink and find a quiet corner.'

'I was just leaving,' Nicholls said.

Koga turned on him, and in the flash before the fixed smile returned, there was a look of contempt in the Japanese's cold, brown eyes and hard, pitiless features. He wasted no time with profound condolences. 'I won't keep you long,' he said, finding an alcove. 'Moore san's death is very regrettable but I am sure it will not affect the excellent relationship between our two banks. To be frank, I relied on his execution capacity very much and his prices were very competitive. As you know the Ohyama bank has many powerful customers and we need as many outlets as possible in all markets.'

'The Ohyama Bank doesn't have problems finding counterparties, does it?' the Englishman said snidely. He knew the Ohyama Bank's name was as reputable as Citibank, Midland and Deutsche and all the first-tier foreign exchange banks in the market, good for one-shot billion dollar deals or more. What annoyed the market was Ohyama's deliberate reluctance to respect a two-way relationship that demanded both parties recip-rocate by making prices when asked. Koga's buy and sell price-spread was often wide and when challenged he would claim there was too much volatility or he would quote for a smaller amount than requested.

Koga sucked in air. 'These are difficult markets,' he said intensely. 'Too many mediocre players chasing the liquidity. My customers want to deal with the real market movers, you, me, a few others, with the balls to handle the big tickets. We must work together with our friends. And Sternberg Chance are close friends.'

Nicholls had to grin, gesturing at the party. 'Most of our staff's from Ohyama. We are more than friends. We are in bed together.'

Koga smiled without warmth. 'I'll instruct my dealers to offer you whatever business we can. There's more than enough around and Ohyama and Sternberg Chance should get what they can.'

'Don't go out of your way,' Nicholls said. 'I'm keeping my head out of the firing line until I've analysed Tony's business profile and understand what he was into.'

Koga smiled icily. 'Then I suppose you will be going back to Hong Kong. I'm sure Moore san left a smooth and clean operation.'

'I hope so,' Nicholls said, easing himself away. 'Otherwise I'll have to stay longer.'

13

Nicholls walked the kilometre from the hotel to the Nichibankan building, the still, brackish palace moat on one side, the solid, old brick offices of Marunouchi on the other. Lights burning in the giant banks and trading companies formed uneven mosaics on the sides of the squat, unimaginative blocks and although it was past eight thirty, Nicholls saw that there were more lights on than off, including, a solitary glow on the ninth floor of the Nichibankan building, corresponding, he thought, to his own office. The guard acknowledged him with a weary end-of-shift nod as he made for the lift. The security light in the reception cast a pale infra-red glow, enough for him to read the numbers on the door code.

The offices were deserted, the outlines of the desks starkly illuminated by the reflected lights of the building opposite. It made him wonder whether he had mistaken the floor when he had stood nine levels below.

'Hello,' he said self-consciously, edging towards his office. He had his hand on the light switch when he noticed the blue-white discoloration at the ends of the four fluorescent tubes half buried in the low, panelled ceiling. As he watched, the brighter parts faded into the hazy grey mass. On an impulse he stood on a chair to reach the lighting rods. They were still warm.

The dealing room was eerily quiet, the brokers' boxes silent, the screens lifeless: the night shift and all the staff who normally worked late had been told to leave early and attend the celebrations at the Ohyama bank party. But somebody was there. Nicholls felt angry and helpless, like the prey who longed to be the hunter, but he was lost in the still strange office, the hidden places unknown to him. It made him defensive. In his business the vulnerable areas were the stacks of sensitive reports on client business and the transaction records on which the integrity of the bank depended. He slapped a monitor screen and dashed to the operations room adjoining the treasury where trades were processed and multi-million dollar payments originated under tight security and discipline. A door slammed, its violent sound muffled by distance. 'Who's there,' he called across the dark space while he searched desperately for a light switch, confused by the unfamiliar layout.

He walked slowly back to the desk nearest the room which housed the transmission hardware. The codes required to transfer two and a half billion dollars a day between Sternberg Chance Tokyo and its customers meant access was restricted to a few trained operatives under the strictest security. Glaring at him on the desk was a torn piece of paper from a computer printout. Its edge had been trapped under the base of a terminal when someone had removed the rest of it in a hurry. He sat at the desk, and began to flatten and smooth the incriminating morsel. A portion of a line of numbers survived, clearly a date and part of what was a foreign exchange deal number. No one would leave a document in that condition: the mutilation would be noted and the file restored. He knew that the visitor had taken the rest of it. He must have left, probably through the reception or the back corridors where there would be an exit to the fire escape.

As he sat contemplating the intruder's motives, Nicholls saw the sliver of wire, barely visible between the keyboard and the terminal where it had been pushed and forgotten in the dash for freedom. Carefully moving the equipment aside, he lifted the pair of eyeglasses from the gaps. They were oversized, as he remembered them, and looking closer he saw they were lightly tinted, their bright red frames inlaid with minute white dots. They belonged to Naomi Honda, the self-assured corporate dealer who had no business being in the bank tonight and definitely not in the operations department.

14

Warron Hanlon, the impressively built chief executive of Sternberg Chance, Japan, a man accustomed to the dignified environment of the upper floors where the corporate finance teams plotted their takeovers and mergers and a small army of bond sales people peddled their wares to affluent investors around the globe, stood like any other forbidden non-treasury personnel, waiting to be recognized and admitted, his shoulders twitching with impatience. He resented not having access to the dealing room code and he rapped again on the glass, ignoring the button which would have triggered a buzzer below the desks of the nearest traders. His narrow, strong-featured face was deeply tanned from the holiday which he had been loathe to disrupt and he pressed it against the glass until he was noticed and the door was opened.

His intense eyes swept the room, but few of the dealers looked up from their screens and the vital movements of a hundred different figures. They were apprehensive, edgy, sensing another assault on the fragile American currency. How long could the central banks tolerate such a weak dollar? It was close to breaking through a technical support level at a hundred and twelve yen and fifty sen and if it did there were no new economic or political factors in the forecasting models to stop it free-falling another five big figures to a hundred and seven yen. Even at a hundred and thirteen yen the once mighty dollar was only worth less than half a cup of coffee, or a few stops on the city's commuter train system.

'Where's Mr Nicholls?' he said theatrically, and then saw the only other Caucasian there.

'Warren Hanlon,' he said.

Nicholls turned, surprised, and shook the other's hand awkwardly from his seat.

'Hang on,' he said, with a dealer's economic wordage. He raised his chin above the console.

'Billy. We've got an order to sell twenty dollars at the figure. If it gets there sell another ten for me. I don't think it'll make it up there though. It's all one way at the moment.' A split screen graph showed a line edging downwards. Taking in everyone on the desk he barked, 'Have you got that guys?'

Kimura and Yamamoto raised a hand without taking their eyes off the screens. Nicholls had to ensure that what he and Billy Soh did with the dollar-yen was known to the dealers handling the other currencies, whose exchange rates would react to sudden changes elsewhere. He flourished a ball point pen at his dealers. 'What have you two got?'

'Short of a buck against the mark,' Kimura mumbled, a pencil crushed in his teeth. Yamamoto said, 'I'm long of five pounds.'

'Good. Watch it carefully. Mabuchi san, would you take over here please.'

The senior treasury man moved from his place at the head of the corporate dealing team, and Nicholls led his chief to his office, offering him the chair he had used to examine the fluorescent lights the night before. He sat behind his desk, changing a page on the Reuters monitor until he was comfortable with the currency listing.

Warron Hanlon had rich, chestnut hair, naturally oily and swept from his low forehead. It gave him a saturnine, somewhat malevolent look and his first words told Nicholls that what he had heard of this powerful director of Sternberg Chance was undoubtedly true.

'I'm surprised you have time to deal,' Hanlon said. 'When I looked for you yesterday your secretary said you'd gone sightseeing.' His voice was uncompromising and threatening.

'That's not exactly the case,' Nicholls responded, the hair on his neck bristling. 'But I did want to see the place where Tony died.' There was something in Hanlon's dismissive, unsympathetic attitude which he saw as a reason not to share his doubts about Tony's death, or his suspicions about the twilight activities of Naomi Honda who he could now see through the window, different glasses clasped in her hair today. He had left the red-rimmed pair where he had found them, instructing his secretary Tomoko Ueda to identify the owner.

'Let's try and keep the sentimentality under control,' Hanlon was saying. 'We're all very sorry about Moore but it's extraordinarily embarrassing at this moment. I can't give you any details but we are in the middle of very complex negotiations which affect our operations in Japan. Moore's death couldn't have come at a worse time. I don't want any more surprises from this department,' he said, implying that the accidental death of a dealer or a minor trading loss would fall into the same category. 'The Press are already scratching at the door. London and I want the lid firmly nailed down.'

Nicholls thought about the journalist Araki, the only person he had met since landing in Japan who was mildly interested in the fate of Tony Moore, and his reasons were purely professional.

'Well, you've seen Moore off,' Hanlon continued placatingly. 'Tell me how you find things in the treasury.'

Nicholls stood to close the doors to the dealing room and the open office, where his secretary sat watchfully within hearing distance. Through the window, he saw a soundless exchange between Naomi Honda and Mabuchi. Billy Soh was on his feet talking intently into a handset. He slid back into his seat and ran his eyes down the screen. The rates had barely moved.

'Tony was a good risk manager,' he began, in a speech he knew he would have to make sooner or later. 'The balance sheet is funded short, but so is everybody's in this market, and we can close the positions out easily. He was borrowing around five hundred million dollars worth of yen on a day to day basis.'

'Christ! Is that safe?' Hanlon said, his eyes narrowing.

'There are no problems with credit. I figure our name's good for up to a billion, billion two hundred thousand dollars a day.'

The terminology of the money markets baffled the chief executive and he made no pretence to deny it. 'What was he doing with all that yen?'

Nicholls opened a hand and counted off his fingers. 'He was borrowing three hundred million dollars worth of yen every day to lend back into the market for up to a month. If the yield curve was static he could earn a quarter, three eighths per cent on the gaps. For the time being I've cut this back by half until I understand the workings of the market here. The rest of the money,' he said, tapping another digit, 'funds the bond trading boys upstairs. We're not in charge of that activity so you'll have to decide whether you're happy to continue with that level of exposure.'

Hanlon scribbled on a block of paper. 'What else?'

Nicholls flipped his own notes. 'He's bought three hundred contracts on the electronic yen futures exchange

101

to hedge his longer term exposures. No position there. You've got a three billion dollar forward foreign exchange book on balance sheet.' He anticipated the reaction. 'It's all squared out, apart from a fifty million position he lets the boys out there play with. The exposure's well managed and brings in around two hundred thousand dollars a month.'

His eyes flashed between Hanlon and the dealing room. He saw that it was now Mabuchi's turn to look worried. Kawasaki from the customer desk was explaining something. Nicholls apologized to his chief executive and tapped on the intercom. 'What's happening?'

Mabuchi answered, agitated. 'A customer just took thirty million dollars at eighty from us. We're trying to get them back straight away as you ordered but we're getting ten point prices. The market's seventy-two eighty-two.'

'Try Citi Singapore and Hongkong, including Sternberg. But tell Trinkel what's happening. Sorry,' he said, returning to Hanlon.

'What was that about?'

Nicholls tried to hold his concern inside. 'When you quote another bank in dollar-yen you make him a five sen spread between your bid and your offer. If the market's uncertain or out of control the spread widens, making it bloody difficult to get out of a position without losing, let alone a profit. At this moment we've given away dollars in exchange for a hundred and twelve yen eighty sen and now the market's offering to sell them back to us, to square our position, at seventy eight sen. That's a two sen loss on thirty million bucks if we have to buy them back now.' He paused to calculate in his head. 'It would cost us six hundred thousand yen, about five thousand dollars. The dollar's still vulnerable so I've ordered the dealers to keep square or short of dollars. But not thirty million dollars short.' He wished he were out with the team and pressed the intercom violently. 'What have you done?'

'We bought twenty-five at eighty-four.' It was Billy Soh, whose voice was tight and controlled. Nicholls did not bother to tell the head of the bank that the loss was now ten thousand dollars, still not excessive.

'Foreign exchange dealing has always bothered me,' Hanlon confessed with a haughty toss of his head. 'All that shouting and swearing and more often than not a lot of money down the drain at the end of it. What was Moore up to?'

If Hanlon had felt any sympathy for their dead colleague, Nicholls thought, as he watched the dark facial shadows changing with each movement of the tall man's head, it had dissolved on that precipitated flight back to Tokyo.

'On a busy day Tony was turning over around a billion dollars, mostly in dollar-yen. He was a market maker in the currencies, like the big Japanese banks. He would quote for one shot up to a hundred million dollars for a bank and unlimited for a customer.'

'Was he speculating?' Hanlon asked grimly. 'How much of that was gambling?'

Nicholls wanted to ask why the head of the operation, even one which employed three hundred people, was so unfamiliar with the part which carried the greatest risk, an ignorance unearthed by this trite and traditional question.

'He took positions,' he explained, 'within the limits the risk management committee in London gave him. He went into the market himself if he thought it right or he ran positions off the back of the deals the customers did with him. Speculation? Sure. About sixty per of Tony's turnover was speculative, the rest came from genuine customer business. Before you get excited, remember that in London and New York eighty per cent of all the foreign exchange deals, hundreds of billions of dollars a day, are speculative. Tony's ratio was better than the market. So was mine in Hong Kong. Ideally, you're looking for a fifty-fifty split between bank and corporate business, but this depends on having a high quality, high volume customer base. Tony had a good balance and it's brought you three million pounds after brokerage so far this year.'

'I want to discuss income,' Hanlon said imperiously, but the moment was lost. The yell from Billy Soh penetrated the partitions. Telephone in one hand, he beckoned furiously to Nicholls with the other, at the same time hollering at the dealers around him. A dozen heads lowered over telephone buttons and Reuters dealing systems.

'We quoted Sankoku Oil ninety-ninety seven in a hundred bucks and he took us. Everybody get calls,' Soh bawled as Nicholls threw himself into a spare dealing position.

Warron Hanlon was soon behind him. 'What's happened?'

Nicholls answered without looking up from the monitors. 'We're now short of a hundred and five million dollars, one of your customers just took us and now we have to get them back in this crap thin market.' He stood up brusquely, brushing Hanlon aside. 'Come on everybody. Get the calls out.'

'Ninety five oh five,' the position clerk Midori Sano hollered in her thin, raspish voice.

Billy Soh shook his head and looked at Nicholls

for inspiration, the tension beginning to show on his normally passive Oriental face. 'The dollar's going bid,' he said.

'Ten point spread,' the English dealer said for Hanlon's benefit.

The next three offers to sell the dollar were fifteen points above the price Sternberg had sold their hundred million. Nicholls waved dismissively at Sano's price. The Japanese dealers flicked into the brokers' lines. Yamamoto's face was flushed with fear when he said, 'No offers out there. Only bids for dollars.'

'Where are these calls?' Nicholls yelled. 'And watch out for the Bank of Japan.'

'The Jap banks are not picking us up,' Soh bemoaned. 'We've got twenty calls out on the Reuters.'

'Billy,' Naomi Honda called, a telephone pressed against the collar of her blouse. 'Ohyama Bank wants dollar-yen in twenty.'

'Tell them to piss off,' Nicholls barked, an image of Katsuro Koga flashing through his brain as he rapped on his keyboard. The market was behaving in a manner that scared him to new heights of alertness; he wanted to see someone else's price for twenty million dollars. Warron Hanlon was not in his sphere of attention and it was an intrusion when the director said, 'You can't ignore the Ohyama Bank. They are our partners and we have to support them.'

'Then why wouldn't they pick us up on the Reuters or the direct telephone line when we called them earlier?' He went unanswered.

'You have to quote them,' Hanlon insisted.

Nicholls shook his head with annoyance. 'Make him twenty fifty.' It was a silly, contemptuous thirty point spread price and well away from where Nicholls perceived the elusive dollar-yen quotation to be. Honda queried it once and then repeated the price into the telephone.

It was an immeasurable instant, one which Kevin Nicholls would relive a hundred times in the next ten hours. Naomi Honda raised her arm straight upwards in the classic market buying gesture. The Ohyama Bank had bought dollars, even at a punishing price.

What's going on? Nicholls computer mind screamed. What the hell does Katsuro Koga know?

'Everyone. Buy dollars,' he ordered. 'We're a hundred and twenty five short.'

A high-pitched, panicked voice screamed from first one brokers' box then the others. '*Nichigin. Nichigin*!' Even Nicholls knew it meant the Bank of Japan. Everyone was speaking Japanese in loud, almost hysterical bursts. He knew what they were saying. The Bank of Japan, and, as the newsflash confirmed, Federal Reserve Bank of the US, was intervening in the Tokyo and other Asian markets to buy the American currency and force its value up. The price line on the graph raced vertically as dollars were hoovered from the foreign exchange system and would only stop when the central banks were satisfied that the current round of speculation against the greenback was stemmed.

'Mine, mine!' the Sternberg dealers screeched, trying to capture the attention of the brokers who could not hold the soaring price long enough to firm a deal. The fractional sen spreads disappeared as banks sought to protect themselves by quoting a full half yen between their bid to buy dollars and their offer to sell. The central banks had intervened at one hundred and thirteen yen and ninety sen and within fifteen seconds, when their intention had shaken the world's dealing community, frantic calls from Asia waking that part of the world that slept, it reached a hundred and fifteen yen. At a hundred and sixteen yen and ten sen, over two yen above the intervention entry rate, the chart line levelled but still edged fractionally upwards. Sternberg's calls were answered and the banks happily long of dollars were content to sell off all or part of their position to the banks and customers which saw the dollar going higher and had to get on the bandwagon. Or to those like Sternberg that had to cover their short position at whatever cost.

'We're square,' Kimura said gloomily, his shirt soaked with sweat, his hair plastered to his scalp. The dealers and their assistants went quietly about the paperwork of their toils. Deals were confirmed by telephone or fax with the counterparties to the trades and operational vouchers completed for the back-office to process into payments and accountants to translate into the books of the bank. No one looked at Nicholls, who shuffled a stack of dealing sheets and worked the raw figures into a calculator. Warron Hanlon stood by a printer, reading the news reports as they were assembled and disseminated by the wire services. His arms were folded, his teeth clenched. Nicholls tore a coil of paper from his machine and led Hanlon to his office.

Hanlon opened his palms and shrugged his shoulders, surrendering to the incomprehensibility of the situation, to the inevitability of the pale excuses that awaited him. He would be disappointed. 'How much has that little exercise in financial machismo cost us?'

'A million five hundred thousand dollars maybe more.' He would waste no time with excuses on the man who had the right to be disappointed but who could not be expected to react rationally. Would he sympathize if Nicholls claimed that the conditions he faced in the market today were abnormal to the point of being impossible? The answer was written in the eyes, in the fidgety anger barely suppressed inside the other man's solid frame.

'We'll pick through the blood and guts when I'm a little less excited but I was going to tell you about the plans I have discussed with Prideaux for the future of the Tokyo treasury. You might not be surprised to know that they don't include you. Don't interrupt please. You'll have your opportunity to contribute to the bank's strategy in due course. We have agreed to transfer Marcus Birkmeyer out to Tokyo on a permanent basis. You will return to Hong Kong and relieve Morgan Trinkel.' The chief executive leaned back, his smug satisfaction barely contained.

Nicholls was keen to recover his authority but the platform of his argument was thin and worn. He tried to maintain a dispassionate response.

'Birkmeyer's a capital markets man. He's a bond salesman. He doesn't understand foreign exchange or the money markets.'

'He's a competent organizer and manager,' Hanlon said, enjoying the other's discomfort and resisting the urge to comment on Nicholls's expertise in that department. 'And he's the man we want to reorganize the Tokyo operation and direct our priorities in other directions. The business today just emphasizes the urgent need to redefine our priorities here.'

'Can I know what these are?'

Hanlon wished he had some papers which he could stack to emphasize the finality of the decision and bring the conversation to an end. Instead, he stood up and smoothed his jacket. 'We are going to integrate the treasury and the capital market function, reducing the market making of your dealing room and give it a more of a support role in the overall structure.'

Hanlon could be reading from one of the jargon-ridden strategic plans which spewed from Sternberg Chance's management office.

'I'd like to talk to Prideaux about it,' Nicholls said calmly.

'You will have your chance. Gervase will be coming out here at the weekend. Please make sure that Moore's things are shipped out and the dealers out there keep their hands off the telephones until then.' He rose to leave. 'And let me have a warts-and-all report on today's fiasco as soon as you can.'

15

Hirata was thirty-two, a patient and cautious man who enjoyed the company of his wife and relished the sight of his three-year-old son, usually asleep in the futon laid out beside his wife's by the time he reached the company-owned apartment in Abiko, a full ninety minutes commute from Marunouchi. Akemi was still awake and while he was bathing she would make a simple meal of grilled fish, rice, soup and pickles for him to eat on the *tatami* mats as he watched the late-night silly shows on television. While he ate, she would lay out his mattress, smelling of freshness from its daily airing on the balcony and then join their son in the room separated from her husband's by a *fusuma* sliding door. She would hear him wake at five the next morning and although he often begged her to rest she would prepare him some toast and coffee before he left to catch an early train.

He had known of Ohyama's reputation when he

joined the bank after graduation from university at twenty-two: he was envied by his peers who had joined other prestigious banks and trading companies but knew that Ohyama was the financial institution everyone else feared and respected. The weeks of physical training at a Japanese Self-Defense Force camp and the deprivations of a Zen Buddhist temple had hardened his body and spirit as intended and reinforced his exclusivity. As a bachelor, the long hours at work, even when there was nothing to do except wait for his seniors to leave the office first, were fulfilling and the daily bouts of social drinking with his colleagues built his friendships and collegiate spirit.

After three years he confronted the reality of life at Ohyama when he was transferred from the long period of corporate training, which had taken him to all of the bank's departments, to the treasury run by Katsuro Koga.

The day before the move was his twenty-fifth birthday and he had celebrated it, and the occasion of his transfer, with friends and, as expected, had been taken back to the bank's dormitory in a drunken stupor. His forgetting to set the alarm, and the negligence of his colleagues in not rousing him, saw him in the bank's head office at nine-thirty, two hours late for his appointment with Koga and in a state of terror and apprehension. He expected censure, perhaps light disciplinary action, not the humiliation the treasurer saw fit to crush his trainee with. Koga hauled him to the pit of the dealing room and in front of three hundred people screamed his abuse at the newcomer, questioning his loyalty, spirit and intelligence and ordering him to reflect on his attitude by staying away from the bank for a week.

On the journey home Hirata ransacked the shambles of his mental faculties to find the strength to die. He sat on the *tatami* mat in the single room he was allocated in the dormitory, a bottle of whisky and a heavy-bladed fish stripping knife to hand while he composed letters of farewell to his parents and the girl he had met at a company party. He was saved by a veteran supervisor who had heard the sentence pronounced and had telephoned the hapless trainee, comforting him by saying that Koga's summary justice was infamous but he would not carry a grudge if the victim showed true contrition.

At four the following morning Hiroyuki Hirata caught a taxi to his chief's home, waiting in the cold and drizzle to be in time to meet his superior as he left by chauffeured car. In stilted, effusively polite language he begged forgiveness, not daring to look into Koga's face but feeling his leer and contempt. 'If you hurry you might make it to the bank before me,' Koga snarled before driving off.

In the next seven years Hirata had applied himself with the diligence expected of him and all Japanese. Fourteen hour days, unpaid overtime, six days of taken holiday a year and sickness borne at the desk. And still Koga drove his team, demanding the total commitment of his dealers as his bank's reputation for the pursuit of profit above all other considerations drew the envy and loathing of the business world in Japan and abroad.

Hirata knew he was not the only dealer to resent the demands of the Ohyama Bank, as enforced with ruthless determination by Katsuro Koga, but he was probably the only one to keep a record of the personal slights. And he had the dossier: a collection of photocopies of confirmations of deals he thought were suspicious; of trades where the counterparty customer was on the credit watchlist but Koga had overruled it and ordered the deal to proceed with the doubtful

111

name; notes and scribblings on the generosity of the brokers, culminating every two years in a sex tour to Thailand for Koga and his close bank friends; the name of a suspected mistress and the bank-owned apartment she occupied.

Hirata's resentment had festered, even as he had risen steadily in Koga's estimation, and when he married Akemi his emotional state was strained to breaking by Koga's next assault on his sanity. A week before his marriage to his thoughtful and fun-loving colleague he was ordered to attend a quickly arranged course on foreign exchange currency options which began two days after his Saturday marriage. His protests were futile, received with the familiar charge of disloyalty, and even the loss of the cost of the Hawaiian honeymoon elicited no compassion from Katsuro Koga.

Then, in January this year, an American, Sam Collier, joined Ohyama Bank on a temporary assignment from his university. His innocuous studies into Japan's monetary system were interrupted by the devastating revelations in the Japanese Press that Ohyama and other banks and financial institutions had been involved in share-price manipulation and the direction of his research became investigative. Hirata, assigned to assist his legitimate research, had befriended him, later steering him towards the shadier side of the country's banking system and coming to see him as his vehicle to exact a deserved revenge on Katsuro Koga.

Now Hirata was bitter to the point of desperation; this latest humiliation would be the last. What would Akemi say when he recounted his interview with the bank's personnel department that morning? She had shared his elation when he had told her that he was being transferred to London, a city she had visited for her graduation tour, and looked forward to their son attending a local kindergarten once she had joined her husband after the customary three month separation. Now she would hear that Katsuro Koga had intervened to pronounce that his treasury staff must show solidarity with their branch banking colleagues and share responsibility for the banking scandals which had drawn public criticism and official censure. Hirata's contribution would be to spend the first year of his overseas secondment alone in London.

He sat at his dealing desk and crushed a smouldering cigarette stub with the blunt end of a pencil, watching the last plume of smoke drift upwards, gather speed and evaporate through the air-conditioning grills in the domed ceiling. The dealing room in the Ohyama Bank was a gigantic high-tech cavern, as deep as three floors and constructed like an amphitheatre, except that the layers of seating were work stations with individual desks, terminals, information monitors, broker voice boxes and a keyboard which gave access to the telephone network and twenty computer systems implanted in each. The centre of the room was a pit where control officers monitored activity, open positions on a bank of screens and vetted the stacks of dealing slips before despatching them to the operations department.

There were fifty dealers left in a hall equipped for three hundred. Some of them were starting the late shift, watching the midday markets evolve in Europe, and prepared to execute customer business and take appropriate foreign exchange positions for the bank. Some, like Hirata, had been in the bank for twelve hours and were waiting for the head of treasury, Katsuro Koga, to leave first. It was nearly seven in the evening local time on the giant digital clocks which curved in two batteries around the world, reminding the staff that there was always somewhere on the globe where money was being bought and sold at any second in the twenty-four-hour cycle.

After a busy but unproductive opening Wednesday had turned into an exhausting, exhilarating day. The bank's aggressive customers, the cash-rich manufacturers and insurance companies, were persistent, pestering, demanding a view on how far the dollar would be allowed to fall before the central banks intervened. Around ten o'clock Hirata was substituting on the set which handled the bank's most prestigious corporate customers, those that Koga took personal responsibility for. He took a call from a trading company and dealt, buying from them five million dollars at some rate or other. At eleven, forty minutes after the Bank of Japan had intervened to force the value of the dollar upwards, Hirata had received the usual fax from the customer confirming his understanding of the deal. To his annoyance, the customer had the deal in reverse, claiming to be the buyer of dollars, seller of yen. Disputes were not unusual in the foreign exchange business, though less between banks as deals were mostly transacted visually on trading screens and could be resolved without great loss to either party. In this case, the customer was claiming he bought the dollars ahead of the intervention, leaving him profitably long of the US currency when it was revalued upwards.

Koga would be livid if a mistake by Hirata embarrassed his relationship with the customer, not to mention the consequences of the loss reversing the deal might generate. What the customer may not have been aware of was the fact that major banks recorded all dealing calls to avoid such potentially costly conflicts, and it was as a last resort that Hirata sat at a console three levels below the Ohyama treasury, earphones clamped on his head, listening intently as one call clicked off and another began. A female clerk had admitted him to the secure room, signed him in and demonstrated the Racal ICR system with the latest activity search function which flashed automatically between calls, ignoring the empty sections of magnetic tape which ran continuously for twenty-five hours before replacement. A standby tape would be running while he interrogated this one. The guardian of this sensitive department settled at a corner desk after isolating for him a thirty minute tract of tape from around his estimated dealing time.

There were not many calls on this particular line and with the machine in search mode he soon heard his own tinny voice, condescending, grateful to the customer for the deal while he silently calculated the sales credit he would get from the market trader for bringing him the volume. He leaned back, hands clasped over the earphones, smiling inwardly as he listened to the voice of the customer dealer leaping at Hirata's bid price, not complaining when he confirmed orally, and very clearly on the tape, 'at fifty-five Ohyama Banks buys five million US dollars.' With the tape still running, the security clerk showed him how to connect a portable cassette recorder to the main-frame equipment and retrieve the exonerating evidence. He was relieved that he was right and would not have to face the trader who would have laid off the deal in the market and positively euphoric at escaping a severe censure from Katsuro Koga.

The tape rolled as he wrestled with a form of words to offer his customer, how to tell the hapless man that he had made a mistake, and if he did not accept Hirata's position a tape of the conversation would be sent to his senior, while still retaining the company's confidence and business. No doubt the customer was revelling in the belief that he had beaten the market. Hirata would have to concoct a cocktail of demeaning and face-saving Japanese, with lots of hissing and stretched expressions.

When his conversation finished there was a disconnection click, then a hum as the machine searched for the next conversation, and then a colleague reserving a restaurant with the economical and careful use of words that comes from knowing the call was being recorded. Hirata was adjusting the time selector on the bank of dials when there was another click of separation, and almost instantly the unmistakable voice of Katsuro Koga erupted and shook him alert. His fingers hovered over the cut-off switch and he looked guiltily behind, where the clerk sat at a desk. He had a legitimate right to be there. He should have stopped the tape when his business with it was finished, but to hear his boss in anonymous conversation was irresistible. It was a brief exchange and made a good, clean recording with only static interference. If Hirata's interpretation was correct, Koga had received an audacious, electrifying message.

He returned to his desk where a night dealer, fresh-faced and lively, greeted him and almost caught him sliding the cassette tape between the folds of a newspaper as he leaned over to receive position sheets and orders and a summary of the day's market movements and customer activity. The newcomer, a painfully thin, hyperactive man from Okinawa, regretted missing the central bank intervention. There was nothing like chaos, and the volatility it generated, to fire a foreign exchange dealer.

Hirata walked to Tokyo Station, his anger swelling to hatred at Koga's latest insult. He sipped from a tumbler of hot sake under the awning of a steamy noodle counter while he imagined the most painful way of killing Katsuro Koga. Another pot of sake calmed him, and in its stimulating warmth he knew he had crossed the ethical line which had held his resentment and frustration in check for ten years and he was now in an unfamiliar world where the demon reminder of his humiliation screamed for revenge. As the train snaked north-west he fingered the cassette in his pocket, the weapon fate had gifted him with to destroy Katsuro Koga. By tomorrow it would be parcelled with the dossier and by Friday his foreign friend would have it.

16

Senior Police Superintendent Fujii was a heavy man, prone to sweaty breakouts, and the only policeman in the divisional force to have used his handgun in the line of duty. He shared with Araki a birthplace in the western province of Shimane as well as a love of sweet sake and the mournful folk tunes which whined of rain and the perils of the fishermen on the Sea of Japan. This pull of common roots fertilized an enduring friendship of opposites: the doting father of three girls, paternalistic upholder of the law and the honest, slightly lost dropout who inhabited the floating world. Araki had followed Fujii's career through the uniformed ranks to his current position as the detective leading a special anti-drug task force with country-wide authority and he now estimated the relationship close if not deep, enough he knew to get him to a murder scene or a gangland bust ahead of the competition without compromising the policeman.

Fujii pleaded ignorance on the death of the British

banker because it had been ruled an accident and the case closed. But he understood Araki's interest when the journalist said he knew there was a girlfriend and she might like a small cash reward in return for some colourful insights into life with a fast-living foreigner. A photograph, even a profile with dark glasses and a scarf, would earn her more.

Her name was Emi Mori, Fujii disclosed, and she had volunteered the information that she knew Anthony Moore and had seen him briefly on the day of the accident, observing nothing unusual in his behaviour. Moore must have started his binge soon after he had left her and joined friends around six thirty/seven in a bar called Romy's. These people, colleagues from his business world, said they had drunk with him until about nine. Some of them thought that Moore was pretty tight when he left; and the woman said in her statement that he was taking a lot of alcohol lately. Fujii would not disclose addresses, telephone numbers or any personal details but if Araki had business in Shimbashi he would do well to visit the Excell Image Agency.

Araki had an image of Emi Mori from the scraps of detail the policeman and the Englishman had discarded and had already drafted her profile for the article he had to submit within twenty-four hours. But he had to see her or a photograph to give him a better journalistic impression. He also had to eliminate the possibility that she was just a disco princess, a naïve groupie, passing fun for the *gaijin* with their padded wallets.

She might be a professional, moonlighting from one of a thousand Tokyo bars and cabarets or a plush Ginza supper club, but he thought it unlikely. The loud, rude girls in the lower strata of the floating world were tied to pimps or street level gangsters while the surgically perfected failed singers and actresses at the luxury end selected their patrons from among the politicians and aged company presidents whose expense accounts could be stretched to include the advisory services of a willowy mistress. Araki was looking for someone who would take fifty thousand yen and grieve publicly in *One Point Finance*, sunglasses masking tired eyes, pale face free of make-up and in her Louis Vuitton handbag a photograph of her perfect foreign lover to remind her of the good times.

Araki knew the unwritten rules perfectly. He would not quote his police source but would communicate any signs of criminal activity he found during his researches.

The street where the Excell Image Agency had its office was typical of the area: a narrow, tidy thoroughfare of six-storey ferro-concrete blocks housing bars, restaurants and coffee shops or the offices of small-scale businesses. Sleek bullet trains glided above at roof level, slowing as they approached Tokyo Station or streaking in a blur of blue and white as they sped towards the south. There were hundreds like Excell, fly-by-night two-man companies with English words like public relations, advertising and image transcribed into phonetic Japanese on their calling cards and publicity material. What they did was to gather models for sex magazines and porno films, leggy promotion girls for trade fairs and young singers for the endless television 'talent' shows whose requirements were an endless supply of adenoidal teenage girls in mini-skirts.

Araki felt a knowing warmth as he took the narrow lift to the sixth floor. If Emi Mori was on the books of Excell Image Agency, he reasoned, it was unlikely she was just a secretary.

He tapped cagily on the frosted pane of the half-glass door, stencilled with the company's name in Japanese and roman script, and was received by a thickly made-up young woman, a head taller than himself, with prominent canine teeth and flowing, crimped hair. She smiled diffidently and led him to an inner room whose walls were inlaid with photographs of attractive girls, some in mid-song, others on the catwork with appropriate pouts. Two of them were identical twins with cropped hair who Araki recognized from their television appearances where they lip-synced their nasalized songs and danced robotically as if they were one. What they all had was a slight chance of a year's fame before the next pubescent acts rolled off the production line like semi-conductors.

He was taken to a private office with a view through panelled glass of an open area where ten or so people worked. The far end was a platform cornered with strobe lights and mounts for cameras.

Tomio Imaizumi had short hair, permed high on the crown of his head except where it jutted forward in a sharp wedge. He leaned back, almost buried in the soft, pseudo-leather chair which pivoted as he moved his body. The walls of his office also had carefully placed photographs, only they were portraits, all of women. They exchanged cards and non-committal bows. The rear side of the head of the talent agency's card gave his romanized name as Tom Imaizumi. Araki had chosen a visiting card he had made when he was writing the story about an actress whose affairs were allegedly close to nymphomanic excess and he needed to get into the film studios. Imaizumi's face creased as he struggled with the deliberately meaningless 'Dynamic Art Culture' phoneticized into Japanese.

'I'm in media and corporate publicity,' Araki said with a dismissive wave of his hand. 'Yamada of Nihon Television's introduction. I'm Araki.'

Imaizumi confirmed his understanding with short, deep gasps of noise and instinctive nods. A later check by a secretary would reach Araki's answering machine which had been primed accordingly. The obligatory and vital contact name escaped Imaizumi. He knew so many people in the media and more than one Yamada. They talked of the weather, as required, of the political scandals which threatened the prime minister and the continuity in government of the Liberal Democratic Party and finally Araki unzipped his briefcase and leaned forward conspiratorily.

'You might not have picked this up yet but there's a round of US–Japan bi-lateral trade talks next month. I can't tell much more and I would appreciate, and expect, your discretion at this crucial stage.

'You have it,' Imaizumi assured him, and they both lit cigarettes in silence while a secretary served coffee.

Araki watched her leave and returned to his charade. 'My company is organizing the inaugural party,' he said, and then whispered. 'At the Okura.'

Imaizumi nodded appreciatively at the mention of Tokyo's most prestigious hotel. 'Very appropriate,' he agreed, 'with the American Embassy so close.'

Araki raised his palms in supplication. 'But please. Even the hotel doesn't know who the party's for. Security, you understand. We've booked the room. That's all they know at this moment in time. What I want to do is hire twenty, twenty-five girls to serve the drinks, pass the canapés around, be sociable, you know, the usual hostesses.'

A broad smile linked Imaizumi's full cheeks. 'I'm sure I can help,' he said, hurling himself towards a shelf of folders.

'There's a small problem,' Araki cautioned before the

entrepreneur could haul his armful of files to the desk. 'The girls must be exceptionally attractive, distract the bloody Yanks and stop them bleating about car imports until the talks start.'

'Absolutely no problem,' the other man said proudly. 'I select the women myself.'

'They must speak English.'

'They can all manage with basic requests. Please don't worry.'

Araki thought of Emi Mori. If she was Tony Moore's close girlfriend he guessed her English would be excellent. He persisted.

'Fluent English is required. My principals want the girls to talk intelligently to the Americans. Lull them with clever chat about politics and economics while their bodies hold their attention.'

'Fluent English?'

'Fluent or very close.'

Imaizumi pressed the intercom. 'Kimiko san. Bring the special files please. The red ones.

'I have twenty-five girls in my special category,' he said, when the two hardcover portfolios binding a collection of plastic envelopes arrived. 'They are, how shall I put it? more mature, more experienced. Probably more at ease among foreigners. They will meet your specifications but I must request a little flexibility on their English ability. Look at this one,' he crowed, extracting two photographs from the sheath. 'A Tokyo university senior majoring in law, available for discreet hostessing. The girl was stunning in a cut-away swimsuit, her legs straight, in western proportions to her trim torso. The other picture displayed her in national dress, enticing and erotic in the tight, wrap-around classical kimono. 'And she speaks English,' Araki said, his eyes devouring the page showing through the plastic – personal details, special skills, conditions of employment.

'All those with special language skills are in this folder They are in demand for international assignments,' Imaizumi said coyly.

'May I look through the files?' Araki asked, adding ominously. 'Of course, I have to look at alternative possibilities. The hotel may even want to supply the hostesses.'

Imaizumi assented gladly, catching the implied threat in his visitor's last remark, and led him to a desk in the outer office, across from a clerk operating a word processor.

Araki tried to appear interested in each file but he pursued only one of them. There was no clear order. He looked for a collation by phonetic arrangements but her name was not there. Should he ask Imaizumi if Emi Mori was available for this commission? He had heard of her talents. Or confess that he was a journalist with a reward for one of Imaizumi's girls?

He decided against both approaches. He saw something protective, almost secretive, in the manner of the talent agency proprietor. It made him instinctively cautious himself. He returned his attention to the files, pausing to admire a child-faced model with waist-length hair and a claim to fluent English and Spanish. Imaizumi was visible in his office, interviewing a woman dressed to impress. Were there other special files, he wondered? He scribbled the names of the girls who would qualify for the fictitious party job, disregarding their figures and other qualities. His notebook had the names of fifteen aspiring talent singers and comedy show stooges who were willing to pour drinks until their big chance came before he found Emi Mori buried in the second portfolio. She was presented like the others, in a swimsuit and in a short cocktail dress. The copy said she liked foreign travel and meeting peoples of different cultures, facilitated, Araki supposed, by her claim to fluent English.

She had a more mature face than the others, her smile more subtle, less deliberate. Her pose, on a couch, was calculated, but looked totally natural. He joined her name to the others on his candidate list and then to his frustration saw that the boxes for her address and telephone number were missing from the personal data. It was most unlikely she would have a telephone in her own name and without her consent he would have to use more devious means to embellish his article, blacking out the eyes and asking the readers rhetorically whether this was the woman who had comforted the dead foreign banker. He slid the photograph of her in her party dress under his notepad, estimating that it was too early for a swimsuit pose, especially one he had not paid for. He waited until Imaizumi was distracted with his visitor before stacking the folders and leaving word with a secretary that he would certainly be in touch after consultations with his clients.

17

All dealers, even hardened veterans like Nicholls, suffer a wrenching, lonely emptiness after a serious hit and his grief was no less genuine or profound than that of the junior trader who gets badly bloodied in the market for the first time. The pain would be soothed with sympathetic words and booze, but Nicholls know no one in Tokyo well enough to drink himself silly with and no one he could trust with his suspicion that the market today had been tampered with. Or perhaps it was just how things were in Tokyo. He had exceeded no dealing risk mandate and broken no ethical rules, but in less than the time it takes to shave he had written off six months of profit by the Sternberg Chance treasury. After Hanlon stormed out he stayed alone in his office all day; even his secretary sensed the gravity of the moment, breaking his privacy only to provide coffee and a box lunch. He sat among the debris of the morning: the dealers' individual sheets listing their buy and sell trades, copies of the deal slips, rudely torn strips of printout from the Reuters dealing system and an early performance calculation from Mabuchi for the whole room. It was close to a two million dollar loss. He plotted the sequence of calls until that moment at twenty-seven minutes after ten o'clock when the Bank of Japan decided to wield the sword. Adrenalin still flowed through his body but he knew he was tiring. When he was satisfied he had a reasonable picture of the morning's events he folded the single sheet into his wallet and left the bank.

He walked for an hour then caught a taxi which dropped him outside a stairway not far from the

Roppongi crossing on the broad road, with its borders of neon stripes and intrusive advertising boards, leading to Tokyo's imitated version of the Eiffel Tower. Elbowing his way through the knots of British, American and Australian money market traders, he reached the smaller bar around the entrance to Mama Gimbasha's, which Tony Moore's diary had appointed as the last place he had planned to be on the night he died.

At the bar, Nicholls greeted Hugh Carter, the broker who had told him that Mama Gimbasha's was the inspiration of a former dealer from the Bank of Tokyo. The Japanese, anticipating his own early burnout, had used his bonuses as equity to invest in a bar where the management would be more tolerant towards the exuberance of the well-heeled financial hooligans whose excesses had led to their being banned from several Roppongi bars.

Carter's bulky form stood in a group under the screen where Telerate prices from the European money markets flashed in the moody darkness. The patron, who was known to his customers as Toshi, served the late shift himself alongside a squat former junior-rank sumo wrestler and team of immaculately groomed, tough but impassive barmen, all of them in dinner jackets. Funky music thumped from cylindrical speakers hung from the ceiling. Like London, Nicholls noted, the in drink was sweet Mexican beer drunk from the bottle with a wedge of lime jammed down the neck. Gold cards flashed across the counter: when broker met dealer the night's drinking could be charged by the middleman to business promotion. The foreign exchange dealers, with their loose tongues, tailored suits and ties twisted rakishly from unbuttoned shirt collars always attracted women. Their productive working lives were short and their health suspect, but while both lasted they were suicidally generous with a wealth their age would not normally provide. Some of the women were brokers and bond sellers and shared the hard talk and drink with the men. Nicholls imagined Tony Moore holding forth in a group of admirers, a large tumbler of iced tonic water in one hand, in the other a cigarette cutting the air as he recounted the details of another killing in the market or one of his adventures in some pleasure palace or another.

Nicholls edged towards a row of stools, returning the admiring glances of a pair of Australian bleached blondes, tanned and broad-lipped, on the fringe of a noisy group of young American bankers. He sat on the only free seat, next to a hopeful Japanese groupie, a leggy, slim girl in culottes and a tight halter-top embroided in gold. A sliver of skin was revealed at her waist when she turned towards the door, implying respectability by pretending to look for a late friend.

Apart from Mexican Corona, the standard drink was cold beer, Japanese or American. He downed an Asahi Dry, the rush of mellow malt giving instant pleasure, and then a second. He admired the bar as the right place to die after dropping two million dollars. There was only one theme in the snatches of talk he sieved through the din: survival in the ferocity of the morning's trading. Nicholls wondered how many of them knew that the man screaming into the telephone lines at ten twenty was sitting at the bar with his third beer and a vengeful heart. Brokers like Hugh Carter would not forget quickly how Sternberg Chance dealers had scrambled desperately for ten wild minutes, trying to buy dollars in a market which had dried up for no particular reason. He ordered a third beer half-way through his second.

Three disco-dressed Filipinos squealed as they nudged their slim hips through the crowd. One of them, a mass of curled, ebony hair and coral-red glossed lips threw him an open-mouth look before reaching a table of braying drunken Westerners. A short, boyish American forced himself between Nicholls and the lonely Japanese woman and bawled his order for ten beers and a gin and tonic and then feigned horror at the bill. 'A cute kid,' he quipped, motioning to Nicholls's bar companion. 'You'd better move pronto.'

His smile died quickly when he was alone again with his thoughts. Another beer appeared before him.

'Man over there,' the barman said economically, indicating Hugh Carter. Nicholls raised his glass in thanks but shook his head at the implied invitation to join the big broker under the monitor where the drinking was very serious. He reached for the folded piece of paper and stared at the annotations. He could have been alone. The noise seemed to recede and even the hazy dullness from the drink gave way to clarity of mind as he studied the chronology of the morning. At twelve minutes past ten Nichii Life Insurance bought thirty million dollars. It took a long three minutes and six deals to buy twenty-five of them back from the market. At ten fifteen Sankoku Oil bought a hundred million. He thumped the bar as he remembered the tumult and the damning absence of Japanese banks willing to answer his call, let alone quote for dollars. At ten nineteen the Ohyama Bank asked for a price in twenty million dollars and when Warron Hanlon insisted they quote their partner bank took the dollars from them. For Ohyama bank, Nicholls scoffed, read Katsuro Koga, chief dealer and plotter who would know exactly what he was doing buying dollars ahead of the intervention. He drained his glass and seethed at the final entry on the roughly written note. Ten twenty, BOJ. It was underlined in red.

He screwed the paper into a ball and almost left it in an ashtray, but even in his resentfulness he saw the folly of leaving his deal details for the market to see and slipped the dreadful evidence into a pocket before sliding off the stool. He ordered a beer for his return and asked the girl to keep his seat free and get herself a drink.

Resting a tired head on his chest, he propped himself against the rim of the urinal. There was a thud behind him and this prompted the man in the second bay to nudge Nicholls and cast a thumb towards the toilet's sole cubicle.

'He gave her ten thousand yen,' the other man said as smirking, he hurriedly zipped his trousers and knelt on the tiled floor to bend his head to the level of the space below the half-door. Nicholls crouched low and together they enjoyed the vicarious pleasure of crumpled trousers and a woman's skirt and panties and the grunts and squeals from within. Grinning, they left together, mingling among the swaying bodies and the heady, smoky perfume of women in a male playground.

The girl's half-sleeve jacket had fallen from the back-rest and lay trapped between the pedestal of the stool and a man's leg. In the restricted space at the bar and with the deliberate care of the mildly drunk, Nicholls stooped low to retrieve the garment, the side of his face brushing a thigh which glistened in the taut silky smoothness of golden tights. She swivelled in surprise and when she recognized her strangely distracted neighbour she guided him to her side again.

'Many people want your chair,' she said, in toneless,

129

faltering English after thanking him. He was not surprised. She had a small face with sharp, high cheekbones and deep, brown, inviting eyes and when she poured his beer with a curious two handed action, her bare arms forced the outline of her unrestrained breasts through the soft fabric of her body-moulded top. She was adorned with neither finger nor earrings but her eyes were shaded in pale blue shadow and a cover of rouge-tinted make-up obscured any expression beyond the thin lips that dipped when she smiled. They were losing the struggle for space and as the crowd pressed inwards the girl's knees slipped between his. His arm was brushing hers and her breath blew warm on his face. With a thick voice he managed, 'Another drink?'

She smiled towards the remains of a Campari soda.

'Can I have something too?' She had found a gap, and stood behind Nicholls, a hand clasped possessively on his shoulder, her eyes on his drinking companion. She was entirely in black: a short-sleeved bolero jacket over a tight black lycra dress in crushed velvet held to a sweetheart neckline with looped buttonholes.

'Don't bother,' Emi Mori said, in the throaty voice Nicholls remembered from their first encounter. She took his glass and emptied a good half-bottle of Asahi beer into it. 'Finish this and let's go to your apartment. I have to talk about Tony.' There was something pleading but at the same time demanding in her voice.

Nicholls drained the beer. His mind was dulled, a few steps away from reality, but he managed a shrug for the disappointed woman he left at the bar, like the predictable ending to a bad film. The cool night air cleared his heavy head. She took his arm with two hands. 'Did you notice the travel bag under the stool?'

she said after a taxi stopped for them and swung around the Tameike intersection. Knowing he had not, she continued. 'There are forty or fifty of them, girls from the country. They've heard about Mama Gimbasha's and the four or so other bars where foreign dealers and brokers drink. They come in near the weekend, pick up a young *gaijin* and have an expensive fun time in Tokyo. They are not hookers.'

'Do they enjoy it?'

'I'm sorry if I stopped you finding out,' Emi said, smiling.

They were passing a point where the vivid neons and the street lights ended abruptly off to the right and a yawning blackness, like the entrance to a cave, covered the short road leading to the dark stairway at the rear of the Hie Shrine.

Tony Tokyo's death bed. Emi Mori's small talk did not acknowledge it.

'I thought you might be at Gimbasha's,' she remarked. 'You dealers find it sooner or later. Usually sooner.'

Nicholls told himself that he should not have been surprised to meet Emi Mori among the boozy, hyper-confident foreign money men. Tony must have taken her to Mama Gimbasha's and the other bars where the outer limits of behaviour were tolerated. Her deceptively vulnerable elegance would have turned the heads of the most depressed drunk and marked her as special.

A few colourful taxis and hired black cars cruised the streets where discreet *geisha* houses, hidden behind high, carved wooden gateways, shared the fiercely bright entertainment district of Akasaka with rowdy hostess clubs and restaurants serving the Japanized versions of the world's diverse cuisine. There were few people about, knots of hostesses in near-silk kimonos

131

or provocative evening wear and men in sports jackets plotting their next move. Japan's army of salarymen, confused and drunk, had responded to the tacit eleven o'clock curfew and left the night to the women they had so recently been pawing.

Emi Mori guided the taxi through the nameless narrow streets to her dead lover's apartment while her companion let his neck loosen and roll along the plastic headrest, his mind a maze of flashing digits, frenzied bids and frustrated offers, of screamed orders and sweaty desperation. The taxi braked sharply on the final corner and when his head rolled towards her with the momentum, she reached for his tie and loosened it. She kept his hand when he helped her from the taxi.

'Shall I collect your mail?' she said, slipping from him to the row of metal boxes screwed to the wall. Nicholls's name had been clumsily handwritten on Anthony Moore's visiting card which was lodged in a slot. 'It's not locked.' The box was large and deep enough to take the airmail versions of the newspapers which Emi plucked from it along with some letters and a packet the size of a hardback book. 'I'd better carry them,' she said, smiling as he aimed a finger carefully at the lift buttons.

'Which floor, Sir?' she quipped playfully.

'I dunno,' he said half in jest. 'How many are there?' The doors closed and Emi Mori withdrew to a corner, her body fitting easily into the angle, her head tucked back, a foot raised with her high-heel clamped to the wall. Her lips were moist and slightly parted. Nicholls's head swam, but his gaze was not drawn to the outline of her thighs under the black dress, stretched taut above her knees or the swell of her breasts where she held the mail tightly to her like a baby. His eyes were on the padded envelope, its contents held inside by two short cords tipped in metal. Another video, another sports tape, sent by a caring friend before word of Tony's death had reached England? He looked up at Emi's face, at the half-closed tear-drop eyes and the fingers of her free hand playing with trails of silky hair against her lips.

It must have been in transit for six days, Nicholls guessed wantonly, as he fumbled for a ring of elusive keys, and if the brokers were to be believed the airport customs had probably delayed its import with a check for pornographic content. Emi stacked the mail against the telephone and after removing his jacket offered him the sofa and some soothing night music from Tony Moore's CD system.

Nicholls, ever the professional whatever his condition, went to his bedroom and checked the rows of money prices from Europe flickering on the squat monitor. The market was alive on another continent and he felt energized by the image, but the drink was working fast, in an absurdly odd way, deepening his fatigue, and making his legs feel heavy as he walked to the couch. Through the half-open door to the entrance the package caught his gaze. She could have brought it into the living room. She strutted around the apartment with the confidence and poise of a close friend or a lover, closing curtains, pumping the cushions and effortlessly manipulating the sound system into life. After lighting a cigarette she dimmed the lights and sank to her knees at the edge of the sofa.

'And now a nightcap. Just the one, I think,' she said smiling.

'You know your way around,' was all he could manage, and she was off again. She half-filled two crystal glasses from a bottle of brandy on Tony Moore's drinks trolley.

'Ice, please,' he said apologetically as she approached him, the glasses held triumphantly aloft.

'Ice? *Hai*,' she trilled like an obsequious waiter and skipped away. He heard the dull thump of the refrigerator door and running water and pushed himself out of the seat and on to the floor in front of the racks of video tapes slung beneath the television. He had to know what the tapes meant to her. Straining to see in the dim light, he ran a finger across the labels until he found one with a hand-written label.

He was barely back on the sofa, and the tape buried under a cushion, when there was another thump as a door closed and she was by his side, sitting on the edge of the couch, her knees towards him, the brandy glasses cupped between orange-tipped fingers. She tapped her glass to his, smiling and encouraging the rich, hazel brandy towards his lips. Nicholls sensed a creeping numbness something different from the mellowing weakness drink usually induced in him, and his mind was following his body in succumbing to it. Emi Mori began to speak fondly of her time with Tony, recalling their last holiday together in Bali, her gaze lost to her memories. He urged himself to stay alert, even as his head dipped involuntarily and the muscles in his legs convulsed painfully. Describing the sunsets and Tony's tenderness, Emi drew closer to him on the sofa, her head resting on the soft stuffed leather backing. At some point the muted beep of a clock alarm drew Nicholls's tiring eyes to the fluorescent glow from the digital clock of the video which was flashing one three zero. If she expected to leave, Nicholls thought of saying, he wasn't physically able to take her home, wherever that was.

His condition was starting to trouble him. His mind and body were at odds. Confused, he tapped his glass again to hers, not noticing that despite the smudge of lipstick on its rim her drink was untouched and sniffed at the deep golden half-moon of brandy before downing it with a jerk of his head. Then he drew breath and said hoarsely: 'You said you wanted to talk about Tony.'

'I already have,' she retorted with playful indignation, 'but I was so boring you weren't listening. I tried to tell you how I felt for him, how I loved him and how sad I felt when you seemed to blame me for letting him drink again. I wanted to tell you it wasn't my fault. I want you to believe me.'

She took his hand, which was cold from the ice, and lifted it to her cheek, her shoulders quivering as she let his fingers trace the porcelain smooth skin of her cheeks and the curve of her neck. Each second drove his blood faster, but as he tried to speak his jaw stiffened and the words emerged in a drunken, slow-motion drawl. His mind jerked between clarity and drowsiness and even as he wanted this woman, his physical control was fading. He looked helplessly at Emi Mori, whose eyes were almost closed, her mouth open, pleading. She was leading his hand to the lace trim covering the looped buttons of her dress and shivered as his fingers brushed the swell of her breasts. The buttons yielded easily and Nicholls cupped a soft mound covered by a flimsy mesh fabric which slipped away at his touch. Her warm breath engulfed him, her tongue finding his and her perfume intoxicating as she murmured in Japanese and kneaded the inside of his thigh. Nicholls knew he was not drunk, light-headed but not drunk, and the spreading surges of numbness and sleepiness which were overcoming him had not resulted from his excesses at Mama Gimbasha's. His fingers pressed into her breasts, across her hardening nipples. Her hands probed, but his flesh felt oddly desensitized to her touch.

'You must be so tired,' she whispered sympathetically, drawing out the 'so'. 'I know how to make you recovered.' Her English faltered but the meaning was clear. She eased herself from him, her dress rolling upwards, skimming her black tights, and letting a hand drift between her thighs. 'I won't be long,' she purred.

Her words reached him in slow motion and when he tried to rise his legs dragged and he stumbled against the edge of the table, shattering a crystal glass as he groped for a hold. He was alone, contemplating the minute balloons of blood on the tips of his forefinger and thumb. He wasn't tired or drunk, he screamed silently to himself, but his mind was slowing as the drug sped through his bloodstream, transmitting a final, desperate demand before the desire to sleep overwhelmed his body's ability to deny it. He fell back against the sofa, his elbow moving the cushion, his left hand clutching the video he had contrived to hide. Pushing himself to his feet, he staggered to the corridor bisecting the apartment. The door to his bedroom was open and a light from the ensuite bathroom drew a triangle on the double bed. Julio Iglesias warbled somewhere behind him and the muted sound of running water from the shower reassured him, spurring him on.

Hands splayed against the wall, he groped his way towards the narrow hall, with its coat cupboard and shaky wooden stand where Tony Moore's best shoes were stacked on the lower shelves and where Emi had left his mail. Unable to stand and at the same time concentrate on untying the metal-tipped laces holding the unsealed flaps of the padded envelope together, he braced himself with his back to the wall and slid to the floor. With the package trapped between his knees and his eyes contorted in a blur of double vision, his hands groped with the strings. Time was elusive, irrelevant: Emi Mori could have showered, draped herself in a sheet and downed a bottle of claret and he would have been no wiser. He would not recall how he managed to push a metal tip through the hole and repeat the action with the second cord and release the flap. Something had snapped inside him. Even in his delusion he was seeing himself as a victim with no idea of the motive of his aggressors. Half drunk by his own choice and drugged for someone else's, he remembered Emi Mori's ridiculous pretence at interest in some English sporting events. If this one was another of the type it now belonged to him, Kevin Nicholls.

The video from Moore's collection was in his hand. He would not remember removing the new tape, dropping it, stuffing the old one into the envelope and sealing it again. A final thrust for survival carried him back to the lounge, the video tape retrieved and cradled like a precious rugby ball, his head swirling with a thousand daytime nightmares. His feet trod shards of glass into the carpet and as he lurched forward the tape bounced out of his hands and fell behind the couch.

Amongst the tumbled images racing dementedly through his brain there was one that would remain after he had slumped into the comfort of the cushions – Emi Mori emerging from the bedroom in a thigh-length pink silk robe, opened to her waist to reveal the curve of her breasts and the glistening skin of her body down to the edge of the dark triangle, where it was held loosely together with a flimsy band. Nicholls was splayed across the sofa, legs apart, arms in disarray. His fantasy faded even as she knelt beside him, her hand inside his shirt, stroking the thick, coarse hairs on his chest and probing inside his trousers. He felt her slap him and opened his eyes, drinking in her perfume for the last time.

18

Hirata ate quickly without much appetite and described Koga's new ruling on his overseas assignment to his wife.

What was a year in the scheme of life? she rationalized, hiding her disappointment. She accepted that while her husband was in London she would dutifully direct their son's education alone and look to her mother for help when the baby was born in seven months. He felt secure in her response, but the impulse for revenge was not expunged by her reassuring reaction and on the pretext of visiting a colleague to discuss an urgent business issue he took his briefcase and drove from his housing complex towards the gingko-lined avenues of Abiko. He needed privacy, well out of earshot of the Ohyama Bank employees and their families who occupied every apartment on the estate.

It was a warm clear late May evening and the places he might have parked were choked with cars and office workers enjoying a last night out before the oppressive weeks of the rainy season began in earnest. He drew into a multi-storey car-park near the south exit of a main railway station, reversing nervously into a space on the near-deserted roof. Unused to furtive conduct, Hirata saw suspicious intentions in the late commuters who crossed his view through the windscreen as he peeled the newspaper apart and shook the tape into his lap. He lifted a radio-cassette player from the back seat and slotted the tape in. He thought the car's stereo system too loud, too echoing for the occasion. He could hear his heart. What if he had misunderstood the context of the conversation? What if the recording from the master tape was corrupted?

Pressing the play button he forwarded the tape until he heard his own voice transacting the disputed deal with the customer. He let the tape whir again in short bursts until he heard a colleague he recognized as Saito booking a restaurant for lunch. He knew he was close and let the spools play at normal speed while his eyes raked the garage. After a short ethereal hiss, and a greeting from the caller, he heard a deep, familiar voice and it prompted a spasm of chilled fear to pass down his spine.

Koga san?' a voice asked.

'*Eh, soo desu*. Ah. It's you. Thank you. I wondered when you'd call. These are difficult markets.'

'They certainly are,' the toneless voice said. 'The next ten minutes could be vital. Please be careful.' There was a sharp click, followed by a metallic emptiness. Fear erupted again and chilled the droplets of sweat on the back of his neck above his collar.

The moment the Bank of Japan threw a grenade into the foreign exchange markets would be relived in the bars and dealing rooms for months, at least until the next time. He recalled the ten, fifteen minutes before that instant at twenty past ten in the Ohyama Bank's treasury. Koga had suddenly left his office and commandeered a dealing desk among the traders. Arms flaying he had sprayed his orders around. 'Buy dollars,' he commanded Sugiyama. 'Citi Sing and Bankers Sing, and get Bank of America, Hong

139

Kong. All big counterparties.' He pointed at a wiry, thin-lipped dealer called Wada. 'Get a price in twenty from Sternberg and take him.' When the central bank began buying massive amounts of dollars, shunting its value up by over two yen, Koga was already sitting comfortably on a five hundred million dollar long position.

A beam of light from a car turning on to the garage roof illuminated Hirata for an instant, causing him to shield his eyes and sink into the seat. When the dark returned he drew on a cigarette and rubbed a fierce day's tension from his eyes with the knuckles of a fist. He knew that the only motives for taking such decisive, dangerously exposed positions in those wild and unpredictable markets could be pure recklessness, or inside information. Koga was neither reckless nor stupid. He was devious, cunning, supremely intuitive and well connected; he would only take a chance when he held three aces in his hand and the other up his sleeve.

The anonymous caller was issuing a warning, which, if heeded could save the recipient of his information from serious losses and if positively misused could earn as much as he needed to satiate his greed. This man, possessing the most sensitive and dangerous information in the financial world, could only be a senior official at the Bank of Japan. What hold, Hirata thought with a mixture of fear and admiration, did Katsuro Koga have over him? The man was risking imprisonment and absolute personal ruin by divulging an imminent move by the Japanese central bank and its worldwide allies. And Koga would join him. He listened to the cryptic exchange again before wrapping the cassette with paper and slipping it between the sheets in a bulky package he took from his briefcase.

19

The vicious hammering of a bell clanger was smacking the fragile shell of his skull from the inside, jolting him to consciousness. Eventually. He groped towards the noise, finally dislodging the telephone. His head throbbed: moving it was an exercise in pain control. He found an angle where it hurt less and cradled the receiver.

'Kevin? Are you all right?' It was Peter Stark, the bank's office manager. 'Kevin!'

'Peter, I'm fine. For Christ's sake, don't shout.'

Stark's voice dropped, almost to a whisper. 'I've been trying to get you all morning. There are problems in the dealing room.'

'What do you mean "all morning"?' Nicholls said, trying to focus on the glare of a bedside digital watch and then noticing the clothes still clinging loosely on him. He carried the phone to the living room, his legs unsteady. The air was stale with spilt liquor, smoke and faded perfume. 'It's one o'clock,' he heard Stark saying. 'In the afternoon.'

Stumbling outside, Nicholls recoiled from the sunlight that hit his eyes like shards of glass. On heavy legs he scrambled in a crazy half-run to the junction where his street met the main Kojimachi road, looking for a taxi in the traffic crawling towards the Outer Moat. Exhaust fumes trapped beneath the overpass choked him, leaving him reeling with nausea.

His private office was crowded: Mabuchi, Kimura, one of his foreign exchange dealers, Stark and the senior adviser, Fujimori, looking trim, as usual, but flustered. It must be serious he concluded as he passed his secretary and entered sheepishly. 'Apologies,' Nicholls managed and to Mabuchi said brusquely, 'Where's the market?'

The Japanese looked through the glass partition and saw his dealers in restful poses, some reading. 'Dollar-mark's steady in a quiet market,' he intoned with barely hidden exasperation aimed at Nicholls for his tardiness and at the loss of face the whole wretched business of Tony Moore and yesterday's hammering in the market had brought upon him. 'Dollar-yen's been moving. Let me check on the present situation.'

'Don't bother,' Nicholls said, looking longingly at his empty chair. 'Billy Soh can look after the FX.'

'Billy Soh's been suspended,' Fujimori said blandly. 'He's with Hanlon san.'

The young Korean-American was sitting at an angle to the oak desk in Warron Hanlon's airy office, drained of his normal cockiness. Hanlon was putting on his jacket. 'Ah-!' he said. 'Rip van Winkel awakes.' Then, with controlled distaste. 'No doubt you'll have the courtesy to explain to me later what the hell is happening in our corpse-ridden, loss-making treasury. Meanwhile, in your absence I've had to suspend Soh for driving the customers away.'

'I've heard,' Nicholls said. 'Can I talk to him alone?'

'Be my guest,' Hanlon riposted, yielding the chair. When he had left, Nicholls resisted the swingback leather chair and took the second visitor's seat.

'What happened Billy?'

Billy Soh was full of anger and close to tears. His English was drawled and flecked with the curt obscenities of his trade.

'Where were you man?' he groaned. 'The market went apeshit around nine. I tried to stay out of it but the fucking customer dealers were demanding prices. I refused to quote after what happened yesterday.'

'Tell me what happened Billy.' Nicholls's voice was cold with impatience, his head throbbing.

'There was a whole bunch of corporates selling dollars when it went through a support level at sixty-five. I was square and wanted to stay out of trouble.'

'So you widened the price?'

Soh nodded.

'How wide?'

The Korean-American looked remorseful. 'Twenty points.'

Five points between the bid and offer would be the norm but at times of intense volatility, when chaos and defensiveness dictated the prices, a ten point difference would be seen as prudent, a twenty point spread told the customers you were not interested in their business. It was an insult. Nicholls remembered trying it on the Ohyama Bank just before the intervention yesterday and had it rebound on him. Billy Soh's head was rocking. 'We have to be nice to them all the time. Show the best prices, no extra spread, like yesterday. Make them a tight price in a nightmare market. So today I said fuck it and looked after my own ass. Some of them called in to complain and we had Hanlon and Fujimori come down and throw me outta the game.'

'You keep saying "them" Billy,' Nicholls said patiently. 'Who are they exactly? The whole non-bank customer list?'

Soh was shaking his head. 'No. There's a block of ten or so big corporate players. We saw the same companies today that came in during the morning yesterday.'

'Who picks up the phone from these clients?'

'Could be Kawasaki, or Mabuchi himself. It's usually Naomi Honda.'

'Two days running,' he commented. 'Do you think they're trying to pick us off, nail us while we're down?'

Soh agreed. 'They seem to hit us when the market's on the edge. Near to data release times or possible central bank intervention.'

Nicholls asked, 'Have they cost us a lot money, apart from yesterday?'

Soh pursed his lips and then exhaled. 'Not when Tony was here,' he said carelessly and then regretted it. 'Sorry Kev, I didn't mean to suggest . . .'

'Forget it Billy. As of now you're reinstated.' Nicholls rose unsteadily. 'I'll work something out with Hanlon. It may mean a formal reprimand.' His voice lacked the coarse severity he would normally employ to censure a junior dealer. How could he do otherwise, having missed the first five hours of the trading day? 'Give me a list of the customers you think you upset and I'll get Mabuchi or Naomi Honda to apologize formally. I'll do it myself if necessary,' he said, leading Billy Soh to the plush reception. The capital market dealing floor was visible through a half-opened door. It was three times the size of the foreign exchange room, housing rows of young, sharp, personable Japanese, and a handful of Caucasians, whose role was to talk, persuade and sell the bank's portfolio of bonds, equities and their derivative products.

'I'll visit each of them myself,' Mabuchi said with obvious reluctance when Billy was back behind his screens and Nicholls had flopped gratefully into his own chair.

'Can't you let Naomi Honda do it?' Nicholls asked, eyeing a column of message stickers on his desk. 'She was the front for us.'

'I have to do it myself,' the most senior treasury

Japanese said through clenched teeth. He was struggling with his English, inwardly detesting the foreigner for the situation he and the bank were in, and squeezed his eyes shut to avoid his gaze. And then, in a voice which implied he had practised the speech for this occasion, he said with controlled bitterness as he left the room. 'It shouldn't be very difficult for you to understand that working in a foreign company is not easy for us. We are Japanese but this bank expects us to behave like yellow *gaijin*.'

Nicholls had never encountered this problem in Hong Kong. The Chinese and the *guailo* each knew their role and if there was a conflict it was resolved amongst the white managers.

Tomoko Ueda sensed his boss's physical discomfort and when he was alone brought him strong coffee. 'I heard you discovered Roppongi,' she said with mock rebuke.

'And more,' he replied, to her puzzlement.

The caffeine stimulated a scant recall of the events of the night before from his tired and battered brain cells which he knew had been dulled by alcohol but thrust into oblivion by a powerful knockout drug. While his head suffered its torment, the images began to ooze through the mist in disorderly scraps. There had been two women he concluded and one of them was Emi Mori and she went back with him to his flat.

'I've put that in your diary,' his secretary said, indicating one of the small heap of yellow message slips. 'Mr Prideaux will be here tomorrow and wants to see you during the morning.'

He called Warron Hanlon and pacified him with word of Billy Soh's contrition and apology to Mabuchi; Braithewaite of the British Embassy could wait, as could a pair of brokers who wanted to 'show' him

Tokyo. His mind was clearing, slowly, his senses sharpening and he was encouraged by the return of enthusiasm to the dealing room. Yamamoto had caught the German mark just above a sharp technical rebound and made thirty thousand dollars before closing out near the top.

Billy Soh came in, obviously cheered to be back at his screens, with a sheet of notepaper in his hand.

'These are the clients who called for prices today,' he said, tapping the paper. 'Those who called on Wednesday before the intervention are on the back. I marked the ones that dealt.'

Nicholls ran a practised eye down the columns. Eight names were common to both lists. 'Is that unusual or is that the pattern?' he asked.

Soh shrugged. 'We've got fifty non-bank customers but only twenty or so are hardcore, dealing twice, maybe three times a week.'

Nicholls said, 'So what pissed you off about this bunch?'

'The same thing that got to you on Wednesday. They lie in wait like fucking sharks. One off-market price, a mistake and they sink their teeth in. Then they're back the next day, even hungrier. Some of the Jap banks are worse,' Soh added.

'Like Ohyama before the intervention,' Nicholls said.

'They're the worst. And we've been told to make a market with them.'

Nicholls leaned back and massaged the back of his neck. 'There's something else, isn't there Billy?'

'I guess it shows,' Soh sniffed. He drew closer to Nicholls's desk. 'What do you know about the *zaibatsu*, or *keiretsu* as they like to call themselves nowadays? Less violent image. Dozens of companies in one big group, interlocking shareholdings, all working together: bank, insurance, trading, manufacturing and all kinds of business.'

'You tell me Billy.'

'Like Mitsubishi, Mitsui, Sumitomo. Take Marunouchi,' he said with a sweep of his hand towards the window and the offices beyond. 'It's owned by Mitsubishi Real Estate, built with steel from Mitsubishi Heavy Industries and supplied with lights and elevators from Mitsubishi Electric. Everything comes from one member of the group or another.'

Nicholls was impressed. 'You know your way around, Billy.'

Soh shrugged towards the dealing room. 'That's the first thing they taught me. Who's in bed with who in business.'

'And Ohyama are one of these groups?' Nicholls asked, familiar only with the Ohyama Bank.

'They're not the biggest in terms of member firms in the group but they've got the strongest financial muscle and they use it. They're the roughest, the most aggressive.'

Nicholls forced a sardonic smile which stayed with him after the dealer had returned to the trading floor. The sting from his parting words still smarted. Confused messages pounded his aching head. Katsuro Koga had tested Tony Moore's successor and found him wanting. A day later, while he lay comatose and shattered, he sends the corporate treasurers from Ohyama companies to bury Nicholls's battered reputation, and only Billy Soh had stood between them. In two days Koga had emasculated the most active British foreign exchange operation in Japan.

He was turning a book of matches in his fingers, brooding over Koga's motives, when he saw the tape slotted among the business books on a shelf. It was an instructional video made for the dealers. As his eyes focused on it the thick, black cloud of bafflement began to disperse. He saw himself scrambling dementedly on his knees in a frantic, pointless hide-and-seek, his confused, poisoned brain locked in combat with his body as he tried to outwit Emi Mori for reasons he could not begin to explain. He recalled handling video tapes, playing with them, hiding them. But it made no sense. Emi Mori remained a mystery, a recurring image which angered and fascinated him simultaneously. As he rocked on his heels an abrupt recollection of her intoxicating flowery perfume and the expert touch of her orange-tipped fingers burst into his mind cracking open a powder keg of jumbled recollections of a night of weird, inexplicable incidents.

20

The air in the apartment was clammy and stale, heavy with the ghostly remains and fragmented images of the evening which Nicholls was struggling to remember and comprehend. He swept some shards of glass from the coffee table on to the carpet and made a mental note to ask the caretaker to arrange an express cleaning service. The corporate video in Tony Moore's old office had stimulated a blanked out spot in his memory, and he was still gathering the shambles of his drugged out recollections when he noticed the couch, slightly askew from the line of the wall. The night's episode still held him in a dreamlike trance and he was apprehensive when he lifted and swung the sofa in one movement.

But it was there, standing on end like a book on a shelf. He released a yelp of triumph.

He slotted the video he had fought to keep from Emi Mori into the player but the moment he pressed the start button Nigel Simpson, the head of foreign exchange trading in Sternberg Chance's London headquarters called. He checked his watch automatically. It was lunchtime in London. Nicholls heard shouts in the background.

'Another Russian coup rumour,' Simpson intoned with his usual implacable composure. 'The mark's getting hammered, of course.'

Nicholls carried the telephone to the bedroom and activated the Reuters monitor. The rumours were appearing as flashes at the foot of the screen.

'Are they for real?' the Tokyo dealer asked economically.

'Doubt it. It's the second this month. Can I do anything for you?'

'I'm pretty well square,' Nicholls said with an ironic smile Simpson could not see, glad that he was gracious enough not to mention Nicholls's hit, word of which would be filtering back to London. 'I've still got a few dollar put options which are on our overnight order list. We made a bit on the mark intraday but took the profit early. Just as well really, with these rumours shooting about.'

'Okay, Kev. Keep in touch.'

Nicholls called the night team in the Tokyo dealing room who reported that the customers were staying away from the mark in Europe time. They had covered a few yen orders but there was no panic in Tokyo. Grateful for that, he laid his exhausted body on the bed by the monitor screen, occasionally turning on his side and watching the fluorescent flickering. At some point his mind began to drift, to hallucinate, as his body relaxed. He imagined he was dealing: he saw himself making foreign exchange quotations in a hotel lobby as people walked by, laughing at him as he searched unsuccessfully for a telephone. How could he deal without a telephone he was asking a receptionist? Katsuro Koga, his old antagonist at the Ohyama Bank was grinning and throwing paper balls at him: Emi Mori was applauding.

A deeper, calm sleep finally overtook him, leaving him dead to the world and to the steady buzz of chatter from the video tape he had left running in the lounge.

21

Koga orchestrated the evening from a lounge seat he shared with the fiercely made-up mama san in a wig which doubled the size of her head and a dark, olive-skinned Thai hostess working illegally on a three-month tourist visa. He manipulated his fifteen dealers at night just as he did during the day, selecting the songs they sang, nominating the performers, slapping his thighs as they struggled with unfamiliar tunes and joining his staff, all flushed with whisky, to bellow good-natured derision. He was still high on the surges of energy that had charged his body all day and now he was thanking, in his own way, his key dealers for their successes, particularly the day before, Wednesday, while reminding them that he controlled their leisure as well as their careers. He had picked a cellar bar in Kanda, where business was never discussed and his team could dominate the karaoke equipment and fondle the local girls and the Thai hostesses whose company he had bought for three hours.

Hirata contrived to join in the fun when trepidation on the the consequences of his actions against Katsuro Koga allowed the jitters in his stomach to subside. What would Sam Collier do with the dossier? Would he believe Hirata's interpretation of the tape? Collier had been researching in the bank at the end of January that year when it was revealed how fully the Ohyama Bank was exposed to private individuals who had invested heavily in a stock market which, like the land they had used as security to obtain the money, had nose-dived. And there were billions of yen in loans to legal entities which turned out to be fronts for underworld syndicates. Finding himself at the core of a national financial scandal which had seen a score of resignations among the senior managers in Ohyama alone and legal action against the giant securities houses, Collier saw himself as a fortunate witness at a dramatic moment. He observed, researched and had his comments and reflections published in Europe and in America. This displeased his hosts and a month earlier, or perhaps the end of April, Hirata thought, Collier was asked to conduct his research elsewhere.

The American's departure had been untimely for Hirata, who saw him as the vehicle for his revenge on Koga. The dossier of notes and secretly photocopied documents with which he hoped to undermine Katsuro Koga and force his dismissal or demotion lacked a real killer punch and Collier might leave the country before he could deliver one. At least, that was until he had the tape of the accidentally heard conversation: the final piece of irrefutable evidence. But what if Collier did not believe that the other voice was a conniving Bank of Japan official disclosing the most sensitive information existing in the financial world? Even as he applauded another incompetent performance at the karaoke machine the doubts flooded around Hirata. By mailing the file he had started the count down to an explosion which no one could stop. When his turn came, he sang in tune to a melancholy melody about lost love and loneliness on a rainy day in Nagasaki.

'Maeda, Hirata,' Koga hollered as the group spilled unsteadily in the street. 'I'll give you both a lift home. I'm getting generous as I get old and feeble.' It would have been inappropriate to refuse, although Hirata knew that if he was lucky with the time he might have caught the eleven five limited express which would have him at Abiko in fifty minutes. 'You sit in front, Maeda.'

Their colleagues made ostentatious half bows towards the black fleet sedan as it pulled into the end-of-the-night-entertainment traffic. Maeda was a senior foreign exchange dealer and close to Koga, even imitating his short temper and mannerisms. Driving into a mild May night, he kept up a patter of flattery which Koga relished. Hirata clutched his soft leather briefcase in his lap, mouthing an occasional agreement. His mind was on the incriminating tape. He recognized the Kototoi Bridge, sniffing the breezy aroma from the Sumida River as they headed towards the Mito Kaido road, and soon the Yotsugi Bridge over the broader, misty Arakawa.

The driver had not spoken at all. His white gloved hands rested lightly on the steering wheel, his broad shoulders spreading across the front seat. Thirty minutes after leaving the bar in Kanda he guided the car in light traffic across the black, sluggish Edogawa River where it marked the border between metropolitan Tokyo and the prefecture of Chiba. There were more darker patches now, where copses, paddy fields and the precincts of temples and shrines began to break up the violently illuminated urban sprawl. Without prompting, the driver left the highway and drew up within minutes in front of Shin Matsudo station, built into a complex of department stores, restaurants and arcades. Maeda muttered his thanks and tottered from the car, turning once to bow staggeringly and then disappear through an automatic gate, still laughing with the silly enthusiasm of the drunk. Again without directional guidance, the driver took his car along a alley of gaudy, gilded love hotels before swinging back on to the Mito Kaido.

Hirata's senses were dulled from drink, but not to the state of stupefaction like his colleagues, and he began to sense unease, alone as he was, apart from the mute driver, with the tormentor he was plotting to topple. Koga's house, he remembered from that awful visit of contrition seven years earlier, was in the northern suburbs of Tokyo and here they were heading into the countryside to the east of the capital.

'Koga san,' he said, with an edge of embarrassed alarm. 'I've caused you so much trouble letting you bring me so far.'

The driver adjusted his position, wriggling slightly. The older man shrugged.

'It's no trouble. I have to attend a wake at my wife's relatives near Abiko so you may as well share the car.'

Hirata acknowledged the kindness, seeing a confrontation now as inappropriate. They passed through Kashiwa, with the Joban rail line visible to their right, almost silent as midnight approached, and on to highway three five six, which Hirata was relieved to see was signposted for Abiko. The two-lane road passed between villages and small dormitory conurbations and long stretches of rice fields. It would be typical of Koga to stop here and throw him out. But Koga's head had loosened and his chin was already bouncing on his chest, a droning snore erupting from within. Hirata could have been alone in the car where the only visible movement came from the bright digital clock which had just flashed to three minutes past midnight. He leaned back, resigned to another twenty minutes on the road.

A slowing, turning motion shook him from his own drowsiness. The car was leaving the Abiko road, curving right towards the bridge crossing Teganuma Lake and making for the home of his chief's relatives on the southern flank of the long, twisting body of water. Koga jerked awake when it stopped on a narrow country road which was beginning to dip. A canal separated the road on one side from a rising bank of dense trees and on the other a flat stretch of cultivated land bordering the lake. The car's headlights illuminated the stanchions of a low bridge and beyond, the flecks of light which Hirata thought belonged to the commuter town of Tennodai, only a few kilometres from Abiko. Then the driver surprised him by killing the lights.

Koga thanked the driver and turned to Hirata, sighing impressively. 'Give my regards to your wife, and come and see me tomorrow. We'll talk about your London assignment. You all did very well this week.'

Hirata was moved to reciprocate his chief's unexpected kindness but the feeling of unease was rising, like something intangible gnawing at the pit of his stomach. There was no house or any other sign of habitation within walking distance of the car. 'Goodnight,' he said feebly.

Koga eased the door against the frame and hurried

into the darkness. Hirata leaned across to secure the door when the car started to roll forward.

'Wait,' he commanded, struggling to grip the latch inside its concealed casing. It was as if an invisible screen had risen between him and the driver, and his words were wasted. The car was inching to the centre of the road when two figures loomed behind the car and then separated to close in on the rear doors, collapsing aside the horrified dealer and crushing him between them. He managed a desperate howl but his new companions simply smiled, and the three were flung against the back seat as the car, lights now blazing, lurched forward. For a while neither newcomer spoke, as if they had simply joined him in a row of three on an aeroplane. Hirata offered a greeting but it went unreciprocated. The driver's head was motionless except for an involuntary nod as the car surged ahead, thumping over a drainage ditch, and turned on to the minor route three five seven.

'Who are you?' Hirata ventured.

'We're friends,' the heavier of the two replied. The other had darker skin on his narrow face and a drawn permanent scowl from thin dipping lips. 'We're going to talk to you later and then take you home.'

'Driver!' Hirata pleaded, leaning forward to lay both hands on the seat-back. 'What's happening?' Silence from the front seat. One of the men gripped Hirata's shoulder with stubby fingers and pulled him back. 'Relax. It won't take long. You'll soon be home with Akemi chan and your cute little boy.'

Hirata's head sank, reality a fading mysterious blur, his mind a labyrinth of confusion. This is how it feels to be mugged, he thought, feeling threatened and impotent. Why should they rob him? Wasn't the driver a colleague, a fellow worker at the Ohyama Bank? And

155

how did they know about his son and his wife's name? 'What do you want?' he demanded, his voice controlled at first but then rising to a desperate howl.

Lit up roads signs told him they were moving south towards Funabashi and the docks of the Chiba shoreline. A window was opened and Hirata sniffed the clean night breeze which he knew would change soon to the gassy, sulphurous odour hanging permanently over the chemical plants and factories around Tokyo Bay. He glimpsed his watch and nervously thought of his wife and how she would not worry until the morning when she would wait for the call to tell her that he had missed the last train again and spent the night in a capsule hotel. He tried at intervals to rationalize with his captors, if that's what they were.

'Look, it's better if you dropped me here. I'll call a taxi.'

'Not much further,' was all he got in return.

The farms, clusters of houses around crossroads and the love hotels soon gave way to Tokyo's dense industrial and port appendage on the Chiba coastline of Tokyo Bay. There had been little traffic in the forty minutes since he was taken against his will but his hopes rose when a police car drew beside them at a traffic light below the Wangan Expressway. Hirata's arms were pinned tighter on either side. The police saw nothing suspicious in a chauffeur-driven car and peeled away without more than a glance.

Hirata's faculties were close to collapse. He saw a huge stadium and then the silhouettes of ships in the bay. The car followed a wharf, where a rusty old freighter rocked dark and silent against its pier, and drifted between warehouse blocks, finally pulling into a pitted alley between two of them. Confused and angry, Hirata allowed himself to be eased from the car and led to the rear door of a warehouse. The grip on his arm was weak and when he saw the metallic, magenta Honda compact next to a loading bay he shook his captors off and pointed. 'Is that . . . is that my car?' he shrieked. 'Where am I?'

He felt painful pressure against the bone in his arm and he was pushed into the warehouse. A thinly spread row of unshaded bulbs lit a passage between stacks of packing cases and boxes to a glass-panelled office. The place smelled of cooled, dried fish. Hirata was encouraged along with a hand in the small of his back but he felt calmed by the relative gentleness of his abductors, sure that they would demand a reasonable ransom which his bank would fund on behalf of his family. Then they and the treacherous driver would disappear. But why hadn't they grabbed Koga? He was worth fifty times more than Hirata. And was that his car outside?

The wooden handrail was essential as the trio arranged themselves to descend a steep set of stairs. When Hirata baulked at the top step and half turned to plead an end to the riddle the hand in the pit of his back closed into a fist and he arched forward as it crunched against a nerve. Only a flash of instinct released a hand which strummed the flight of metal columns before catching one of the thin piles and arresting the violent fall, but the weight of his tumbling body wrenched free his tenuous grip, buckling his legs and spinning him in free-fall down the final steps to the cold concrete floor. Strong arms lifted a bewildered Hirata onto heavy legs and half-dragged him between the industrial piping and a massive cooling turbine which emitted a monotonous rhythmic throb.

At the end of the underground machinery room was a rest area for the engineers, with a table with criss-crossed collapsible legs, a television with video and a sink unit stacked with the utensils for making tea and quick, boiled noodles. There was no illumination except for the infra-red glow from the warning lights on the machinery which picked out the featureless forms of three men standing in wait for the newcomers. Hirata's escorts exchanged curt greetings with them and sat with him in the darkness at the table. His initial disbelief was evaporating and a fully conscious realization of his situation overtook him, pushing him from nervous disbelief towards fear and its ultimate expression in terror and panic. His sphincter loosened and he felt a warm dampness in his groin. He blinked repeatedly until the three other figures manifested themselves like apparitions from the hazy pink greyness.

'Hirata san,' one of them said with disarming pleasantness, taking the fourth seat. He was short and smartly dressed in a salaryman's dark blue suit and plain tie. 'My name is Shimizu. I do apologize for keeping you away from your family and assure you the delay will not be long.' He intertwined his fingers and brought the double fist together in a movement which cracked his knuckles, jolting Hirata. 'I'm sorry I can't give you a name-card, but you would honour me by handing over the tape.'

Hirata spluttered, half in comprehension, half in disbelief.

'The tape,' Shimizu repeated patiently. His voice had a strangely high pitch. 'The cassette recording you made at five thirty-seven yesterday.'

'You're mistaken,' Hirata managed, staring at a spot on the table while he summoned up courage. 'I demand to be released. This can cause you a lot of trouble.'

Shimizu snapped his fingers. The television flashed alive, and Hirata was looking at himself from ceiling height in hazy black and white with a slow moving line rolling down the screen. The security clerk was helping him operate the mainframe recording equipment before she retreated and sat beneath the camera which was activated when anyone entered the sensitive area. Staring at the screen, Shimizu spoke to Hirata, a malicious smirk on his broad face. 'The next bit's good. Look. You're making a recording onto the little cassette deck.'

'Where did you get this film?' Hirata blurbed. 'That's confidential material belonging to the Ohyama Bank.' Unseen by Hirata, a man walked into the crescent of light cast by the television monitor. A shock of permed hair crowned his small, oval head and a scowl of pleasant expectation erupted on his tanned, unshaven face. Shimizu raised a calming hand towards him and then turned to Hirata again. 'What did you record?' he said with alarming menace.

Hirata shrugged. 'I had a dispute with a client so I had to check the telephone recording. In this case I was right and if I couldn't persuade the customer he had made a mistake I would have to send him the tape.'

Shimizu leaned forward, his hands splayed on the table. 'What else did you record?' he growled.

Again the chill of fear swept through Hirata's body. 'I had to listen to parts of other conversations until I found what I wanted. There was no other way.'

'But what did you record?' Shimizu insisted.

Hirata's stomach loosened as the nightmare continued. The stutter in his voice betrayed the swelling panic. His heartbeat was audible.

'Somebody booked a restaurant. Was it Saito? There was a private call.'

'What private call?' one of the faceless men shouted.

'Quiet!' Shimizu ordered, and with his face close

to Hirata said: 'Did you listen to it? To this private conversation'

His breath was heavy with garlic and liquor. Hirata drew back as he replied. 'I heard my general manager, Koga san,' he said calmly.

'What did you hear?' his adversary said. 'Precisely.'

'I respected his privacy.'

'Good. Very good.' Shimizu stood and circled the table, pausing to accept a cigarette from a shadowy figure, before rounding on his captive, his face twisted with anger. 'Now give me the fucking tape!'

Hirata's mind raced in confusion. He wanted only his freedom, to escape from a situation he still only half-believed was happening and he saw in his fear his wife and child and wanted to be with them. He knew he had underestimated Katsuro Koga; that his personal vendetta had nowhere to go. His mind raced: the tape would reach the American in the mail that morning. Hirata could not recover it until much later and he did not want to compromise Collier. He chose to stall. 'It's in my desk in the dealing room.'

Shimizu made three distinct movements before he struck. He transferred the cigarette to his left hand, bunched the free fist against his chin as if in contemplation and then spun in a lightning pivot. The outside of his hand hit Hirata's cheek, splitting the skin and dislodging three upper teeth. The banker's eyes popped in surprise as his chair levered backwards. His arms flayed hopelessly, seeking a hold, but his head struck the bare, concrete floor and he felt the sting of the blow which had rasped his face and tasted the warm, sweet flavour of his own blood.

He was in the chair again, his head rolling free, his senses numbed. A disembodied voice was repeating, 'Where is it?' Another raised Hirata's head with a fistful of hair. 'He needs bringing round,' he said, releasing his stunned captive and filling a tumbler at the sink. Hirata lifted a heavy head and looked pathetically at his tormentors. He took the water full in the face. It smeared the blood and dried tears, soaking his dishevelled suit and turning his shirt pink. He was too stupified to scream. He was broken. 'Can you hear me?' Shimizu intoned.

Hirata's head moved imperceptibly.

'I now want the tape. It's not in your desk, your car or your house,' he said, enjoying Hirata's look of horror. 'Your lovely wife wasn't at home when we called to check the gas leak. Pity really.'

'The *gaijin* has it,' he managed, a thin trail of blood spilling from his broken gums.

'What foreigner?' Shimizu said, his oily nose close to Hirata.

'The American. The man who used to research at my bank.'

Shimizu nursed his knuckles, contemplating another strike, this time into Hirata's narrow rib cavity, but his two cohorts at the table raised comprehending hands.

A door clanged somewhere above the dull noise of the generator. The two sentinels, Hirata's abductors, reached instinctively inside their jackets, fingers resting lightly on compact revolvers. They moved apart, into the dark recesses of the subterranean powerhouse. Hirata prayed to the Shinto deities that the footsteps belonged to the police, but his head sank again when he saw his captors relax as two figures approached, one a woman, and they exchanged stiffled greetings. The woman stayed out of view, speaking to the group in urgent bursts.

'Does he have it? Have you got it?'

Her companion was a tall man with a mournful

expression and piercing eyes. A Burberry raincoat over a three-piece business suit rested on his shoulders. He approached the table and inspected Hirata's pathetic figure.

'Where is it?'

Shimizu answered. 'He gave it to the American.'

The newcomer made a wry face. 'How the hell could he,' he said, still staring ahead. They all looked perplexed and waited for Hirata.

'It was posted yesterday.' he groaned.

Where?' Shimizu demanded.

'In Abiko.'

Hirata became irrelevant as the group went into a tight huddle.

'It could have arrived during the day. Late delivery,' one of them said.

The woman stepped forward. 'Get someone to the apartment. If the caretaker hasn't got the package already it'll be in the first delivery tomorrow.'

Shimizu glanced back at Hirata with a contemptuous look before speaking to the man who demanded answers and solutions.

'The police are still looking for the American and one of his relatives has turned up to help.'

'Just get the tape,' the newcomer ordered.

The woman shrugged. 'It shouldn't be a problem.'

They began to break up, moving like silent shadows, ignoring the prisoner Hirata. As if it were an afterthought, the imposing figure draped in the raincoat turned towards the table, where three men semi-circled the prisoner. As he moved, his left hand slid from the fold of the coat. Hirata was mumbling incoherently through the painful swelling on his face and with the eye that was not quite sealed by the blow he watched his oppressor chew the cauterized gristle where the tip of his small finger had been.

'*Yakuza*,' he breathed, but he only heard it in his mind.

22

Jenny Collier leaned into the short, steep hill which curved between tidy shops, fast-food noodle and curry stands and subdued stairways to members only drinking clubs. Her brother had rented a comfortably cramped Western-style apartment in a squat four-storey ferro-concrete block which vibrated slightly when Toyoko Line trains passed on tracks below a stepped embankment.

A young uniformed Japanese policeman on a bicycle wobbled to a halt beside the imposing, mournful foreign woman and greeted her formally. She reciprocated with a dry, lifeless smile. The arrival of the missing American's sister and the fuss she and the American Embassy were making prodded the Tokyo metropolitan police into a number of face-saving measures including a regular high-profile patrol near the man's apartment which Jenny Collier visited every day to collect the mail, hoping forlornly to find her brother there. The two-man squad in the Daikanyama station police box had been told to recognize her and assist if required.

The twenty-two-year-old duty policeman, Ikeyama, had seen the clean, white Toyota turbo saloon, with its ostentatious tinted windows and spoiler, twice; once when it drove past uncertainly and now, parked in the recess of a driveway with its shadowy occupants

163

making no moves to leave the car. But he did not notice the solid man in the salaryman's dark blue suit who stood with his back to the Collier block sipping a vitamin drink and reading the sports pages outside a general goods store on one of the corners of the imperfect intersection of four narrow streets. One of his practised, rapid side-glances caught the figure of Jenny Collier collecting a package from the caretaker and the turning of the page flashed a positive message to the white Toyota. A longer gaze followed the policeman's departure.

Jenny carried the bulky envelope to the cramped, lonely apartment she visited every day, always hoping to find a repentant brother but staying for an hour or so to open his mail and peruse more of the research cuttings, photocopies, reference books and magazines which cluttered the room he called his study. She had thought of leaving the Ginza hotel and moving into her brother's rooms but the atmosphere was as dark as her spirits and while her money lasted she would stay where she could walk among the lights and the polite, helpful people on the streets around Ginza.

Today the new package was as disappointing as all the rest, until she found the note in English and a cassette, which turned out to be a series of short conversations in Japanese and no trace of her brother's voice. But somebody must think he was in Tokyo and this thought lifted her hopes. She had to know what was in the unintelligible papers, but who could she look to for an honest, unbureaucratic and quick response? The people she had met in Tokyo passed across her mind's eye and what she saw depressed her. The officious staff at the American embassy; the dismissive, arrogant Japanese police, the embarrassed university professors who wanted to distance themselves from the errant

164

foreigner. Sam would be back, they all said, just show a little patience. A white foreigner can't disappear in Japan.

She found Kevin Nicholls's business card among the stack she had gathered in the last three weeks. Everyone in Japan gave her their card before speaking. She had found Nicholls genuinely pleasant, curiously unintimidated by her brash American facade but not interested in her as a woman, as if he had his own unspeakable problems. She wanted to respect his privacy but her level of desperation had become intolerable.

'If you're alive Sammy,' she intoned solemnly to the worn family portrait she kept in her purse. 'I'll find you.'

Some of the newly arrived papers, written, apart from a strange message in English, in scrawled, meaningless Japanese, had the name of a bank in English script and a logo at the foot of the page. Nicholls said he worked for a British bank. It was a flimsy link, but she was desperate. He was not in his office when she called and her next stop was the American Embassy where a functionary had rung the hotel to tell her they would like to talk about some new theories which might explain her brother's disappearance. Nicholls was still busy when she made her second call to his bank and she left a message for him.

The slim, young man placed his sunglasses carefully on the dashboard, emitted a burst of instructions to the impassive driver and when he was sure the patrolman had departed he slipped from the car. He caught the waiting figure of the man with the newspaper in a swift glance and crossed the road, sidestepping through the airless, damp gap between two buildings to reach the iron fire escape which opened onto an alley leading to the railway embankment. The charcoal-grey suit he had worn and dozed in for two days was rumpled and stained with sweat. The reinforced jacket dragged from the weight of the Japanese short-sword fitted beneath his armpit as he edged lightly up the steps, unobserved he hoped, to the third floor landing. Smirking as he caught sight of the strip of bare concrete and the third door along, he waited in the overhang and checked his watch.

In the Daikanyama station police box, its sparse furnishing comprising a desk, two chairs and a wall map of the area, patrolman Ikeyama waited with the telephone cradled on his shoulder. The call was local, to the sub-police station in the Hachiko Plaza in Shibuya, a kilometre and a half away. He could have ridden there in the sunshine, glorying in the commendation to come, but he had to be seen to be efficient, in view of the criticism the force had suffered. At last the reply came, and his heart raced. The suspicious car, the white super-charged Toyota, was registered to a real estate firm in Ebisu, which itself was a subsidiary of a general trading company in Osaka. The file on the southern Japan company was flagged on the central police computer as a front for an underworld syndicate.

Officer Ikeyama pedalled hard between wooden houses, his body heating from the effort and the pump of adrenalin. At the same time, a patrol car was leaving Shibuya, its siren blaring.

The second hood, a Japan-born Korean called Tai Il Kim, moved inside the shop, fingering the magazines as he watched the police officer manhandling his bicycle against the entrance to Jenny Collier's apartment block. He cursed in Japanese, the only language he knew, an impotent whimper under his breath. He had no way

166

to warn his companion without wrecking the mission. The tape, their *oyabun* leader had told them in front of Hirata's miserable, moaning body, had to be found and nothing should stand in their way, least of all the law.

The white Toyota was two blocks away, its engine rippling, pointing to the open road, waiting for them. Patrolman Ikeyama struggled with his own thoughts. He wanted both the *yakuza* vehicle and the American woman off his territory. When he reached the front of the apartment he saw the car with the smoked glass windows had gone. He sighed once, deeply, with relief. Now he wanted to see Jenny Collier escorted to a taxi or the train station, whatever she wanted. The porter said she rarely stayed in her brother's apartment more then thirty, forty minutes. He glimpsed his watch. She would be leaving soon, he guessed. In the lift he practised aloud what he would say. 'Please. I wait for you. Please. I wait for you.'

Yokoi, the *yakuza* entrusted with the retrieval of the damning tape, felt the hilt of the knife, excited by the ribbed ivory, and loosened it from its sheath. He moved out of the shadows onto the balcony and then instinctively back when the lift at the other end of the landing whirred to a halt. A policeman emerged, tall young, perspiring and nervous, his hand around the holster of his service revolver. He knocked on the American's door and was admitted. Yokoi's resolve, like Kim's, was heightened by the uncompromising threat of what would happen to them if the tape was not recovered. He looked at his watch again. Kim would be near the lobby, guarding the escape route. He would like to have him, or his gun, but if he could surprise the policeman, and he certainly would, his blade would be enough. Again he moved into the open corridor.

Kim heard the siren well before the black and white car screamed into sight, brushing pedestrians aside and stopping where his own car had been. All four doors swung open. He stepped from behind the column which supported a canvas canopy over the entrance. He thought of his colleague Yokoi, willing him to have the tape, and walked at a carefully relaxed pace round the curve of the road as the four officers moved towards patrolman Ikeyama's bicycle. Yokoi was near the door on the bare concrete third floor landing, his knife now unsheathed and rubbing the side of his trousers, when he too heard the siren tail off below him. His grip on the blade tightened and for an instant he considered pressing on with his deadly mission.

Witnesses aroused by the incident would recall seeing a man in a suit, descending the fire escape noisily and dashing between the buildings until he scrambled dangerously across the Toyoko Line railway tracks.

Jenny Collier struggled to make sense of the shouts, the incomprehensible, rattled chatter into walkie-talkies and the swelling number of police and curious residents. An officer with a useful knowledge of English said there were bad men in the area but the danger had passed. Ikeyama, and his senior officer who rushed to the scene, recognized that a *yakuza* contingent had visited their territory but saw no reason to connect it with the distressed American they had pledged to assist. Jenny Collier gladly accepted a ride to the American Embassy in Toranomon where news awaited her of the latest sighting of her brother. Her hopes were not high.

23

Nicholls wrapped his jacket around a chair. The red-framed glasses still stared at him from the top of his Reuters screen, almost mocking him. His secretary had carried them round the bank, looking for an owner, but they went unclaimed after two days. Naomi Honda, if they were hers, was flaunting a plain, smaller pair with dull-silver rims.

'Very soft dollar overnight,' the keyed up, slight spot dealer, Kimura, remarked when he saw Nicholls settle into his office at seven. In thirteen and a half hours, at eight thirty in the morning Eastern Standard Time in Washington, the announcement of US durable goods sales for April was expected to show another sharp fall, triggering a reaction in the money markets, ruining the traditional Friday lunchtime drinking session in Europe and keeping late shifts in position in Asia.

'I know,' Nicholls said. The young trader did not know his temporary boss had checked New York daytime activity on Moore's bedside Reuters screen twice during the night and followed early Sydney and Wellington business in the taxi on his pocket mini monitor.

'Maybe dollar interest rate cut today,' the young Japanese offered, handing Nicholls the day's technical charts for the yen and the mark against the dollar.

'I don't think it'll come today but the market's started to discount it. Bond prices are really firm. Have you got a position?'

'I'm short of two dollars and I'm well in court,' Kimura said proudly. 'I executed some New York orders and kept a small position from one.'

Like Moore, Nicholls would not allow large position-taking by the general traders in early morning illiquid markets when there were few banks yet quoting in Singapore, Hong Kong or Tokyo. But it motivated the dealers to run speculative positions instead of having to cover every deal immediately and so he gave them a limit of five million dollars for out of hours trading provided the deal resulted from a customer approach and was not a position instigated by the dealers themselves.

The market in Japan was quiet ahead of the American figures though there were probing calls from specialist fund managers in New York, sharks looking for a quick kill with blocks of a hundred million dollars. Nicholls quoted them wide, the memory of two days earlier still rasping. At nine thirty he called Mabuchi and the taciturn accountant from Yorkshire Derek Lemon, who kept the financial books of the branch and reconciled the dealers' claimed income with the figures which emerged from the computers, for a postmortem on their black Wednesday. Then Billy Soh put his head round the door.

'Thanks again for getting me outta the shit yesterday, Kevin. Appreciate it. I've got a position in mark yen out there and they won't watch it for me, but I'd really like to talk in private. There are things going on here and they're getting to me.'

'Sure. I don't know what my plans are yet for the weekend,' Nicholls said, 'Prideaux might want to visit Mount Fuji or something. Leave me your home telephone. Maybe we can get together over the weekend. Really in private.' Soh went over and scribbled onto a memo pad. 'And Billy,' Nicholls said as the tall figure of Gervase Prideaux appeared at the outer office door, 'keep this stuff about the Ohyama companies to yourself.'

'You bet,' Soh said from the door. 'With these human bugs out here we don't need direct telephone lines into the Ohyama Bank.'

'Gerry. Good to see you,' Nicholls said.

The tall head of Sternberg Chance's global treasury tossed a tired response. After leaving Nicholls in Hong Kong he had travelled to Sydney and then to Wellington. He had tuned his mind for a thirty-hour two-stop flight home from New Zealand in the first class cabin of a British Airways seven four seven when Warron Hanlon tracked him down to disclose a major foreign exchange loss, suggesting strongly that he went home via Tokyo. His irritation was barely hidden beneath his customary joviality.

'Hardly the best of circumstances. What was the bottom line? A million and a half dollars?'

'A bit more. Almost two.'

'Jesus! I sent you up here to hold the fort, not blow the bloody place up. It's hard enough to make money in this city and now Hanlon tells me your loss will push the branch into the red in May. What the hell were you doing?'

Nicholls was bristling, sensing the quickly taken glances from the traders through the dealing room windows. He wondered if they were sympathetic. 'I can't excuse the bottom line and I'm sorry if you've been embarrassed,' he said genuinely. 'If one of my dealers dropped a million dollars, let alone two, I'd send him home for a rest or I'd fire him if he'd exceeded his mandate. But on Wednesday the market behaved like I've never seen before.'

Prideaux spoke, his state of mind still sharp in spite of all the air travel. 'I thought there were no excuses for the loss.'

171

'There aren't, but let me put a few things on the table which might help my successors to stay out of trouble.'

'Go ahead,' Prideaux said wearily, his mind already made up, decisions taken.

'I could have coped with the pressure out there on Wednesday, but I wasn't helped by the general manager, who happened to be in the dealing room, ordering me to quote into it.' He looked at his rough cut papers. 'Let me talk you through the big hit. At twelve minutes past ten I quoted the branch's big customer, Nichii Life Insurance and they take twenty million dollars. At ten fifteen Sankoku Oil takes a hundred dollars. The traders are trying to get prices to buy back the dollars but don't get picked up on the direct lines and can't get prices for big amounts through the brokers. It's a total aberration. Like the banks have been warned off. The market's choked up. I've never seen it before. Four minutes later at ten nineteen the Ohyama Bank comes on the Reuters for a price. He was one of the banks who wouldn't pick up my calls. I wanted to cut him off but Warron Hanlon ordered me to quote and guess what? He took me for twenty bucks. Aggregating my other positions, I'm now short of around a hundred and twenty-five million dollars and no sellers for more than five million at a time. At ten twenty, a minute after I deal with Ohyama, the Bank of Japan comes in and smacks the sellers, like yours truly, probably the biggest seller in the market at that moment, hoovering up every fucking dollar they can and in ninety seconds the dollar's worth two more yen and that's what I had to pay to square my position.'

Prideaux crossed his legs and brushed at an imaginary crease in a lapel. He said, 'You're saying there was something out there, other than market forces.

Is that it? These customers and banks you dealt with knew what was going to happen.'

Nicholls nodded. 'Could be.'

'Don't get me wrong, Kevin,' Prideaux said, opening his palms, 'but perhaps they were following things a little more closely. You'd been in Japan less than a week. Not long enough to get to know how things work here or who's conspiring with who. Maybe Tony's death took it out of you. Blunted your edge. You were always close to him.'

Nicholls stood up and faced the dealing room through the glass partition.

Prideaux went on, 'What was Mabuchi doing when all this was going on? Didn't he warn you?'

Turning to him Nicholls said, 'There are thirty-seven people behind me in the treasury. Nine of them, including Mabuchi, worked for the Ohyama Bank and either resigned to come here or were seconded to us on the basis of this close business relationship you all claim we have with them. Mabuchi seems like an honest guy but I don't know where his loyalty lies. He's not gone out of his way to tell me who the baddies are in these markets.'

'I don't think you can make a case out of one incident,' Prideaux remarked stifly. 'Even an expensive one.'

'But there's more,' Nicholls said, retaking his chair. 'A lot more. One of our traders out there, the only non-Japanese it turns out, was quite properly quoting wide in another rough morning yesterday and lost the business. There were complaints from the customers and these reached Warron Hanlon who suspended the dealer. You can gather that I wasn't in the room at the time but I supported Billy Soh. When he showed me the list of clients trying to deal into the volatility there was Nichii Life Insurance again. Sankoku Oil and Nakahata Corporation. We all know that Nakahata are up there with the other Japanese trading companies like Sumitomo and Mitsui Corporation but I wasn't aware they were at the core of the Ohyama group. There are forty odd firms tied up with the usual cross shareholdings, intra group sales and so on and I am told that the bigger Ohyama companies are our customers.'

'I'm still not sure what you're getting at,' Prideaux said.

They waited while Tomoko Ueda served coffee, Nicholls using the pause to confirm the calmness in the markets before returning to Prideaux.

'Billy Soh objected to quoting four Ohyama companies yesterday, which was correct in view of Wednesday's disaster. We were a hundred grand ahead and square, not taking any chances. Half an hour later, when Billy Soh was getting a bollocking for protecting the bank's interests, the Bank of Japan came in again.'

'I didn't read about any intervention yesterday,' Prideaux protested.

Nicholls was tempted to lecture his chief but explained economically. 'If they want to send the market a message that the BOJ is prepared to intervene they make it known through the brokers that they are checking the prices. It doesn't calm the speculation. It's just a warning not to go against the Bank of Japan and it doesn't cost them anything.'

Prideaux tapped his forehead with a closed fist. He said, 'If I understand you, you're suggesting that Ohyama companies have access to inside information from the Japanese central bank and used it once against you on Wednesday and tried it again, unsuccessfully, yesterday.'

'That's about it,' Nicholls said.

Prideaux was unconvinced. His coffee cup rattled as he shook his head vigorously.

'There's one more twist,' Nicholls declared. 'Tony called me the day before he died and told me about a half billion dollar deal about to hit the market. It was a selling order. I sold a few myself and sure enough in twenty minutes the market was swilling in dollars and down it went.'

'It's not unusual to warn your overseas colleagues if you're going to handle a potentially market moving deal, is it?' Prideaux said. 'You don't have to disclose the client on the other side. Just advise them to exercise caution.'

'Of course not. But the unusual's started to become the norm here. I gathered the dealing records for a week ago Wednesday. I went through the computer printouts, then two hundred dealing tickets and just in case I looked in the drawers for hidden tickets. No five hundred million deals have been booked in Sternberg Tokyo for six months.'

'What are you saying?' Prideaux asked ominously.

'Either the company that initiated the deal or the bank that executed it thought enough of Tony Moore to tip him off.'

Prideaux was genuinely outraged. 'That's unethical and absolutely unacceptable.' And added, 'If it's true.'

Nicholls reached behind and lifted the red glasses from the Reuters monitor. He ran his fingers around the rims. 'You know what's so bloody weird Gerry?'

Prideaux shrugged. 'It's all weird, but tell me.'

'When Tony gets a tip-off there's a big deal in the market it makes him a bucket of money; when I'm on the receiving end of somebody else's inside information I get screwed for a couple of million dollars.'

Prideaux was shaking his head before Nicholls had finished, irked by the slight but unmistakable inference that one of his senior dealers was corrupt. 'Tony had great connections here,' he said forcefully. 'He'd been here almost a year. He was bound to have better contacts than you.'

'Maybe,' Nicholls conceded, retreating from a debate on Tony Moore's dealing ethics.

Prideaux felt smug in the belief that he had carried the exchange. 'Time for lunch,' he said, tapping his watch. 'We'll work out the specifics of your move out of Tokyo later.'

When his chief had left, Nicholls went to the dealing desks, refreshing himself in the markets, calling the brokers, banks in Hong Kong and Singapore and working on a currency options ploy based on the technical chart forecasts. Returning to his office when the foreign exchange markets closed for lunch in Tokyo, Tomoko Ueda brought him a box meal of *teriyaki* fish on rice, with a little pocket of coloured pickles, and fresh green tea. His mind wandered mentally to Hong Kong and Tony as he ate: to that last big deal they had discussed during a bout of feverish trading. The memory of that deal had returned when he sat alone in the hotel on his first night in Japan and now, after finding no record of the deal in the books of the Sternberg Chance branch in Tokyo, he realized Tony had been relaying a warning. He had given him the details of a deal about to hit the foreign exchange market, a deal big enough to move the rates dramatically. Somebody had cautioned Tony, who was kind enough to call Nicholls.

The loose ends were still bothering him as he sorted through the small heap of yellow telephone message slips. He selected one which took him back to a very pleasant late snack earlier in what turned out to be a lousy week.

24

Jenny Collier took a deep, therapeutic breath, suppressing the anguish which threatened to destroy the last of her inner strength. It was not only the curious incident at her brother's apartment, or even his continuing absence, that had begun to unnerve her. It was the state of not understanding; of being in an endless, unlit tunnel; of questions met with blank stares or embarrassed, empty smiles and the official suggestion that her presence in Tokyo was hindering the search.

She fanned the papers onto the bed in her hotel room, as if the action would help her decipher the columns of hieroglyphics and the perplexing English words and phrases scattered among them. The Japanese police had invited her to bring them to their headquarters and the American Embassy had requested a copy. She was sitting on the bed, impatient, frustrated and lonely, a slim cassette tape in a hand, when the telephone rang.

'Jenny? It's Kevin. Kevin Nicholls.'

'Kevin. I'm so glad you're there. I'm hope you remember me. I should have called to thank you for the dinner on Monday.'

'That wasn't necessary,' Nicholls said genuinely. 'Of course I remember you.' The ready smile, edged with sadness, and the way she touched his arm with those slender fingers to emphasize a point were the high spots in what was becoming a nightmare assignment. 'It was

177

me who should have called you about your brother.' He looked at the mosaic of flashing lights on the telephone console. They seemed to be mocking his professional failure. 'I've been a bit occupied.'

Jenny Collier's voice deepened as she spoke with controlled urgency. 'Kevin. I need help and I don't know where to go.'

'If I can,' he began.

'I think you said you did something in banking.'

'That's right,' he said, remembering how his miniature monitor had intrigued her. 'But not your high street type.'

'There'll all the same to a simple girl from Chicago,' she quipped and then grew serious again. 'Sam, my brother, got a packet of papers in the mail today. And a cassette tape. Some newspaper cuttings.'

There was a break on the line and he knew she was struggling with her emotions.

'It's all in Japanese, except for a message in funny English to Sam. Some of the writing's on a bank's headed notepaper. That's the bank connection I'm afraid.'

'What did it say? The message in English,' Nicholls asked gently. Another short break told him she was searching through the papers.

'"This is the last chance for me. Please tell the truth about my company,"' she read aloud. 'I don't know what the hell it means but maybe there's a clue to Sam's plans. Hell, I don't know.'

Nicholls tried to rationalize and placate, saying, 'The police can help you better than me,' and he offered feebly, 'especially with the Japanese.'

He sensed her frustration boiling, evident in the gaps between words, in the intense pitch of her voice.

'I just don't know, Kevin. They've gone through

Sam's things in his apartment, all his notes, letters, research papers, and I've heard nothing positive from them. I know if I give them this dossier I'll never know whether it's helpful or not. The embassy's worse. They assure me we're not dealing with a Third World country here. The cops will do their duty and anyway a white foreigner can't disappear in Japan. Kevin. Is there someone trustworthy at your bank who could run his eyes over the papers in Japanese for me? It sounds desperate but I have to try everything.'

'Of course,' he said. He had been in the bank less than a week and there was only Fujimori with any fluency in English and he would not put himself out for Nicholls or his friends. Neither would it be smart for Fujimori or anyone Japanese here to see another bank's documents, whatever their contents. A desk-set bleeped. 'Just a second, Jenny,' he said, covering the mouthpiece.

'Nicholls san.' Tomoko Ueda's voice called. 'There's an Araki san on the other line. He says he met you at the Hie Shrine.' Of course he remembered the helpful, inquisitive journalist with the lived-in suit and similar face. And then, with his dealer's instinct, he saw a buyer and a seller and a solution to Jenny Collier's dilemma. 'Take his number and I'll call him back in two minutes.' He clicked off. 'Jenny. Sorry. I think I can help, but I have to ask you to come to my apartment. There'll be a Japanese reporter from some rag magazine or other. He's helping me with my own mission; I'll get him to help you. I think I can trust him.' He gave her time to think but her pause was only to breathe her relief.

'Thanks Kevin,' she said softly. It took him two minutes to transmit tortuously his address to the American woman.

'Any time after six,' Nicholls said, not too keenly he hoped.

'This is Araki,' the toneless voice said, 'we met . . .'

'Where Tony died. Yes I remember,' Nicholls said brusquely. 'Did you dig up any more shit on us for your magazine?'

'A few things,' Araki answered drily, 'principally a lover, a young model. I want you look at her photograph. Maybe confirm the identification. A picture of her in Moore's flat? I'd keep your name out of it.'

'What's her name?' Nicholls asked.

'Mori. Emi Mori. Is that correct?' Nicholls's expression was sour. Keep him on the hook, Nicholls thought. He needs you to remove that last suggestion of doubt. 'It could be,' he said. 'Bring the picture to my flat tonight.'

'Thank you Kevin san. I'm bowing into the phone as we speak. Can you feel the sincerity?'

They both laughed and then Nicholls said, 'I need something from you,' and the silence through the line was loaded.

'If I can,' the Japanese said finally.

'I want you to read some papers, they're in Japanese, and tell a friend of mine if they're relevant to her research. It shouldn't take long.'

'No problem,' the Japanese said briskly, relieved that the reciprocity demanded did not sound onerous. Then Nicholls remembered the video again and tapped his head with a clenched fist in frustration. Whatever Emi Mori had put in his drink was clearing slowly, leaving his mind in short bursts of lucidity and then clouding it again. He had run the tape last night but had fallen asleep after taking the call from London. What the hell had she given to leave him drowsy after thirty-six hours?

Emi Mori had left with the padded envelope, unaware that he had managed to replace the new tape with an old

180

video from Tony's collection. Possession of the video had to be the reason for her to dope him. Perhaps the drug had worked its way through him. Finally. He saw the pieces sliding together to make a a frightening picture. If Emi Mori had played the old video already she would know it wasn't what she expected and might attempt to retrieve the new one. She had returned one set of keys to him. Maybe she had another. He had been out of his flat for eight, nine hours. The tape was in the machine.

'One more thing,' he said urgently, thinking quickly now and realizing the futility of trying to explain the situation to the police, even through a Japanese intermediary. 'Can you get away now?' he said to Araki.

'Now?'

'I need somebody to fill the space in the lobby till I get there.'

'Is this something to do with Tony Moore's accident?' the Japanese said, his attention suddenly gripped with interest. He sensed an advantage.

'Might be. I really don't know,' he said honestly.

'Let me have a piece of it.'

'I might just do that,' Nicholls said, keeping vengeful thoughts to himself. He read out the address. 'Hang around the lobby, note anyone who doesn't look like a resident. There are only six apartments and five of the tenants are *gaijins*. Can you do it?'

'I'll see you there.' There was a click on the line.

25

Tomio 'Tom' Imaizumi chewed on the earpieces of his glasses and circled the long-haired teenager in the red, rear-zipped ribbed mini skirt and the clinging black sweater which managed to enhance what were little more than fatty swellings beneath it. She smiled inanely as an assistant measured her waist and legs, inside and out. She was not tall but her uncharacteristically short torso and a line with little hooping of the legs gave her the right proportions for the programme Imaizumi was pre-auditioning for. It was an after-midnight soft porn spot in the guise of a comedy game show but it had a good rating in the insomniac student sector and Imaizumi submitted a regular stream of hopeful contestants from his books, with an acceptable one-in-ten success rate.

'Now,' he said. 'Giggle, but don't cover your mouth, and turn confidently with your back to the camera. Plant your feet and then unzip your skirt slowly.' He felt the roots of his short, permed hair tingle. 'Remember, there's a guy lying on the floor looking up three skirts and he'll decide which of you has got the best ass. OK, try it.'

She had practised at home a hundred times and performed a fluent twirl for him, releasing the well-oiled zipper and stepping smoothly out of the fallen skirt.

There was a sharp knock on the door of the meeting room and Emi Mori leaned in. She ignored the buttocks and the strip of silk thong that parted them and spoke to Imaizumi. 'I believe it's time for the development meeting,' she said coldly.

'Is it?' he said. 'Of course it is.' The soft, full pockets

of skin, close enough for him to see the tiny blemishes and depressions, had distracted him into missing the urgency in his visitor's message. He handed over the audition reluctantly to the two female assistants. 'Thank you Miss . . .'

'Fukuda,' one of them prompted.

Imaizumi led Emi Mori through Excell Image Agency's untidy business office and into his own. Two keys on a ring hooked to his belt were needed to unlock a solid door which opened into a short corridor narrowed by a row of steel filing cabinets. Another door clicked open after Emi Mori had entered a four digit code into the keyboard implanted in the wall. In the soundproofed room, which hummed from two banks of recording equipment stacked against two walls, a man in creased sweatshirt and jeans, with hair pulled sharply back into a finger of pigtail, sat at a personal computer, headphones clamped to his ears. He greeted the visitors without standing. Emi Mori took a copy of *One Point Finance* from a department store bag and slapped it onto a table.

'Have you seen this?' she said intimidatingly to Imaizumi.

'Yes I have, and I've complained strongly to the editor.'

Emi Mori, in a double-breasted coat suit over a white blouse slashed with orange and black, dismissed the futility of this gesture with a flick of a wrist. 'How did this journalist Araki get hold of my photograph?'

Imaizumi explained how the man with a convincing story and representing an enterprise which was verified by the voice on an answering machine persuaded him to open his portfolio of escorts with specialist talents, like the ability to speak good English. Emi Mori eased herself onto a corner of the table. 'And how did he know about your agency? I only use it for official purposes, to establish a legitimate place of work. I have no calling card with this address on it.'

Imaizumi took this in and then turned his lean, high-domed face slowly to the woman. 'Did you tell the police when they interviewed you about Tony Moore?

She nodded slowly and meekly, then said, 'But they wouldn't pass anything on to the Press, especially not a rubbishy weekly like *One Point Finance*.'

'They might. Journalists tend to have good contacts in the police. A quiet word dropped over a drink would be enough to reciprocate some favour or other.'

Emi Mori's dress fell apart at her thighs when she crossed her legs, revealing a shimmer of tights. 'How do you think he got interested in Tony Moore? Has there been a leak?'

Imaizumi leaned against a filing cabinet. 'That's what our people will want to know. I hope it's only the *gaijin* interest. If he takes it further he might try to contact you in person. If he does you must tell our seniors. Let's hope he doesn't, for his sake.' The man with the pigtail took off his earphones and swivelled on his chair. He said to the woman, 'My database here is still missing the last tape from England. I hear you did the job yourself, and well it went I understand.' His face hardened. 'If it fell into the possession of the wrong people it could hurt us.'

'I know that,' Emi Mori said, dropping from the table. 'London side sent the last one to his apartment address as usual, but the man the bank sent out to replace Tony Moore somehow got hold of the keys and moved straight into the place. I died a little when I saw this guy sitting there. What could I do? I had to think of something tolerably credible so I said I'd come to pick up some old British videos for sentimental reasons. I took a handful of old clean tapes but this new fool got suspicious and switched the video that arrived on Wednesday.' She shook her head in frustration. 'I managed to get to the apartment with him when it arrived but he must have swapped it when I went to the bathroom.'

'Do you think he watched it?' Imaizumi asked.

'The dose of chloral hydrate I put in his beer in that Roppongi bar should have erased his memory for a week. But he was strong, all muscle, not like Tony. He kept awake long enough to suspect something.'

'Will he recognize you if he watches it?'

'I kept my back to the camera and let the girls work on the subject.'

'Who was it?' the techician asked.

'He's the assistant to the head of investment policy at the Kokusai Mutual Life Company. All pension funds and premiums go through their department. They're the third largest insurance company in the country so you imagine for yourself what we're talking about.'

'How will he be approached?' said the pigtailed man, whose name was Koizumi. 'if we don't have the ultimate inducement to encourage his co-operation.'

Emi Mori adjusted a band of silver bracelets and then examined the tangerine tips of her fingernails in the half-open fist she had made. 'It has to be decided.' she said, and then captured Imaizumi in a penetratingly serious look. 'We have been instructed to meet at seven tomorrow. The issue of the tape and other unpleasant developments will be discussed.'

Imaizumi smiled his acceptance, cursing to himself and casting his thoughts back to the university dropout with the perfect backside who said her artistic interests and ambitions went beyond taking her skirt off on television and that she would like him to observe and assess her skills without the embarrassment of his staff in attendance. She would have been his Saturday night.

Koizumi said, 'I hear there's another job coming up.'

'That's right,' Emi Mori declared, reaching into a deep shoulder bag for a sheaf of papers. 'It has to be done sooner than we would have liked. And here in Japan. Are you ready?'

Koizumi unlocked a box, selected a floppy disc, slotted it into his desktop computer and opened a new file onto a spreadsheet with the category headlines running vertically. 'Go ahead, give me the profile,' he said finally. As Emi Mori read each piece of detail Koizumi repeated it and tapped it into a keyboard.

'Name: T. Michael (Mike) Schweiker,' he intoned as he typed. 'Nationality: American. Age: forty-two. Interests: fishing, food, wine. Education: Bachelor of Science from Stanford University, MBA from Harvard, sponsored by the Federal Reserve Bank. Career: Entered the Federal Reserve in Washington DC after graduation,; vice-president and staff assistant to the Federal Open Market Committee in Washington DC and currently senior vice-president of the Federal Reserve Bank of New York.'

Schweiker was married with four children. His point of vulnerability was an illegal time deposit of US$100,000 with the Liechtenstein Peoples' Bank, Cayman Islands Branch, Grand Cayman. The opinion section read: Tight income/expenditure ratio, frequently works weekends (genuine); competition extreme for next upward move. Wife aggressive for his advancement. Will be stretched by future private education costs. No mistresses or sexually involved girlfriends. Eats with attractive thirty-year-old secretary once a month – lunch. She accompanied subject on Federal Reserve mission to Europe in December 1990. Likes Tex-mex and Cuban food (speaks Spanish, see undergraduate minor). May have received massage attentions while drunk during business trip to Asian Development Bank conference in 1991 in Manila. His compromise would be eased by monetary stimulus. Has high alcohol tolerance. Use awareness of Cayman deposit cautiously. Sensitive approach advised.

Koizumi entered the details and waited by the printer. 'How was he identified?'

Emi Mori said, 'Our main contact in Japan confirmed that Schweiker plays a key role in the co-operation between the Federal Reserve and the Bank of Japan. I'm told he's the senior vice-president in charge of the dealing activities in the Federal Reserve Bank of New York. It puts him in charge of executing the orders of the Chairman of the Federal Reserve and the US Government Treasury Secretary.'

Koizumi made a puzzled face. The woman saw it and looked at Imaizumi for an explanation.

'I'm not a financial expert either,' he began, 'but the Federal Reserve's like the Bank of Japan. They decide whether interest rates go up or down and where the ideal exchange rate should be. They talk to each other a lot, co-operate, try to keep the yen and the dollar in some kind of controlled range.' He sucked in air and grinned. 'If you know when they are going to change a rate or take some other measure you jump in ahead and put your money in the right place.'

Koizumi was not completely convinced. 'It takes me days to move my money from one account to another,' he grumbled.

'The professionals move money in seconds,' Imaizumi

said definitively. 'And Schweiker can give our people those seconds. He is the last important link.'

'I'm sure our friends know what they're doing,' Koizumi said. 'I hope they realize that the more people we dangle like puppets, the more chance one of the strings'll snap.'

Emi Mori's expression was blank when she answered. 'That's not your problem.'

Koizumi turned to his monitor and keyboard, his mind back to the technical difficulties of capturing T. Michael Schweiker on film at the right moment. 'Just tell me when you want the event,' he said.

Emi Mori checked her diary. 'Wednesday. In five days.'

'And where?'

'The staff officials supporting a G-Seven international finance conference in Tokyo will arrive here during the week and attend private meetings with their international colleagues before the main talks.'

'G-Seven?' Koizumi interrupted again, his face twisted. Emi Mori looked to Imaizumi for an explanation.

He said, 'The Group of Seven. The finance ministers of the main seven economies, Japan, America, Britain, France, Germany – Italy and Canada are the others I think. They get together when necessary and talk about currency problems with the central banks, like the Bank of Japan. I understand the strength of the yen is the main topic but I am not an expert on the subject. Japan is host this time and the participants bring a full staff with them, people like Schweiker, who work in the central bank of their country.'

'Thanks,' Koizumi said. 'Sorry, Emi san. Please continue.'

'There will be a small party in the main rooms of the Asakusa guest house on Wednesday to which

Schweiker has been invited by our seniors who know him from the past. He will be assessed during the dinner and if his behaviour is appropriate he will be taken to the bamboo lodge for more suitable pleasures. There will be three women in attendance. I am one of them. The others also speak English and Lisa Hamazaki speaks fluent Spanish, like Schweiker. Megumi Arai has studied in California and understands wine.'

Koizumi smiled inwardly, relishing the chance to see Lisa Hamazaki again. Her Mexican father had given her skin the colour of milky coffee and an exquisite body imbued with the Latin passion to enjoy it without inhibition. Megumi Arai possessed a perpetual interest in the maleness of foreign men, however physically repulsive they were, and they liked her exquisite Oriental femininity, although it was contrived, and mistakenly believed her curiosity derived from their irresistible masculinity.

Imaizumi ran an eye over the Schweiker details on the monitor. 'What if this fat American doesn't appreciate the finer points of the *shamisen* and the tea ceremony. He might prefer to go to Roppongi on Wednesday night.'

Emi Mori straightened her suit. 'He's already accepted. This is the most important assignment so far. Our senior principals host the evening and they will bring our good friend from the Bank of Japan. He will leave as soon as appropriate but his presence will give the evening an official seal as he has similar responsibilities to Schweiker. I'm sure the American will not overlook an opportunity to meet such a senior official.'

'And if he doesn't take to Lisa?'

Emi Mori thought about a cigarette but knew it was forbidden in the air-conditioned machine room. 'I see him as a man who loves his wife and children in a

189

sort of tired American way, who cherishes the perks that the travel side of his job brings him and saves his waywardness for those times. He probably doesn't play around much sexually but gets his satisfaction from expensive food and wine. Megumi will quench his appetite for food and Lisa will melt him.'

She gave them each a waist-up photograph of a heavy set man with thinning hair and thick eyebrows and turned after reaching the door.

'I repeat. This is a vital assignment. A friend inside the American central bank is the final piece in the network. Your best efforts are expected.'

26

Araki was sitting in the bright lobby, scribbling furiously. His article, short of substance but long on innuendo about the night activities of the foreign dealers paid over half a million dollars a year plus benefits, was on the Thursday presses with a provocative photograph of an unidentified woman believed to be the lover of a dead money market trader. He saw a follow-up story and he wanted to know more about the lifestyle of the foreigner and in particular meet the Japanese woman who lived off it. The only commodity he had to trade was money, which would not impress the dead man's successor but would tempt the woman who had rejected the route her society had planned for her in favour of the fast, sexy life she believed the *gaijin* could give her, if only as an interlude.

Nicholls shook his hand and gave a passing *konnichiwa* to the nervous caretaker who was not happy with the presence of the unkempt visitor and the attention the death of one of the foreign guests was bringing to the company. Police, women of a certain kind and now journalists with unshaved faces and rude manners. The arrival of her temporary tenant was only mildly comforting.

'Any callers?' he asked, ushering Araki to the lift.

'There were actually,' Araki said. 'A couple of men were talking to your caretaker about you when I got here. They said they were detectives.'

Nicholls turned to the woman but spoke to the journalist. 'What did they want? They've been round to see me already. Last Monday, in fact.'

'They wanted her to let them into your apartment. Apparently there's been some new findings on Tony Moore and they wanted to look around his place again.'

Nicholls frowned. 'So what happened?' he said impatiently.

'I butted in and said I was waiting for you, that you were about to arrive and you could let them in personally.'

'And?'

'They said they were busy and will call you later.'

'Thanks for that,' Nicholls said, as he urged the lift upwards.

'What's going on?' Araki asked, his journalist's curiosity aroused.

Nicholls's recollection was still clouded, it had taken almost two days for its memory to jerk back into life. He gave Araki a potted version of his second meeting with Emi Mori but could not fit in any depth of detail.

'Leave your shoes on. There might still be some broken glass around,' he warned, making for the television. Araki inspected the functional, leased furniture, the framed photographs, easy expressions of Tony Moore's personal life.

'You won't find any pictures of Emi Mori.' said Nicholls, pressing the eject button and extracting the much-wanted video cassette from the slot. It was warm. 'I fell asleep and left it running,' he confessed.

Araki grinned, wondering with rising interest why Nicholls's first action was to clutch a video tape like some precious jewel.

'It must have been a great party,' the Japanese said. 'Mysterious tapes, broken glass, record player still on.' He pressed a button on the music centre and sniffed the air that Nicholls had been too tired the day before to refresh by simply opening a window.

'Cacharel with a dash of cognac and old tobacco.' The last observation prompted him to produce a crumpled packet of Hi-lite cigarettes.

Nicholls slid the windows apart and was engulfed by the billowing curtain. Araki knelt in front of the television and examined the tape. 'British VHS. Converter on the video. Are you hiding it from your wife?'

'Play it,' Nicholls said.

'Is that what you wanted me for? To see how the *gaijin* live and write some more bullshit about the orgies?' Araki pressed buttons and the television flashed alive. He stabbed the video machine and the screen erupted in a black and white haze, followed quickly by a helicopter's view of the huge sports stadium.

'Not your usual porno venue,' the Japanese said with disappointment.

Nicholls chuckled. 'That's right. I almost died for a fucking film of an English soccer match.' Players in white and red strips limbered and loosened and scampered in miniature. 'I must have fallen asleep soon into the tape last night. I don't remember much after the kick-off. Let the tape run. Drink? Beer. Whisky. Anything.'

'Beer, please. What do you mean you almost died for the tape?' the Japanese said, following Nicholls to the kitchen and sensing another story. 'What exactly did Emi Mori do to you?'

'Nothing. Just a sick joke,' Nicholls said, clutching a pair of misted tins and carrying them back to the television. 'You called me,' he said, recoiling at the pressured spray when he pulled the tab and conscious that Jenny Collier's arrival was minutes away.

Araki drew a photograph from his jacket pocket. 'Was this Anthony Moore's lover?' he asked, holding the stolen picture between the tips of two fingers.

The soft-focus image did no justice to the delicate features of the woman who had teased and tormented him. Nicholls's body stirred. The curves of her glossy, living body were outlined beneath the satin dress, cut low to the swell of her breasts. It had been a dream until it exploded into a nightmare. His hands had explored her. He knew it had been real.

'Is it her?' Araki said again, mistaking Nicholls's lustful, ambiguous contemplation for doubt and calculating the horrendous consequences if the article, on the printing presses at that very moment, suggested libellously that the innocent model in the photograph was a groupie for a bunch of *gaijin* bankers. He breathed noisily in relief when the Englishman nodded.

'Where did you get it?' the dealer asked.

Araki said, 'From what I can loosely call a model agency. She was on their books as a bi-lingual party hostess. The photo's appeared with my article today. We've blurred out the eyes because she hasn't given her permission. She doesn't even know about it but I

193

had to be sure she was the girl who was with Moore when he started his last binge.'

'This is crazy,' Nicholls said, mental and physical fatigue still fueling his irritation. He snarled at the Japanese.

'Tony didn't drink. It made him puke. Anyway, why's a financial rag interested in the accidental death of a foreigner?'

Araki smiled ruefully. 'We, *One Point Finance*, are at the personal end of the market. We put faces to the marker movers. Some are greedy, others devious or outright crooks. Our banks are the biggest in the world and you foreigners have praised them for years as the power plants of Japan's success. Now we find that many of them, especially your partners at the Ohyama Bank, have piled up massive loans to dubious land-rich characters who shoved it into the stock market. Some of the speculators have crime syndicate connections. When I hear Ohyama I grab my pen.'

I'd like to grab something else, like a primed missile, Nicholls thought, reminded of two days of nothing but Ohyama. He said, 'That still doesn't tell me why you're stalking Sternberg.'

'There are rumours that Sternberg Chance will be the first Japanese-owned British bank. That interests the Press. When one of their staff gets drunk and dies in the arms of a mysterious Japanese mistress that interests me.'

'You've got it wrong,' Nicholls said, shaking his head in frustration. 'Tony couldn't have stood up with any booze inside him, let alone walk around a shrine in the middle of the night.

'But that's what the police autopsy said.' And Araki added. 'Did you find the stick?'

A soccer player was being carried off the field:

his face, contorted with pain, filled the nearly silent screen.

'It was probably cremated with him. Nothing surprises me in this country,' he said, making for the kitchen with two empty beer cans. The doorbell rang. 'That'll be Jenny Collier.'

'I'll get it,' Araki offered, stopping the tape.

When Nicholls returned they were chatting like old friends.

'How do you get around this goddamn city?' Jenny was complaining. 'No street names, crazy numbering and people laughing when they send you the wrong way.'

'You have to know where you're going before you go,' said Araki, smiling only when her quizzical look turned into a broad grin.

She wore a black sweater with three broad white hoops and loose-fitting trousers: her figure, Nicholls noticed, was again hidden enticingly in comfortable clothes. He knew she felt safe in their company, her suffering masked behind an easy smile and ready conversation.

'Functional bachelordom,' she said, nodding with mock criticism at the unimaginative furnishings.

'Give me time,' Nicholls quipped, handing her a glass of chilled white wine. 'On second thoughts, I'll be gone in a couple of weeks. You'll have to help me get through Tony's cellar, mostly Napa Valley chardonnays, but there's some good claret too.'

'I think you need a rest, Kevin,' she said. 'You look like a wet day in Chicago. Have you been overdoing the sake?'

'No, just a little woman trouble.'

'I hope you're around long enough to meet my brother,' she said with forced cheerfulness. She glanced at the silent images on the television. 'I'm sorry if I'm disturbing you. Are you guys settling down for a TV dinner together?'

Nicholls grinned, and led them to the table in the dining alcove of his L-shaped apartment. 'We were watching a video, a present in the mail for Tony Moore.'

'Tony Moore?' she said, without further interest, removing from her briefcase a plastic folder of papers. A slim audio cassette tape rattled as it slipped from the package on to the walnut table. Nicholls remembered that out of concern for her feelings he had not disclosed his own mission when they met at the foreign correspondents' club. 'This was his apartment. He was my missing person,' he confessed. 'Well, more than missing. I'm sure you'll find your brother's pursuing his research with a fawning butterfly from Roppongi.'

She seemed to understand. 'Oh I'm sorry,' she said. 'And I've brought you my silly problem.' She splayed her fingers and motioned at Araki and the sheaf of papers he had begun to sift. Her elbows were anchored to the table and she chewed on the knuckles of her clenched hands, a picture of hopelessness and dejection. Nicholls was moved to take her arm. Araki coughed theatrically.

'Is there anything to eat, Kevin?'

Jenny sprang alert. 'That sounds like my cue,' she said, seeing the kitchen through the opened door.

'I bought a few things for the fridge,' Nicholls called after her. 'The beer was getting lonely.'

Araki turned to Nicholls, his voice serious, alert and quietly excited. 'Where did she get these?'

Nicholls explained how the package had arrived that morning for her missing brother.

'It must reassure her to know that at least one

person thinks he is still in Tokyo,' the Japanese said, pushing a sheet of paper across the table. 'See anything familiar?'

Nicholls was about to offer it back, the mesmerizing mass of hand-written and word-processed ideograph characters totally unintelligible until Araki directed his eyes wordlessly to the roman script at the foot of the page. Beside the words was a reproduction of the logo depicting a mountain of three peaks, a tiny facsimile of the graphic symbol of the Ohyama Bank and the network of industrial and commmercial giants sharing the name of the Big Mountains. It was as familiar as the three diamonds of Mitsubishi and the three lines of Mitsui.

Nicholls smirked ironically. 'I can't get away from the bastards.' He aimed the remote control at the video unit and pressed the play button. 'What's it all about?' he called.

'I don't know yet,' Araki said. 'This guy, something Hirata. I can't read the characters for his given name. Hirata's not happy at Ohyama. What do you say in Britain? Pissed off?' Nicholls nodded. 'He figures he's been victimized at work and he's had enough. He's collected a pile of papers about his bank and he sent it to Sam Collier. I'll have to look at them in detail but it seems strange he should send them to a *gaijin* who probably doesn't read or speak Japanese.'

The rich smell of frying meat and onions wafted from the kitchen. 'I helped myself to more wine, Kevin,' Jenny Collier called.

Nicholls turned to Araki. 'Jenny told me her brother was doing some research earlier this year with a Japanese bank. It must have been Ohyama. He was also selling the occasional article, mostly Japan-bashing for the US Press.'

'It still sounds like a desperate move by Hirata,' Araki said.

Nicholls replied: 'Perhaps he had no one else he could trust.'

'Can I change to whisky?' Araki said, brushing a film of tobacco ash from the table and lighting another cigarette. 'If it ever got out that Collier used his Japanese source's name in an exposé of Ohyama internal practices,' he continued, pulling on the cold concoction Nicholls had prepared, 'Hirata's in trouble.'

'He somehow trusted the American I suppose,' Nicholls suggested.

'Sloppy joes,' Jenny announced proudly, spooning the ground beef, tomato and spicy filling into sesame-coated buns.

Nicholls raided Tony Moore's wine cellar, actually layers of wire mesh in a cool clothes cupboard in his bedroom, and returned with two bottles of Fleurie. There was a curious synergy between the pressurized British dealer, the desperate American executive and the Japanese purveyor of sleazy exposés. By the time the food was finished and most of the wine drunk they knew each other's stories, the men becoming helpless with laughter at Jenny's stories on the testing of baby foods and then sombrely pledging themselves to help in the search for her brother. The American woman was encouraged by the papers from the Japanese banker and the generosity of the two men she hardly knew. Her spirits reached a three week high.

Araki looked at his watch. 'If you don't mind I'd like to study the papers and the tape at home,' he said to Jenny Collier. He did not say that he had seen things in the papers to shake him. He had to be alone for a night session. Jenny had no objections and exchanged

198

telephone numbers with the Japanese. They agreed to meet the next day, Saturday. He laboriously plotted on paper the route Nicholls should follow when the Englishman said he would attempt to manoeuvre Tony Moore's car around the monster that was Tokyo.

When Araki had left, Nicholls stacked the dishwasher and was peeling the foil off a bottle of dry white Moldavi when Jenny Collier's deep Chicago drawl echoed through the apartment.

'You guys are sick!' she bawled with pained disgust. Nicholls joined her in front of the television which had been playing the soccer video for almost two hours. The vigorous athletic figures had transformed into athletes of another skill. A skinny, bespectacled Oriental man lay, or more acurately squirmed, in loosened clothes on an American king-sized bed with two Caucasian women, one in black underwear, the other in a white, lacy patterned bra and camiknickers. A third woman sat on a stool at the foot of the bed, her naked back to the camera.

'Some sports tape,' Jenny said, taking a new glass of wine.

'Have you changed it?' Nicholls said.

She shook her head. 'It just went fuzzy and then this started.'

The woman in black cast a furtive glance towards the camera's assumed position, went off screen for a few seconds to reappear with a bottle of champagne in one hand and the stems of three tulip glasses between the fingers of the other. She poured the drink ostentatiously while her colleague, a blonde with a tiny waist, let the fullness of her bra mesmerize the Oriental as she made a scene of unbuttoning his shirt and loosening his belt and trouser zip.

'There must have been more like this,' Nicholls

guessed aloud, trying to explain Emi Mori's interest in dated British sports tapes, and he kept to himself the thought that she must have been shocked to see a stranger in Tony's apartment before making an awkward, deliberate attempt to remove the dirty videos, including the one they were watching. Jenny said, 'It's ingenious the way they spliced the porno film on to an innocent tape like that.'

'You're right. It's to fool the customs at Narita and seems to have worked a few times. Araki told me they are tough on porno in Japan, especially pubic hair. They employ teams of students to black out imported copies of *Playboy*.'

'Weird,' Jenny groaned. 'Perverted.'

'They would have confiscated this one,' Nicholls said as the central character lost his shirt and trousers. The shoulders of the woman with her back to the camera moved as she reached for something on the bed. Nicholls's voice tapered to a drawl, his eyes, his concentration on the hand moving across the filmy, satin sheets.

'It's not a porno movie,' he murmered. 'It's a set up.'

Jenny moved closer to the edge of the couch.

'The camera's not moving,' Nicholls concluded. 'It's got some kind of wide-angle lens and it's shooting straight, through a two-way mirror. And how many porno actors wear undershirts on screen?'

'You think it's blackmail?' Jenny Collier said incredulously.

'Probably. Look at the women. They're working on the bloke but making sure his face doesn't get covered.'

'You've been right until now,' the American said. 'But he's gonna get smothered to death if he's not careful.'

The woman in black, with thick, bundled hair had leaned over and unclipped the brassiere of her agile partner, unleashing the firm, full breasts which she fed to the man on the bed. His legs rose and fell as his body responded to the sexual onslaught; a hand found a satin crotch and was trapped by two determined thighs while dextrous hands stripped him of his underpants. The mysterious, half-naked woman, her back still to the camera, was like a film director, choreographing the pleasure scene. When the man was naked, she reached for a small bottle, a move which sharpened Nicholls's attention, and handed it to the woman in black underwear. Nicholls froze the frame with the handset.

'This stuff makes you horny?' Jenny said, placing a hand on Nicholls's shoulder. For an instant he thought she was serious but when he reached for her he saw behind the smile and the swirl of the lush blonde hair her hidden fatigue and desperation. She grinned. 'Maybe not. You don't look too good yourself.'

'You're right,' he chuckled, stopping the video. 'I'll find out what happened another time.'

'No. Don't come with me,' Jenny said. 'It's not late and they tell me it's safe out there in the streets of Tokyo. Crime's against the law.'

Exhausted, but exhilarated by her company, Nicholls accompanied her to the road and flagged a taxi, agreeing they would meet at his apartment the following day and drive to Araki's home together.

He hurried back to his empty living room, juggled the remote control in his excitement but finally had the last scene in frozen hold. It had progressed a few frames in the process. The hand of the woman with the secret identity had released the bottle and at the instant before it withdrew out of view in front of her the fingers were clearly visible. Nicholls was kneeling before the television, his own right hand touching the image on the screen. The woman's fingers were tipped in bright orange, just like Emi Mori's.

27

Araki had not made straight for his home in Nerima after leaving Nicholls's apartment but, seeing it was past ten thirty, had run towards the main road, desperately in need of a taxi. When he flagged down a cruising private cab, he urged the driver to get him to a Kabuki-cho intersection soonest, knowing that he would not gain admission to the club after eleven. It was a short trip in the moderate evening traffic and it gave him time to find the page in the Hirata papers again and draw a rough circle round the name that had screamed at him from the rambling accusations. It had not been a mistake. He had read the Chinese characters correctly.

The neon forest east of Shinjuku Station turned the warm evening into blinding day. Kabuki-cho, a planet of cellar bars, restaurants, hostess-packed cabarets, peepshows, no-panty coffee houses and their exotic variations marshalled into safe patches of playground by a thousand troopers from fourteen *yakuza* crime syndicates. Around seven the salarymen had gathered for another night of male bonding or customer entertainment and lone males looked for companionship in the dial-a-date booths while two hundred love hotels waited a short walk away to help them consummate their success. Young *yakuza* in garish happi coats lined the narrow streets and bawled the delights within the walls behind them. But it was already approaching the unwritten curfew and cheerful groups of well-dressed drunks were meandering towards the station. Araki found the club behind the main drag which passed in front of the Koma theatre. It was in a building split from its neighbours by damp alleyways and not far from the Roman, his own Shinjuku watering hole.

Benkei Onodera acknowledged Araki with a friendly grunt, his square head bouncing on his thick, muscular shoulders with only a thin trace of neck. He stood inside the curtain, arms across his chest, and ran an eye over the customers as they entered. It was not a demanding job. The occasional drunk had to be admonished but in general his guests obeyed the signs on the walls to remain silent and respectful during performances. Araki moved to speak but Onodera begged a few minutes delay. He never tired of the part of the show where the stripper, in this part of the rotation a flame-haired Rumanian with small, pointed breasts and the narrowest of waists, twirled at the climax of her act and invited the audience around the raised circular stage and catwalk to pay two thousand yen to photograph her genitals with the house Polaroid. A young salaryman paid his money and snapped the gypsy's stretched vagina while his immediate neighbours craned forward with the intensity of examining gynaecologists. Men talked quietly, their cigarette smoke shimmering in the beams of the arc lights that washed the stage.

'Haven't seen you in Shinjuku for a while,' Onodera said at last, revealing a set of raspy, discoloured teeth. Araki coughed into the cavern's noxious air.

'I have a safe bar to drink in but some places are still a touch hot,' he said, his stiff neck flaring. The pain as the baseball bat cracked into his ribs and the asphyxiating surge of mud into his mouth when the boot of the Yanagida gang psychopath thudded into his face were as vivid today as they had been on that filthy night three years earlier. But he was safe in this tacky strip club in the five block franchise of Onodera's Kamigawa Rengo, a minor affiliate of the south Japan power group, the Igarashi-kai, with its twenty thousand loyal gang members.

Araki felt not a little sympathy for this slow-witted punch-permed street punk who, moving oceans of money in cash in a society suspicious of cheques and distrusting the confidentiality of banks, was the dope in the middle in the Momoyama affair. He was the bagman, scurrying around Osaka with the forged certificates of deposit and the cases of cash this collateral generated from the Ohyama Bank and which paid off the forgers and his own syndicate. Caught stuffing a coin locker with three hundred million yen he could not explain he served eighteen months of hard labour when the forgeries at the savings and loan bank were exposed and the chain which led straight to the top of the Ohyama Bank revealed.

Onodera could only blame himself. He was an old-fashioned mobster. Recruited at sixteen from a teenage motorcycle gang he threw himself into the part: the tendered permanent wave, white socks and shirt, outsize black suit, heroic tattoo which over the years spread to cover his entire torso. And of course the swagger. He collected protection money from *pachinko* pinball parlours and compliant cabarets but with more muscle than brain was lately used to intimidate the stable of two hundred Thai and Filipino women his gang controlled in the Osaka area. The popular weeklies had speculated that Michiko Momoyama had turned to her friends in the Igarashi-kai when she needed a little distance between her and the forgers.

When Onodera left prison he was fêted in the time-honoured way in a top hotel but he noticed gaps in the ranks. The government had at last taken measures to restrict the business of Japan's mockingly visible organized gangs, enacting a new anti-gang law which might at last bring the three thousand gangs and their ninety thousand members to book. As a recognized mobster with a criminal record Onodera could no longer enjoy the protection of what was now a designated crime syndicate. He was a tattooed dinosaur, ripe for the hunt and extinction. He saw some of the new *yakuza* at his welcoming party. Sharp business suits, neat unpermed hair, clean records and a white Mercedes or BMW to take them to negotiations where drugs would be dealt, stock prices manipulated, women bought and sold and guns peddled with their colleagues from Seoul, Taipei and Manila.

Some of his old friends bought themselves out of the gangs, others disappeared, while Onodera departed amicably, staying in the gang orbit by taking a job as a bouncer in their Tokyo outpost but paid by the club and owing allegiance to no one. The perm had almost unravelled and he was saving for the operation to graft a piece of a toe to the gristle on the tip of the little finger of his left hand where he had severed it in his ritual gesture of atonement.

Araki read the night's programme while Onodera watched the last public voyeur with his head between the redhead's legs. There was a Thai to come, and then an Australian, a Korean and twins from Kyushu. When Araki was writing the Momoyama case he had scooped his rivals by intermediating between his contacts in the police and this hoodlum who was destined to take the rap for the gang he represented. He divulged nothing in court which would implicate Michiko Momoyama but fed Araki information which helped the police case and they both believed his sentence was lighter than it might have been. The duty and obligation account was written in Araki's favour and the journalist had come to redeem it.

'I want to talk to Momo chan,' he said, as the strobes flashed again, raking a demure dark-skinned Thai girl in bolero top and tight, sequinned micro dress.

Onodera's shoulders heaved and his craggy, pitted face broke into a chilly smile. He said without malice, 'You tell me. I'd like her scrawny neck in my hands.'

'You wanted your dick inside her once,' Araki said, defusing the implication of failure with a proffered cigarette.

'We all did,' the reformed *yakuza* growled.

'Some guy at the Ohyama Bank was getting it. That's what they said at the time. Do you know if it was true?'

'The fool must have got something for his money. How much did his bank pay out?'

'Seventy thousand million yen.'

A spotlight flashed across the beads of sweat on Onodera's forehead before enclosing the stripper, now down to a mauve bikini, in a funnel of pink light as she spun and girated to a medium beat French love song.

'I've never seen money stacked like that,' Onodera said, raising his hand to his waist. 'It came straight out of Ohyama's Osaka branches.'

Araki said, 'Ohyama foreclosed on the loans to Momoyama and I expect they're still trying to unload the property and shares and all the other crap she bought.' Onodera was not listening. He did not understand. Ohyama Bank were vindicated, judged

206

to have lent money in good faith, unaware that the collateral was forged. There were two other cases before the courts where equally important banks had been duped and like Ohyama they were censured but not indicted. What Araki and the prosecutors, and even Onodera, suspected was the strong probability of collusion between someone in the Ohyama Bank and the peddler of the phoney certificates of deposit. Someone high enough in the Ohyama hierarchy to influence the bank's internal credit evaluation of the borrower and agree the massive loan to an individual. Michiko Momoyama.

'The bastard woman really used me, and didn't even get done by the police. She said she didn't know that stuff from the two guys was forged. What a bitch. I took them two suitcases of money myself to pay for the fucking things.' He saw the willowy Thai girl was swaggering along the catwalk like a model, bikini top in her fingertips.

'Get yourself a beer from the machine,' he invited. 'I've got to work. Follow me.'

They entered the narrow control room by a short staircase at the back of the salon. 'Applause please.' The gruff, intimidating voice of Onodera, bouncer turned master of ceremonies, filled the room. 'And now gentlemen,' once the enthusiastic handclapping had died, 'the moment you have waited for has arrived.' Hands reached into the air from every side. The entertainer was sprawled on the raised floor, resting on her elbows and raising and lowering each leg in turn, her eyes on the ceiling, her night-black hair grazing the ground. 'Who shall we chose tonight to satisfy the endless desires of this volcano of passion from Bangkok?' Onodera droned. The girl managed a dry, cheerless smile. A man with a boyish face waved

207

a ticket towards the booth. 'He knows I decide,' the ex-mobster chuckled, clicking off the microphone. 'He's here every Friday. I let him do it now and again, once a month. He's getting better. It stays up and he lasts longer. He likes the Thais.'

'What about the guy with the red face over there? He looks keen.'

Onodera shook his head dismissively. 'He's half drunk and his pals are putting him up to it.' Onodera selected a bemused salaryman in glasses with a neat, conventional haircut who looked surprised to be chosen.

'Did you ever hear the name Koga?' Araki asked when Onodera had shut down the equipment.

'Koga, Koga,' Onodera intoned. 'Not an uncommon name.' He had a strong Osaka accent and had not rid himself of the gangster's guttural drawl.

'He's a big mover in the Ohyama Bank's head office.' Araki swallowed from the tin of Kirin and passed it to Onodera, who raised a palm and filled a glass from a Nikka bottle hidden below the control desk. The whisky loosened him.

'I know,' he said.

Araki smiled. 'Was he screwing her?'

Onodera released a guffaw that sealed his eyes. 'If you'd given a woman enough money to buy half of Hawaii you might expect more than a box of rice crackers in thanks.'

Araki joined in the joke and then pressed. 'Did you see them together? Near a love hotel maybe.'

Onodera turned a hard, pitted face to his interrogator. 'You were not interested in her sex life two years ago.'

'The phoney CD's and your bags of money kept us busy.'

'The whore really used me,' Onodera repeated to himself.

On stage, the performer and her stud were naked, kneeling towards each other. She removed a cloth from a basket of necessities and enveloped his genitals, cleaning and massaging life into them while he stroked her breasts beneath the curtain of hair flowing over her shoulder. Onodera modulated the music to a heavy throb. Otherwise the room was quiet: it was a very serious moment.

'Where is Momoyama now?' Araki demanded gently.

'I don't know,' Onodera said in low level street language.

They watched the fitting of the condom in silence. 'But I might let you know if I hear anything.'

Araki passed him a number.

The woman writhed convincingly and the unashamed salaryman pumped solidly before collapsing, spent, in sweaty unison. The front row craned and everyone applauded when the act was over.

Araki stood to leave. 'Do you still have the gun?' he asked innocently.

Onodera feigned shock. A few months before his arrest he had bought a nine millimetre Beretta semi-automatic and two thirteen round clips from a Taiwanese in Fukuoka, giving him the ultimate status symbol in gun-shy Japan. He did not need it now, in his new, reformed life, but he still kept it and the clips in a holdall in a station coin locker which he changed every three weeks.

28

Jenny Collier needed space, physical and mental, somewhere to take stock, to gauge where she was in the long,
unending nightmare. She was no closer to finding her
brother than she had been when she arrived at Narita
airport three weeks earlier. The sudden eruptions of
optimism were as ephemeral as the morning mist in
Tokyo. The American Embassy had heard that a lone
Caucasian male had esconced himself in a Franciscan
monastery retreat in the mountains of Nagano, north
of Matsumoto, and only a plea from Jenny herself
would persuade the monk in charge to bring their
putative recluse to the telephone. 'Si?' a voice said
reluctantly, after a ten minute pause on an open line.
Listening on an extension, the embassy officer covered
the receiver and groaned. 'Your brother doesn't speak
Spanish, does he?'

The papers Nicholls's friend Araki had just perused
revealed little of interest to her and promised even less
when they met again the next day.

'*Koko kudasai*,' Jenny said, in simple but effective
Japanese.

The taxi driver braked hard, stopping near the
entrance to Hibiya Park, a rare tract of greenery in
the grim metropolis, which she could cross leisurely in
fifteen minutes, reaching the Dai-Ichi Hotel in another
five. The park had once formed part of the Imperial
Palace grounds but was now a swathe of tendered
gardens, placid ponds with lilies and languid carp, and
banks packed with shrubs and trees, all connected by
broad avenues and hidden paths. It was a place where
lovers found a rare kind of Tokyo solitude, clinging

together on the benches in the darkness. The air was cooler away from the traffic, refreshing her spirits. At least, she reasoned, the sender of the strange package believed her brother was alive and in the pressurized Englishman and the Japanese journalist she had found something close to friendship. She walked easily, the eerie silhouette of Japan's beehive-shaped parliament building still visible behind her on the Kasumigaseki rise, guided towards her Ginza hotel by the flashing neon sunset in the distance above the tree line. A full, bright moon in a cloudless sky illuminated beds of azaleas and banks of dangling wisteria.

She skirted a pond, its border of gingkos and dense larch trees absorbing the rumble of traffic pausing and then reached an open lawn surrounded by benches. As she passed a deserted bandstand, where four narrow paths converged, the only sounds she heard were the metallic squawk of a truculent blackbird and the crunch of other feet on the gravel. She turned, as she would instinctively in Chicago, and released a scream before she was hit, a piercing cry which shook the hidden lovers out of their embraces.

It was a fierce rush from behind, like an American football tackle on a quarterback. Her left side absorbed the force of the fall, the shards of gravel rasping the skin on her arms and legs. She lay stunned but conscious, limbs immobile, waiting for the inevitable assault on her body which she was too weakened to prevent. The leather briefcase had slid from her grip into a gutter where it was retrieved on the move by a man whose companion was walking unhurriedly away, into the trees. Relieved, she twisted painfully, wondering how she had managed to live twenty-seven years in Chicago without getting mugged.

29

It was midnight before Nicholls snapped his bedroom Reuters monitor alive. The London market was winding down for the weekend after a brief but violent surge of trading when the American durable goods figures were announced at one thirty in the afternoon. He called his Tokyo dealing room and instructed the two night shift traders to go home after they had squared his currency options position around the levels shown on the screen. Then he changed for bed with vivid images in his mind drifting between Jenny Collier and Carole Chai. That's what the weird, camouflaged video tape's done for you, he grinned.

It was eleven fifteen in Hong Kong when he dialled the Happy Valley number and heard her voice, first in Cantonese and then in softer English, telling the caller she was not able to answer the telephone at the moment. He hung up without leaving a message. His stay in Tokyo was hardly the refreshing break he had anticipated. Each day had brought a new assault on his confidence. That very day had not improved after his frank talk with Prideaux, who gave him a bland assurance that he would treat Nicholls's remarks as confidential and bear them in mind when issues regarding the relationship with Ohyama Bank and its group were under negotiation.

He had begun to wonder which way his chief would lean, how deep his allegations had penetrated, and he received an indication sooner than he expected. Prideaux had lunched with Hanlon and his senior adviser Fujimori and afterwards returned to the treasury to present Nicholls with the skeleton of a plan which would emasculate Sternberg's Tokyo dealing operations and bring Ohyama even closer to sharing the British bank's goals. He would not go into detail at that stage but it involved the establishment of a joint funds management enterprise aimed at responding more readily to the needs of customers to move their investments to higher yielding currencies and instruments.

What it meant to Nicholls was a dynamic operation whose wealthy private customers could gear up an initial ten per cent margin of a million dollars to take a position of ten million or in the case of corporates a deal of half a billion dollars could be generated on a five per cent margin of twenty five million. There had been Press and market speculation for months that Ohyama might be moving to buy the British merchant bank, and Nicholls assumed this was part of the grand plan. Prideaux would not expand, only confirm that the market-making role Tony Moore pursued in the Asian time zone would not continue and so would Nicholls please pack Moore's personal effects and arrange his own departure so that Marcus Birkmeyer could arrive and move in as soon as was feasible.

The afternoon's trading had produced steady income on the back of customer business. The dollar had stayed in a half yen range ahead of the American figures and attention in Europe was moving in on the dollar's value against the German mark. He had left early to find Araki at the apartment. Had the strange Japanese prevented another search of Tony's apartment? Odd thoughts were gnawing him, arousing illogical suspicions. Real policemen would not have come on a mission and then abandoned it. Were they friends of Emi Mori coming for the tape? Were they looking for something else? He had to look through Tony Moore's papers when he obeyed Prideaux's instructions to pack them up for despatch. At least it was the weekend.

30

Jenny Collier's call drew him from the shower.

'Jenny, what's the matter?' he said urgently. Her words came in gasps between sobs. 'Where are you?'

It took a moment for the outburst to subside. He heard her taking a very deep breath and then finally she was calm enough to recount the mugging in Hibiya Park. Before he could ask she told him she was bruised and ached down one side but apart from that she was fine. 'Has that guy called? Your Japanese friend. I'm sorry I missed his name.'

'Araki. No. I'm waiting for him.'

'Kevin. Can I come over anyway? This place is getting me down.'

'Of course you can. I'll come and get you. Are you sure you can travel?'

He heard a sniffle. 'No problem, but don't come for me. The police are coming round to the hotel to interview me in a few minutes. They were very kind last night. I'm sure they won't mind bringing me to your place when they've finished. The hotel's getting pretty fed up with me and the police. Anyway you should wait around for Araki san's call.' There was another short break before Jenny said: 'Are you sure you don't mind driving over to Araki's place?'

'Don't be silly,' he responded. 'See you soon.'

Of course he did not mind. A day with a beautiful woman, even one with an unending problem, and now battered from a random mugging, was a welcome way of putting the week behind him. He also confessed to more than a passing interest in the contents of the papers her brother had received from a disgruntled Ohyama Bank dealer. Any dirt on the bank that had skinned him might be useful when the losses he made on Wednesday came before the formal inquest in London, which he knew they would.

When Jenny Collier mentioned the police it reminded him of the two alleged detectives who tried to get into the flat. Coffee in hand, he found the calling card of the police interpreter Mochizuki, who, with a senior officer, had brought Tony Moore's belongings but his call to the police headquarters in Kasumigaseki reached a Saturday shift officer who repeated simply *wakarimasen*, a word Nicholls knew meant he would never get through to an English speaker.

With his time left in Japan very limited, and conscious of Prideaux's request, Nicholls sat at Tony Moore's desk and bookcase and set about packing books, photographs and letters into their original shipping boxes which he had stored in the second bedroom. He flipped or turned each item listlessly, seeing in each the image of his dead friend whose remains, in their shrouded urn, fitted comfortably into the corner of a packing case. While he worked he let Tony's last few home-recorded videos run on fast play. The memory of Emi Mori still haunted him. Had he dreamt those things she did to him? If there were more revelations like the sex trap on the tape she had drugged him for and almost got, he had no intention of leaving them for Birkmeyer to salivate over. It was more in Araki's line, Nicholls concluded with a grin, and decided to give him the view of Emi Mori's back and orange fingernails. He tossed junk mail and bills and other demands aside, along with letters he concluded would be of no sentimental value to Moore's sister, if she could be found. Most of them were from women, and he smiled when he recognized the married writer of a particularly unrestrained missive.

He went briefly to the Reuters monitor in the bedroom where the New York Friday closing prices were still displayed. In a few hours the only quotations on the screen would come from Bahrain and other minor centres in the region where business in the foreign exchange markets would continue over the Christian weekend, although with small trading volumes.

Back at Tony Moore's desk, he found one drawer held a heap of folders containing official looking manila envelopes whose contents revealed more legal exchanges between the firm representing Tony and the lawyers acting for the estate of Miranda Hooks, the woman who had died in Tony's car crash, and letters from an assistant district attorney representing the state of New York. It was an orderly file, unusual for Tony, Nicholls thought, but perhaps a reflection of the gravity of the contents. It ran sequentially, from shortly after the accident to a letter from his lawyer in London dated April the seventeenth, about a month before Moore was last seen alive. The contents clearly documented the build-up to the serious letters that must have been posted after Tony's death and which he had read on that first day in the flat. One letter, in carefully phrased legalese urged Tony not to engage in direct communication with the appellants and informed him that a claim for damages of ten million United States dollars had been received from Miranda Hooks's family. 'Is that all?' Tony had written in pencil in the margin. His lawyer was concerned that Sternberg Chance were being cited as partially culpable in

Moore's behaviour because he was driving back from an office function in New York when the accident happened and the compensation claim reflected an element of corporate responsibility.

But what drew Nicholls's fixed attention was the sheaf of letters embossed with the official eagle of the FBI. He had known about the indictment, the charge of manslaughter and drunken driving which would have put Tony in jail for years as there were no mitigating circumstances. Tony had somehow managed to flee the country, another felony, and for two years was pursued by the American government and the parents of Miranda Hooks. Their claim for ten million dollars was wrapped around the copy of an order demanding his extradition to New York. The handicapped dealer had given Nicholls only a sketchy picture of the events which followed the accident, and few of his colleagues pressed the issue. He let rumours fly and die while the real situation evolved within the bank's legal department.

'I'm pretty sure I know what pushed you over the edge', Nicholls said, addressing Tony's ghost in the bottom of a packing case. Did you get your taste for booze back to give you the guts to top yourself after one last binge? Or was it really an accident when you fell down those steps? He laid the legal papers on top of the urn. Nicholls calculated Moore could have raised around three million dollars from the sale of property and other assets in the mainland UK and by draining his hidden deposits in Guernsey and Switzerland, but another seven million would have left him in debt for ever. And then there was the small matter of half a decade or more in jail. He bound more papers in rubber bands and stacked them in the chest.

The last drawer contained more papers, some crumpled maps and, under them, as if hidden for security, he found Tony's travel documents: a frayed British passport, an out-of-date international driving licence, some used air ticket stubs and a vaccination certificate. He was certain he had looked through the drawer before, if only a perfunctory prowl, when he first moved into the apartment, but had not noticed the passport.

Depressed by the task he had nearly completed, he looked forward to Jenny's early arrival. Knowing it would ease her tension if he took to Tony Moore's car as if he were familiar with its locks and buttons he decided to check it out before she arrived. Before leaving the flat he stacked the video tapes, which had revealed no further erotic scenes. Emi Mori, he realized, had removed exactly the right ones.

A single bulb crudely lit the stuffy, dusty basement garage where saloon cars filled three of the six spaces. Tony's was a metallic grey, two-litre Mitsubishi Diamante, hemmed between a wall and a deep blue BMW. He pressed what he thought was the alarm on the key ring, sweeping the car with it. It had no effect on the vehicle, but instead activated the entrance, which cranked upwards noisily on its pulleys, letting into the garage a swelling tunnel of light. Tony's car, he estimated, had been motionless for at least ten days, and a generous film of dust corroborated this, but the engine bit quickly from a healthy battery.

The automatic transmission did not bother him and the dials were fairly standard, with most functions electrified. With a prudence he retained from driving wrecks in his youth, he let the engine ripple and went to check the tyres. He edged around the car whose metallic sheen was dulled by its coat of powder and grime. The tyres looked fine, but his eyes were drawn to the car's expanse of trunk. It seemed polished, reflecting the pale light which filled the garage, while the rest of the car was a dull matt. He rubbed his fingers across the shiny metal, intrigued by the contrast. A heaped ridge of dust ran along the base of the rear window.

If events were causing him to become paranoid, the feeling was strengthened by his discovery of Tony's passport, a document which had eluded him until today, and now his car which was not quite looking right. It was clear the boot of the car had been recently touched, or tampered with, at least since the dead man had last used it. But it hadn't been driven. He leaned into the car through the driver's door and pulled the release handle, watching in the mirror how the trunk sprang sharply open and bounce on its hinges. The dust of barely a full day slid away. Nicholls peered at the unsurprising contents: a litre of oil, a jack attached to a tool box, a tin of wax and a spare wheel set into the boot well. On a bed of rags he saw the same type of long-handled feather duster he had been amused to see the chauffeurs using on their company cars in Marunouchi. Very useful now, he thought smiling, and lifted the long, fluffy contraption from the boot. The black, knotted rod had been hidden beneath the duster and half-covered by the rags.

He stared at it for an instant and then lifted Tony's walking stick as if it were made of glass. He rubbed its smooth, comfortingly gnarled surface and sniffed at his own incompetence for not having checked the car earlier. The police must have looked it over when they first investigated his disappearance a week earlier. But he knew someone else had been there since. He flipped the ridge of dust piled along the based of the window before slamming the trunk shut and walked up the ramp into the refreshing sunlight, where he surprised a matron scooping up her dog's deposit in her surgical gloves. She inclined her head dutifully towards him and smiled. The gate inched down behind him as he stamped the ground with the stick in frustration. There were somehow too many questions to answer before he left Japan involuntarily and the oddball journalist Araki would have to hear *his* story as well as Jenny Collier's.

31

The monotonous, rumbling din of the pile driver began its relentless thumping at eight, pounding the foundations for a new high-rise mansion which would cast a permanent shadow over the old, weathered wooden house wedged between the columns which supported the Senkawa-dori road across a five road intersection and a ring of drab, ferro-concrete tenements and offices. The dull thuds woke Araki who had fallen asleep in his wicker chair, the Hirata papers scattered around him and a burned out cigarette lying in the scar it made in the *tatami* reed mat where it dropped. He poured hot water into a pot of two-day-old green tea leaves and was revived by the bitter brew and the nicotine surge of a fresh Hi-Lite. He collected the old man's newspaper from a hole bored into the concrete wall which was joined to the low porch by a staggered row of mossy stones and was opening the broadsheet before he slipped his clogs at the door, but he knew realistically that the story would not make the newspapers until the evening editions. Seventeen million readers of the two largest dailies, the *Asahi* and *Yomiuri*, and a dozen tabloids would carry the same story about the discovery of the corpse of Hiroyuki Hirata. His last testament, a desperate message to the missing American Sam Collier, lay at Araki's feet.

It was close to midnight when he left the reformed gangster. Young night people were replacing the salaried army who had left their stepping stone pools of vomit in the streets leading to the stations. Araki was burning with enthusiasm. He changed trains at Ikebukuro but interrupted his journey only long enough to eat curried noodles at a stand-up counter beneath the tracks. He was charged up to work, to piece together the bits of the fascinating puzzle which Hirata had scattered over thirty bits of paper. When he finally moulded his body into the old man's wicker chair with its pull-out leg rest, it was with a chain of cigarettes, a tumbler of warm sake and the raunchy badinage from the late night chat shows on channel four for company. He had not wanted to add to Jenny Collier's personal anguish, or risk a sharp rebuke from the short-fused Briton, by showing the intensity of his excitement at reading the Hirata papers. In the fear, the hatred and the accusations Araki saw the germ of major story. Amid the invective directed at his boss, the frightened banker seemed to be hinting at an important, imminent event without knowing exactly what it was.

The cassette conversations were in unintelligible technical jargon yielding nothing, but the hand-written text was a primed missile of slanderous invective aimed at the man's superior at the bank, someone called Katsuro Koga. Hirata accused him bitterly of a vendetta provoked by nothing more than personal aversion and a military-like fondness for humiliation by bullying, falling just short of actual physical violence.

Hirata's only recourse, his sole source of pleasurable revenge in a society which expected him to *gaman*, to endure, for the sake of the whole, was to lay out the charges for a researcher-journalist like Sam Collier, hungry to expose Japan's darker side. Araki read the list of indictments, some of which pointed to trivially personal, almost spiteful, punitive rules, like having Hirata stay in the dealing room, even when he was not on the night shift, until Koga left; others itemized humiliating punishments for minor dealing mistakes and accused Koga of reneging on promotion and career promises.

Hirata had been close enough to Koga to see receipts and internal memoranda and copy them discreetly. There were copies of the money transfer slips evidencing payments by the Ohyama Bank to an Osaka leasing company Hirata alleged was a front the bank used to channel loans to a network of real-estate dealers, at least two of which were themselves fronts for *yakuza* crime syndicates. Press cuttings exposing the Osaka firms' dubious business accompanied the payment vouchers.

There was an organization chart for a new, unexplained company which featured some foreign names, receipts for bar bills and other payments whose origins were unclear and internal notes which would only mean something to a banker with proper training. But Hirata saved his high octane vitriol for a three page rant on Koga's private life. Araki broke off to draw the warped rain doors together against the night echoes from the overpass. From the television a panel of personalities evaded the anti-pornography guidelines, which would have forbidden a simple graphic exposure of a telephone sex-to-order service, by discussing its moral implications and legality in a concerned way as actors in a film showed how the business worked.

He warmed another pot of sake and returned to the ramblings of Hiroyuki Hirata. The Ohyama Bank man's charges of philandering by his boss were naïve and the names of inns and hotels used by Koga, and an apartment owned by the bank, would hardly give Sam Collier the evidence for a shattering exposé. He must have been confident that Collier could find a trusted and competent translator because his handwriting gradually deteriorated, each Chinese character running clumsily into the next, as if he was running out of time before an important meeting. His written English must have been limited as he attempted only a few words. In several places he wanted to write 'mistress' but could only manage its literal transcription from Japanese as 'Number Two san'. The only other piece of English script, in a lone sentence near the end of the last page which warned Collier that Koga was working on a big play in the foreign exchange markets, brought Araki upright. He held the paper towards the timid light from the bare overhead bulb and read, 'Miss Momoyama is here again'. Before his mind could begin to take in what he had just read his attention was distracted by the monotonous drone of the television newsreader. '. . . identified from documents as Hiroyuki Hirata, a section manager at the Ohyama Bank. His body was in his car when it was found by police divers in the sea off the Wangan Makuhari dockside an hour ago. A Metropolitan Police spokesman at the scene was unable to say whether the incident happened as a result of an accident or a suicide death. An autopsy will be conducted during the day.'

Pacing the room in disbelief Araki wondered how he would tell Jenny Collier that the man who had reached out to her missing brother was now himself worse than missing. Finally he fell into the chair again his body drained by fatigue. 'So Momoyama san's back,' he told himself, as sleep closed in. 'And bribery, lies, deceit and mountains of money with her. And now there is a body.'

32

'Strange Death of Gaijin Banker' read the blocked out portion on the cover of *One Point Finance*'s new edition. Araki had pieced together a biography of Moore from harmless reports slipped to him by Police Inspector Fujii, but conscious of the readership's absurd and superficial curiosity in foreigners, at once mesmerized by them and at the same time frightened by their freedom, he focused on the assumed life of a foreign male bachelor with three million yen a month to spend and no living expenses except for food, drink and laundry. He portrayed Moore as 'Tony Tokyo', cutting a swathe with his golden samurai sword across Roppongi and Azabu and picking at will from a camp following of Japanese groupies drawn to the neon playland by the glitz and the *gaijins*, which brought him nicely to Emi Mori.

'Was this Tony Tokyo's mistress?' he wrote under the stolen photograph of a demure 'aspiring talent' with her eyes hidden behind a black rectangle. His rudimentary research had divulged a handful of the Roppongi dives which kept open until dawn and his imaginative power described the white *gaijins* and the drink that fuelled their lavish lifestyle, and the excesses which led to

Tony's death. A sense of tragedy was summoned by his picture of the *torii* gate tunnel shielding the steep, sharp-edged stone steps at the Hie Shrine where Moore fell to his slow, lonely end after a typical night in Tokyo. A researcher at *One Point Finance* had padded his draft with a paragraph on what foreign exchange dealers did and Araki had managed three references to Sternberg Chance's close business relationship with the Ohyama Bank, whose principal secondee to the British bank, Masaaki Fujimori, refused to be interviewed.

He had two hours before the tormented, glamorous American woman and the hyperactive English foreign exchange dealer, not much different from Tony Moore he guessed, were due at his house. Before he saw them he had to catch the editor of *One Point Finance* before the staff drifted home around lunchtime. Thick, oily coffee in Nerima had kickstarted a body which had slept like a corpse in the curves of the old chair and the mind-expanding inferences of the Hirata testament gave his senses the stimulant they needed. All he required now to take the evolving story further was money.

One Point Finance occupied two floors out of the eight in an anonymous ferro-concrete block built on an impossibly narrow plot of land in Nihonbashi, the old merchant quarter adjoining prestigious Marunouchi and now home to the securities houses orbiting the stock exchange and a mosaic of specialist trading companies, printers and provincial banks. Editor Hirosawa sat behind glass panels giving him a total view of his journalists and editors. He preserved the formality and total conformity of the big-five university alumni he had left behind on the *Japan Economic Press* and now a near middle-aged writer with long hair and a moustache, wearing a baseball warm-up jacket and running shoes lowered his demanding standards and strained his tolerance.

'Well done,' Hirosawa said reluctantly but genuinely, his magazine open on the desk. 'Thank you for delivering a vivid and interesting article at such short notice. Funada san called this morning to express similar sentiments. It was extremely professional and we have to admire your contacts with the authorities. 'He raised his palms towards the part-time journalist and quipped, 'But I don't want to know them.'

Araki smiled and set off confidently. 'Thank you. I'd like to table some ideas for a really great story.'

'There's been a complaint,' Editor Hirosawa declared firmly, ignoring Araki's proposal and sliding his glasses easily off a flat, flared nose and peering at his notes. 'A Imaizumi san of Excell Image Agency called. He said that the picture used in yesterday's story about Anthony Moore was reproduced without permission.' Araki rubbed his upper lip and looked sideways. 'We covered her eyes, left her name out,' he said defensively. 'I don't think her mother can recognize her. What else could we do?'

'Did you have to steal it? That's what he said. Said you took it by some devious method. I thought you said it was a standard publicity shot.'

Araki's warm feeling was evaporating, along with the possibility of a follow-up article.

'It is. It's a posed shot taken by a professional. If it's a problem I'll send it back with an apology.

'Please do so.'

'I don't think we'll hear from that particular cuties' talent agency again,' Hirosawa said releasing a wry smile. After all it was Araki, the man who he knew by reputation would benignly lie, cheat and steal to embellish and authenticate his work. He also knew that he would put his job on the line if he sniffed a conspiracy, a deliberate cover-up or a politician with his hand in too many pockets and even risk his physical well-being as a still stiff neck from a killer's attack with a baseball bat testified.

Seeing the editor's satisfaction with the article, Araki again pushed for more work. 'If I can find Emi Mori, throw her a few ten thousand notes and a bikini spread in colour she might produce the meaty stuff on life with Tony Moore.'

'I don't think so,' Hirosawa said his smile fading. 'It's a shame in a way Moore wasn't murdered. Then you could turn private detective again and upset us all.'

Araki smiled weakly. 'I agree,' he said, enjoying Hirosawa's suspicious frown at this easy acquiescence. 'So I have another proposal.'

Hirosawa swivelled towards the window of soft sunlight and leaned back, his closed eyes towards the ceiling. 'Any *gaijin* in it?'

'Only indirectly,' Araki said blandly, extracting the notes he had made from the Hirata file. 'It's about a thirty-two-year-old salaryman driven to his death by hard work and harassment.'

'Who was he?'

'A foreign exchange dealer at Ohyama Bank, name of Hirata.'

Hirosawa twisted and sat upright. 'I saw it on the news this morning. They pulled him out of the bay yesterday. Probably suicide. The story's only just broken. You can't have had time to interview the corpse.'

'I want to revisit the Momoyama affair.' the journalist said.

Muffled rings and muted conversation invaded the silence as Hirosawa stroked the soft skin beside his lips.

He said tentatively, 'You mean Michiko Momoyama?' and nodded the reply himself. 'If I remember right she was implicated with the Ohyama Bank. Is that the connection, the link with Hirata?'

'I'm not sure yet if it's the old story or a new mess,' Araki said.

'You said there's a *gaijin* connection. Another banker?'

'Not exactly. He was doing research on Japan's financial system and seems to have turned investigative journalist.'

'You said "was". Is this *gaijin* dead as well? Two dead *gaijin* in two weeks might stretch my readership's interest a touch thin.'

'He might be,' Araki confessed. 'But could be in hiding. His name was Sam Collier and he was sent a file alleging odd happenings at Ohyama.'

'And Momoyama?'

'I'm not sure. That's why I want to talk to her and find out.'

Hirosawa stood up and stretched his arms above his small wiry body. He stalked past Araki and looked disinterestedly at the outer office. 'She caused a lot of trouble in financial circles,' he said at the glass panel. 'A lot of top men locked their doors and stayed away from the Ginza for a long time. It might not be appropriate to disinter the ashes from the tomb.'

Araki raised the proposal to a plea. 'Hirata's dead. Collier's missing and I don't fancy the Ohyama Bank's Koga san will open his files to me.'

Hirosawa turned to Araki. 'Koga? There is a Koga at Ohyama. What was his given name? Katsuro. Katsuro Koga.'

'You know him then?' Araki asked

'Not personally. He gave a talk last month to the

Japan Press Club on the role of the yen in the world's financial system. Very fluent, very articulate. Very bullish for the yen.'

Araki felt cheered. 'This one's got potential. Big finance, a dead trader, a woman. There must be a politician in there somewhere.'

Hirosawa returned to his chair. 'What do you know about foreign exchange?' he asked, his scepticism drawn in the frown and the narrowed eyes.

Araki shrugged. 'If the yen's strong, imports are cheap, except they're not because the government won't let us buy cheap foreign goods and America gets angry. If the yen's weak we export more, except we export more all the time and America gets even madder.'

'That's what I thought,' Hirosawa complained. 'Nothing.'

'I'll learn as I go along,' he said confidently, thinking of Nicholls.

Hirosawa reached for the telephone. 'Let me talk to Funada at the *Press*. I don't want to tread on toes.' He showed Araki a profile, a hint picked up by the journalist who buried his hands in his pockets and made for the main office, to the desk of a career veteran with a grey jersey under his suit jacket who was sitting with his back to the warmth of the window. His cloudy eyes were rimmed in red and his skin was sallow and lined.

'*Kondo san, genkiso,*' Araki said brightly. 'You're looking fit. Not working hard enough.'

The older man huffed and tapped a stack of papers. 'Look at this lot. These youngsters just don't do their research properly. They don't understand what the competition's like out there.' Araki listened to his familiar banter with patience, because that was the tired old man's job. To read the manuscripts, check the facts quoted and re-word any potentially libellous statements into suitably foggy prose. Araki leaned towards him. 'I saw an old friend of yours last night. Name of Onodera.'

Kondo hissed and crooked his neck. 'I remember,' he said fondly. 'Fourth-rate pimp who thought he was a *yokozuna* grand champion among *yakuza*.' His grim chuckle turned into a cough. 'He wouldn't even rank at sumo's skinny schoolboy level.'

'He's going very straight at the moment,' Araki declared.

There was a tap on glass behind him and Hirosawa was beckoning from his office. He broke away reluctantly and the editor met him at the door. 'Leave Momoyama alone,' he said tensely.

'What?' he groaned in disbelief.

'Our parent newspaper does not feel it appropriate to create inconvenience to the banking sector when they are trying to reconstruct their businesses in difficult circumstances.'

Araki leaned on the door. 'I'm not talking about bringing down the banking system. I have serious written allegations about Katsuro Koga which may concern a man's death. This has to be important.'

'Why don't you talk to the police?' Hirosawa said.

'Because they're allegations, perhaps the ramblings of a demented man. This is not America. The local police won't touch white-collar crimes. They direct you to the Prosecutors office who won't investigate unless they have a watertight case, you know that. All I've got is allegations. Serious allegations.'

'We are not commissioning a private investigation,' Hirosawa said with uncompromising finality. 'Momoyama is history.'

Araki slapped his thighs in a useless gesture of futility and a few paces from Hirosawa turned back saying, 'If I come up with anything will you look at it?'

'Perhaps,' the other said, closing his door.

Araki went to the floor below, to the library of books and cuttings sharing space with quiet cubicles. The plain young woman in charge recognized him and smiled him a row of uneven teeth with prominent incisors. 'I enjoyed your article,' she said genuinely.

'That's kind of you.' He looked around conspiratorially and leaned across her desk. 'I'm working confidentially on a follow-up,' he lied. 'I have to look at the Momoyama files. Do you recall the case?' Of course she did, and guided him between the tall, metal filing cabinets.

It was the most outrageous scandal in a year which saw Nomura Securities, the world's largest share dealers providing investment advice to an underworld syndicate and their fellow securities houses actually compensating their major customers for losses incurred after the crash of the stock market in October 1989. Chairmen and presidents resigned and await a quiet rehabilitation without loss of face. But Momoyama was different. Michiko Momoyama owned a dozen expensive restaurants, exclusive cabarets and private members' clubs in Osaka and she held a discreet interest in more than a hundred pleasure salons in the lower depths of the floating world throughout the Kansai area. When the affair broke the prosecutors could not believe that the Ohyama Bank, Japan's rock-solid, prime financial institution, the third largest in the world, had lent seventy billion yen (over half a billion American dollars, the foreign Press calculated gleefully) to a forty-year-old bar owner with a carefully cultivated past. And then it turned out that the security accepted by Ohyama from Momoyama consisted of three certificates of deposit, CDs the money market called them, evidencing the existence of seventy billion yen with a small savings and loan bank in Osaka. The three CDs were forgeries; the money did not exist. Momoyama used the Ohyama loan, and more she raised from mortgaging her real estate, to invest in the mighty stock market bubble of the eighties. She also bought a pair of Monet landscapes and an early Van Gogh, none of which was disposable for even half their purchase price within a year. When the Nikkei reached meltdown at the opening of the nineties, speculators like Momoyama were caught short of cash as the market worth of their assets shrank and the banks, themselves in need of cash as the value of their vast holdings of securities collapsed, eroding their capital base, demanded repayment.

Momoyama was finally arrested, but what Araki and a meagre handful of inquisitive journalists in Japan demanded to know was how come an individual qualified for a seventy billion yen loan, even with real collateral let alone a stack of forged money market instruments? Did she have a powerful sponsor in the Ohyama Bank? they asked without response.

Araki carried the two bulky hanging files to a refrigerator top in a kitchen alcove and stripped through the chronological record of notes, photographs and newsprint cuttings, wondering how long he had before Hirosawa read his intentions. There were photographs of Michiko Momoyama in formal black wedding kimono and in a series of sombre designer outfits at her trial, together with a clinical dissection of her life. She started her career in the *mizu shobai*, the water trade as the entertainment industry is known, probably in a soapland massage parlour in Kobe, and by the age of twenty-two was the mistress of the sixty-year-old president of the biggest iron and steel company in southern Japan. She served him for twenty years and he died in her bed, leaving her land and enough hidden cash to build a residential block for foreigners and doctors and a four-storey complex in Umeda with a specialist restaurant on each floor and a sauna and health centre in the basement. It was believed there was a child from the long liaison but its whereabouts or even existence were never confirmed. Momoyama's dead patron's friends became her customers and there were rumours of a new sponsor.

It would not be surprising. At forty she was attractive in a classical Japanese way, with a narrow angular face like a courtesan in an Edo period wood-block print, and a long pale neck. Araki found a cutting from a Tokyo soft porn weekly which suggested her new patron was a director at the Ohyama Bank. He smiled when he saw the allegation was in an article he had by-lined himself. He had forgotten. Half an hour's delving in the files refreshed and revived his recollections of the scandal but produced no clue to Michiko Momoyama's present whereabouts and the last reference was already a year old.

He did not hear the custodian of the files approach. She must have been there for a while, waiting sheepishly for an opportunity to interrupt. 'Excuse me,' she whispered, her eyes on the floor. 'Those files are required urgently by the Editor.'

33

'It's scary on this side of a car,' Jenny Collier said, a map open in her lap, as Nicholls nudged the Diamante in three lanes of traffic through Shinjuku. 'I didn't even know they drove on the left here. Hey, is that the Marui department store coming up? You've gotta turn right.' He swung the car north onto Meiji dori. Jenny said her injuries were not hurting, claimed they were more colourful than painful. A deep purple, almost black bruise ringed a swollen, half-closed eye and a slight graze below the bruising was beginning to form a soft scab. The grass verge in Hibiya park had limited the damage but her head hit a rusty hoop of iron bordering the lawn as she slithered on the gravel.

Nicholls glimpsed the drawn, battered face in a sideways glance and reached to squeeze her hand. 'We'll find your brother,' he said. 'Araki said he'd found something in those papers and wanted you there.'

Apart from the a headache and a sore elbow Jenny was unruffled and philosophical. She returned his tenderness with a smile and said: 'It never happened to me in Chicago because you always expect it and look out for it. Guess I believed what everyone told me about Tokyo being the safest city in the world and I got careless.' She lowered her sunglasses gingerly from a crown of golden blonde hair. It was a warm, very sunny day and she wore a plain, white sweatshirt and her casual jeans.

They drove through a Tokyo that seemed a light year away from the broad avenues and towering buildings at the heart of the city. With Jenny Collier directing they crossed an unending clean, green and grey urbanscape of low houses, shops and offices, of claustrophobically narrow roads edged and straddled with overhead cables, where people dodged vehicles, telegraph poles and advertising signs. An hour after leaving Nicholls's apartment they were in Nerima, where life throbbed around the station, and followed Mejiro dori avenue, with the Seibu Ikebukuro line railway on their right. Jenny switched to Araki's hand-written map and as they approached the ramp which carried the road over the railway tracks she pointed vigorously.

'Slow down. Don't cross the tracks. Take a left over there, before the barber's pole.' Fifty yards later, where the rows of packed houses in the narrow lane ended, replaced by the columns which carried the Senkawa dori road over the Nakamura-kita intersection, the American said, 'Pull in over there.' Nicholls parked beside a battered Toyota Corolla on a strip of dirt bordering a deep excavation which was dotted with heaps of iron rods and concrete mixers. 'Is that it?' she said, with a trace of disbelief.

The old double-storeyed wooden house, with water stained, sand-plastered walls, stood alone on the edge of the construction site and its outer ring of offices and tenements, and almost under the overhanging wings of the elevated road. The upper floor sat like a square lid on the main building topped with an angled roof of ochre brown overlapping tiles. They approached through a latticed gate in a low wall and saw that the house was raised on short stilts with a veranda on three sides. A pair of cherry trees and hardy shrubs struggled for light above the patchy grass and rich emerald green moss.

'What's his first name?' Jenny asked, seeing the journalist waiting under the rickety porch.

'The men here don't seem to use them,' Nicholls said.

Araki seemed to be beckoning, his expression insistent. He peered across the front wall, where the cars were parked and into the shadows beneath the expressway before closing the door behind them. He relaxed once they were inside the old house.

'The owner won't sell out to the developers like the others did,' Araki said, as his visitors removed their shoes in the dark entrance. 'They offered him close to a hundred million yen. That's about a million dollars,' he said for Jenny's sake. 'But he won't sell, so they're building a pair of apartment blocks around him. I'm looking after it until he comes back next year to die. We Japanese need to plan,' he said, seeing Jenny Collier's astonishment. 'He's eighty-two and staying with his son who's a friend of mine.'

He led them along a corridor like a tunnel, whose wooden floor boards were cold and uneven, through a stiff sliding door framed with squares of blotched opaque rice paper to a large room covered with soft *tatami* reed matting which opened onto a patch of walled-in yard. The gravel had once been raked symbolically; now it was untended, leaving it uneven and spiked with weeds. The room also suggested a temporary tenant. Apart from a desk and a low table holding a television and video his daily needs – books, papers, a comfortable wicker chair – lay around on the *tatami*. An alcove housed the only decoration, a fading *sumie* ink drawing of a bamboo cluster. He invited his guests to sit on the matting and slide their legs beneath a low table and into a sunken well where their legs met. Apologizing for the absence of back-rests he brought them coffee in unmatching cups with no saucers.

When Jenny raised her sunglasses and lodged them in her hair Araki gasped and started to reach out to touch the bruising. 'What happened to you?' he said, pulling back. Jenny relived the taxi ride, the decision to cross Hibiya Park and the attack, the snatch-and-run robbery, the kindness of the police and the doctor and nurses who treated her.

Araki sank into a pensive spell, negotiating a cigarette in slow motion. Finally he said, 'What was in the briefcase?'

'Nothing. That's the great thing. I used it to carry the file that Sam got in the mail that morning to Kevin's place. The police found it outside the park. Those guys were so mad there was no money in it they slashed it into pieces with a knife.'

'You were lucky they didn't use it on you,' Nicholls said.

Araki was not listening. He shuffled from the shallow pit. '*Komatta na*,' he murmured to himself, then made for the corridor.

Jenny Collier's eyes followed him. 'Did I say something wrong?'

Nicholls shrugged. 'I don't think so.'

A noise like a steel bolt being driven home ricocheted through the old house. Araki returned and stole across the room, passing the foreign couple and heading for the house's flimsy wall whose rain doors and windows had been drawn aside, leaving only a light framework of insect netting in the vast gap.

'What did you say in Japanese?' Jenny asked concerned. 'Com . . . something.'

Araki drew the mesh apart and turned round. '*Komatta*. We've got trouble.' He stepped into a pair of clogs, moved swiftly across the neglected patch of garden and lifted one leg on to the stump of a long-rotted cherry tree, easing his face above the tiles which topped the weathered concrete perimeter wall.

Satisfied, he returned to the house and began tugging the warped *amado* rain panels from their sockets in the wall cavity. 'Kevin,' he called, pointing. 'Pull the other panel out from over that side and the window with it. Search for them with your fingers in the cavity, then lift them into the runners on the floor.'

The wood was stiff and swollen with age and dampness and when they came together Araki locked them into the frame of the house with upper and lower clamps. The sliding doors on one side of the room, now lit with the bare bulb hanging above the *kotatsu* pit, opened reluctantly, and Araki found a full-size baseball bat which he laid beside the table when he joined the others.

'I don't know what you're doing but you're sure getting me scared,' Jenny Collier said, as Araki bent his legs into the gap below the table. His eyes were shadowed and red-rimmed, his expression solemn. 'You don't look so good yourself,' she added.

'I was up most of the night with this,' he said, patting the Hirata file. His face became grim. 'The men who attacked you were not common muggers. We don't have much street crime in Japan. They were professional criminals. Probably killers from one of the *yakuza* syndicates.'

'Yakooza?' Jenny attempted.

'Japanese underworld. Our mafia,' Araki answered economically, keen to put his findings to them. 'What they wanted was these, the Hirata papers and the tape.' He tapped the folder, then opened it, letting the cassette slip on to the table. Nicholls thought at first he was affecting his dramatic posture, but the Englishman sensed the air was sparked with tension. Araki looked at Jenny, whose injuries began to throb as a spasm of fear shivered through her body. 'You brought the file in that black briefcase to Kevin's. I skimmed through it and then I took it home with me. They must have been disappointed when they found you were carrying an empty bag and you're lucky they didn't check it while you were on the ground or they would have persuaded you with that knife to tell them where the file was. From what you both say I think they've now made three attempts to retrieve it.' He let her absorb the gravity of his remarks and then explained. 'Jenny, you said there was a commotion at your brother's apartment yesterday morning. The police chasing somebody. I'm sure the police have been watching the apartment quietly since your brother went missing. I think they accidentally foiled a first attempt at getting the file when it arrived in the mail.'

Nicholls said, 'That's two, with the mugging. What was the third attempt?'

'Those two men who were at your apartment yesterday. I'll call the police for you but I'm a hundred per certain you'll find they were not the real thing.' Nicholls knew that if they were trying to get into his apartment their target was a video tape. He kept that piece of knowledge from the Japanese while he wrestled with the possibility that there were now two groups interested in his world: one trying to recover a compromising video, the other looking for a folder of papers.

Araki was saying, 'They probably waited outside and saw Jenny arrive with the briefcase they assumed contained the papers they had tried to get from her earlier in the day.' He tapped the baseball bat fondly. 'And, since they know that I was also at your place yesterday, it won't take them long to deduce that I'm the one with it. They might have tried to follow me when I left Kevin's place last night. I'd read something in the papers and I had to check it out urgently, right away.' Araki's face creased with his own rising misgivings. 'They could have grabbed me,' he thought aloud.

Nicholls thought of unburdening his own darker doubts about the walking stick when Jenny Collier clamped her hands to her temples. 'What's going on?' she cried, swallowing the sobs surging inside her. 'I only came here to find my brother and now I've been mugged in this goddam crime-free paradise. My only Japanese friend is making out like John Wayne at the goddamn Alamo and Kevin here's into porno videos and Christ knows what else. What's this stuff about Tokyo being the safest city in the world?'

There was a muffled rumble outside, sending a vibration through the house. Araki flinched, reaching for the bat, and then realized it was the engine of a heavy earth-mover starting on the construction site. Nicholls produced a handkerchief and held it to Jenny's eyes, avoiding the colourful swelling. He felt her legs press against his below the table.

'I'm sorry Jenny,' the Japanese said, 'but there's more and it gets worse. There's no point in trying to hide it if it leads us to your brother. Can you handle it?'

Jenny sniffed, and then nodded.

Araki removed the Hirata folder from the table and replaced it with the Mainichi newspaper which he spread to a page with a photograph of a car emerging from the sea, hanging from a crane as if it had been executed. 'The car belonged to Hiroyuki Hirata,' Araki explained, 'the man who sent those papers and the cassette to Jenny's brother. He was tied to the steering wheel and the police and his colleagues at the Ohyama bank believe he was under such severe stress from overwork that he killed himself, tying himself to the

column in order to strengthen his resolve.' Araki closed
the newspaper and continued gravely. 'Hirata was last
seen at eleven thirty on Thursday night when he was
left near his house by his chief after a party of bank
colleagues. Your brother, or in his place you, Jenny,
received a package from him in the first delivery on
Friday morning. It must have been mailed some time
on Thursday morning as it arrived so early the next
day.' Araki sucked in air loudly and crooked his head.
'What I was asking myself all through last night was
this. If Hirata mailed the file on Thursday, how come
the people who were trying to get hold of it knew that
it would be at Jenny's brother's apartment the next
morning?'

Nicholls contributed the obvious after a short pause.
'Because, presumably, at some point during the day he
met them and told them what he'd done.'

'Precisely,' Araki said.

'My God,' Jenny groaned. 'I can't cope with this.
These gangsters got hold of Hirata, forced him to tell
him where he'd sent this stuff and then drove him into
the sea. Is that what you're saying?'

The air in the closed room was stagnating and the
smoke from Araki's fresh cigarette hung around the
light bulb. The Japanese dropped his head.

Jenny said, 'So Hirata wanted to give my brother
some information which he thought Sam could use in
his research.'

'Not only research, Jenny,' Araki said. 'Your brother
was stringing for some American news agencies.'

'What does that mean?' Nicholls asked.

Araki said, 'Like freelance writing. If a newspaper
in Chicago wanted a one-off article on a particular
financial topic they might contact someone like Sam
Collier, a known expert.'

241

'That's right,' Jenny added. 'Sam would send us copies of the things he wrote for the media.'

'As I see it,' Araki said. 'Hirata got to know Sam when your brother was researching at the Ohyama Bank. Fairly well it seems. He refers to "Sam" in the papers and asks him to tell the world what it's like to work at a Japanese bank and for someone vindictive like his boss.'

'That's hardly worth dying for, or being killed for,' Nicholls said.

Araki opened the folder and turned the pages to the end.

'It's in the last three pages. The paper's still crisp so it was written recently and there are mistakes in the characters. It tells me he was writing quickly, as if he was desperate to finish it. It's almost all in Japanese. Again, he's in a hurry and remember, he's found something and wants to expose it for his own reasons. He assumes Jenny's brother can have it translated by someone trustworthy. Perhaps Sam could do it himself. He is saying that his chief, a very senior man in the bank, is not only making his life a complete misery but he's tampering illegally in the financial markets. That's not unusual in itself in Japan. We try to manipulate everything, from politics to the foreign markets we sell into overseas. But he alleges that a known fraudster is in action again. He's not absolutely certain so he hints at it. His only words in English are here, look.' Araki ran a finger down the hieroglyphics then twisted the page around to show how Hirata had written sideways in English to maintain the line of the column.

'Momoyama is here again,' Jenny read. 'What's Momoyama?'

'The foreign Press at the time called her Miss Peach Blossom,' Araki said grimly. 'The translation is really "peach mountain". Michiko Momoyama. Two years ago she was the most written about woman in Japan. She used half a billion dollars of embezzled money to speculate on the stock market and was finally exposed when the bubble economy collapsed and the banks wanted their money back. But it had vanished into stocks and land whose value had collapsed. She didn't serve a day in prison and has disappeared. Most of the money Momo chan spent came from the Ohyama Bank. According to Hirata she's back and if it's true we are talking big money.'

Nicholls said, 'Surely Ohyama wouldn't get their fingers burnt again?'

Araki managed a wry smile. 'Michiko Momoyama is very likely the current mistress of Hirata's boss, a director of the bank.'

Jenny Collier shifted her position on the cushion.

'Sounds like one powerful gal. But as Kevin says, there's still not enough for my brother to expose in any serious way. Hirata's only making allegations.'

Araki's unkempt hair fell across his scalp as he leaned to move the last page into the light. 'Let me translate the last paragraph. "Sam san, please listen to the tape. It was made today, Wednesday. I do not have time to isolate the conversation but you will hear my chief talking to somebody for about twelve seconds. I suppose the other man made a mistake by calling into the bank on a recorded line. I cannot trust anyone here to help me but I think the problem is very serious. I'm not certain but the other man in the conversation might be in the Bank of Japan. It's too complicated to explain what they are talking about in writing but I will meet you soon and interpret the meaning. It is extremely serious."'

Araki closed the file and looked at Nicholls. 'I don't

243

understand the technical jargon on the tape, Kevin, so I'm asking you to listen to it with me because you are also a foreign exchange dealer, like Hirata.' Nicholls nodded his agreement. Araki continued, 'Thank you. I'm not a crusader, don't have much of social conscience as you'd know if you could read some of my crap magazine work, but there's guy here who's died because he wanted to speak out. I'll take it a bit further, if only for Hirata.'

The room was silent, save for the distant throb of machinery. Nicholls drew himself to his feet and stretched, stabbing the unpainted ceiling with his fingers, his head a hand's length from a cross beam. He swore to himself and stood, arms folded while Jenny composed herself to say what he knew she would.

'Maybe two people have died,' she said bravely, her voice cracking again.

Araki took her wrists. 'We don't know that Jenny. Sam might be anywhere. Needs some space, peace to write, cut himself off for a while. I'm like that sometimes.'

Jenny repaid his thoughtfulness with a sad smile but knew he did not believe it himself. A stray strand of hair stuck to her bruised cheek. She said, 'Hirata believed that my brother was alive when he sent the tape and the file, but those other guys were not fooled. They knew Sam was not around to receive the papers and they knew where to go to find them. He was researching in that bank for months. They must have seen what kind of stuff he was putting in his articles for the American Press. I think he got too close to something big and they . . .' Her voice became a quiet sob.

Then she recovered and said with bitterness, 'Who is this guy in that bank, with his mistress, his bullying and cheating and his hired thugs and killers?'

Nicholls knelt on the matting and flipped the accusatory papers. 'I've got an awful feeling I know him.'

'His name's Koga,' Araki said. 'Katsuro Koga.'

Nicholls gave a weary shrug. 'It had to be him.'

'How come?' Araki asked. 'How do you know him?'

'There are over a hundred traders in the Ohyama dealing room but there's only one that fits poor old Hirata's description. Koga's a heartless thug. And he's dangerous. I've traded with the Ohyama for years and had a few tough run-ins with Koga. One very recent.' He paused for a moment, then said, 'Let's hear the tape.'

Araki slid backwards from the table. 'Not here. I don't want to alarm you but it's not safe here.' He found an old sports bag in the wall cupboard and was packing it with clothes when the telephone rang. It was a brief conversation, not an exchange. '*Hai, hai, hai,*' Araki repeated, scribbling somethings as he nodded into the handset. 'Thanks. I'll talk to you soon.' Replacing the receiver he was facing a menacing Jenny Collier who had risen painfully to her feet.

'You *are* alarming me,' she said. 'Why can't we just go to the police?'

Araki sidled to the shelves and finally found a matching pair of socks. Without looking at her, he said, 'What could we say? That we have some papers from a dead man who was probably killed for writing them and now the *yakuza* are chasing us for it. It might help them solve the mystery of Hirata's death but there's nothing indictable in the dossier. Nothing to guarantee we can keep our bodies in one piece today. Hirata thought your brother has the ability to do what he himself can't, to expose a serious financial scandal. But he warns your brother to be careful several times

245

in the papers, now it seems he wasn't worried enough for himself. He stopped a protest from Nicholls. 'I'm meeting an old friend tonight. He's a senior police inspector. I want to stay healthy until I see him. It'd be stupid to take a chance of a visit from the people who did that to Jenny.'

The American woman moved a bruised cheek across her fingertips. 'I'll go along with that,' she said.

Nicholls shrugged.

'I know you think it's melodramatic,' Araki said, reacting angrily and stabbing a finger towards the Englishman. 'You've seen what's happened to this house. It's marooned behind a wall between a road and a hole in the ground. Hirata's killers can park under the expressway, sneak through the gate and creep round the wall completely unseen. I don't want to sit here and wait for them. I want to feel my wheels under me.'

Jenny raised her hands in surrender and turned to Nicholls. 'Let's do what he wants,' she said, irritated. 'Then we can talk it through with his cop friend tonight.'

'OK' Nicholls agreed. 'Let's do it.'

Araki sighed with relief. 'Thanks. Now Kevin. What are you driving?'

'A grey Mitsubishi four door.'

'OK. Follow the columns of the overpass left until you reach the intersection. Go straight across and turn left where you see an Idemitsu gas station. I'll meet you there. Keep the driver's seat free and let me take over.'

'What are you going to do?' Jenny said, gathering her things.

'I'm going through a gate in the back wall and then down what used to be an alley. Now it's part of the construction site. If there's anybody waiting for us they can't hide there. I checked. They'd stand out against the workers.'

The foreign exchange dealer and his injured companion managed a limp wave in response to Araki's extravagant gesture of farewell from the porch.

'Is that guy for real?' Jenny said, as Nicholls grimaced and edged into the endless Saturday traffic of largely spotless, late-model two-door cars inching towards the crossroads. There was no lane jumping and no one honked. Finally, when a multi-coloured canopy of flags and balloons indicated the petrol station he said, 'At the moment he's all you've got.' He threw her a glance. 'If Araki's right about your brother, I'm very sorry.'

'Thank's Kevin. I don't want to believe him but I do. I know his motives are not the purest but the guy's got to make a living and I think he's genuine. He's the only one I've met so far who is.'

Nicholls pulled in behind a green utility van on a typical Tokyo two-lane road with no pavements.

'What about me?' he said with mock annoyance. Jenny smiled at the oversight and leaned across to kiss his cheek. Turning his face to meet her he saw a white Mercedes crossing the vision of his rear view mirror. It bumped across a drainage ramp and glided towards the petrol pumps. Then he saw Araki rounding the corner and moved to the passenger seat while Jenny went to the back.

The journalist took the wheel and turned sharply into a side road, throwing his passengers across the car. Araki spoke as Nicholls clamped his seatbelt. 'There was a white Mercedes with tinted windows in the gas station back there. Look out for it while we drive.' Jenny leaned forward 'Why? What's with a Merc?' 'It's the *yakuza*'s favorite car, especially in white.'

247

He drove for fifteen minutes, criss-crossing a twenty block area and finally drawing on to the gravel forecourt of the Nanzoin temple and into a corner well hidden from the road by a rim of thick, lush greenery. He took the Hirata tape from the pocket of his baseball warm-up jacket and slotted it into the cassette deck on the dashboard. Jenny Collier leaned forward, her elbows on the heads of the front seats. 'The tape actually finds the conversations,' Araki told her. 'There's only a slight gap between them on the recording, however far apart they had been in reality.'

Nicholls knew they were dealing conversations. Short, concise, no pleasantries.

'Can you explain something to me?' the Japanese said, stopping the tape. 'What do they mean when they say "six two six seven"?'

'It's the dealing price. Six two means sixty-two sen. In Japan you only use the single digits, and that's your bid for dollars. Six seven is sixty-seven, what you would pay for dollars. Then you add the yen big figure.'

'I need to learn more,' Araki said confidently, restarting the tape. 'The Koga conversation is coming up now, right after Hirata's own exchange with his customer.' They listened silently to the dead dealer. He had a weak, highly stressed voice. Jenny shook her head, feeling the terrible fate that was to await the brave, unwitting man. There was a sharp rasp as the tape jumped to the dealer making a restaurant reservation. Then came the voice of the man Hirata had accused of coercion and serious financial irregularities.

Araki translated, 'The caller says, "Koga san?" who says, "Yes. It's you. I wondered when you'd call. These are difficult markets." The other says, "They certainly are. The next ten minutes could be vital."' He depressed a button and repeated his translation. 'That's it. Does it mean anything to you?'

'Could do,' the Englishman said, feeling the warmth of Jenny Collier's breath as she leaned forward with an intense, earnest look on her face. 'It's the kind of banter we have all the time. If you know something about a big deal that'll move the market price of a pair of currencies and want to warn a friend or a customer without divulging your source you tell him to be careful because there's a big buy or sell order about. But this conversation is very strange.'

'Why?' Araki said.

'Because Koga hangs up immediately, as if he'd been given a message and had to act.' Nicholls fixed his gaze on the cracked, mushroom crown of a low, stone lantern in a clearing in the trees. Before Araki could break the silence he made a fist and brought it down on the passenger dashboard. The car rocked on its suspension. 'Bastard, the cheating bastard,' he rasped, the venom oozing through clenched teeth. Jenny gripped his shoulder; Araki shuddered at the outburst and checked their surroundings, clear but for an elderly couple who arrived in a compact Subaru with flowers for their family grave.

Without turning to Araki in the driver's seat Nicholls said, 'Did Hirata note the time of the conversation? That's how you search for a conversation. You estimate when you had it and then interrogate the computer running the tape system.' Jenny passed the dossier to Araki who turned to the end. 'It was timed at ten eleven.'

Nicholls's anger broke through. 'And one minute later he buys twenty million dollars off me and lo and fucking behold within seconds the Bank of Japan is in buying every dollar in sight and I'm buried because I can't get square.'

249

'Kevin!' Jenny jumped at the Englishman's vehemence.

'Koga's got a mole in the Bank of Japan dealing room. It's called insider trading and it's illegal, even in Japan I suppose.'

Looking at Jenny and then Nicholls, Araki said, 'That's what Hirata suspected. I don't understand well about foreign exchange, but you are saying that Koga deliberately bought dollars from you, knowing that its value would shoot up almost straight away.'

'If this tape is genuine and the other guy's in the Bank of Japan, yes. Koga set me up. He screwed me,' Nicholls said, and then apologized to Jenny for his rudeness.

'That's OK. Did you lose a lot of money?'

'About two million dollars.'

It was Jenny's turn to swear; Araki asked him to repeat it, thinking he had said yen.

The journalist looked at the notes again. 'Hirata says he believes the other person is in the Bank of Japan.' He looked across at Nicholls. 'Couldn't it be just a friendly business relationship?' he asked.

'Not at eleven minutes past ten last Wednesday,' Nicholls scoffed.

Araki started the engine and slipped it into reverse, the wheels spinning before biting into the gravel. 'Let's eat something,' he said, steering into the road.

Jenny made a puzzled face. 'I only know what I read in the newspapers: I'm with Araki san on this. Tell me Kevin, I thought the Bank of Japan, like the Federal Reserve in the States, only intervenes in a crisis and these don't happen every day. Is it really worth the time and money, and the risk of disclosure, to have an informer in the central bank?'

Nicholls twisted his head and said, 'I would think that Koga and his bank, and the other Ohyama companies which were acting on guidance from Koga, probably made a hundred million dollars between them. That alone's worth waiting for. But the other value of the mole is to have a constant feed of information on what the men who control the currency and therefore the heart and lungs of the economy, are thinking and planning. Your informer might tell you, for example, that the Bank of Japan has agreed with the US central bank to let the yen drift higher over three months, say by four or five yen, in a quiet, controlled way. With that information you could buy a pile of yen against dollars and bank a fortune if you've got the guts to wait it out.'

'OK.' said Jenny, adding to herself. 'I wonder how Koga turned somebody into a traitor.'

34

Araki wiped his greasy fingers on his trousers and pushed the debris of his chicken lunch to the empty part of the table. 'What will you do now?' he said to Jenny Collier when Nicholls had gone to buy coffee. She thought for a moment, toying with a crumpled paper napkin.

'I'll go back to Chicago and tell my parents their son is dead. Those bastards would never have let him live. Look what they did to that poor guy Hirata. I must go and see his widow. Would you help me please?'

'Of course I will. The first thing we'll do is give Hirata's file and tape to my friend in the police. I can trust him to use it properly, get it put in front of the public prosecutor. But you must be careful Jenny. I think you realize what we are dealing with here. It's not a small time fraud by a pair of crooked accountants. It's a major conspiracy by people with vast financial resources to monopolize the country's lifeblood and, as you people in the West are starting to understand, they have close links with the *yakuza*. They are no fictional characters Jenny. They are everywhere, more and more infiltrating legitimate business with the connivance of the so-called economic and political leaders. They own vast chunks of Hawaii and have investments in hundreds of American and British companies. And who do you think owns that *pachinko* pinball parlour we just passed near the temple and who recruits the labourers for that construction site behind my house? The *yakuza*. Please stay close to Kevin until you leave.'

The American woman had strong features and was a head and shoulders taller than Araki, but when she turned her ice-blue eyes and sad, pale face to him, she appeared vulnerable and close to tears. 'I'd like to stay close to you, too.' She managed a smile at his discomfort and said, 'And I'm worried about Kevin.'

'So am I,' Araki admitted, as the Englishman returned with three paper cups of coffee. His face was drawn, his mind working on something elsewhere, like how to nail Katsuro Koga to a dealing desk and pass a splintered broker's box through his body.

'How are you doing Kevin?' Jenny asked, a hand over his.

'I'll manage, thank you.' He faced Araki. 'We can't let them get away with it. They're murderers. They killed Hirata, probably Jenny's brother and I wouldn't be shocked if Tony got taken out because he wouldn't co-operate with Koga's cheating.'

Araki walked once around Nicholls's car before

letting them all in. 'I'll drop myself at home first and let's meet up later,' he said. 'My reformed *yakuza* friend called just before we left the house and told me where he thinks Michiko Momoyama is living under a new identity. I want to check it out before I start writing and then I'll meet you both in Shinjuku, around ten if that's all right, and we'll speak to my friend from the police. What are you to going to do?'

Nicholls responded, strength and purpose returning to his voice. 'I'll tell you in a minute.' He dialled a number on the car telephone and heard a young child's voice answer. '*Moshi, moshi,*' it said in hesitant Japanese.

'Is your daddy there?' Nicholls said.

'*Chotto matte kudasai.*'

Then he heard Billy Soh's strong American accent.

'Hi Billy. It's Kevin. Can you talk?'

'Sure. We've just had lunch. Going shopping next.'

'A few things have happened since yesterday. An Ohyama bank dealer has died and I think it might have something to do with my problems.'

Billy Soh's voice became distant, then defensive. 'It was in the Japanese papers this morning. My wife, she's Japanese, showed it to me. He killed himself through overwork. There's a quote from Koga saying how valuable he was but the stress from long days was getting to him.'

'He didn't kill himself,' Nicholls said, 'but that's something else. We were going to meet over the weekend to talk over what's bothering you, can you meet me for a drink tonight? Something's happened and I have to know more about the people in the dealing room.'

There was silence on the line.

'Billy. Are you there?'

'Sure Kevin. It'll have to be quick. We have a dinner date at seven thirty.'

'How about six. In the ground level bar of the Capitol Tokyu Hotel.'

'Sure. That's not far from my place. Isn't that where Tony died?'

'It's the hotel on the hill next to the Hie Shrine where they found him, right.'

'See you there,' Soh said and clicked off.

'Can we make that a threesome?' Jenny said, with a trace of desperation Nicholls recognized. He turned and smiled his agreement.

At some point, as Araki steered the Diamante past a grove of gingko trees on a plot of powdery ground in front of a kindergarten, the breeze carried a sweet fragrance of woodsmoke through the window. He was ebullient. 'I think we can get them,' he said. 'This guy Koga, who you know to your regret Kevin, has got a hold over an influential dealer in the Bank of Japan and he's helping Koga rig the market. Koga has *yakuza* friends who are policing the operation and probably arrange the compromising of the bureaucrats. The Peach Lady, Momoyama chan, might be the catalyst. She's no stranger to big money. I need to find her again with Koga and link them both with one or other of the *yakuza* syndicates.'

Approaching the Idemitsu petrol station again, the traffic thickened, and the Nakayama-kita intersection was choked. They purred in the jam for ten minutes until Araki stopped the engine. Traffic on the overhead section roared, but beyond the gridlock below it a muted cacophony of sirens wailed. Jenny rested with closed eyes against a rear window.

'Kevin,' Araki said uneasily as they waited in the jam, 'can you smell something?'

'What's the matter?' Nicholls said apprehensively when Araki lowered the window and then started the engine.

Jenny sprang alert, sensing the tension.

'Can't you smell it?' Araki said. Exhaust fumes from the idling traffic lingered in the still air but did not mask the smell of burning wood. 'Hold on!'

He forced a gap in the line and the car erupted with a squeal into the oncoming lane which was slowly draining the blocked intersection ahead. He switched on the beam and pressed the horn, forcing the oncoming cars into the shop frontages as he drove the car forward in the wrong lane. Jenny screamed; Nicholls clutched the armrests and pressed an imaginary brake pedal. The garage was ahead.

'Come on, come on!' Araki urged as a small utility truck refused to give way. It pulled over reluctantly, its driver cursing soundlessly behind the windscreen, but not enough for him to pass without bending his car's right side mirror back on its rubber hinge. Nicholls winced and the underside of the car hit the bump of the ramp as it entered the garage.

Araki stopped beneath the hanging petrol pumps and left it with the three attendants who surrounded it with buckets and cloths. He waved them away and led the two foreigners as they half-ran towards the rising noise of the sirens and the people being drawn to the scene. When they reached the columns of the overpass and the bending road that led to Araki's house they saw the smoke where it had drifted and become trapped below the elevated road. He elbowed a passage through the crowd which had

255

been stopped at a police cordon. The near hysterical Japanese with two tall *gaijin*, quickly becoming as much a distraction as the fire, persuaded a uniformed officer with a clipboard to let him and his companions be taken under escort nearer to the incident.

The flames crackled, spitting embers into the air, as they consumed the weathered wood, but it had not taken long for the house to collapse. The fire vehicles parked on the road and the building site were playing their hoses on to the burning heap, dampening down the half burnt beams and twisted framework which were all that remained of the old house. The *gaijin* and the policeman shielded their faces against the ash and smoke hanging listlessly over the area.

Araki stared at the debris and thought of the old man who owned it. The wall had stayed intact except for a gap where the firemen had used a bulldozer from the construction company to open an access for their equipment. Araki's battered Toyota car had been removed without much damage and stood forlornly out of danger, covered with ash. Jenny Collier gripped his arm as a propane gas tank in the smoking heap exploded into a final defiant flash of cobalt-blue flame.

35

They watched a troop of children, their heads down, intently reading the fortune messages bought from a dispenser, while a pair of newlyweds summoned the gods in front of the offertory with a tug of the bellrope and two sharp claps. The rich canopy of greenery from the tall cedars, maples and fragrant pines cast jagged shadows across the gravelled courtyard. Jenny took Nicholls's arm, sharing his subdued mood and sensing in the touch his hidden tension and apprehension. After leaving Araki deep in his own gloom and anger, they had driven to Jenny's hotel in the Ginza and while she changed from casual to a morale building outfit for the evening Nicholls walked through the lively back streets to the Imperial Hotel to read the news agency printouts and buy a British newspaper.

Arriving early to see Billy Soh, Nicholls walked Jenny Collier through the greenery of the Hie Shrine. The destruction of Araki's house had somehow numbed her own physical and mental anguish and she found the strength to walk and linger on the chipped, slippery steps where Tony Moore died before leaving under the massive *torii* portals and making the short walk to the Capitol Tokyu Hotel on the hilltop. Soh was watching the entrance from behind a magazine. He was wearing a light sky-blue jacket, tie and charcoal-grey trousers in anticipation of the dinner party to follow and had an uneasy, nervous look about him. He was half-way to the bar, with its view of the Japanese garden and carp pond, before exchanging curt greetings with the newcomers. By arrangement with Nicholls Jenny excused herself and made for the shopping arcade. A corner table behind the piano gave them a measure of privacy.

'What happened to your friend?' he said, his eyes admiring Jenny's long legs and lively cascade of hair as she retreated.

'Hit her face on a door frame,' he lied. 'Japan's not built for people like us.'

The Asian-American's expression collapsed.

'We've both got things to talk about, Billy' Nicholls said after ordering beer. 'Why don't you start?'

Soh lowered his eyes and toyed with a coaster. 'Don't get me wrong, Kevin,' he said uncomfortably. 'It's nothing to do with you, or what happened on Wednesday.' He studied a spot on the table. 'I'm resigning,' he said finally. In the silence, a demure waitress in a crane patterned kimono poured their frothy beer. They touched glasses and sipped.

Nicholls said, 'I'm sorry you're going Billy, but I wish you well. I won't be in charge of the room here myself much longer so I won't try and persuade you to think it over again. But I think you've done a good job for us in Tokyo and if there's something I can do to dissuade you, tell me what it is.' He knew there wasn't. The code was specific. If a dealer was valuable to an institution because of his contribution to the bottom line a counter-offer might be in order. But the ethics of the situation dictated that once he had resigned any loyalty and commitment he had shown in the past were irrelevant. Billy Soh would not be allowed into the dealing room again unaccompanied. He would be taken there on Monday with a plastic bag and his personal possessions emptied into it under supervision.

'Where are you going?' Nicholls asked.

'To Hong Kong. I'd rather not say which bank at this point.' He sucked the foam from the beer.

Nicholls left his untouched. 'What pushed you over the edge Billy? Was it Tony's death or just a better offer? Did you get pissed off working with the Japanese?'

'I've been thinking about a move for a while,' the Korean-American admitted.

Nicholls fixed him with his dark, intense eyes. 'You'd better tell me what was bothering you while we're both still here. I'm going back to Hong Kong next week myself.'

'They got to you pretty damn quick,' Soh drawled lazily.

'I'm pretty certain Koga and his Ohyama dealing teams around the world are trying to manipulate the market,' he said, a solemn expression frozen on his face.

Soh smiled ruefully.

'I was trying to convey that impression to you but I didn't know whether you were going along with them.'

'Hanlon made us quote them last Wednesday, a minute before the Bank of Japan came in. Is he working for them?'

Soh's face twisted. 'Maybe, maybe not. I never got that close to our top management. Sternberg has always looked on Ohyama as one of its top two Japanese customers so it's hard to tell whether a decision is made for relationship purposes or because we're colluding with them on some scam or other. But I wouldn't trust that adviser guy, Fujimori.'

'I don't. Let's talk about Tony. I knew him a long time and we had our moments with the brokers before we both grew up and they put us in charge. We got our share of presents, a day at the races or the dogs, a bottle or two of scotch, but we never took money or gave them an inch when we negotiated brokerage. Do you think

Koga over at Ohyama came up with something Tony couldn't resist?'

Soh sucked in air like a Japanese. 'Ohyama always seemed to be a step or two ahead of the rest of us when the markets were tough. We put it down to their aggressiveness and sheer skill. It used to piss me and Tony off for a long time, but lately, I'd say since the start of the year, Tony was more relaxed about it. We also started to make money consistently. Our customer list grew and most of it was filled with Ohyama group firms like Nichii, Sankoku and the rest. We always quoted them the best prices, even in volatile markets, and I got shouted at if I didn't. And Tony started to enjoy things more. He read the market better, took some positions which worked out.'

Nicholls cut in: 'I got a piece of one of them a couple of weeks ago. It made me a lot of money.'

Three well-dressed matrons, each with a pair of glossy carrier bags, were enjoying a giggly late tea at the table nearest the dealers. Nicholls turned back to Soh. 'Did you believe Tony was colluding with Koga?'

He drained his beer and checked his watch. 'I dunno,' he said.

Nicholls's frustration surged. 'Look Billy. You came close to making some serious allegations to me about the Ohyama group and you've been trying to talk to me in private. I know that half a dozen people are seconded from the Ohyama Bank on a more or less permanent basis but I reckon the dealing room's been infiltrated by someone who works directly for Koga. Could be Mabuchi, Kawasaki, Hashida, anyone. Could be all of them. It might have been Tony but he walked out of this hotel drunk and died. Koga made me a tacit approach at the Ohyama party and I didn't exactly fall over myself to accept it.'

'And you paid for your rudeness with a coupla million bucks,' Soh added sympathetically.

'If he was trying to get rid of me he was successful,' said Nicholls laconically. Soh buttoned his jacket and made to leave. 'You're finished in Sternberg Chance Billy, and this might be the last chance we have together in Tokyo before you head for Hong Kong. I've got this feeling you're holding something back from me.'

Soh was standing, fingering his jacket lapels, his face creased in denial. 'I'm outta here Kevin and I'd rather leave quietly, take my shit with me and start again in Hong Kong.'

'C' mon Billy,' Nicholls said through clenched teeth. 'You've already told me Koga and those Ohyama corporates, who probably deal off his advice, were always ahead of the rest us. I'm just about convinced from what you've said, and what I've found out, that there's more than just a cosy business relationship between us and Ohyama Bank. Was Tony helping them by washing deals through Sternberg? Record deals through a foreign bank for some regulatory purpose?'

Soh looked around.

'For Chrissake Billy! Tony's dead and there's a woman over there looking for a brother who's missing, maybe because he was making a case against Ohyama. If you know anything you've got to tell me.'

Soh settled back into the chair.

'OK Kevin. You're right. But I've got no proof anyone in the office's working for Ohyama. Sometimes it just seems so. I can't say I'm unhappy to leave them all behind. I might have got a touch paranoid in the last two years in Japan. I'm an American citizen but the Japanese see me as foreign, Asian and Korean. That's three strikes and I'm out. That stuff bothers the Japanese. Behind the smiles and the bowing they dislike the outsider, although it helps if you're white.' He grinned. 'So I might have seen things there that weren't real. Anyway, Tony always took me seriously and treated me like the others and I respected him a lot, at least until this fondness for the Ohyama group began to obsess everybody. There were times I thought we were all working for the goddamn Ohyama Bank.'

'What are you getting at Billy?' Nicholls said, seeing Jenny Collier talking animatedly by the concierge desk.

'I might be wrong, but try this. Every Sunday a dealer comes into the bank to check the unexecuted orders which are sent out of New York branch when they close on Fridays. If there's some news during the weekend that the dealer thinks might move the market so that one or more of the orders might reach their trading levels early on the Monday he will fax them to New Zealand where one of our correspondent banks can watch them for us before we open here. It's just a prudent measure that Tony started. Otherwise we'd have to have someone come in at five o'clock on Mondays and Tony decided it wouldn't be worth it for the one or two deals out of the hundred or so we usually get from our New York.'

'It's your turn tomorrow,' Nicholls said jovially, 'and you want me to take your place.'

Soh did not return the smile. 'That's the point. It's not done on a rota basis. The same person volunteers to give up part of every Sunday. If you're looking for an Ohyama mole try asking Naomi Honda, at the bank tomorrow afternoon.'

They shook hands and walked to the hotel entrance. 'I'll come in on Monday to sign off,' Soh said in a cheerful and unburdened way as he left. It crossed Nicholls's already confused mind that Soh might not have a job to go to and simply wanted to leave Tokyo because it was getting too hot for him. Was he an Ohyama implant? Had he deliberately pretended to bad-mouth the Ohyama group customers because he thought Nicholls was becoming suspicious?

Meanwhile, Jenny Collier was turning heads in the lobby. She was wearing a fuchsia-pink shot silk skirt above the knees and a matching jacket nipped in the waist with peplum. The outfit curved around her figure. She caught his admiring look as he led her to his table. 'It's the last outfit in the rotation,' she bemoaned. 'I changed a hundred dollars yesterday and they gave me eleven thousand two hundred yen. A hundred and twelve yen to the buck for traveller's cheques. What can you buy with that?'

Nicholls grinned, and watched the waitress add Jenny's whisky sour to the running bill which she rolled and left in a decorative jar on the table. 'It might just cover this bar bill,' he calculated.

'How did it go with the guy from your bank?' Jenny said, stirring her drink.

'He's resigned. I think he felt excluded from what they were doing at Sternberg.'

'Including murky deals with Koga at Ohyama.'

'Very likely,' Nicholls admitted. 'Ohyama are using Sternberg Chance as dealing outlets. They have to deal with as many counterparties as they can to keep a credible presence but we're one of the tame ones. We deal any time, any price.'

Jenny had no idea what he meant but settled back as a thin man in a dinner jacket, with oiled wavy hair and a fixed bemused smile placed himself with a flourish on the piano stool and went straight into his cocktail lounge repertoire of easy-on-the-ear Beatles tunes, beginning with 'Yesterday'. The pianist rolled with the rhythm, beaming into space as his musical cliché rippled round the lobby bar. Jenny's eyes closed, but not with rapture. Nicholls touched her hands with his and waited for her composure to return. She did not look up when she spoke but her voice was firm and controlled.

'I'll pack a few things of Sam's tomorrow and leave on Monday. Get back to Chicago and the baby food, tell Mum and Dad. It would be nice to have something he treasured, like the graduation ring they gave him.' She tasted the drink, her lips lingering on the misted flute, leaving a faint strawberry half-moon on the rim.

What's happened here is unreal,' she declared finally. 'And now that poor guy's house has been torched. I mean, we were in it three hours before. What kind of people are we dealing with? It's worse than Chicago. I can usually tell who the baddies are there.'

'I don't even think Araki realized how dangerous the Hirata papers were,' Nicholls said. 'I hope he lets the police take over.'

'He doesn't seem that kind of guy. He takes it all very personally. What time are we seeing him?'

Nicholls glanced at his watch. 'Nine, nine thirty. He went to tell the owner of the house the bad news, and then follow a lead on the Peach woman.'

'He's crazy.'

Jenny refused another drink and suggested dinner. Nicholls signalled to the waitress with the bill and a ten thousand yen note. 'By the way,' the American woman said. 'You remember in that foreign correspondents' club where I met you I gave you a photograph of my brother Sam on the off-chance you might come across him?'

'Sure,' Nicholls said, pocketing his change.

'Do you still have it?'

'I do. Why?'

'I've been showing his picture in all the hotels, bars, places like the Press Club, where Sam might have been recognized. No luck so far but it won't hurt if the concierge here sees it.' She tapped her cream shoulder bag. 'I left my picture in my other bag. While you were with your friend from the bank I also talked to the bell captain and the head man on reception.'

Nicholls grinned. 'I saw you. You know how to hold a man's attention.'

'Stop that,' she chided, relishing the change to a lighter mood and Nicholls's hint of affection. They walked slowly towards the desk anchored just inside from the double automatic doors. 'I thought it might help if I asked them about Tony, save you a bit of heartache.'

'That was very thoughtful. What did they say?'

'There was an incident a week ago last Thursday. A large foreigner was here with three Japanese, a woman and two men and the *gaijin* got very drunk and awesomely raucous.'

'Was he thrown out?'

'Politely requested to respect the other guests.' Jenny remembered the words employed.

Nicholls held back, grasping Jenny's arm, as he searched his memory for the police report which the British consul or the policeman had read to him. As he recalled, no one had come forward to say they had been with Tony on his last night after he had left Hugh Carter and a bunch of brokers at a bar called Romy's. A diary entry had put his next stop at Mama Gimbasha's, but no one remembered seeing him there. He was rubbing his misgivings into his chin when Jenny Collier said, 'Come on Kevin, give me the photo.'

The head porter wore a grey longcoat with gold

buttons and a half-size top hat with braiding. Trained to exercise his elephantine memory of guests and visitors with discretion, he had easily succumbed to the American woman's questioning and plea to view the picture of her brother. Nicholls rifled through his wallet and finding no photographs remembered the slim Sternberg Chance diary he carried in an inside pocket of his jacket.

'Lucky I brought it,' he said, opening the diary and extracting two photographs, now dulled around the edges, one of Jenny's moustached brother and the other a portrait of Tony Moore he had removed from a frame in his apartment. He handed Sam Collier's picture to the porter who held it at a distance.

'He might not have a moustache now,' Jenny said, her eyes wide with hope.

'Excuse me a moment,' the Japanese said, and he walked to the reception desk where he talked to two of his colleagues and twice looked over to where the foreigners waited hopefully.

'I've never got this far before,' Jenny said excitedly, crossing two fingers like a child.

The hotel head porter returned. 'Yes madam,' he said correctly, 'this gentlemen has been in the hotel recently.' He did not smile. 'And you are correct. He was clean shaven'.

Jenny clutched the photograph with two hands and breathed in deeply to quell the emotion she could feel rising inside her. Nicholls smiled for her and while she readied herself to release a torrent of questions, he passed over the photograph of Tony Moore. The head porter beamed. 'Ah Tony Tokyo.' Then his smile vanished as he remembered. 'We are very sad about him. Moore san was our valued customer.'

Nicholls said, 'My friend here told me you said that

266

Tony was here last week and embarrassed himself. You had to ask him to leave because he was drunk.'

The Japanese looked at both of them and then crooked his head and sucked in air through the corners of his mouth.

'Perhaps I should apologize for him,' Nicholls offered.

The head porter politely retrieved Sam Collier's photograph from Jenny and Tony Moore's from the Englishman. He laid them on the counter of his booth.

'I'm sorry for my English,' he said. 'Let me take away any confusion.' He covered Tony's face with a hand. 'I think I told your friend here that there was a large foreign gentleman here last Thursday who was regrettably causing a disturbance. I have not seen Moore san personally for several weeks but of course he might have come to the restaurants on other floors or one of the bars downstairs. Perhaps Mr Moore was here last Thursday.' His hand moved across to Sam Collier's photograph. 'It was this gentleman who was here last Thursday with some Japanese people, unfortunately drinking very much and disturbing the other guests. I'm afraid we had to ask him to leave the hotel.'

Nicholls did not register Jenny Collier's scream or a hundred faces turning their way. He was conscious only of the warmth and scent of her body as it heaved in torment against him and the moistness of her tears when she plunged her injured face against his neck. He stared over her shoulder at the hanging sign in the distance, above a row of uniformed clerks, and where it read 'reception' he could only see in his own confusion and anger the word 'deception'.

36

Asakusa, with its theatres and old city crafts and restaurants bordering the evocative Sumida River was not Araki's territory, although to his literary heroes of earlier decades it was the spirit and heart of old Edo, the *shitamachi* downtown of what is now modern Tokyo. Where once the merchants and the poets came to visit the licensed brothels and tea houses, now the visitors bought cakes, fans and temple souvenirs. Araki walked under the vermilion statues of the gods of wind and thunder which guarded the alley of shops and stalls leading to Sensoji Temple. The smell of smoke clung to his clothes and his Nikon, which had thankfully been under a seat in his car, hung heavily from a shoulder.

Standing by the huge copper crucible of smouldering incense, watching visitors to the Hall of the Goddess Kannon waft the pungent smoke over their bodies to ward off illness and other adversity, Araki thought about his short visit to the owner of the house which now lay in a burnt, ruined heap. The old man was sitting on the wooden veranda of his son's house, a blanket on his lap although the sun would warm him for another hour, and he wore a winter *haori* jacket over a brown *yukata* and long underwear. A tattered straw hat shaded his small oval face where patches of grey stubble grew through loose, leathery skin. Araki had knelt on the stiff boards and held his head low, almost touching them, in apology.

The violence of the day haunted every step he had taken since leaving the blazing wreckage of the house the old man would never return to. He reached over the incense and wafted the smoke towards him rubbing it vigorously over his body, a desperate petition for divine help against the methods and sanctions he knew the seekers of the Hirata tape were willing to employ mercilessly. He almost wished he could give it back to them, to mail it as Hirata had, but he knew he was tainted, doomed he might say, by the information it contained, however little he may have understood it.

He knew a handful of *ryotei geisha* houses remained in Asakusa, quiet, discreet reminders of the past now trapped in the concrete prisons which enclosed them. Before the war they had lined the Sumida River, where guests and their companions could carouse before mooring their boats on the steps of the *ryotei* and continue their pleasures inside. Now the river was walled against floods, or widened with parkland, and the *geisha* houses on its banks gone. Except one. Onodera had repaid his *giri* obligations to Araki with the location of an unnamed *ryotei* in Hanakawado, at the end of a narrow lane between Edodori avenue and the Sumida Park. Finding the quiet lane from Onodera's instructions was not difficult, but Araki passed it by and turned towards the river at the Kototoi bridge approach. He doubled back along the riverside walkway and sat in the early evening darkness under the sheltering canopy of a fully grown cherry tree. If Michiko Momoyama was reincarnated behind the two metre earthern-style wall topped with blue tiles she would be protected inside and out, most likely by the thugs who had attacked Jenny Collier, killed Hiroyuki Hirata and destroyed his house. He wanted a photograph of her, whether or not she was involved in the Koga plots as Hirata alleged. He wanted Japan to know where the woman who had humbled the mighty Ohyama Bank and probably seduced one of its powerful directors had made her new base.

From the safety of the river bank, where lovers and families enjoyed the mild weather and a rare view of open Tokyo, he saw the roof of a main building facing the river and two subsidiaries houses flanking what he assumed was a garden. On either side, crowding the *ryotei*, were the plain, windowless sides of two modern buildings, one a featureless office block, the other a four-storey complex of plain, grey apartments. With the access lane beyond, and the strip of park by the river, Araki saw that this small old world patch of congested urban Tokyo was a rarity, almost an aberration. It could not be overlooked from any side; it enjoyed absolute privacy.

He left the cover of the tree and crossed to the road which ran by the wall of the *geisha* house. Not entirely private. A lamp in the garden cast an arc of light up the side of the apartment house, picking out two flights of a zig-zagged iron fire escape. If he could reach one of the higher landings, permanently in darkness, he would be less than sixty metres from the house, with a view of the porched entrance roof and overlooking the veranda and garden of the main house.

A man, turned out neatly in the way a guest of the *geisha* would dress, stepped from the darkness of a corner doorway. He acknowledged the driver of the black Mercedes and spoke into the handset of his portable telephone. A minute later a Nissan President passed the same spot and rolled towards the house where its passenger alighted, unseen by anyone other than a middle-aged woman in a patterned kimono who greeted each guest inside the porch of the latticed gate with a deep bow. Emi Mori stood beside her, wearing a plain black cocktail dress with a double necklace of pearls and dangling pearl earrings. Her

270

hair was loose, and hung in a glossy trail across a shoulder.

Osamu Takagi shrugged the raincoat he had worn in the car from his shoulders.

'Is everybody here?' he asked the older woman.

'Koga san, Imaizumi san,' she recited. 'Shimizu san is at the gate.'

Takagi was tall, stooping slightly in the corridor: he had light olive skin spread tautly over his finely boned face. His eyes were clear and piercing. Their slippers gave on the polished dark wood of the corridor which led through a sliding *fusama* door into the main *tatami* reception room, decorated with hanging scrolls, a cascading flower arrangement and an old, gnarled pine bonsai in the *tokonoma* alcove. The front wall, facing the river, was drawn open to the warm May evening. A malt whisky was served by a maid moving silently among the group who assembled on the terrace, where lamps lit the garden beyond a bamboo rail.

A fusuma in the side wall was drawn aside and Michiko Momoyama glided into the room, the hem of her rich silk silver-blue kimono rustling on the *tatami* matting. Her angular face and long, delicate neck were powdered white, matching the edge of her silk undergarment which showed above the top fold of her kimono. The men bowed a brief familiar nod and the maid appeared at her side with a flute of champagne.

'Mother,' Emi Mori called. 'You're looking marvellous.'

Araki retraced his route to the bridge and back to the alleys leading to the riverside park, looking for a way to reach a vantage point on the fire escape of the apartment block next to the *geisha* house. To reach it up the outside steps would have taken him close to the guarded entrance of the *ryotei* restaurant, where he would face a second threat of detection when he tried to climb to the unlit third landing without being seen. Instead, he found the unprotected entrance to the apartment block, meeting only a mildly drunk salaryman returning home, and used the stairs to reach the balcony shared by the units whose front doors opened on to it. He followed the sign to the emergency staircase and paused, breathing deeply and craving a cigarette, to let his heart settle.

From the iron railings Araki looked down on the exquisite, illuminated Japanese garden of the *geisha* house, seeing clearly the mottled orange and black backs of large carp twisting among the lilies and between the four legs of a tall, snow-viewing stone lantern. Uneven stones set in *sakuragawa*, pebble-sized gravel surrounded the pond and separated it from banks of azaleas, a ring of maple and cherry trees and a grove of tall, elegant bamboo. His eyes followed the path to a veranda where three men and a woman, her back to him, were talking. He was pondering his options when the group withdrew inside. Brushing the wall with his back, he moved softly down the rusty stairway to a landing half-way between floors at the point where it turned on itself and dropped to the next balcony. There he slumped to the floor, leaning against the bare concrete wall. Panelling covering the lower half of the landing's railing protected him from view as he assembled his camera, attaching a two hundred millimetre telephoto lens and calibrating the exposure and speed.

A long, low table was laid out for a full *kaiseki* dinner, each place with ten dishes. The two women had doubled their legs beneath them while the men squatted. Takagi finished a piece of pink, fatty tuna wrapped in *shiso* nettle and drained a thimble of sake, which Emi Mori refilled immediately. He let them eat without enjoyment, watched their individual levels of discomfort. Finally he scraped the last of his rice and ate it noisily. Shifting on the cushion, he pushed the bowl forward to give his hands room, then addressed the table at large when they had fallen silent.

'Very damaging problems have arisen this week and they could have been avoided.' There was menace in his words and several people at the table tensed. 'The last tape from England was extremely important and has been lost. I understand the circumstances of the loss and expect an appropriate expression of responsibility from the agent in England and in Japan.' He looked at Emi Mori.

'We did not think the replacement would move into Moore's apartment so quickly,' she said defensively.

Takagi said, 'What made him switch the tapes?'

'Perhaps he was suspicious when I pretended to be interested in keeping some of Moore's videos as a keepsake.'

Takagi's cold, piercing eyes raked the room. 'When can I expect to be told that you have recovered it?'

Shimizu answered in the same polite, disarming way that he had used in interrogating Hiroyuki Hirata. 'We were unable to get into the apartment on Friday. The journalist was sitting in the lobby.' He looked at Emi Mori. 'I believe our British associate from the bank went to the apartment this morning while the *gaijin* was in Nerima. He had obtained a key from the real-estate agent without causing suspicion. Regrettably, the video tape wasn't there, or the cassette tape we have been looking for. There was nothing in that journalist's house either. The tape's not in his office in Sternberg Chance so I assume he's carrying it around with him. I also conclude that he's watched it.'

'Are you in it, Emi san?' Takagi said.

'Yes, I am guiding my girls directly but I do not show my face to the camera.'

Michiko Momoyama smiled proudly at her daughter.

Takagi made his conclusion. 'If the Englishman keeps it he'll probably use it just to amuse his friends. He won't know any of the people on it and will have no reason to find out who they are. If he follows this scenario he will live.'

Katsuro Koga raised his chopsticks. 'My contacts in Sternberg Chance tell me that Nicholls is being forced to leave Japan next week. I approached him informally to assess the likelihood of his joining our projects.' He hesitated, and thought about a sip of whisky. 'But he reminded me how much money I'd cost him in the past and made it clear he'd rather sleep in a shark pool.' He smirked. 'I regret I was a little severe with him.'

'About three hundred million yen's worth of severity,' Tagaki said. The table shared the humour of the moment. Then his mournful expression returned. 'And what will the scenario be if he's shown it to that journalist, Araki?'

Tomio Imaizumi was half-way along the table, beyond Emi Mori and Shimizu. He leaned forward to be seen by Takagi. 'We don't know if he plans to do another rubbishy article about *gaijin* bankers or whether he's found something interesting on the cassette.'

Takagi laid his left hand, with its shorn finger tip, on Emi Mori's. 'You were very careless, Emi chan. For a second time.'

Michiko Momoyama came to her daughter's defence in a deep and sensuous voice with a wispy Kyoto lilt. 'Emi could not know this man would tie her with Moore and set out to find a picture of her.'

Takagi conceded the point and spoke to Imaizumi. 'Your negligence in letting Araki see and even take away her picture could be very costly.'

Imaizumi's head was close to the lacquered table top as he hissed a long apology.

Toying with a chopstick, Takagi speared a piece of pickled carrot.

Shimizu said, 'We must not forget that the caretaker in the American's mansion block said the package that arrived for him was a large, fairly heavy envelope. That sneak Hirata may have written an explanation and stolen some of Koga san's documents, as well as the tape.'

Koga dismissed Shimizu's speculation. 'I have always been very careful.'

'But that does not apply to your important contacts in the Bank of Japan,' Takagi broke in.

Koga's nostrils flared. 'He was suicidally stupid. He claims the nominated line was engaged and he needed to convey the intervention message with extreme urgency. Which was true. It was unfortunate he came in on a recorded dealing line. Hirata's intervention was pure coincidence and very bad luck. For him and us.'

Shimizu let Emi Mori fill his sake cup. 'When we moved on the house this morning,' he said, 'we found neither papers nor the cassette. Araki and the *gaijin* had given us the slip and I believe they took whatever Hirata despatched with them.'

Takagi's face creased with misgivings. 'Surely he couldn't comprehend what was behind the conversation.' He turned to Koga again. 'You said you only exchanged a dozen words and the real message was coded.'

Koga's face hardened. 'My fear is that he might ask the Englishman, Kevin Nicholls, to interpret it. It's a very implausible possibility, but he just might unravel the sequence, particularly if he knows I might be on the end of his discoveries.'

'Can't we influence this man Araki?' Momoyama suggested. 'All men have their weak points. Money, something else.' She smiled across to Emi Mori. 'Who is he? What is his background? Where is he going to sleep tonight?'

Araki shifted his position, his tailbone throbbing. There had been no movement in the garden but in front of the *ryotei* a figure patrolled the lane, silhouetted in the hazy moonlight. Light filtered from all three wooden buildings, and from the orange-tiled house nearest to Araki's precarious hideaway the smothered sound of a *shamisen's* ripe twang invoked the image of an earlier age. He brought his face close to his watch and as he leaned forward a movement in the lantern-lit garden caught his eye. He slid to the railing, rested the Nikon's long lens on a crossbar and trained it on the indistinct form of a man who had moved into the light from the furthest of the lesser buildings. Araki turned the focus slowly, begging the man to dawdle, to emerge from the distortions made by the branches of trees he passed behind. He pressed the shutter, the wide spread of flash contained by the enclosure of the landing. He pressed again when the man, large and awkward, stared into the pond and again when he looked towards the main house where he could hear the muted sounds of people talking. Then the subject of the camera reeled and disappeared behind the bamboo grove. Araki fell back and sat in a corner on the landing, listening to his heart beating.

In the lane, Yokoi had walked to the main road and back, stopping to buy a cold coffee drink from the machine outside the general goods shop and ripping off the tab in the lamplight of the gateway to the *ryotei* house. The cone of pale light was bright enough to hide the microsecond flare from Araki's camera, not far above him.

Tomio Imaizumi drew a folded piece of paper from his suit pocket and, with the others listening earnestly, condensed the profile of the journalist who had violated the security of his office. 'Araki's forty, from Shimane Prefecture, a Keio honours graduate, fluent English-speaker and divorced. His fifteen-year-old son lives with his mother and they all live with her parents. He was dismissed from his first job in a national newspaper for screwing the personal secretary to a government minister and lying about his source when the information she gave him was published.' Imaizumi's face made an ugly smile. 'He worked for the *Tokyo Weekly*, exposed the Matsuhashi drug finance ring, and was dismissed, this time for for lack of co-operative sincerity, meaning he went off like a detective and caused his company severe embarrassment. He has a free will and no particular loyalties or ties. He teaches English occasionally, has no money, drinks heavily and was hired on a one-off basis by *One Point Finance* to look into Tony Moore's banking lifestyle.'

Michiko Momoyama teased her bunched, auburn-tinged hair and tilted her delicate face upwards.

'I remember him,' she said. 'He used to follow me around Osaka when I had my problems. He was quite ruthless and wrote extremely nasty things about me.

277

Everywhere I went he was there.' She caught Koga's eyes in a sweep of her head. 'I had no real private life for a whole year.'

Takagi said, 'Will the destruction of his house be a sufficiently clear message for him to desist from further interest in our affairs?'

Imaizumi exchanged eye contact with Momoyama and Shimizu before answering Takagi. 'What we know of him suggests he gets tenaciously involved in his stories. A friend of mine in the media told me Araki turns stories into one-man crusades if he thinks there's a cause. He has been physically punished by his adversaries on several occasions.'

Takagi frowned, his head crooked. 'You're saying he might not have got the message,' he remarked. 'His house destroyed, and all.'

'Precisely.' It was Imaizumi, and Shimizu agreed.

Takagi adjusted his position on the cushion and straightened his back. The Takagi-gumi, as his tight, criminal syndicate was known to the police and media, was not built on a grand scale like the Yamaguchi or the Sumiyoshi criminal group. The police estimated it had less than a thousand members throughout Japan, but it was considered by crime analysts to be the smartest. Osamu Takagi was happy for the big five gangs to take most of the official and public criticism and fight each other in territorial disputes.

The youthful sixty-year-old *oyabun* was quietly changing the direction of his operation, spurred by the massive bubble of opportunity thrown up in the last half of the 1980s. He hived off prostitution, loan-sharking and protection to sub-groups and invested resources into more lucrative, less violent sources of income from real estate turnover, share stuffing and art dealing. Fortune, in the persuasive form of Michiko

Momoyama, brought him to Katsuro Koga and the ambitious project he had devised to manipulate the world's foreign exchange markets and at the same time swell and launder Takagi's massive cash-flows. The loyal tattooed army his father had built was generating so much money in the syndicate-managed clubs and bars and the stimulant drug racket that he sometimes struggled to invest it discreetly.

He kept Shimizu and his small team, trained and armed to protect him against the gangs that would attempt to encroach on his territory and to exercise a degree of force in the normal course of business when matters reached that unfortunate necessity. He had found it distasteful to watch as his followers forced the stupid, misguided man from Koga's bank to admit he had taken the sensitive cassette tape. His death was regrettable. Now, though, Takagi was hiring people like the two redundant employees from a top flight securities firm who had been made scapegoats when their company was discovered to have been forcing up stock prices in collusion with another *yakuza* syndicate which was also moving into white-collar criminal business.

His eyes leapt from one person to the next as he spoke. 'The success we have achieved from our financial activities has been immense. I will not give you the amounts because you know that the operation is less susceptible to infiltration or accidental exposure if we keep a wall between our different contributions. But it has been three years since my modest organization decided to move into areas where we would need the expertise and co-operation of citizens in the more acceptable sectors.' He motioned to Koga and Imaizumi. 'I am very proud that a member of our country's parliament owes his total allegiance to me. Five hundred of my men have retired to join other families or leave our honourable brotherhood altogether. Only my friend Shimizu san and his followers retain the traditional skills of my father and grandfather and I suppose a thousand men still wear our badge.' Shimizu nodded. 'We no longer do this,' Takagi said, holding up his withered finger. 'Or our different respectful bow. I claim some credit for this foresight. My lawyers now believe the police will not use this new spiteful anti-gang law to designate my organization as a "criminal entity" but this good fortune depends on maintaining a clean record. That is why the mistakes and failures you have described tonight fill me with anxiety. We must quickly and quietly plug the holes in this operation. Please finish your food and drink and I will talk to each of you privately.'

Limbs aching as he crouched on the platform, Araki zipped his jacket against the fresh breeze. The party in the main building of this exclusive restaurant was restrained: elsewhere the man he had photographed appeared fleetingly again from one of the separate lodges where a light burned behind a window of *shoji* rice paper and a lone *geisha* practised her *shamisen* in the other. But this hidden nest of quiet privacy would be perfectly understandable if Michiko Momoyama was using it as a cover for whatever other business interests she was now pursuing. Another fifteen minutes and he would leave for Shinjuku and what might be his last moments with Jenny Collier and Kevin Nicholls. He had a few clothes in a bag, the money for the Moore article and a car. The need for a place to stay was distracting his mind from the incredible discoveries of the day, and their awful consequences, when movements in the house brought him again to a crouch against the bars across the cold landing.

Two men, in business suits and smoking, walked slowly in garden clogs from the terrace. They stood against a rockery with vivid pink azaleas growing between the stones and turned towards the house in three-quarter profile. The camera flashed twice. Two women appeared on the veranda, leaning on the bamboo fence. One of them, in a kimono which began in azure silver-blue at her throat and gradually reached a deep blue-turquoise below the knees, dropped morsels to the carp below. Through the camera's telescopic eye she was unmistakable. In his head a voice screamed at him to take the picture and run. Somebody would catch a movement half-way up the side of the building or the flash of the camera, however concealed it was.

The shutter clacked once, capturing Michiko Momoyama and a younger woman in black whose profile was masked by a cascade of hair. He adjusted the focus but she stayed anonymous but somehow familiar. Looking around once, he rose to his feet for a clearer shot, the lens heavy in his cupped hand, the viewfinder hurting his eye.

'Our new unit will be called Pacific Impact Trader and will be established in Hong Kong in two weeks.' Koga said, as he strolled the sweet smelling garden with Takagi. The staff will gather there a week Wednesday.'

'Including Momoyama san's guest?' Takagi asked, stooping to stroke a cushion of white azaleas.

'Correct. Our Hong Kong subsidiary, Ohyama Finance International will subscribe two million US dollars as capital and Sternberg Chance's Hong Kong subsidiary another million. You will transfer five million from your United Nippon Fund in the Cayman

Islands and this will be the company's first customer. Note that PIT is an offshore unit, as are its shareholders. None of them falls under the regulations of the Japanese Ministry of Finance. That is crucial. We cannot operate this kind of company in Japan. It is permitted in America but we will concentrate on the yen from Asia and so have chosen Hong Kong as our base. If circumstances change in Hong Kong we can move to another location.

'Members of the Ohyama group and Sternberg Chance will leave surplus investment funds with Pacific Impact Traders as if it were a normal management outlet. The funds will be used entirely in the foreign exchange markets to respond to the special information we will receive from time to time from our implants in central banks and major financial institutions. PIT will use the funds it receives as collateral and place it with a selected group of banks as margin which they will allow us to gear up ten, fifteen times, and so trade in chunks of a hundred million dollars or more. With the right information and a hundred million of our own funds and those of our clients we can easily raise a billion dollars and move the whole market our way. The chief dealer will receive eight per cent of all profits, and the other two, three per cent each. They will also receive a salary and living expenses. Dividends will have to be paid to the two shareholders but beyond that all other income is our profit. Yours, mine, Momo chan and everything is offshore. All the money flows around the world completely outside any one country's control.'

Takagi's face was a picture of smug satisfaction. 'And all our special sources of information are in place?'

'Almost. We have eleven in Japan, including the Bank of Japan. Our contact at an American investment house regrettably took his own life last month and we have not yet identified a suitable replacement. We have three in England, of course, that includes the central bank, and two in Germany. I have been looking for a special recruit in the Federal Reserve in the US for a long time. The big banks and investment houses are covered but we need a central banker for those key changes in interests rates and times of intervention in the foreign exchange markets. Momo chan is arranging an encounter for a senior Fed member who's attending the G-Seven finance ministers' conference in Tokyo this weekend. He's been carefully vetted and I'm sure he'll join us.'

They turned back to the house. Koga frowned. 'I'm still concerned about Moore's replacement, Nicholls. Perhaps I hurt him too much and he's thirsty for revenge. I can't be sure he'll take the pain and walk. He's one of the best dealers I have ever come across and I think it would be strange if he did not suspect something.'

'You said he's leaving Japan next week,' Takagi remarked.

'Yes he is, but unfortunately he's going back to Hong Kong. There's a strong possibility of a casual meeting of old friends and adversaries. I am still trying to influence Sternberg into transferring him to London. After all, he did lose a fortune.'

'Can we take that risk,' the taller man said when they reached the terrace.

Koga's head twisted as he tossed the alternatives around. 'Can the market take another dead British dealer?'

Takagi saw the silhouette of his dangerous, faithful subordinate in a panel of *shoji* frames.

'I'll talk to Shimizu,' he growled.

37

In the street, guarding the *geisha* house, Yokoi rocked on his heels, close to reaching his threshold of boredom. He craved food and strong drink. His replacement, a clean cut young thug from Shimizu san's hometown near Kobe, was late and an apology would be exacted. He did not enjoy these nights on security duty, stripped of his sunglasses and knife and made to wear a cap like a chauffeur and so complement the appearance of respectability of a *geisha* house which only three days earlier had entertained two cabinet ministers and their mistresses. Here he comes, he murmured to himself, swaggering like a cheap pimp.

'Oi, Koike, you're late,' he said, tapping his watch and stepping out of the light of the gateway. It was only an instant, but they both sensed it. A sudden, instantaneous change in the darkness. A flash. The two looked around and then up. Koike saw a movement on the balcony of a fire escape ladder not illuminated by the garden lamps.

'There's somebody there. Let's check it.'

Araki heard the rough voice as he pressed the shutter and saw two figures making for the narrow alley where the fire escape touched the ground. His abrupt jump rattled loose joints and his footsteps resounded on the metal as he leapt the steps in twos.

Yokoi collared the impetuous youngster. 'There's a stairway in the building up to the balconies. Get around the front and cover it and don't get too aggressive. Yet.'

Koike peeled back and ran to the main road while Yokoi started up the fire escape. From the garden of the *ryotei* Shimizu saw the movements of shadowy figures on the side of the apartment block. He motioned Takagi and the others inside and flipped a switch which doused the garden lights.

'Call for the cars,' he said calmly to a man with a round, hard face who appeared in the room and to the others he ordered. 'Please leave quietly. We cannot take any chances, even if it's only a kid snooping on us.'

Araki looked down from the balcony. Someone was walking slowly up the fire escape steps, as if uncertain whether he had imagined the disturbance or whether there was danger to him in the dark. Then there were voices on the balcony, a woman welcoming her returning husband. 'It's only nine o'clock. How early you are today.' His options limited, Araki breathed deeply and stepped from a cavity in the wall, turning the film rewind on the camera as he fast-walked along the exposed corridor, nodding at the faces watching him from a closing door. He passed a lift and by the time he reached the access stairway he had used earlier his pursuer was at the other end of the balcony. Araki looked once towards him and then threw himself at the bare concrete stairs, each heavy landing jarring his leaden, abused body, his heavy camera smacking on the handrail and stabbing his ribs. Lungs pumping with the strain he found himself at the entrance to the building where a group of young housewives chatted in the road.

Koike had the apartment front in his vision and he slowed his pace to avoid attracting attention from the salarymen and young revellers on the street. A man with a high-powered camera appeared from inside and nudged through a group of women. Koike quickened his pace, pumping his arms and shoulders in keen anticipation of the action to come.

Araki gave himself the dangerous luxury of a moment's thought. To go left or straight would take him back into the orbit of the *geisha* house and no doubt more pursuers. He set off to the right, intending to plunge into the lanes and alleys which would take him back to the Kannon temple precinct and the Kaminarimon gate where he had left his car.

Yokoi was helpless with rage as he thundered down the staircase. His eyes darting everywhere, he rammed contemptuously through the cluster of housewives, scattering a shopping bag and ignoring the anguished protests. He saw his colleague was running towards him, his left arm outstretched and jabbing the air. He set off in the same direction and saw a man with a camera jigging through the heavy traffic on Edo-dori avenue. The man was older than him and not very agile and by the time Yokoi had himself dodged the slow moving traffic he knew he could catch him.

Araki stumbled forward, his breathing becoming tight and raspy. He knew if they caught him in a quiet place they would not be content to search him and take the film. If they were *yakuza* they would leave their mark. His only chance, he rationalized, was in the mosaic of passageways and narrow lanes which fed the main roads. He broke one way, then another, hoping that instinct was taking towards the shops and the crowds around the temple.

Koike cursed when the traffic cost him precious seconds and chose an opening between two arcades of shops without having either Yokoi or his target in sight.

Yokoi's face was creased with anger as he was forced to stop and elect one of three directions.

His hand strayed instinctively to the place inside his jacket where he would normally carry his beautiful blade.

Araki saw the break in the houses ahead, an opening he knew marked the Asakusa Park complex with its temple, shrine and pagoda, and the security of the crowd. He was disappointed. There were few people enjoying an evening stroll in this rare open space, and the stalls and shops were closing. He paused under the roof of the open shelter housing the huge basin of cooling incense ash, where only a few sticks were still smouldering. Hidden lighting bathed the intricate carvings on the Kannon Hall but the gravel precinct where Araki assessed his next move was in deep darkness. He heaved, drawing welcoming breaths into his aching lungs. He did not see the hand that came out of the night and seized his neck from behind, pressing into his windpipe and stifling the scream that fought to erupt. He was pulled helplessly backwards, tripping and falling with his assailant against the patina on the copper vessel. The heavy camera slid down his arm and cracked against a concrete step.

'Who are you?' Yokoi was saying as they sprawled in the cover of the shelter, but he had released his grip, and Araki's arms were flaying with the instinctive ferocity of a trapped animal, bouncing off the *yakuza* without hurting him but enough to confuse and distract. Yokoi aimed a fist from below which thudded into Araki's jaw, thrusting the journalist backwards. He could only manage a muffled groan. A passing couple saw a scuffle between two drunks and hurried on.

A shopkeeper saw a strange incident and rang the police, but they would be too late. Araki would not remember how long the assault had lasted. It seemed an hour but was only a few frantic, unreal seconds of nightmare. The punch had helped lift him upright and as he scrambled for a hold on the rim of the incense container he felt the weight of the Nikon whose strap was still in his right hand. His back was half turned to his attacker but his scope of vision caught the man rising awkwardly to his knees. In a manic, reflexive fight for survival, he spun like an olympic hammer thrower, the camera flying with centrifugal intensity. The protruding lens struck Yokoi on the soft, vulnerable bone on the bridge of his nose while the body of the camera smashed into his left eye.

His piercing scream was heard by Koike who had entered the park near the five-storey pagoda. The young hood called out for his colleague and ran in one direction and another before rushing across the gravel to find his senior alone, doubled up and clutching his face, which was a mask of blood. A low, continuous moaning completed the pathetic scene. He heard voices from the temple's shopping arcade and lights came on in the distance. He lifted Yokoi, whose face was split open below his left eye blinding him with blood, and bundled him into the darkness.

38

Emi Mori whispered to her mother and while Michiko Momoyama looked anxiously towards the neighbouring buildings before shuffling back to her visitors, she hurried across the garden in the feeble moonlight to the smaller building beyond the grove of mature bamboo. The mood of Japan ended at a small *tatami* reception room, simply adorned with an arrangement of white flowers. Crossing it quickly in bare feet, she descended a short flight of stairs into a studio decorated in Western style with thick wall to wall carpeting and electronic gear stacked on aluminium-framed minimalist furniture. *Shoji* screens had been removed from the window overlooking a narrow extension to the garden and patterned curtains replaced them. Pulling the drapes together she dimmed the lights over the low lounger sofa, tidied the foreign magazines and newspapers she found under the baggy cushions and removed the empty tonic water bottles littering the side table. She entered another room through a passageway and saw his clothes on the duvet of a short-legged bed. The bedroom had the same basic metal-framed furniture for the bedside and dressing tables and the only colour aside from the plum-purple duvet was white.

She heard water splashing in the bathroom and peeked in to see his outline behind the frosted glass of the shower closet. Turning away from the bathroom, she quietly removed her earrings and necklace and unhooked the sheer black dress, letting it lie where it fell while she admired herself in an expansive wall-mirror facing the bed. She ran her hands through satin-soft hair and removed a comb, then swirled her head, playing with the tresses that fanned into the cleavage of her black lace bra. Her free fingers strayed over the front of her briefs. Then stronger hands gripped her from behind and warm, moist musk-scented skin pressed against her. Her hands fell and her eyes closed. His fingers rose from her waist and flirted over the velvet smooth cups, feeling her small breasts swell inside them, the tips hardening to his touch. Emi Mori clenched her teeth and reached around for his buttocks, skimming his rough hair with her fingertips and then pressing between them and triggering in him a spasm of excruciating pleasure which arched his back.

'You're early,' the heavy man whispered.

She raised her eyelids and watched his broad hands playing over her body. 'There was a little problem tonight,' she said hoarsely.

'Serious?' He buried his face in the flowery fragrance of her hair and kissed behind an ear. The flimsy bra slipped over her breasts as her slender body began to move with his. 'You must leave Japan soon,' she breathed, her eyes following his finger-tips moving downwards. Then they were inside her and it was too late to talk as her body heaved and gave in to his caresses. They lurched forward, hitting the mirror and bouncing upright again. Emi's hands firmed against his buttocks, easing him lower. Then she reached down from the front, beneath her opened legs, to take his hardness and thrust it under her damp panties. She gasped as he shifted and settled deep inside her; and then she was in the air, skewered, inseparable from him as he turned and carried her to the bed like a trophy borne before him.

Behind the mirror, in a cupboard space between the rooms, Michiko Momoyama stood quietly, holding a glass of champagne to her lips, and watching her daughter with a fixed, admiring smile.

39

The pleasure seekers, mostly white-collar males and young office women, turned Shinjuku's Kabuki-cho into another relentless, orderly Saturday night and even the first promised droplets of rain had a certain programmed inevitability.

'We must be near,' Nicholls said hopefully. The fierce, perplexing neons and unintelligible signs, which hung almost the entire height of every building, seemed to mock them.

Jenny held on to him with two hands, as she had all evening since they had left the hotel. Blinded by anguish, mentally drained by the awful realization, she had insisted on visiting again the place in the Hie Shrine where she was convinced her brother had met his death, desperate to somehow unscramble an incomprehensible series of events which had suddenly brought her mission and the Englishman's together. Nicholls had tried to comfort her, saying it still could not be certain that it was her brother who had been taken helpless to the steep, deadly stairway, but she saw in his kindness his own lack of conviction.

Their appetites dulled, they picked at hamburgers at Shinjuku Station and then edged through the crowds, where the women giggled innocently and pointed at the good-looking foreign couple they thought might by actors or models. The men may have thought they were seeing their ultimate blonde fantasy, mistaking the dark

291

glasses which, with her long tresses, hid Jenny's bruises and grazes, for artistic affectation.

'That's got to be it,' she said, turning Araki's map and leading them out of the soft rain and into the entrance of a narrow, nondescript ferro-concrete building which housed cafés, intimate bars, a pink touch-touch salon and a mahjong parlour. Jenny matched Araki's jottings with the three simple characters on the neon stand sign intruding into the passageway. It was in the basement and when they slid the door aside the bar fell silent. A short, flabby woman wrapped in a garish kimono and topped with a great bunned *geisha*'s wig flapped a stubby hand across her massive bound chest.

'No *gaijin* san, sank you,' she bawled in English, exposing a double row of uneven, gold-capped teeth. A pair of men sat at the counter, which was backed by rows of bottles with the names of their owners scribbled on a special label, and all but one of the booths contained red-faced men now staring towards the door.

Nicholls swallowed his anger. 'I want Araki san. A-ra-ki,' he intoned. The woman's eyes almost closed as she hissed in ignorance. One of the men slipped off his bar stool. 'He's looking for Araki,' he said in Japanese, with a strong lisp. And to the newcomers, 'My name is Abe. I am a friend of Araki san.' There was a brief conversation among the Japanese and Abe said finally, 'Mr Araki is coming soon.'

'I know that,' Nicholls said unkindly, as they were escorted to the empty booth. A large pot of warmed sake was placed before them and Mama Yoshida, as the old retired hot-spring entertainer was called, expressed her apologies through Abe.

They had arranged to meet around nine thirty and it was now after ten. Jenny drained a thimble of sake and sank her head against Nicholls. 'I've had it,' she said sadly. 'I don't have any more tears, Kevin. I'm exhausted and the goddamn yen's wiping me out. I want to go home but I can't now. It wasn't your friend who rolled out of that hotel, drunk as a skunk, it was my brother. I'm sure Sam was set up and there's not a goddamn thing I can do about it.'

A young waitress in a blue and grey country *happi* coat with matching headband placed a menu self-consciously on the table.

'I'll take that,' an oddly garbled voice said behind her. Araki sidled next to Jenny, his hair matted, his clothes peppered with rain. 'I'm sorry I'm late. I had to see my friend in a club near here first.' His right cheek was a raw red swelling which dragged his mouth grotesquely to one side. His baseball warm-up jacket was torn at the elbow and his hands were grazed and dirty. The cut to his nostril had stopped bleeding, but it had left his wisp of moustache matted and stained a dark brown. From his seat he greeted everyone in the bar and invited the solid man who had sat with Abe at the counter to join them, introducing him as senior police superintendent Fujii. He had a small square face, and his high nose and loose skin around the eyes gave him a Western appearance. The skin on the crown of his head, where it met his cropped spiny hair, was beaded with sweat.

Araki talked in his disjointed way to the policeman who punctuated the account with worried hisses and what to Nicholls sounded like seriously critical remarks. The girl decorated the table with bottles and snacks and poured Araki a generous glass of whisky water, which stung and dribbled from his mouth on his first attempt to drink it. The journalist turned to the *gaijin* and repeated in English the account of his evening squatting on a fire escape and his confrontation with the security guards from the *geisha* house. His mouth was painful and the words emerged slurred.

'Gangsters. The *yakuza* I told you about. They were shouting at each, and at me, in their own rough dialect.' He wiped saliva from the corner of his mouth. 'I assume they're from the same syndicate that attacked Jenny and destroyed the old house. And sent their more personable colleagues to try and get into Kevin's apartment yesterday.' He gestured to the police officer. 'The Tokyo metropolitan police wouldn't search a place without a warrant or at least permission and they wouldn't walk away like those two did. Your visitors were bogus.'

Jenny said, 'You're certain that you saw that woman, Peach Blossom, Mountain, whatever, in the garden?'

Araki tapped the pocket of his battered jacket where he had managed to keep possession of the film during the fight. 'I can't be certain until I have the photographs back tomorrow. I've just left the film with a trustworthy friend. What I saw was an elegant woman, I assumed she was the formal house madam, entertaining guests in the kind of place where they never insult the visiting host guest by giving him a bill on the spot. It was Michiko Momoyama and that place was not just another evening in one of the last traditional *geisha* houses in Tokyo.' He rubbed a tender cheek. 'Those nasty little street punks proved that.'

'Will the police go in for a look?' Nicholls asked.

Araki tossed an aching face towards Fujii. 'Not yet, if at all. They can't go in unless they believe a crime has been committed or have a good reason to think a suspect is hiding there. I must persuade my friend here that there's some sort of criminal conspiracy going on and the schemers include a respectable major bank.'

'But the guy who attacked you might be inside the place,' Jenny offered.

'The man who caught me was unarmed, he was clean, otherwise he would have killed me. And even if they found him he can claim that he was chasing an intruder and have me arrested for assault. I should have told you that I left half a million yen's worth of camera equipment in his face.'

Nicholls was riled. 'But what about Hirata? Are the police investigating his murder?'

Araki spoke to Fujii. It was a short exchange and the conclusion clear to the outsiders. 'Suicide,' he said.

'We know that's not true,' Jenny said on behalf of the three of them. 'Haven't you told him about those papers, the tape. The poor guy must have told his killers where he'd sent them and then they made his death look like suicide.'

Araki translated the policeman's explanation. 'The Ohyama Bank, presumably Katsuro Koga as the spokesman, has made a statement about the dead man's recent unpredictability and symptons of severe stress. His wife has also said that he has been very nervous recently.' He raised a hand to delay the protests he knew were about to erupt from the *gaijins*. 'I'm not defending my friend or the police in general,' he said, 'but there has to be a clear crime or the suspicion of a conspiracy. I will give the police the Hirata papers and the tape and let the public prosecutor decide whether there's a case to answer.'

'So that's it then?' Jenny said with a mocking shrug towards the uncomprehending policeman. 'The case just fades away and the cops leave the town to the bad guys.'

Araki's back straightened and his face contorted with pain when he spoke to Fujii. Then he turned to Jenny. 'I intend to find a publisher to print what we believe to be the truth.'

'Will your crusade put the Ohyama guys and the *yakuza* in jail?'

'I doubt it. My task, because I need the money as well, is to get at the truth through the media. It's often the only way in Japan.'

'Well, we've got some more work for you and the prosecutor,' Jenny declared, steeling herself against the inevitable pain to come. 'See if you can handle this,' she said, her fingers spread on the table. 'When I met you through Kevin you'd written about his friend Tony Moore and I was looking for my brother Sam, and you kindly read through the papers Hirata sent in case there was something in them to indicate where he might have got to. When we talked it over this morning we all three, deep down, believed that Sam *is* dead.' Her words emerged like a long question. Then she paused and choked back her emotion. 'Somehow, the things Kevin and I both came to Japan to do are linked.' She let the words sink in and then said: 'Kevin and I believe that Sam's dead and Tony Moore is alive.'

Fujii sensed the change and tried to lever a translation from Araki, who looked at Jenny, stunned, his swollen face insistent for more.

'Sam was in the hotel that night,' Jenny said, 'with two Japanese men and a woman. He was drunk, noisy and they asked him to leave. I don't know where he'd been in the two weeks before that but I'm convinced the person they found with Tony Moore's wallet and keys was my brother.'

'What happened to Moore?' Araki asked sceptical but intrigued, a cigarette still unlit in his lips.

Nicholls said, 'He faked his own death. He put himself around Tokyo in the days before his disappearance pretending to be drunk, so people would remember they'd seen Tony in that state when the police were investigating his death. Jenny and I believe it was her brother who wandered, that's not right, who was carried, cajoled, or whatever, by his drinking buddies into the shrine around midnight and shoved down the steps.' He looked at Jenny who nodded glumly. 'He didn't have a chance. And, of course, our adviser from the Ohyama Bank, Masaaki Fujimori, was standing by to identify the body as Moore's. Nobody else got a chance to look at it or attend the cremation. Fujimori was waiting to do everything. The Japanese police, my embassy, everybody took his word as the truth.'

Araki exhaled, seeing his own failures in the evolving tragedy. Then he faced Nicholls across the table. 'So Emi Mori wasn't just Moore's girlfriend, she's mixed up with the Hirata – Ohyama business.'

Nicholls smiled ruefully. 'I don't know if she was, is, the girlfriend or not but she just about told me the day I moved into the apartment that Moore was alive.' He punished the beer with a long draught.

'How do you mean, "told" you he was alive?' Araki pressed.

'I should have got it straight away but I was fresh off the boat. I was sitting at that dining table, where you sat on Thursday night, when she came in using her own key. When she realized somebody was in the place, the lights, television were on, she just called out, like you would, sort of instinctively, naturally. I guess she thought that if there was someone there it could only be Moore, although she had to know he was hiding somewhere more secure. She had to think pretty damn quick when she found me.' He sighed. 'Everything else fits. You remember the walking stick? The black one we looked for at the shrine. I found it yesterday in Tony's car. There was a good layer of dust everywhere, except on the boot. And the passport turned up too. It wasn't on the body, although a lot of Tony's stuff was, or in the flat and I'd made noises about it at the bank. Word must have got back to Tony and lo and behold those little things turn up, probably brought round thoughtfully by Emi Mori when she drugged me. They were really trying to make it appear that Tony had died and might have got away with it if someone who knew him less well than me had come to Tokyo.'

While Araki begged a break to translate for the police superintendent, Nicholls saw Jenny Collier's uninjured eye was red-rimmed and shadowed. 'How are you doing?' he said softly.

She shrugged, and fiddled with the miniature bow on the collar of her silk blouse. 'I'm fine,' she lied. 'And I'm going to see this out. I'll tell my company I'm not coming back for a while. Hell, they can fire me if they want. I'll have to find somewhere cheaper to live, but I'm sticking around until I convince these guys my brother was murdered.'

'If Araki san can stay alive that might be sooner rather than later,' he guessed, and then remembered the urn in his apartment, packed and ready for despatch as the remains of Tony Moore. Araki turned to them again.

'Fujii san wants to know why Tony Moore should want it to appear that he's dead.'

Nicholls said, 'Tell him that the US government have applied to have Tony Moore extradited to New York to go on trial for manslaughter, drunk driving, illegal flight and half a dozen other charges related to the accidental death of a girlfriend in his car.'

'It's still a bit drastic, isn't it? To have to "die",' Araki suggested.

'The woman's family are suing him for ten million dollars. That's one point one five billion yen for Fujii san. Add that to a five to ten years in jail and you can see what his options were. He had no close family, no responsibilities in England. As one of the best foreign exchange dealers in the world he's worth about two million dollars a year in personal earnings. Ten years in prison, and the suit, would set him back at least thirty million bucks. He's around thirty-one now and wouldn't want to spend the next fifteen years earning nothing, that's if he manages to avoid prison. But he must have something going with Koga and the Ohyama people.'

Nicholls's voice was falling off as he thought aloud.

'What are they up to? They're getting inside information from the central bank. How?'

Araki was struggling to interpret the Englishman's ramblings when Nicholls thumped the table.

'The videos. They've got the key players on tape.' He grinned at Araki. 'I've been carrying the bloody evidence around in my hands for two days! You remember the soccer on the video. You left before it got to the good bit. You've got to see it.'

They looked towards the squeals and protests as a party of young, flushed salarymen were escorted unsteadily to the door by two hostesses, their mothers for the evening. One of them, with prominent teeth and glasses that slithered on his nose, spotted Jenny Collier and lurched over to the table. 'Farah Fawcett body,' he managed, breathing stale sake over Araki. Superintendent Fujii smiled with understanding and drew himself up to the innocent drunk. 'Go home and kiss your wife for me.' The man was led away, giggling, by his friends.

Araki turned to Nicholls. 'I'm not going to translate

that. I'd like to see the video first.' And then to Jenny Collier. 'Fujii san advises you to return to America as soon as possible.'

'Tell the superintendent that I want to see my brother's murderer under arrest first,' she said firmly.

Araki translated unwillingly, after which the policeman fixed Jenny with a sweaty scowl, and growled in broken English. 'Japan, tourist, businessman, safe, no problem, no rape. But now *yakuza* come. Very dangerous.' He jabbed a finger towards Araki opposite. 'He good man, but stupid. Please go home America.'

Nicholls said, 'Can't the police give us protection from these *yakuza* characters.'

Araki looked despondent. 'They're an institution in Japan. They bring a certain harmony. Who do you think keeps the peace in this part of Tokyo? The police pick up the lower ranks if they step over the line and disturb the public, or use guns on each other. Otherwise they keep a certain distance.'

'They just disturbed your harmony pretty badly,' Jenny said.

'I haven't had time to identify the group yet,' Araki said. 'The police recognize about four thousand organized gangs in Japan with a hundred thousand members. Many of the syndicates are affiliated with each other to divide the country and the businesses. They're all different. Some have unbelievable political connections, some are more violent than others.'

Fujii made a remark which Araki translated. 'He says the situation for all three of us is very serious. We are in danger. You two should leave Japan now.'

Jenny leaned over the table, her sharp aquiline nose stabbing towards Fujii. 'I am not going home until the scumbags in Ohyama and those fucking gangsters are in your jail.

300

40

'Don't hurt the door by slamming it,' the journalist ordered as Nicholls shut Jenny into Araki's Toyota. 'Lift it at the last moment.'

Jenny cowered in the back, hugging herself against the chill the rain had brought and the desperation inside her. First stop was Nicholls's apartment and when they reached the lights on the Sotobori Avenue Jenny leaned across to the passenger seat. 'Kevin. I can't face that hotel room tonight. Can I stay over?'

Nicholls looked round. 'I didn't want to suggest it,' he said with a sympathetic smile, 'in case you served me with your usual American harassment writ.' She slapped him playfully.

Araki drew up outside the Kojimachi apartment and Nicholls's body was almost out of the door when the Japanese lisped noisily, 'Kevin. I have a problem.'

'What's that, mate?' the Englishman said.

'I can't face that pile of charcoal tonight. Can I stay over too?'

Nicholls exchanged glances with Jenny, who collapsed on the rear seat, laughing genuinely for the first time in days. He leaned back into the battered Toyota and scuffed the driver's hair. 'No you can't you bastard. If it wasn't for you we'd all be happily ignorant and safe.'

It was close to midnight when they entered the apartment, Nicholls promising Jenny the guest bedroom and Araki the couch.

'Are we safe here?' Jenny said, eyeing the dark, sterile rooms with apprehension.

'It'd be tougher for them to get in here, not like my

old shack. And we're safer together,' Araki reassured her. 'Fujii san will ask the Yotsuya police to pass by the block every half hour or so. Car and bicycle.'

'He's a good guy to know,' Jenny said, 'but what do we have to do to get these crooks caught? Get kidnapped ourselves?' Speaking out of frustration and fatigue she did not wait for an answer. 'I'll take a shower, guys,' she said wearily, as her two men settled before the television and video unit with the tape Nicholls had kept out of the possession of Tony Moore's girl. Araki had found Moore's scotch and Nicholls cracked open a bottle of Australian chardonnay.

'When are you going to give her this?' Araki said, stopping by a packing case and gesturing to the box in its white linen wrapping. Nicholls threw him a glance as he fast-forwarded the video and said gloomily: 'I suppose we're almost certain they're her brother's ashes. She's going to take them when she leaves. When she's ready.'

Araki squatted on the carpet beside Nicholls and said: 'If you're right about Emi Mori being more than a bean-curd brain talent model I now understand why her company, Excell Image Agency, were agitated. They tried to put pressure on my magazine when they recognized Mori's photograph with my article. I'll have to check them out again.'

Nicholls suddenly turned on him. 'You're crazy to get involved with these people. Look what they've done to you and to Jenny. You were bloody lucky today. Next time they'll be ready for you.'

Araki added a natural scowl to his distorted face. 'I'm going to be here when you've both gone,' he said hoarsely. 'So will Koga, Michiko Momoyama, Emi Mori and their mobster allies, laughing at us. And there'll be more Sam Colliers and Hiratas. Sure, I

302

could walk away from it, like you'll do, but every time I pass a branch of the Ohyama Bank I'll think of that unfortunate guy and his widow and children. Did you know she was pregnant? What are you going to think when you get Ohyama on the phone in your dealing room? "What can I do for you, Koga san? Shame about Hirata wasn't it? Tying himself to the steering wheel of his car like that and driving off the pier. Got badly bruised on the way down, I hear." Sorry Kevin, I'm going to provoke them into making more mistakes. You and Jenny prompted them into a few just by turning up in Tokyo when you did. But that phone call from the cheat at the Bank of Japan was their biggest error and Hirata, for his own reasons, leapt at it. And look what they did to him for it.'

The frenzied miniature soccer players fizzled away. Nicholls pressed the play button, and in seconds the enormous bed and the bemused Oriental with his three women filled the screen. He indicated the woman with her back to the camera, sitting on a stool at the foot of the bed and wearing only a short skirt. 'I think that's Emi Mori,' he said. 'Now notice how the camera doesn't move, it's fixed behind a mirror or something. The women always manage to keep the guy's face on view. His head's propped up on the pillow.'

'Except when they're doing things to it,' Araki observed. 'Lucky bastard. He's starting to overcome his Japanese shyness. What's she doing to him?' They watched him surrender his clothes and allow the woman in black underwear with the boyishly bobbed hair to lick champagne from his body while the brunette in white lace kept his hands employed.

'Do you think that's the Bank of Japan man?' Araki asked, draining Tony Moore's scotch.

Nicholls shook his head. 'I don't think so. If Hirata

was right, and I know to my cost he was, the BOJ mole has been in action for at least two weeks. Koga's going to have a few friendly contacts in other banks and probably the big corporate capital movers. This guy's in heaven at the moment but he's going to get a surprise call soon asking for his co-operation.'

'Maybe not,' Araki remarked.

'Why?'

'Because we have the video,' Araki said, pouring a refill. 'Where do you think it is? A hotel.'

'It's a big room, can't see the ceiling. Look at the pictures on the wall. They don't look like hotel decorations. Might be a country house. He was probably being entertained by the Ohyama Bank while on a business trip with colleagues. He wouldn't be travelling alone but somehow he was cut out from the group and led astray.'

Imagining the capacious dimensions, the height of the walls and ceilings, what looked like oil paintings near the bed, and the ornate, matching bedside tables triggered the memory of a weekend conference at the country manor house belonging to Gervase Prideaux in Berkshire: a landscaped garden running down to a pebble-bottomed river and a private nine-hole golf course in the grounds. It was a Japanese man's fantasy world and with its stock of malt whiskies and fine wines it was the place where Sternberg Chance take their reluctant business targets to clinch a deal. It never failed with the Japanese.

Nicholls and Araki were engrossed in the part where the two active women knelt aside the Japanese and fondled each other and were cheerfully unaware of Jenny Collier's barefoot approach. It was the fragrance of a washed and perfumed body that turned their heads.

'Can I borrow this?' she said, wearing a man's large,

cotton shirt and stretching the hems as she waited for approval. 'I couldn't find anything else suitable. There's some pyjamas in the drawers but they're like a tent on me.' In spite of the bruises she looked and felt refreshed. She knelt on the carpet and drank from Nicholls's glass of wine. 'Carry on boys, you've got scantily dressed women all around you now, including a real one. Don't get nervous.'

The two men grinned, Araki painfully. If Nicholls's body had become immune to the mechanical, loveless sex on the screen the fresh warmth of Jenny Collier by his elbow made him stir uneasily. The video rescued him.

'Here it is,' he said. 'Watch the woman on the stool. She's been tickling his toes and helping the girls with their potions but she's never turned to face the camera. She's going to hand the girl on the right a bottle of cream or something.'

The woman stood up, clad only in a mini-skirt, and reached out. Nicholls froze the frame where she released the bottle, her hands fully splayed. 'Look at the colour of her fingernails,' he said. 'They could be red or orange, depending how the colour adjustment's set. The two times I met Emi Mori she had orange nail varnish and the first time she had an orange sweater and the same colour earrings.'

'I bet you don't remember what I was wearing the first time you met me,' Jenny chided.

The film continued. Emi Mori, or whoever it was, sidestepped out of the camera range, leaving the object of their attentions spread across the bed with a silly, satiated grin on his face.

Araki managed a hiss. 'I'm sure she's Oriental from the hair and the shape of her torso and buttocks. From what you said Emi Mori did to you to try and get hold of this video, I'm ready to believe it's her or one of her conspirators.'

Jenny filled the glass for Nicholls. 'Did you sleep with her?' she said in a matter-of-fact way.

Nicholls thought for a moment. 'You know what?' he said. 'If I see her again I'll have to ask her.'

'Let's turn in,' Araki said. 'I'm beat and I ache everywhere.'

'What's the plan for tomorrow?' Jenny asked, assuming they would still have the same commitment to justice as they had showed in the bar.

'It's already Sunday,' Araki said, getting wearily to his feet. 'I'll leave early for Shinjuku to pick up the photographs I took in the *geisha* garden. I have another small task to do near here but I suggest we meet at your brother's old apartment, Jenny, and go through his things and see if there's something to tie him to the people we suspect of murdering him. Leave me the address, please.'

Nicholls said, 'I'm going to the bank in the afternoon. I think that one of my dealers is working for the Ohyama Bank. She comes in every Sunday to tidy up the New York orders. If you two want to come with me and see how the market works you're welcome. After all, this whole bloody business is about making millions of dollars by manipulating my industry.'

The other two readily agreed.

'That's fixed,' Araki said, tossing the softest cushion to the head of the couch. He turned to Nicholls. 'Kevin. Please lock the door.'

41

Jenny crossed the room quietly and closed the curtains against the glare from a street light. Araki was doubled up on the narrow couch, snoring in bursts, a blanket on the carpet. She knelt by him and rocked his shoulders gently, her battered face and blonde hair close to him. An eye opened and then closed in disbelief. 'The other bedroom's empty,' she whispered. 'You'll be much more comfortable there.' He was led meekly, dragging his blanket, to the guest bedroom where he collapsed pliantly onto the bed, still believing in dreams. Jenny covered him and closed the door.

Eyes closed, hands clasped behind his head, Nicholls's body refused to drift into sleep. His mind raced, as if he were following the overnight progress of a bad dealing position. He knew that to deal successfully amid the mental violence of the money markets he had to suppress a layer of emotions, particularly purgative outbursts of anger. But Tony Moore's deceit had torn away the restraining membranes of his temperament and exposed unfamiliar urges. Moore was alive, perhaps laughing at him, his old friend who had grieved for him and paid homage at the place where he died. But it was all beginning to fit: that phone call to him in Hong Kong from Moore, hinting at an imminent central bank intervention and the thinly covered suggestion from Katsuro Koga at the Ohyama Bank party that Nicholls continue the fine dealing relationship he enjoyed with Moore. And even Prideaux, the supreme head of Sternberg Chance's treasury operation, was enthusiastic for him to talk to Koga as soon as he had found his feet in Tokyo. What

Nicholls had thought was to be a holding operation in Tokyo, spiced by a bit of friendly rumour trading, was becoming a malevolent web of blackmail, insider trading and murder. Incredible ... His anger and vengeful instincts swelled to the surface.

A luminous glow, a sliver of light, showed beneath the bedroom door. She sidled in. He was lying on his side, nude apart from a sheet tugged over his middle. She turned off the strange screen of numbers and sat against him on the edge of the bed. 'I'm exhaused, Kevin,' she whispered. 'Beat. I want to sleep but I can't bear to be alone anymore. Not after today. Can I lie here for a while?' He opened his eyes, smiled and reached up to brush a stray strand of hair from her bruised cheek.

'You were wearing a creamy, beige number, no belt. Didn't flatter you.'

She smiled. 'Does this?' she said huskily, guiding his fingers to the buttons of her shirt.

42

Jenny Collier had been identifying what she would take back with her to Chicago from her brother's abundant collection of books and magazines, most with a Japanese theme, stacked in Sam's cramped one bedroom, Western-style apartment. They were packed around the desk Sam used in the office-living room. She had mostly kept notebooks, photographs and letters to him which she had found around the apartment. She was showing Nicholls the family photographs when Araki arrived, unshaven, wearing the same tattered, smoky clothes as the previous day, and carrying an envelope and a small sports bag. He had already left Tony Moore's apartment by the time Nicholls and Jenny Collier woke, with not a little shame, their legs entangled.

'Look at these,' he said enthusiastically, using a saucer for an ashtray and spreading his hard-earned photographs and their enlargements on the dining table in the kitchen.

'What did you use?' Nicholls asked, selecting a pair of photographs and taking them into the natural light beaming through the kitchen door's half window to the balcony. The rain had passed by dawn, leaving the air pleasantly cool and brilliantly clear.

Araki drew deeply on his Hi-Lite. 'A two hundred millimetre lens on my Nikon. My ex-Nikon. Asa four hundred film.'

'But you needed the flash,'

'Right. I was as close as I could get. On a fire escape about fifty, sixty metres away. The garden was well lit but I wanted clarity.'

'You did well.'

Araki joined him and looked around his shoulders. 'It almost got me killed,' he added. 'Which are you looking at?'

Nicholls held up the pictures of the two women on the veranda above the carp pond.

'Meet Michiko Momoyama,' Araki proclaimed proudly. 'Embezzler, fraudster, manipulator of men and currently madam in charge of a very expensive Japanese guest house. It's so exclusive it has no advertised name.'

'Are you're sure it's her?' Jenny asked, bringing them coffee. She admired the line of the kimono and the elegance of the wearer in the complete picture. The enlargements captured the subjects from the waist upwards.

'They're turning grainy at this magnification,' Araki declared, 'but that's her. I haven't seen Momo chan for at least two years but you can't mistake that neck, that lovely long nape. She's straight from an *ukiyoe* print.'

'Is that the big thing around here? Necks.' Jenny wondered.

'Used to be,' Araki said mysteriously.

Nicholls held the picture at arms length and then closer.

'Is that Emi Mori with her?'

'You're the only one who's met her and, how shall I put it, knows her intimately,' Jenny said.

'There's not much to go on from Araki san's photos,' Nicholls protested. 'Her hair's hiding her profile. It's the right style, though. Long and cut straight across the front. She wore it like that when she took me out of Mama Gimbasha's. The body size and shape look similar, but I couldn't swear it's her.'

'Do you recognize either of these?' Araki said, spreading the photographs of the two men who had strolled the garden in intense private conversation and turned towards the house, giving the journalist a good three-quarter profile. The shorter of the two wore a double-breasted suit and even at the distance his well-preserved, deceptively youthful features showed through with clarity.

Nicholls studied the pictures in the light and then sat at the table where, after more close, but unnecessary scrutiny, he pronounced with an ironic grunt, 'Katsuro Koga.'

Araki leapt from the chair and punched the air. '*Banzai!* We've got the bastard,' he shouted.

'Calm down,' Jenny said, juggling the bits of logic in

her head and frowning as she tried to assemble them. 'Koga might be at the *geisha* house at a genuine business party. From what you said, Araki san, the Peach Lady was punished for her part in the phoney certificates of deposit racket years ago and is now running a legitimate restaurant business in Tokyo. Koga is just another client.'

Araki came off his high but he was still enthusiastic. He was shaking his head slowly, even as Jenny was speaking.

'It wasn't disclosed at the trial,' he said, 'but I now know that Momoyama became Koga's mistress at some point and as a director of Ohyama Bank he was in a position to influence the credit decision and lend billions of yen to her, which she blew on the stock market. The collateral, of course, was forged. She has a strong, unbreakable hold on him, probably the only person in Japan who has, and now they're working together to control Kevin's money markets. Whatever they're doing they believe it's worth killing for. If I can identify the other man in the picture, or the other woman with Momoyama, I can remove your doubt, Jenny.'

'OK,' she conceded. 'Any idea who he is?'

He thumbed the coarse image and crooked his neck. 'He's in his fifties, very well dressed, hair groomed with care and he's got a worn, pitiless face. His hardness came out well in the picture. He's definitely not the governor of Chiba prefecture. If he's a *yakuza oyabun* I can find out who he is.'

He took his cigarette to the window and peered around the edge of the drawn curtain into the street. Jenny joined him. 'What are you looking at?' she asked nervously.

'That corner,' he said, pointing to a staggered

intersection made by a modern glass office block and apartments with shops at ground level. 'A very vigilant policeman was suspicious about a Toyota turbo watching your brother's apartment from there. He foiled the *yakuza* attempt to intercept the Hirata package when it was delivered. You were very lucky.'

'Araki, Jenny!' Nicholls hollered from the kitchen. He was arranging the six exposures of the solitary man. 'Are these three from the garden as well?' he asked.

'Yes. He didn't stay long. He may have been out there for a while before I noticed him.' The grainy image was dark, almost a shadow. 'He didn't come right out from behind the bamboo and other obstructions and stayed well away from the house, as if he was having a quiet stroll but wasn't a guest at the party. Then he went behind the trees, presumably into the house on the far side.'

'Was he doing anything, like pruning the trees?' Jenny suggested.

'He just messed around for a while,' Araki said.

Jenny picked up two of the enlarged photographs. 'Look at the proportions of Koga and his friend and then this guy on his own. He's taller, wider.'

They were struck by the same exciting notion and scrutinized the man from every angle.

'Did Moore have a beard?' Araki inquired.

'Never, as far as I know, but he might be growing one now if he's trying to hide his identity.'

'It could be shadow,' Jenny offered. 'You said he stayed out of the light.'

'I can't say for sure it's Tony but I can tell you the guy in these pictures is not Japanese,' Nicholls said.

'A *gaijin* guest then,' Jenny suggested.

Araki sucked in air. 'The only circumstances you'd find a foreigner in a *geisha* house would be as a

312

guest. The *gaijin* in the picture's dressed casually. Open-necked shirt, casual trousers. He's not a guest.'

Jenny was not convinced. 'Aren't *geisha* houses little more than brothels, in one way or another. He could be taking a break from relaxing with the girls.'

Araki was mildly irked by the ignorance of his companions, a potentially dangerous shortcoming when the *yakuza* have your address.

'The old-style *geisha* house is not a brothel,' he proclaimed indignantly. 'The women in them, and there are only fifty or so real *geisha* houses left in Japan, are trained from their early teens in traditional Japanese music and dance and how to entertain a powerful man in an unobtrusive manner. It is expected that at some stage she takes a politician or a businessman as her patron and he will keep her. Very expensively, I might add.'

Jenny asked, 'Is this Momoyama place a real *geisha* house?'

Images of the streets of the Gion quarter of Kyoto from old wood-block prints flashed across Araki's mind. 'The buildings are magnificent and the garden is a beautiful example of our classical landscaping. But the place is a sham. It's a cover for Koga and Momoyama's latest conspiracy.'

'Is there any way we can get the police to go and look for Tony and any other evidence they've got hidden away?' Nicholls wanted to know.

Araki scoffed. 'I can't think of one,' he said, gathering, the photographs. 'I guess I'll have to go in myself.'

Jenny stood before him, hands on hips. 'Are you crazy? Look what they've done to you already. They'll kill you next time. I wouldn't be surprised if they're looking for you now.'

'They are,' Araki said impassively, fetching the holdall he had arrived with. He removed a shoe box and placed the envelope of photographs on the bottom of the bag. 'And Kevin as well.'

Nicholls said, exasperated, 'Why me? It's you two who want to stay around and take on the local mafia. What have I done?'

'You can get in Koga's way again,' Araki explained. 'You could undermine whatever he's planning. And we have to get Fujimori into the open. He made sure Koga was aware of everything you've done and how close you've been getting to breaking into their little arrangement. We know he's a liar because *we* are convinced it was Sam Collier. He was befriended by the people who got him drunk, pushed him down some steps and stuffed his clothes with Tony Moore's things when they were sure he was dead.'

Nicholls leaned from his chair. 'Before we accuse Fujimori, is there a slight possibility he made a genuine mistake? The injuries to the body were so bad that he said it was Moore because it looked reasonably like him? And the contents of his pockets just confirmed what he thought?'

'Very unlikely,' Araki said firmly. 'If there was the slightest doubt about the identity of a corpse, an honest man would never have been so certain as Fujimori was. You said he signed all the papers immediately and had the body cremated as soon as it was legal to proceed. He made the decisions himself, quickly, absolutely no thought for what the family might want. Because it didn't matter. It wasn't Tony Moore.'

Nicholls grudgingly agreed. 'So if he's one of them, whoever *they* are, he'll know by now that you've found their hideaway. And when they find no film in your camera Fujimori's going to know just how pissed off they are and what they intend to do about it. And here we are waiting for another suspect to come in and measure us for our coffins. Bloody hell!'

'You'll have to come clean with your suspicions about your bank's dealings with the Ohyama Bank,' Araki said. 'If there are any honest people in Sternberg Chance they'd be devastated by your allegations. Can't you stir the market up a bit? Cause a reaction.'

'I'll have to think about it,' Nicholls said, knowing Araki was right. But the inclination to spoil Katsuro Koga's plans had moved beyond being a mere revengeful fantasy. The coming week, with the arrival of the finance ministers of the industrial world, would bring the money markets to life and he, Katsuro Koga and a hundred and fifty thousand dealers in thirty countries would take their turn in the twenty-four-hour trading cycle, ready to pounce on any fragile nuance emerging from official statements or act on the rumour of their choice. Nicholls knew that if Billy Soh was correct his first objective had to be to neutralize Naomi Honda, whose loyalties he was convinced lay outside Sternberg Chance, and persuade Billy Soh to postpone his resignation for a few days.

They took delivery of buckwheat noodles and *katsudon* pork cooked with egg and ate while sorting through Sam Collier's stack of photographs, each taking a bunch. Jenny had already read every piece of her brother's written work and his letters but there were photographs of him with people he had met in Japan. Araki might know how to follow up these tenuous connections, many of them no doubt now forgotten by everyone in them. Sam had travelled throughout the country, snapping indiscriminately in the style of a tourist with a basic camera, but writing on the back the date and place and if there were people their names in the manner of a professional and the researcher he was. The portrait photographs were passed around the table. Jenny twisted a chopstick listlessly through her rice as her companions shook their heads at the parade of anonymous people beside her brother in various scenic spots or at parties.

'It doesn't say who the other two are,' Jenny said, passing a photograph of her brother, laughing with a Japanese couple, to Araki. The journalist leaned forward, glaring at the images until his skin felt cold.

'It's Hirata,' he said painfully through his aching jaw. 'I don't know who the woman is but the man's Hiroyuki Hirata.' He passed the picture to Nicholls. The gaudy glasses were missing, replaced by the pair of sun-shades which occupied a familiar place on the crown of her head.

'And this is the lady we're going to see today,' the Englishman said. 'Meet Naomi Honda.' Three heads came together to contemplate the trio, arms over shoulders, enjoying the fully opened cherry blossoms of April.

'Don't get too excited,' Nicholls cautioned. 'After all they all coincided together at the Ohyama Bank. Naomi Honda trained there for three months while Jenny's brother was researching.'

Araki said, 'You're right, of course. But two of the people in the picture are now dead. I'm sorry Jenny. We must find out how well they knew each other and there's somebody who might be able to tell us.'

She went across to the box Araki had removed from his holdall. 'New shoes?' she said. He turned from the window, where he had been watching the intersection again, an odd look of surprise breaking his unshaven, injured face. 'That's right. I got a bag of clothes out the old house but no shoes.' He walked to the desk, repossessed the shoe box and returned it to the sports bag. He saw Jenny watching him, her nose hitched upwards, an enquiring look on her face.

'What's the matter?' the Japanese asked.

'Nothing. But could I ask you what you wear with green leather open-toed sandals with three inch heels that weigh at least two pounds?'

Nicholls peered into the bag and whistled. An outline of a woman's shoe was drawn on the lid with a colour-code tab stuck next to it. Jenny put a friendly arm around Araki's shoulders. 'We won't embarrass you,' she laughed. 'Just feel free to borrow my clothes any time you like.'

Sheepishly, Araki extracted the box again, removed the lid and drew aside the folds of cloth wrapping.

'Shit!' Jenny said.

'Christ! Is that thing real?' Nicholls gasped.

Resting in the container, along with a double rack of stubby bullets in their own square box, was an automatic. Nicholls edged around it as if it were about to spring to life. 'Where the hell did you get that from? I thought you said there weren't any handguns in Japan.' He waited for the reluctant response.

'The *yakuza* gangs are armed,' Araki said meekly. 'Only handguns. And they use them on each other mainly. I have a friend, Onodera san. He was a minor *yakuza*, a bagman and general fall guy. He was imprisoned for his part in the first Momoyama affair. He's quit the formal gang scene and now manages a Shinjuku strip club on his former gang's territory. When he retired he bought the gun for insurance from a Taiwanese sailor running guns into southern Japan. He keeps it in this bag and moves it every few weeks between different coin lockers. He gave me the key last night before I met you and I picked it up this morning at Yoyogi.'

'And he's a friend of yours?' Jenny said bewildered.

'We drink together occasionally. The policeman Fujii san sometimes joins us. It was him, Onodera san, who tipped me off about Michiko Momoyama's whereabouts. Now he's lent me his gun.'

'Some way to go before I figure out this country,' Jenny drawled, staring at the automatic. 'It's more like Chicago every day.'

'Do you know how to use it?' Nicholls said.

'I've no idea,' Araki confessed. 'I've never touched a gun before, let alone fired one.'

Jenny asked, 'So what are you going to with it when your next *yakuza* heavy comes at you with a sword? Stick it up his nose? Somewhere else?'

'I'll deter them with it,' Araki proposed, straight-faced and serious. He reached for the box.

'Hold it!' Jenny ordered. 'Don't get near it. Is it loaded?' Araki shrugged his shoulders.

He reeled as Jenny brushed passed him and with her back to the others turned the box so that the barrel pointed to open space. Gripping the handle she tugged the gun gently from its hold and after checking that the safety catch was engaged cradled it upright in her left hand. She pressed the magazine release on the leftside of the hilt below the trigger guard and caught the magazine in her right hand as it slid from the handle. It was empty. Finally, she pulled back the slide, exposing the muzzle, and locked it in place. 'There you go,' she said confidently. 'Nothing in the magazine, nothing in the chamber. The baby's clean. Here look.' She tossed it to a startled Araki who caught and held it out as if it were a live snake. The two men looked at each other.

'Did they teach you this at the baby food company?' Nicholls asked with grudging admiration.

'Let me tell you. I lived four blocks from the

wrong side of Chicago until I was seven and I haven't moved very far since. When I graduated from university my dad's present, was a self-defence course, including shooting.' Retrieving the gun from Araki, she released the slide lock and pretended to aim and pulled the trigger. 'Nine millimetre, double action Beretta eighty-four, semi-automatic. Not a great stopper but very accurate,' she informed her startled companions. 'I've used the ninety-two model at the range but this one's sexier, shorter barrel, lighter. Nice walnut grip.' She closed an eye and looked along the three dot sights. 'So what are you going to do with it, Rambo?' she said to Araki. 'Serious offence, you know. Possession of an unlicensed, unregistered, and probably stolen gun, even if you only plan to wave the thing.'

Araki took the gun and said, 'Whatever I do with it I ought to know how it works.'

Jenny waited for an admission that he had made a mistake and a promise to take the gun back to its owner's coin locker. It did not come.

'You're serious, aren't you?' she said at last. He shrugged.

'OK. Gather round children, and don't touch anything yet,' she commanded.

With the two men leaning forward intently, Jenny wiped her hands against her jeans and then cradled the gun in her left, pointing with her right. 'This is the safety catch. If you leave it where it is now the gun will never fire. When you want to fire, press it down, otherwise leave it where it is and you won't shoot your own ass off.' She let the men hold the gun and manipulate the safety catch. 'Now the slide,' she said, taking the weapon. 'Hold the gun upright like this and then put your other thumb and forefinger on the two grips. Pull the slide as far as you can. Like so.

In this state it won't lock back because the magazine's not in, but the hammer's cocked. See.' She pulled the trigger and the hammer fell with a sharp click. 'Try it guys.'

'What does it do?' Araki asked, pulling the slide towards him and releasing it, reaching a fluent action.

'A lot of things. It ejects anything in the chamber. Empty shells or unfired rounds. And the forward action will draw another round from the magazine, it'll also cock the hammer.' The two men practised until they were comfortable with it. Jenny said, 'When the magazine's in and you've loaded the gun by pulling on the slide, the hammer'll cock automatically each time you fire. Now you're ready to take on the *yakuza*.' Then she demonstrated the handgrip. 'Basically, you rest your gun hand on your free one and you can lock thumbs if you want to. If you have the option of firing standing up, put equal weight on both feet and aim for the centre of the chest. Ease the trigger back slowly and evenly, like you're squeezing the whole grip. Don't jerk or your aim will be off. There's not much of a kickback on this model. Go ahead, get used to it.'

She put them through the safety and firing procedures in turn and they practised until she was satisfied they fully understood the danger and the consequences of a mistake.

'Surprisingly little pressure needed on the trigger,' Nicholls observed, taking his turn and imagining another spot on Koga's anatomy to fire at. He passed it to Araki.

'You've got the idea. Araki san,' Jenny said. 'Now make the gun safe and give me the magazine.'

He released the slide and locked the gun on safety.

'No need for you to practise this part,' she said, tipping a box of ammunition onto the table. 'You shouldn't need more than one clip, I hope. So I'll do it.' They watched as she pressed the rounds on to the head of the spring through the narrowing top of the magazine. 'It'll take thirteen shells,' she commented, 'but I'll give it twelve. Might avoid causing the gun to jam.' When it was fully loaded she tapped it gently against the palm of her hand. 'Gets the rounds to move to the rear of the clip so they feed properly. Most jams come from bullets that don't feed smoothly.' The loaded magazine in one hand, she looked at the men sternly. 'If you ever have to load this thing you've got to do it gently. Hold the magazine straight, don't force it in, and wait until it clicks quietly into place. OK?' The student gunmen said they understood.

'Right,' she said. 'I'm going to leave the slide released and the safety on. If you have to fire the gun, and heaven forbid it, you put the magazine in, pull the slide back and release it and deactivate the safety. Then there's only the trigger.'

Araki put the gun into the shoe box and weighed the magazine in his palm before wrapping it in a sock and laying it against the barrel. He seemed relieved when the lid of the box was in place and a few items of clothing covered it.

When Nicholls looked at his watch and suggested it was time they moved to his bank, Araki said to Jenny: 'Can I go through your brother's notebooks and writings at my leisure? There might be something in his recent work to hint at future trouble. Perhaps I'll come back here after Kevin's bank. If you let me have the key I can stay over and get started on my own analysis of the Hirata–Ohyama situation.'

Why not, Jenny thought. She had been told the rent was paid to the end of the month and she had never wanted to intrude into Sam's apartment while there was

321

a chance he was alive. Now she knew he was dead, but she had another reason not to take up residence here. She exchanged smiles with Nicholls who was packing a small bunch of photographs from Sam's collection into an envelope.

'We've found something very interesting to show my loyal dealer today,' he said.

43

Nicholls checked his companions through the Nichiban-kan building's Sunday security desk and escorted them between the rows of eerily silent office machinery and work stations to his locked office. Naomi Honda had not arrived, and might not do, he supposed, if she was part of the Koga intrigue and Araki had stirred the poison enough in the *geisha* house to trigger a containment plan. Or perhaps they would not have to react, knowing how little real evidence the journalists and the *gaijins* had.

In the dealing room Nicholls switched on a Reuters monitor and Araki made notes as he used the analogy of the street trader willing to buy and sell the same product to explain the workings of the foreign exchange market where the commodities were currencies. 'Naomi Honda comes in on Sundays,' he said, 'because if something's happened during the weekend – could be anything, a Russian coup, an assassination, a statement by a central banker – it could affect the exchange rates, but whatever happens in the world we have to act on the orders our customers and branches left with us on the previous Friday. These orders usually stipulate the rate

322

the customer wants to deal at. If we fail to execute the deal when the rate is reached in the market the customer might claim we were negligent and demand we fulfil the orders at the prices he asked for, which of course could cost us a lot of money if the market price has moved against us. This could all happen before we can deal here in Tokyo and we don't have an operation further east than here. So she'll sort through the orders, a lot of which may have started in Europe, went unexecuted in New York and were then sent to the western Pacific. If she's concerned that some of them might reach the market prices, where they have to be executed as done deals, before Tokyo opens, she'll send them to a bank in New Zealand where they'll watch them for us.' He fetched a sheaf of papers from a fax machine and swiftly ran over the columns of figures. 'Of course, during the week Auckland and Sydney overlap with the US markets' close on the previous day. We have an early shift during the week to cover the gap with Tokyo but Tony Moore wanted to be sure we had the weekend orders under control.'

Jenny, in familiar jeans and a loose, v-necked mauve sweater, sat on a desk and threw her head back. 'So Naomi Honda has a perfect opportunity to know what's in the desks, in the systems, in the customer lists,' she concluded.

'That's believable,' Nicholls agreed. 'Koga, Fujimori, and whoever else is in this racket, would want a Japanese speaker to support Tony Moore directly in the dealing room. The Ohyama group got the closest prices from us, the best service and the anonymity that they could not achieve through the incestuous Japanese banking system.'

'But where does Tony Moore go from here?' Jenny asked, in a voice edged with bitterness. 'He's "dead", for all intents and legal purposes, and I assume he can't work openly in Japan.'

'I don't know,' Nicholls confessed, returning the faxes to the machine. He paced the room and then turned on the others. 'He's one of the best dealers around, and as you said, Jenny, he couldn't work here again. Or in any of the big financial centres really. He was too well known. If it *was* Tony in that *geisha* house last night it means Koga's planning to use him somehow, and that's somewhere outside Japan. I'm damned if I know where.'

'We have foreigners under strict control here,' Araki said. 'The police know where the illegal Iranian, Filipino and Bangladeshi workers are. We need them on the building sites and in the docks so they're allowed to stay for the normal ninety days of their tourist visas and then deported after they're caught for staying on. Then we let some more in. But your friend has abandoned his passport and his alien registration card. If he's found by the police the whole plot fails and they'll tie him to Jenny's brother because we've already told them as much through my friend inspector Fujii san.'

'So how will he get out?' Jenny said. 'In a crate of frozen whale meat?'

'I've no idea,' Nicholls admitted.

Araki sat at a desk, mesmerized by three screens of coloured numbers and graphs, and held telephones to both ears. He looked up at Nicholls. 'Is this all worth killing for?'

'Speaking personally, no,' the Englishman said. 'But it obsesses an awful of people and has corrupted some of them. Every day, around the world, five hundred billion US dollars – what's that? half a trillion dollars – every day close to half a trillion dollars moves between banks like Sternberg and Ohyama. This operation in

Tokyo does at least a billion and a half a day. Can you both imagine that amount of money? No one controls it. It flows freely from country to country looking for weaknesses to exploit and strengths to latch on to. And it brings down the governments who think they know what's going on. Only about ten, fifteen per cent comes from an underlying commercial, real business deal. The rest is hot money. Speculative money out to make more money. What kind of people do you think are in this market?'

'I thought the central banks controlled the foreign exchanges,' Araki said. 'Isn't that why they're meeting in Tokyo this week. What's it called?'

'G-Seven,' Nicholls scoffed. 'Governments believe they control their own currencies and that's why they're willing to waste billions of dollars from their country's foreign exchange reserves to intervene in the markets. It's a macho sort of thing. Governments always think their countries' currencies are worth more than they really are. It might work for an hour, or a day, but in the end it's people like Koga, and me I suppose, who decide what the pound and the yen are worth. At any moment, somewhere in the world, a smart, twenty five-year-old mathematician is working on yet another programme to plot the movement of currencies and ways to make money from it.'

'It's immoral,' Jenny said. 'I work my butt off for the dollars you guys are trying to screw.'

Nicholls felt it hard to disagree but his mind had been jogged by Araki's remark about the G-Seven finance ministers' meeting. Deep in thought, he withdrew to a window and stared at the quiet streets of Marunouchi nine floors below. In the sheer silence of the empty building the faint, metallic clash of a door closing automatically on its spring turned their heads towards the outer open office.

Jenny joined him and took his arm. 'Don't be hard on her,' she urged. 'You don't have proof that she works for Koga.'

From where he stood he could see the red-rimmed glasses on the shelf in his room. An envelope of photographs he had brought from Sam Collier's apartment rested on a shoe box in a sports bag beside the desk.

Naomi Honda saw Araki first and assumed that as the evening cleaners were better turned out than this scruffy, middle-aged unshaven man in the torn jacket and dirty sneakers he must be a burglar. Nicholls intercepted her, immediately impressed by her poise and knowing smile.

'I'm sorry, I didn't know you were coming in today,' she said.

'We had lunch in the Press Club,' he lied, introducing her to Araki and Jenny. 'I wanted them to see the office, even without the action.'

Her lively eyes danced and she adjusted her glasses instinctively, tossing back the trails of crimped hair which touched her shoulders. She was dressed for Sunday in a blouse of bright abstract patterns and casual pastel blue trousers.

'There shouldn't be much to do,' Nicholls said. 'Let's have a chat when you've finished.' She left his office and he said to the others. 'Wait for me in the downstairs coffee shop of the Palace Hotel. I'll be an hour or so. I'll bring the shoe bag.'

Closing the doors to the back office and the treasury, Nicholls unlocked Tony Moore's private cabinet, with its personnel records, and removed a file he had studied many times since disturbing the intruder after the Ohyama anniversary party.

Naomi Honda shuffled the messages and underscored a selection of transactions which she input into a personal computer terminal. Her clear-framed glasses rested in her hair as she tapped the keyboard. She did not make any telephone calls and stayed in the dealing room for thirty minutes, finally despatching a facsimile message. It was in her hand when she joined Nicholls in his office.

'New Zealand?' the Englishman said, beckoning her to the chair by his desk. If she stretched she could touch a pair of red designer glasses on his Reuters monitor.

'Yes. National Bank. There are several deals close to their levels.'

'It's very noble of you to volunteer every Sunday. I'd find it a damn nuisance.'

Naomi Honda showed him a profile and a fraction of hesitation which told him she had seen her lost property. 'I live quite near the office,' she volunteered. 'The other side of Shiba Park, near Tokyo Tower.'

'Why didn't you claim these?' Nicholls wanted to know, motioning to the glasses. He spoke with subdued yet unmistakable firmness.

'I didn't know you had them,' she tried. Her English had that slightly rounded American accent he had come to recognize in Emi Mori, Fujimori and others.

'My secretary showed them around the bank a week ago. There were no takers then.'

'I guess I forgot about them,' Honda said unconvincingly.

He let her live with the lie and then said: 'I'm thinking of making some changes in the dealing room before I leave. If you've got time I'd like to talk about your role in it.'

The Japanese dealer crossed her legs, her shoulders heaving as she took in breath. 'Please,' she managed.

'When I leave I will not be replaced by a hands-on dealer manager and the room here will be more geared to exploiting the customer base rather than our speculative positioning.' As he was speaking, to a woman he was sure knew more about the direction his bank was about to take than he did, part of his mind was tracking Tony Moore. Dealers who moved markets, who brought down currencies and sometimes governments with them, do not retire to run a garden centre in Devon. Where are you going to turn up next Tony? And what as?

'As the senior Japanese, Mabuchi san will have to run the whole dealing room and leave the corporate treasury, the four of you, to run as a separate team under a new head. I have to nominate a leader.'

'I hope I'm a candidate,' she said with controlled eagerness.

'I see you've trained in London. Six months to last summer and before that three months with Sternberg Chance of Canada in Toronto,' he read. 'You've done the Citibank Bourse course and a three month attachment to the Ohyama Bank. When was that? The Ohyama secondment.'

If Naomi Honda was beginning to perceive a more sinister reason for the interview it was not apparent in her confident poise in front of the *gaijin*. Her experience overseas had served her well. She said, 'From February this year.'

'Did you work directly for Katsuro Koga?' Nicholls asked.

'Not for Koga san. I was attached to one of the corporate teams.'

'Was it a team with Hiroyuki Hirata in it?' woman lowered her head in thought and then ren bered the name. 'The poor man who killed himself ast week. No, but I met him of course.'

'Have you worked on spot trading?' Nicholls asked, meaning the foreign exchange desks where the dealers watch the evolving markets and determine the price to quote directly to another bank or to a corporate customer via a treasury salesperson like Naomi Honda or Mabuchi.

'Only as an assistant to the trader.'

'I want you to work with Kimura on dollar-yen from tomorrow. Billy Soh will take your place on the customer desk.'

Her dark, deep eyes hid whatever fury burned behind them. A meagre tip of the head signified her acquiescence and she rose to leave.

'Before you leave,' Nicholls said, 'would you please bring me the transaction printouts for the Ohyama Bank and all the companies in their group. Sankoku Oil, Nichii Life and the rest.'

Naomi Honda stopped by the door. 'Is there a problem?' she asked.

'I'm not sure,' Nicholls said indifferently. 'The turnover is exceptionally large with this group. I want to reassure myself that the credit lines are adequate for a customer of this importance.' That pretext was intentionally unconvincing. It would not fool her and when she returned with the printouts the cracks in her hitherto imperturbable Oriental facade broke through. She said: 'The Ohyama group are my customers. It might be strange if they hear another voice without prior advice.'

'Billy Soh is very competent,' Nicholls said defensively. 'And his Japanese is very good. I'd want him

.o bring his market experience into the customer field. I will be moving most of the staff below senior dealer tomorrow.' Again there was a modest inclination of the head.

'By the way,' he said, as she gathered her handbag and jacket, 'when you worked in the Ohyama Bank I think you met an American who was doing research in Koga san's treasury, name of Sam Collier?'

'Did I?' She was startled. 'I don't recall him.'

'I'm sure it's you.' Nicholls took the manila envelope containing Sam Collier's photographs from Araki's holdall and emptied them on to the desk. He picked one out. 'That's you, isn't it?' he claimed, holding a picture of a group posed in front of a gigantic bronze statue of Buddha. 'Sam Collier's the only foreigner in it and there are only three or four women. You're taller than the others and you stand out because, well, you're more attractive. You're next to Collier.'

She smiled weakly and examined the images. 'It could be, I suppose.' She laid the picture on the table after giving it an indifferent glance.

'Is this one clearer?' Nicholls pushed another photograph towards her. 'There are only three of you in it.' She lingered on the likeness in order to create a plausible excuse for her lapse of memory. Nicholls said, 'It's a beautiful background. Are they cherry trees?' Naomi Honda stood between two men, one of them Sam Collier, her arms around them. They had been drinking and eating beneath a canopy of fully blooming, richly pink cherry blossoms, a traditional pastime in a few raucous days every spring.

'I'd almost forgotten,' she declared, forcing a grimacing smile. 'The Ohyama dealing room invited me to

330

their cherry blossom viewing party in Kamakura. It seems such a long time ago.'

'It's less than two months,' Nicholls said taking the photograph and looking intently at the images. 'Is that Sam Collier?' he asked handing it to her. Naomi didn't take it.

'It seems so.'

'And the Japanese is Hiroyuki Hirata.'

'I don't know his first name.'

'I accept that,' he agreed. 'Now, Honda san. Tell me if the Japanese in this photograph is Hirata, the dead corporate dealer from the Ohyama Bank, or not.'

She did not give him the pleasure of seeing her in any more discomfort. Ignoring the picture, she drew on her jacket, and made to leave. 'Of course it is,' she snapped brusquely. 'Can I leave now, please? I have an appointment.'

Nicholls escorted her to his outer door. 'Don't forget these,' he said unsmiling, and handed her the pair of red-framed glasses.

'How did she take it?' Araki asked as they walked the sparsely populated underground corridors below Marunouchi.

'She couldn't deny the red glasses were hers and I didn't have to accuse her of trying to remove or hide documents that night after the party. She knew I knew. I then had her bring me up-to-date turnover figures for the Ohyama Bank and its group. I'd already seen them. I just wanted her to know I suspected something.'

'And the photographs?'

'She was evasive for a while but the photograph under the cherry trees knocked her out. She first met

Jenny's brother and Hirata when she worked with the Ohyama Bank for three months.'

'Do you think Koga turned her into one of his people and sent her back to Sternberg?' Jenny asked.

Nicholls gave the sports bag to Araki. 'Almost certain, but I'll find out tomorrow when she's had time to report to whoever's pulling her strings. It's going to be hot around Marunouchi tomorrow. What are you going to do?' he said to Araki.

Araki bought a subway ticket for Shibuya. 'I'll draft something about this – what was it? – G-Seven meeting. See if I can cover a few of the things you told me about intervention, manipulation, that sort of thing. I'll go over it with you before I try and sell it. Tomorrow I'll find out who Koga's talking to in the *geisha* house photograph. I'll call you when I know something.

'I'll also take Jenny to see Hirata's widow. Can I have the photographs please, Kevin? Be careful both of you and don't go anywhere without telling one of us. Perhaps I'll have a doctor look at my jaw too before we meet up tomorrow night.'

Jenny Collier leaned down and kissed his sore cheek softly at the ticket barrier. 'Use Sam's things, please. And his clothes if you can find something to fit.'

44

He rolled on his side and shut down the redundant alarm, which would have woken him in five minutes at four o'clock. Jenny's body moved with his as if tied to it and she murmured a sigh of subconscious protest when he slipped from the bed. There had been a frightening and passionate violence in her lovemaking as if she was making a frantic and desperate attempt to expunge and obliterate a nightmare vision she knew could only be postponed. It was followed by shallow, convulsive sleep during which her hands searched for him when their bodies were apart.

From the bed he switched on the Reuters monitor awaking its fluorescent glare. The screen was still showing the closing prices in Bahrain, the only foreign exchange market to make prices on the weekend, although the bid and offer spread was wide and the business sparse. Very early start-of-the-week indicative prices in the South Pacific probed around a weaker dollar against the yen and the mark although it was too early to see a pattern. He returned the room to darkness and kissed the gently purring body in his bed. After showering, he made coffee and called a number in Westchester, New York from his alcove dining space.

'Alan? Kevin here in Tokyo. Are you in the middle of Sunday lunch?'

Nicholls did not believe the head of Sternberg Chance's US operation was part of Tony Moore's phoney death and reincarnation scheme; while Moore needed a cage to contain his passions and excesses, Alan Pike was a family man whose mild temperament had often been mistaken for weakness. Still, he was wary of disclosing the manoeuvres he had planned for the day, even to a Sternberg Chance colleague.

'Just finished, old buddy. We eat early in the States. What's happening out there?'

'I can't see much happening ahead of G-Seven,' Nicholls said cagily, 'but there might be interest in the dollar in the run-up.'

'Can't see it myself,' Pike said. 'But there'll be some big punters out there. Watch yourself.'

Nigel Simpson, head of foreign exchange in London, was out to dinner the Spanish au pair said, although they normally stayed in on Sunday nights. Nicholls asked to be connected to the answerphone, where he left a message he knew to be untrue. 'It's five o'clock Monday morning in exotic Tokyo. Yen looking a soft early on. Dollar might rebound before G-Seven. Call you later. *Sayonara*.'

Jenny was stirring when he took her coffee half an hour later.

'God almighty,' she stammered, seeing the smartly dressed and shaven Nicholls through sleep misted eyes. 'Is this hell or what?'

'Big day ahead,' Nicholls said sitting down on the edge of the bed. She reached and held him, almost painfully tightly.

'Remember what Araki said,' he warned. 'If you plan to go out give one of us a call.'

45

Mabuchi hid his displeasure behind an impassive mask of compliance. 'There might be some uncertainty among our customers,' was the limit of his protests.

'It won't be permanent,' Nicholls had declared. 'But I want the dealing staff on the different desks to get a better knowledge of the products and techniques of the others. My successor may wish to change this but at this point let's have them share their expertise.' He had sketched the changes on a notepad and would formalize them with an internal memorandum in due course, if he was allowed to stay long enough. Shortly after eight o'clock, when the first probing requests for quotes from banks and customers in Australia were coming in ahead of the official Tokyo opening, Midori Sano, the foreign exchange position clerk, had moved to the forward FX desk, replaced by the intense and attractive trainee Yukiko Eto from Hashida's yen interest rate management team. Kawasaki filled the gap left by Eto on the money side. Naomi Honda was receiving a condensed lecture on the broker network and dealing strategy from Kimura on the spot desk while Billy Soh was reviewing the client lists. He saw Nicholls beckoning from his office.

Nicholls took a coffee gratefully from his secretary Tomoko Ueda and when she had gone said, 'Thanks for putting off your resignation for a week, Billy. You may not need to stay that long. I understand your reasons for going and I won't try and persuade you to stay, but I need your help today to bring the Ohyama situation to a head. I can't explain without prejudicing your position but things have moved on since we met on Saturday.'

Billy Soh was talking, agreeing to co-operate and stay as long as it took. Over his shoulder, Nicholls could see Naomi Honda on the spot desk, standing as she spoke on the telephone. She was dressed for business in a slate-grey suit and a high-necked blouse trimmed with a red floppy bowtie. The lost glasses, found by Nicholls and returned to her the day before, had been left at home. He wondered what she had done when she had left the office. Who had she called from the privacy of her apartment to say that the replacement chief dealer was breaking up the team before he could be sent back to Hong Kong in some disgrace and that he had possession of a photograph of her with two men, a Japanese and an American, who were both now dead? He suddenly thought of her staff file and something he had missed yesterday.

When Billy Soh rose to leave, Nicholls said, 'I'm on dollar-yen today. Whatever price I make you for the customers, don't look surprised. Just quote it. OK?'

Soh nodded.

'And Billy. There are rumours that the Bank of Japan might bring down interest rates today.'

Soh flapped a dismissive hand. 'Bullshit. No chance. Everybody sees a lower dollar, not a lower yen. Why should they do that? They've come down twice already this year.'

Nicholls smiled. 'Listen carefully Billy. We've heard that the Ministry of Finance is desperately concerned that the Nikkei share index hasn't recovered enough and might collapse again. And world sentiment moves with the Nikkei. They tried forcing the securities houses to buy but they haven't got any spare money or credibility since the crash. How can the Ministry of Finance stimulate buying? Lower the intervention rates. Kick-start another bubble.'

'Absolutely impossible,' Soh remarked slowly, his chin rising and falling as he began to comprehend. 'Am I hearing this here first?'

'Could be. But you know what the market's like. Rumours all the time.'

This was true. The market lived on an edge, where a rumour or a fact had equal power until the hearsay was dismissed. This led dealers to obey the maxim, 'Buy on the rumour, sell on the fact.' Soh could not remember how many times President Reagan had died or how many heart attacks he had suffered. At least six of each he thought.

'Tell the corporate customers you have heard it and give them the reason I said or anything else you can think of. After all, the government here won't give a fuck about the dollar if the fabric of their fragile economy is in danger. It's a plausible rumour, better than most. Check casually with Hashida. Ask him to ask the *tanshi* money brokers. That should stir things up. We'll know we're doing well when the rumour comes back to us.'

Billy Soh was not convinced, and very unhappy. He brushed the edges of his thick, wiry hair behind his ears.

Nicholls said, 'On the back of the market talk I'm going to buy dollars this morning.'

Soh cursed in his own knowing way. 'Shit. Buying on the rumour, eh? Your own rumour. That's a new one.' Then he became serious. 'If you're found out, you're dead, Kevin. Starting a rumour you know to be false could get you charged with very unethical, very unprofessional conduct. Criminal maybe. If they trace the rumour back to you you're finished in the market. Might not even get a job with the brokers.'

Nicholls steered the young dealer towards the door.

'Thanks for the warning, Billy. I know the rules and understand the implications. Too bad there are people out there who don't.'

Before finding his dealing place in the trading room, Nicholls called his own replacement in Sternberg Chance Hong Kong, Morgan Trinkel, transmitting the same veiled forecast which contradicted all market sentiment. Then he locked the outer door of his office from the inside and entering the dealing room he approached Hashida, whose desk faced the door to the general office. A button under the desk controlled the entry mechanism. He ordered the dealer not to admit anyone without first speaking to him. Anyone, he repeated. Taking his place at the empty desk between Naomi Honda and the volatile Yamamoto on the foreign exchange trading desk, he quoted for business on the Reuters and through the brokers. In an hour he had built a chunky long dollar position of fifty million on a series of small ticket trades at an average cost to him of a hundred and fourteen yen and fifty seven sen. He called ostentatiously to Mabuchi, asking if there was anything behind the persistent rumours of official interest rate cuts.

'I'm hearing same thing,' the most senior of the dealers said, a puzzled expression on his face.

Telephone in hand, Nicholls turned to Naomi Honda. 'Call Ohyama Bank and get a price in a hundred dollars,' he ordered abruptly and then returned to his call.

Honda used the Reuters. There was a nine-second silence.

You're thinking about it, aren't you Koga? Nicholls said to himself. Are the rumours true? You're mega short of bucks, aren't you? Shouldn't you be buying some back? If the rumours are true it'll cost you a fortune if the price rises and you have to cover. Come on you bastard, you've had ten seconds. Have you got the balls to quote me or not?

'Fifty three fifty eight,' she read aloud.

'Take him,' he uttered without looking at her.

'At 114.58 i buy dlrs 100 mio,' she typed.

Nicholls stifled a wry smile, imagining the dealer over at Ohyama screaming for outgoing calls when he realized the price was going to go up and he was another hundred million dollars short. Koga would be nearby, his mind racing to assess the situation. Nicholls struggled not to look sideways as Naomi Honda finished entering and agreeing the deal details with an anonymous trader less than half a mile away. What would her face tell him if he could study it?

The business activity schedules she had brought him yesterday, and which he had analysed that evening while Jenny dozed on the couch, revealed that spot foreign exchange turnover with the Ohyama Bank averaged five hundred million dollars a day since the start of the year, ninety per cent of which was initiated by the Japanese bank. In earlier times he would have asked: why didn't we call them on a fully reciprocal basis? Now he knew the reason. Sternberg Chance in Tokyo was a puppet for the Ohyama Bank, for Katsuro Koga, a brothel to be visited whenever he wanted and for whatever purpose. Tony made reasonable but not spectacular money, the whore's fee, and this disguised the income he was giving up in order to service the Ohyama Bank and its group companies.

All of these entities, he discovered, were under critical credit watch by the world's banks as a result of the collapse of the asset-inflated bubble economy, bringing down as it did the grossly over-priced stock market. The severe recession which followed had eroded corporate capital bases and forced the manufacturing and trading firms into announcing record falls in income and profit and companies which were synonymous with Japan Incorporated like Sony and Nissan to declare real bottom-line losses. Whereas the world's active dealing banks had cut or cancelled the formal, authorized limits which specified the upper levels at which they would trade with the Ohyama group, faithful Sternberg Chance maintained or actually increased the ceilings. They own us, he was telling himself, as Billy Soh stood and called out to him.

'Dollar yen in twenty for Nakahata.' Nakahata Corporation's credit limit appeared on Soh's screen and he checked it before speaking. He reminded Nicholls it was the giant trading company arm of the Ohyama group.

Nicholls questioned a broker through the flexible, drooping neck of the microphone and then raised his voice calmly to Soh.

'Make him sixty eighty.'

Mabuchi thought about a comment but desisted.

Now Nicholls could not resist a furtive glance towards Naomi Honda. Come on, dammit. React to an insulting twenty point spread for the Ohyama group trading company.

'Nothing there,' Billy Soh bawled.

Nicholls had Kimura and Yamamoto buy five more lots of ten million dollars. 'We are a hundred and ninety five million long against yen,' Yukiko Eto informed him.

Kimura felt the cold sweat pricking his cropped, prematurely grey hair. The background noise on the open broker lines was increasing. The dollar was going bid.

Billy Soh rose again. 'Sankoku Oil in a hundred bucks.'

Nicholls tensed, his eyes raked the screens, his ears

searching in the din for direction. Another big Ohyama group company scrambling for a price. If he quoted the interbank market rate the customer could buy dollars from him by giving him one hundred and fourteen yen and seventy sen per dollar and if they sold him the dollars he would pay them one one four yen and sixty five sen. An image appeared of a Wednesday less than a week earlier when he had quoted this same Ohyama company a give-away five point spread.

'Sixty-eighty again.' It was almost a curse. Soh shouted the price down the telephone line. Yamamoto was quoting dollar-mark through Mabuchi to a Hokkaido regional bank. Most of the room was watching Billy Soh who was covering his free ear against the noise from the brokers' boxes. He clicked the line dead to the customer. 'Sankoku ask if that's the right price.'

Nicholls looked over the monitors. 'Tell him that's our corporate price in a very volatile market.'

Soh acknowledged the comment and activated the line again. He was still talking as he shook his head.

An American funds manager was quoted for dollars against marks and dealt in fifty million dollars on a five point spread. Yamamoto dealt the opposite way round in the interbank market and squared the trade as Nicholls had instructed. The dollar was now being bid for at one one four yen and seventy five sen. Nicholls calculated he was over two hundred and thirty thousand dollars in profit. But it was not the profit motive that had driven him to break the market trading rules.

Sawada on the forward foreign exchange desk shouted above the noise. 'Reuters news alert.'

Nicholls read the brief statement which had flashed on to the foot of the screen of dealing prices. 'Bank of Japan may cut official discounts rate to help stock market recovery.' And weaken the yen by making it less attractive for investors to hold, Nicholls added in his mind. There was no attribution to the statement. It was nothing more than a substantiation of his own rumour which had covered the money markets and reached semi-official status in less than ninety minutes. The request he was expecting came as he stood calmly, one arm aloft checking the situation on each desk.

Naomi Honda read from the screen. 'Dollar yen in a hundred for Ohyama Bank.' Her delicate fingers rested on the keyboard, her face turned impassively towards the *gaijin* who had tormented and humiliated her.

Nicholls had the price but he would have his nine seconds back. He wondered if Koga's man in the Bank of Japan had tried to call him, to deny the rumours, to insist there were no plans by central bank to cut rates. Koga probably accused the hapless fool of lying, threatening him with the video of his sexual antics if he did not get to the root of the rumour which had taken hold of the market.

The dollar's still bid, a voice ripped through his brain. 'Make him seventy-two eighty-two,' he barked, and then raised his arms to the room like a choir master. 'We're selling dollars. Two hundred million to go. Get to it.' He folded his arms and stood by Naomi Honda. 'Come on Koga san,' he said inaudibly to her screen. 'I know you've been buying dollars in and it's cost you a packet, over a million to square I should guess. Are you still short?' Nicholls's wide quote was as close to an insult as he could get without questioning Koga's parentage. A ten point spread for Sternberg's closest Japanese bank relationship.

'Off that,' he growled to Honda, cancelling the

quote because the other side delayed their response unreasonably.

'They've gone anyway,' Naomi Honda said, her rage absorbed as she responded with the others to the call from Nicholls to sell dollars and square their position. He wondered how long he would have to wait before his first irate visitor arrived at the dealing room door and who it would be.

Figures appeared on the split screens, quotations from banks called by codes in groups. Dealers shouted the prices towards Nicholls, reading the monitors or repeating the telephone quotes. Kimura flicked the row of broker buttons, demanding levels.

'Give him!' Nicholls ordered, or dismissed the price with a flourish of his wrist.

The dollar was still riding the rumour, but in the minutes Sternberg Chance had unloaded a hundred and fifty million into the market the bid price was softening.

'What have you done?' he said curtly to each of the dealers and repeated their replies to Yukiko Eto who kept the running total.

Billy's Soh's face was furrowed from spasms of nerve-racking tension as he waited for responses from Hong Kong and Singapore. The dollar had topped out, and Sternberg had caught it at the peak. He had sold twenty million each to the Union Bank of Switzerland and Bank of America in Singapore and another twenty million to Dresdner in Hong Kong. He had a Canadian bank in Sydney on one screen and a Japanese bank on the telephone. The Japanese dealers had sold lots of five and ten million to banks in Tokyo. At ten fifty-two the Bank of Japan made a formal denouncement of the rumours that they were about to reduce interest rates. They could have quashed them earlier, they must have heard them, but operating procedures in the bureaucratic maze required consultations with the Ministry of Finance, from where any changes in the delicate exchange rate mechanisms would have emanated, and an inquiry into the origins of the false stories. Relations between the ministry and its executive arm in Japan were permanently strained to the point of mutual distrust and the rumour was allowed to grow and fester until it attained the status of Japanese government policy, influencing, as it spread through the time zones, the entire trading pattern of the world's foreign exchange market while the consensus and status-minded officials in Japan disavowed all blame.

Yukiko Eto added a ten million sale by Kimura to her position and with Nicholls standing near said, 'Two hundred and twenty sold.' In the rush to cover, the dealers had oversold by twenty million dollars. 'Leave it short,' Nicholls ordered as Yamamoto prepared himself to call out to buy dollars. The market was selling dollars again, steadily but without fervour as the taste of the rumour lingered, and the US currency was drifting down to a level slightly above its opening, before the rumours had begun to grip. The pessimistic dollar sentiment had returned, but the market feared that there was support for the dollar and many players were covering their short positions, even taking losses in the process. Nicholls took the profit on the twenty million dollar short position and added it to the money he had made from selling two hundred million cheap dollars at the top of the brief buying frenzy he had created. He returned the room to normalcy by directing the dealers to job in and out of the market, earning a few points on each trade as the dollar settled in a steady trading range.

He was transmitting these instructions when the commotion he was expecting erupted outside the dealing room and drew him from the trading desk. He made it obvious he was making the visitors wait as he congratulated the dealers and guided Mabuchi and Billy Soh to the privacy of a corner drinks dispenser.

'I want no further trading with the Ohyama Bank today or any company related to it,' he commanded, reeling off the names of the firms in case the message was unclear. When Soh had left he said to Mabuchi. 'Escort Naomi Honda from the dealing room and take her to Personnel. Tell her she's being transferred to other duties and until these are announced she is suspended from treasury activity, including entry to the dealing room. Send her home.'

Passing the locked treasury entrance, he motioned his visitors round to his office, which he made a point of unlocking only when they were at the door, and were shuffling impatiently on the other side. 'I thought you'd gone home,' he said to the flushed features of Gervase Prideaux. Beside him was Masaaki Fujimori, his prominent, purple lips closed, the usual benign smile secreted somewhere behind a severe, unhappy expression, and the imposing frame of the local chief executive, Warron Hanlon.

'I'm staying for the G-Seven,' Prideaux said. 'I hope to talk to the Chancellor at the Embassy reception and meet that new chap in the Bundesbank. Masa's going to entertain the number two in the Fed with a senior Bank of Japan official. I hope to be able to join them.'

Nicholls buzzed through to his secretary for a cold drink and coffee for his three visitors.

Hanlon exchanged an impatient glance with Fujimori. Prideaux saw it and assumed a tone of frustration and disappointment when he spoke to the chief dealer.

'We're going to re-focus our treasury business strategy for Japan and in view of recent events here we're bringing the plans forward. Warron has already given you an outline. Tokyo will be marketed as a specialized centre to deal only with our corporate customers and those central banks around the world who want us to intervene in the foreign exchange market on their behalf. Market making and speculative punting by the traders outside London and New York will be restricted.'

'Like last Wednesday, and, I presume today,' Hanlon said.

Nicholls ignored him; he was enthralled by Prideaux, and urged him inwardly to continue.

'I know this may damage your reputation professionally Kevin, once the immediate motives for the changes leak into the market, as they inevitably will, but I will certainly do my best to cushion the blow. As Warron or Masa will tell you, our plans for Tokyo supersede individual considerations.'

He spoke again about the central banks, his contacts, his ambitions and the important role for Masaaki Fujimori: the more he said the more the clouds lifted. Nicholls knew that the imposing Japanese, formerly of the Ohyama Bank, had intentionally identified the body of Sam Collier as Tony Moore and after reading Naomi Honda's personnel file again he had remembered something about Tony and now knew how he was going to leave Japan. But was Prideaux the senior Sternberg link?

Nicholls was still high from the morning's dealing, the glow of adrenalin-fired confidence which would not be quelled. 'Thanks for keeping me informed,' he said. 'I'd like to stay myself until the conference finishes. The markets could be extremely volatile, what with rumours and leaks, even before the official communiqué.' He did not miss the flashed meeting of eyes between his visitors. 'I hope you didn't mind waiting just now. The security in this place has been atrocious. I believe that confidential information has been passed to another bank by a member of staff here. I have had to suspend one of my dealers pending an enquiry.

'There's also been unhealthy overtrading with a particular group of customers who've been given massive rebates in the form of trimmed prices or non-application of the agreed profit margin. Reductions in the credit facilities approved in London have been overruled at senior level and we are continuing to deal here with companies which are on the highest credit watch alert. Oh, and one of the best dealers out there is about to resign.'

He was not ready to disclose that he was engrossed in what he now knew was a related intrigue which had led to two murders, a phoney disappearance, a drugging by a blackmailing beauty, a loaded gun to be used against the local gangsters who had already beaten up two of his friends and burned a house down.

Fujimori was nodding uncomfortably.

'I'm sure you didn't come to talk about G-Seven and I have to get back out there,' Nicholls said caustically, gesturing to the dealing room. 'It's been one helluva morning. Some crazy rumour about yen interest rates going down. Anyway, we made about four hundred thousand dollars for your bottom line.'

Tomoko Ueda returned and laid out the refreshments. She slipped a sheet of yellow notepad paper with a half dozen telephone messages under Nicholls's eyes. The only ones he saw were from Jenny Collier, which Ueda san had spelled with three 'r's, and Araki.

347

Warron Hanlon patted his rich, swept-back chestnut hair into place and crossed his legs impatiently. He motioned to Fujimori. 'You tell him Masa. I've been through this before and I couldn't get through to him then.'

'It's about the dealing again,' Fujimori said, with uncharacteristic reticence. 'I have received a number of complaints about the prices quoted this morning to our valuable customers. I am sure you know which ones I'm talking about.'

Nicholls elbowed the top of the desk and cupped his chin, rocking his head wearily. 'I quoted appropriate rates to clapped out companies that were using Sternberg Chance, with our compliance I might add, to deal with us because nobody else would. By my calculations, Sternberg has cheerfully given away about three million dollars this year in subsidized dealing rates to the Ohyama group companies. I also know there were times when Ohyama shared inside information with Sternberg Chance to their mutual profit.'

'What do you mean, "with our compliance?"' Hanlon trumpeted. 'Tony Moore never said anything to me about rebates.'

'Tony was bent,' Nicholls said patiently. 'He was colluding with Koga at the Ohyama Bank and they were washing all their *zaitech* speculative business, and their group's, through this branch.'

'That's preposterous.' Hanlon said, turning his body away.

Nicholls faced Prideaux. 'Gerry, you sent me here to make sure the place was run properly after Tony's death. On my second day here I catch one of the dealers trying to remove deal information and the next, after I told Koga I wasn't going to establish a so-called special relationship with his bank, he takes

348

me to the cleaners for nearly two million dollars. I was set up.'

'I don't believe any of this,' Fujimori exclaimed angrily. 'The Ohyama group are our most valued customers. We are working on a number of important joint ventures with them and our relationship will be closer in the future. Or it would have been if they hadn't been insulted by Mr Nicholls.'

Nicholls listened to the man he knew to be an accomplice to murder and was glad he did not have Araki's deadly sports bag. Thanks to his beautiful, sad, bereaved Jenny Collier he reckoned he could have the magazine in the automatic and under Masaaki Fujimori's chin in five seconds. Then he'd know who got Sam Collier drunk and pushed him to his death and whether the *gaijin* in the *geisha* house was Tony Moore. He'd find out who tied Hirata to his steering wheel and slipped the handbrake. He glanced across shoulders and saw the puzzled look on Naomi Honda's face as she was escorted away by Mabuchi.

'And in this respect,' Fujimori was saying, 'a sincere expression of apology must be given to Mr Koga at the Ohyama Bank and our valued customers at Nakahata Corporation and Sankoku Oil and to Nichii Life Insurance whose call was not even accepted.'

'Not from me,' Nicholls insisted. 'I will write a report to you, Gerry, as head of the bank's treasury, and copy it to Warron, the Board and the bank's auditors.' He had wanted to play his hand, tell what he knew, while he had the local and head-office senior management as his audience but Prideaux's choice of words, and whatever might be behind them, had caught him unprepared. Hanlon was either stupid or genuinely unaware of the special arrangement Fujimori and Moore had with Koga and the Ohyama group. True on both counts he decided. Prideaux replaced him in his suspicions. If he was involved, why had he sent Nicholls in from Hong Kong if there was a risk of exposure? The traders were gathering in small groups in the dealing room, throwing occasional glances at Nicholls's office.

'We can't make decisions in this fishbowl,' Prideaux said, lifting his frame and smoothing his lightweight double-breasted suit. 'I believe Warron asked you last week to ease down on the trading while we get Marcus Birkmeyer here to replace you on a permanent basis.'

Nicholls said, 'I made in two hours this morning what those fifty yuppy securities sales people upstairs make in a month, that's when they're actually making money. I could've made as much as Koga last Wednesday if I'd got his contacts.'

'That might be so,' Prideaux said from the door, 'but I have to decide on some appropriate response to the Ohyama group and to your activities today.'

'You'll have my story, Gerry,' Nicholls said, showing them out. As they left, he touched Fujimori on the arm and held him back from the others. 'A small thing, Fujimori san. Where was Tony cremated? You were kind enough to attend the ceremony on the bank's behalf. The least I can do is pay whatever respects are required.'

Fujimori smiled benignly. 'That's very thoughtful of you but not necessary. Ceremonies of respect take place in the Buddhist temple or in the home. The crematorium is there only to prepare the body for its final journey.'

Nicholls said, 'I appreciate knowing that. Saves me making a fool of myself.'

Fujimori saw Nicholls's expression harden.

'For the record, where was it?' the Englishman demanded.

46

'I called him twice,' Jenny said. They were passing through Matsudo City and Araki's old Corolla was protesting at an incline. 'I left a message for him too,' he said. He wore a black sweater with yellow slashes courtesy of Jenny's dead brother but he had not found the American's razor for his patchy stubble. It was Jenny's first trip in the semi-urban country around Tokyo and she was drawn to the rich greenery and the rural tidiness of the hamlets.

'I don't really understand what Kevin does,' she confessed, 'but there were a whole lot of zeros on those numbers.' She wore a simple, plain black dress buttoned to the neck for the sad visit to the home of Hiroyuki Hirata's widow. 'I hope he doesn't do anything stupid. He was pretty worked up yesterday.'

'He's a very impulsive *gaijin*,' Araki said. 'But he's competent. The problem is Koga. He's an extremely dangerous man and with Michiko Momoyama involved there is no real limit to their ruthlessness.'

The dormitory town of Abiko was a two hour drive from the capital in the crawl of an average weekday and the austere tower blocks named as the Ohyama Residences One and Two were deserted, with the menfolk at work and the children at school, apart from knots of housewives with their babies and shopping. Faces turned towards the striking foreigner whose golden hair bounced on her shoulders, a rare white visitor to their company housing complex.

'Her name is Akemi,' Araki relayed. 'She's thirty and

there's a son of three called Shigeo. Her husband was cremated yesterday. The official verdict will say that he took his own life. She remembered Sam when I telephoned last night because he'd been to their apartment in Abiko.'

They took a lift to a balcony of doors and small, barred kitchen windows which reminded Jenny of a row of prison cells. Akemi Hirata's face showed her fatigue in the hollow, shadowed eyes and deathly complexion. But her long, straight hair was brushed to a rich sheen and made into a neat roll of curls across her forehead. She managed an apologetic smile as Jenny clumsily removed her shoes and had to stoop through the *fusuma* sliding doors separating the comfortably cramped and immaculately tidy rooms. Jenny watched as the two Japanese fell to their knees, Araki's head bobbing as he murmured condolences, apologies and offers of support.

In a corner of the living room, where the table on its squat, truncated legs was laid with cups for *ocha* green tea and delicate, wrapped cakes, a Buddhist altar had been assembled. Above the urn, which would be interred after the customary forty-nine days in the family temple grave, was a portrait photograph of Hirata, the corners draped in black. A bronze dish for incense and a bell for summoning the spirit of the dead completed the altar, which was surrounded by flowers. When finally they rose, Araki went to the altar where he lit an incense stick, tapped the tiny bell and bowed, hands together, before the ashes of Hiroyuki Hirata. The widow dusted her hands on a plain apron and extended her hand to Jenny.

'I am Akemi Hirata,' she said in pleasantly accented English, and motioned Jenny to sit or kneel at the low table. Araki joined them. 'I am very sorry for your brother. Araki san explained to me.'

'I am sorry for you too, Akemi,' Jenny said compassionately. 'I think they were friends.'

Akemi Hirata smiled weakly. 'Collier san came here sometimes. We Japanese do not know foreign people so it was difficult for me. But your brother was very kind. My son liked him very much.' The visitors looked for the three-year-old son but he was at nursery school. His mother poured hot water into the blue and white ocha pot while Araki spoke to her in Japanese.

'Akemi says that Sam was last here a month ago,' Araki translated. 'On a Sunday. He drank with her husband and played with Shigeo and then they worked on a magazine article Sam was writing. Her husband was helping with the practical banking aspects. He believed Sam was alive because he asked her to mail a package to him last week. I told her that Sam has not been seen for three weeks and that you received the papers and the cassette at his apartment. I explained in general terms what her husband's state of mind appeared to be from the documents.'

Akemi Hirata broke in, speaking in mournful English. 'My husband had much stress at his bank. Koga san is a very bad man. Why did he not like my husband? Hiroyuki always in trouble. Koga san always . . .' she looked to Araki for help in Japanese. 'Humiliate,' he said. 'Humiliate him, and other people too.' They spoke again in Japanese while Jenny copied Akemi Hirata by lifting the tea bowl and resting it on the palm of her left hand as she drank the clearish, bitter green brew. She was opening a powdery cookie when Hirata's widow's sad brown eyes swelled with tears and she slumped foward. Jenny moved around the table, and caught her by the shoulders and held her. Araki shifted uncomfortably.

'Her husband did not kill himself. She's sure of that. He was a family man and that was another reason Koga criticized him. They were looking forward to bringing up Shigeo in London for a few years. He lived for his son.'

'And the future baby?' Jenny said.

Araki looked down. 'She lost the baby last week.' He went to look for an ashtray.

'Are you all right?' Jenny asked when he came back. He nodded and refilled the cups. Akemi Hirata braced herself and apologized.

Araki spoke to Jenny. 'She thinks the apartment was searched last Thursday while she was out. Nothing was missing and she had already posted the package to your brother. A neighbour saw her husband's car leaving the parking lot in the afternoon. She couldn't see the driver but it wasn't her husband because he was at the bank and later at the party with Koga and their team. And are you ready for this?' he said, drawing deeply on the cigarette. 'Your brother brought a girlfriend with him when he came here a month ago.' He gestured to the widow. 'She said they were very friendly, very happy together. She can't remember her name.'

Jenny's jaws fell open. 'Do you think . . .?'

'Do you have Sam's photograph? The one with the three of them.'

Jenny delved in her handbag where she carried anything that once might have helped find her brother and might now identify his killer. She extracted the picture of Hirata with Naomi Honda and Sam, smiling

354

in the April sun under the cherry blossoms, and handed it tentatively to his widow.

Akemi Hirata smiled with sad understanding warmth. 'She was a kind person. Your brother liked her very much. I really cannot remember her name.'

'Honda,' Araki prompted. 'Naomi Honda.'

Revving the Toyota on to route three five six, Araki said, 'I bet everything I have that Naomi Honda was on vacation two weeks ago when no one knew where your brother was. She was keeping him out of circulation, maybe at a hot spring somewhere, trying out a large size, virtually new suit from Tony Moore's well-stocked rack. And when the moment came for Moore to lose his identity she delivered him drunk at the Capitol Tokyu Hotel, ready for the sacrifice. A substitute for Tony Moore who wouldn't have been missed if you hadn't arrived. I'm sorry, Jenny.'

'That's OK. But it'd be an interesting bet to win,' she grinned, twisting round. 'I don't recall you having many recognizable assets after the fire.'

'Good point. What are you looking at?'

'Ten days in Tokyo's made me paranoid. A white BMW. Tinted windows. Unless they're everwhere, I've seen this one three times. It's about ten cars back. Got any power in this thing?'

47

Tomoko Ueda avoided his eyes when she brought him coffee and two envelopes. Before leaving for the day, he asked her to find out if Gervase Prideaux was still in the bank. From the thicker of the two envelopes he pulled the notes he had signed for as expense money, counting them before filling his wallet. He read the contents of the other by the window. In the early dusk the street below was filling with office women heading for the underground and Tokyo Station. Billy Soh had presented his resignation, cleared his desk and had left Sternberg Chance for ever. Nicholls had thanked him for the extra day and agreed to meet him later, if other matters did not interfere, at Mama Gimbasha's where Soh was celebrating with the brokers and other market friends. Mabuchi was alone in the dealing room except for the two night shift dealers and Hashida from the money desk and when he saw the secretary leave he knocked at Nicholls's office and entered.

'A good day for the room,' he said, accepting the chair. 'There are so many rumours all the time. It's difficult to make money in these markets.'

'It's a lot easier if you've got direct lines into the Bundesbank and the Bank of Japan,' Nicholls said venomously.

'That's impossible,' Mabuchi said with a sucking noise. 'We all have contacts in the central bank but they would never give insider information.'

'It happens everywhere in the financial system. In Britain. It's commonplace in the equity markets in Germany. I don't think Tony Moore was getting it directly from the BOJ but your former boss Koga at the Ohyama is.'

Mabuchi smiled his contempt at the assertion. Or was he masking his own involvement, Nicholls wondered? He said, 'I know that Tony was getting the jump on central bank announcements. I got a piece of one of them just before he disappeared.'

'Disappeared?' Mabuchi said, struggling with the meaning. Nicholls let it pass. Then he said, 'I don't hold you responsible for what's happened in this dealing room but what I want to know is when did Sternberg Tokyo's favourable treatment of the Ohyama group begin? Was it before Tony arrived two years ago?'

The Japanese crooked his head and hissed in a way which had come to infuriate Nicholls in his short stay in Tokyo. Grimacing, he tossed the second envelope towards Mabuchi. 'Read that,' he ordered politely, but with an edge of force, and smiled inwardly when Mabuchi's expression showed that he thought he was joining Naomi Honda amongst the unemployed.

Mabuchi's eyes narrowed in concentration. 'I'm sorry,' he said finally and returned the letter. Gervase Prideaux had signed it but Nicholls wondered whether he or Hanlon had come up with the form of words which effectively finished his career with Sternberg Chance, ordering him to return to London for redeployment without going to Hong Kong first. Would he please hand over the keys to Tony Moore's apartment and car and collect an air ticket for British Airways' direct noon flight to London on Thursday?

'So I'm out in three days,' he said to the Japanese. 'If I go quietly I'll be allowed to resign for personal reasons and they'll give me a reference. If I continue to press for a review of our dealing relationship with the

Ohyama group of companies I'll be put on disciplinary and eventually fired.'

'Perhaps you are lucky to leave the group,' Mabuchi said enigmatically. 'It's very difficult for the Japanese staff to work in these conditions.'

Nicholls banged the desk with his fist, frustration rather than anger. 'Since when? When did you, I mean Sternberg Tokyo, become a puppet for Koga and the Ohyama *zaibatsu*?'

Mabuchi rolled his hands together, craving the tactile support of a cigarette. He allowed his head to hang to one side. 'It must have been after New Year. All the credit lines to every Japanese customer were reviewed. The financial condition of many companies was very bad after 1990. The American credit agencies lowered the ratings of the banks and they had to pay more for the money they borrowed.'

Even more than before, Nicholls knew. The Japanese, always takers, as in many things, of funds, and lending proportionally less back into the market, had always had to pay up in the market for their borrowings. A sixteenth, sometimes an eighth per cent more. And in foreign exchange and derivatives the companies began to struggle to find banks willing to take the risk of dealing with them in big amounts and for very long periods beyond the limits of the economic forecasts.

'But a special case was made of the Ohyama Bank and its group in Tokyo. The limits were not touched. In fact, many were increased, particularly for foreign exchange.'

'And at the same time,' Nicholls added. 'You were told to cut your profit margins and deal with them on finest interbank prices, even the shipping firm which is being kept going by its main banker, the Ohyama

Bank of course, which has put in a moratorium on debt repayments, including interest.'

Mabuchi nodded. 'The room was making money.' He raised a placatory hand. 'I know it should have been a lot more. I think that this distracted the auditors from realizing how much we were subsidizing our business with Ohyama.'

Nicholls remembered a letter from Moore's lawyers dated December last year in which the punitive damages of ten million dollars had first been mentioned. 'And Tony Moore drew closer to the Ohyama Bank from about this time,' he suggested.

Mabuchi said, 'Yes, he became a friend of Koga san.'

The eleventh floor was quiet but business in the mergers and acquisitions took place behind locked doors and Nicholls saw the slivers of light at carpet level as he walked to the suite of management offices which Prideaux had made his base during this prolonged visit to Tokyo. The dealer found his chief in a meeting room of the intimate type with its own telephone, fax, television and mini-bar.

'Would you like a drink?' Prideaux offered, about to refill his own glass with scotch. He declined and sank into an armchair, the letter hanging from his fingertips. Prideaux, in shirtsleeves, looked drawn, his lanky frame stooped as the man he intended to dismiss sat before him with a composure he found threatening.

'Where's Tony Moore?' Nicholls demanded to know.

Prideaux sat opposite and smiled maliciously. 'He's dead. You've got his fucking ashes on your bedside table.'

'It's not Tony,' the dealer said drily. 'It's an American called Sam Collier who upset your friends at the

Ohyama Bank when he was researching there and discovered how Koga was trying to manipulate the foreign exchange markets.'

'Don't be stupid. You can't manipulate a multi-billion dollar a day market. There are too many players.'

'Not if you have inside information from the central bank.'

Prideaux fell silent while he conjured a reply. 'How often can that be significant?' he asked dismissively. 'Three, four times a year.'

'You only need half a minute's advance notice once a year,' Nicholls said. 'Like the other day when I lost close to two million. Koga spread the word and the whole market died on me after he and his Ohyama friends had stuffed me with a position they knew I couldn't get out of. He knew the Bank of Japan was about to intervene. I figure Koga's group made fifty million dollars before the rest of us realized what was going on.'

'Hard to substantiate,' the tall director said, sipping uneasily from his glass. 'And how does poor old Tony figure in this?' Nicholls's eyebrows rose. He leaned forward and spoke intensely. 'Because Tony was the vehicle. When Ohyama's dealing in big numbers everyone tenses, quotes him wide, because they know he's a shark. If he deals through Sternberg Chance it's different. We have a better reputation, better distribution capability, better prices in the market. I'll have that drink now,' Nicholls said, helping himself from the black-labelled bottle on the top of the refrigerator. 'But, of course, you know that Gerry,' he said, turning on his chief. 'You came in hard today and gave me a bollocking for treading on those cockroaches at Ohyama. That's when I knew you were in with them. You can't justify the volumes our Tokyo branch was doing with Ohyama Bank, or the risk on some of the group names which isn't reflected in the margins we should have been adding to the prices we quoted. I don't know how Tony's going to re-emerge but I'm telling you now that at least two people have died for getting in the way of whatever Koga and Tony are planning and I'm going to blow the scheme before I leave Japan.'

Prideaux dismissed him with a sneer. 'I've got a death certificate, autopsy report and you've got his bloody ashes. As far as the world's concerned, he's dead.' He sipped his drink and waited for the response from Nicholls which did not come. He pressed on, digging himself, Nicholls reasoned, a little deeper into into his personal slippery-sided hole. 'And how could I be involved in it? I sent you to Japan to hold the fort, for chrissake.'

'You had to do something, Gerry,' Nicholls answered, 'when Tony went missing. You had to be seen to be responding to the crisis. I was nicely placed in Asia to get here quickly and you probably thought I would be impressed and write a gushing report on the profit levels and Tony's role in it and then strut back to Hong Kong so that you could plant another Ohyama clone in his place. You've already got Fujimori, of course. I was almost taken in by the smarmy liar. What did you say in my office just now? Masa's entertaining someone from the Fed before the G-Seven? Is he already in your bag or is Emi Mori polishing her nails for the big night? Maybe you don't need him. I forgot, you're downscaling the Tokyo operation. Where are Ohyama going to take their business in the future? Our New York and London offices don't have the same special relationship with them and we certainly don't in Hong Kong.

He shrugged and rose, tucking the letter into his

inside pocket after flourishing it at Prideaux. From the door he said: 'I know what motivated Tony to fix his own disappearance, I know how his death was arranged and I believe I know where he is. I also know how he's going to get out of Japan. You might mention all this in passing when you see Koga tonight for dinner and while you're at it pass on my regards to Momo Chan, the Peach Lady.'

48

'Is it still there?' Jenny said, hoping for a firm negative.

Araki shifted to the inside lane and caught the white car's distinctive grill in his mirror as it made the same manoeuvre six cars behind them. 'Is it them?' she asked, and when she turned to look her eyes fell on the sports bag sitting heavily on the rear seat.

'Don't know. Could be a rich kid in his toy. They just drive around all day. Not going anywhere.'

'Let's hope so.'

Araki increased the volume of the radio when it changed from traffic and weather information to a special report on the financial markets. He listened and then translated. 'It says there was chaos this morning in the money markets on rumours of domestic interest rates coming down. The Nikkei stock index jumped and then fell back when the rumours were denied by the Bank of Japan. I hope it wasn't another of Koga's games.'

'That's why Kevin couldn't get to the phone, I expect,' Jenny said.

The road dipped in a gentle descent to the Edogawa River and as they drifted in heavy traffic between lights, Araki said, 'I need a telephone. I should have an identification on the other man with Koga in the garden and we ought to tell Kevin about Naomi Honda and your brother. Get him to check the holiday rota. If she was away from the bank at the same time as your brother was out of circulation, I think that proves what Hirata san's widow said about their relationship. There's no doubt she's Koga's mole in Sternberg Chance. Kevin was right and I think he's in great danger.'

'She was also his honey trap for my brother,' Jenny said bitterly. 'And I can't wait to make her acquaintance again.'

They crossed the Shin Katsushika bridge, returning to metropolitan Tokyo, and Araki drew into a petrol station which made a corner with the Mito highway and the road which followed the Edogawa River moving south from Kanamachi. 'Watch out for that white car,' he said after stopping on a gravel path away from the forecourt. He made for the red telephones outside the pay booth and shop.

The passenger door groaned as Jenny forced it open. She walked to a stand-up advertising sign for engine oil which revolved in a gentle breeze at the entrance to the garage. To her right, exhaust fumes shimmered over the bridge under which the unseen brown mass of the Edogawa moved silently towards its end in Tokyo Bay, almost within sight. There was no sign of the BMW in the crawl of vehicles. She sighed with relief. She had maligned an innocent road user whose menace was nothing more than an illusion, another stab at her sanity.

Arms folded, she turned away from the road and thought of the letter she had mailed that morning to her parents in Chicago, telling them their son had died in Japan, and saying that she would return with his ashes. In it she had described the unshakeable, good-looking Englishman Kevin Nicholls who spoke like Michael Caine, drank off a couple million dollars he lost in his business during the morning and went back to work the next day with less concern than if he had spilled coffee on his trousers. She did not tell them he had the urn but was too nice to admit it contained her brother's remains and not those of the man he had come to Japan to replace. She wrote of the strange Japanese who, indirectly because of her problems, now owned only a scrapyard car, a pair of trousers and a couple of shirts but was ready to take on the local version of the mafia with nothing more than honesty and a sense of justice in his arsenal. She did not mention the gun.

Beyond the pumps Araki, motioned to her, a thumb in the air in triumph, and then dialled again. She smiled in his direction and waved, then strolled back to the road, stretching her limbs after the confines of the Japanese apartment and Araki's early-model car which was wearing badly from all angles. A chemical tanker thundered by, belching fumes which made her retch and lean on a post which marked the garage entrance.

As the air cleared she saw the full beam glare from the headlights of a car cresting the hump of the bridge and moving towards her slowly, on the hard shoulder of the highway as if it were damaged and about to stop. Cars and trucks sped past but she was transfixed by the distant coruscating shimmer which on the dip revealed the distinct form of a white BMW.

'Oh God!' she appealed and waved towards Araki, who was beyond calling distance above the din from the road. Then a high-sided truck pulled alongside the pumps, cutting him from view. She picked up pace towards the Corolla, all the time looking sideways at the car whose sheer white roof was creeping steadily towards her on the Mito highway. She could have hit it with a stone but instead tore at the driver's door on Araki's car and forced herself in, her knees thumping the dashboard painfully until she found the bar below the seat and jacked herself backwards. Even then it was tight; but she was operating by instinct.

The car lurched when she turned the key. 'Goddam shifts!' she cursed, not having driven a manual car for four years since a vacation in France, and before that a boyfriend's sports car in college. Clutch in, ignition again and a scream as she raced the engine, a gear at random from the upper left and the wheels spun on the gravel, hurling sharp pellets at the fence before catching. She reached Araki with one punishing roar in first gear and leaned across to help the door open with a desperate shove from the heel of her hand.

'Get in!' she ordered, as customers and attendants stopped to watch. Araki was about to protest when he saw the brilliance of the headlights entering the garage and the car they belonged to. The Corolla was moving before Araki had the door closed and it thumped over a ramp and swung left, moving south on a narrow road with the river in view beyond the lip of a concrete flood barrier.

'Where's third on this goddamn thing?' she shouted, watching the pursuing car grow in the rear-view mirror.

'It's stiff,' Araki barked, 'go straight to fourth.'

Jenny threw him a nervy glance.

The river bank broadened into back-to-back dusty baseball diamonds and soccer pitches between open, rough grassland used for golf practice. The road rose to where they were almost level with the tiles of the houses on their right. Jenny tore round a utility truck and drew a blast from a sluggish bus as she ignored a red light at an empty crossing and hurled past it. The BMW was caught by the sparse oncoming traffic and fell back. 'Is this another Chicago skill of yours?' said the journalist with grudging admiration, his hand shaking as he found the seat-belt clasp.

'Survival. I know what those guys are capable of. We're the ones in the way now. They won't just knock me over and take my bag. They frighten me and I don't like men to do that. Do mine, please,' she said, pulling the belt across her body. 'Where are we going by the way?'

Calculating the closing distance, she used the gears to surge past a high powered saloon and cut in before a refrigerated truck, its horn blaring, its brakes screeching, thundered by, a whirlwind of crossdraught air jolting the old Corolla. Araki's feet lunged for imaginary brakes and his bowels loosened. The road straightened and they could see the chasing car every time it drifted sideways and then back in frustration, unable to overtake the few but slower vehicles between them. He pointed ahead.

'Railway bridges across the river. Could be near Koiwa. It's very built up. If we can stay ahead of them on this open stretch we should reach the train stations near the bridges. There's always a police box near them. Or we can throw ourselves into the crowds. But we don't stand a chance if they catch us down here when we have to stop.'

'We do have a chance,' Jenny growled, urging more power into the car. 'Load the gun.'

Araki's neck twisted as if wrung. His mouth dropped open. Jenny Collier's skin was moist with sweat and the veins in her temples bulged on the surface. 'Load

the gun,' she grunted, 'or hold the steering wheel while
I do.' She had to slow behind another car before
crossing lanes and skimming it violently in second
gear. Ahead of them, in the distance, red brake lights
told them the traffic was backing up where the road
joined the main route fourteen; and there were heavy
vehicles approaching on the other side of the road.
Jenny's eyes were everywhere. In the mirror the BMW
was overtaking a car and closing. Araki reached for
the bag.

49

Katsuro Koga replaced the handset of the secure, unre-
corded line with a restraint he could barely sustain and
then prowled the control centre in the pit of the tiered
dealing room. He had ordered his dealers in prudence
to cover part of the massive short dollar positions he
had been quietly building ahead of the G-Seven meeting
as the rumour gained a momentum of its own in the
foreign exchange and the interest rate money markets.
It had to be Nicholls. That early call from Sternberg
Chance, their purchase of a hundred million dollars
against all the market indicators, should have warned
his dealers that someone was sending Ohyama Bank
a dangerous signal. Minutes later they were picking
up ridiculous stories about falling yen interest rates
and could not afford to ignore them. Koga ordered
his dealers to cover and he estimated the scramble to
buy dollars in the rising market had cost him well over
a million.

He could not have known for sure whether the

unsupported hearsay flying across continents had not been just another rumour. The intentions of the Ministry of Finance might not have reached the executive level in the Bank of Japan where the new rates would be posted. If the central bank had been advised then surely his captive representative there would have called.

Koga sensed that the man was showing signs of nerves. He had asked for a rare, secret meeting, and when they met in a back room of a quiet, back-street broiled eel restaurant near Nippori station he told Koga he had been uneasy since the intervention a week earlier and the tragic death of an Ohyama dealer two days later. He was sure there was no connection, but the Press had picked up the death of a British dealer and related it to the pressures and profits in the foreign exchange markets. The ambitious, flawed man drank domestic whisky until his inhibitions evaporated and he begged to be released from the nightmare his one indiscretion, a year earlier during a fact-finding tour of Europe, had trapped him in.

Koga explained the impossibility of this course, the event had taken place and regrettably could not be erased from the record. As he led him wearily to a taxi with a vague suggestion that Lisa Hamazaki might welcome another, more private rendezvous, Koga tossed a folded, unmarked manila envelop containing two million yen in new ten thousand notes on to the seat beside him. 'Get yourself a new car,' he suggested. 'A deserved bonus for a trusted friend. And don't forget, I need you on Wednesday at dinner with our friend from the Federal Reserve.'

The man from the central bank let his body sag into the seat, his neck muscles loosening. There was no way out of the trap the Ohyama Bank had drawn him into. A confession would be appreciated and expected but it would mean the absolute end of his career and most likely imprisonment, and that was not worth the pleasure he had contemplated at seeing Katsuro Koga in the hands of the prosecutors. He fingered the envelope, remembering his attempt to call Koga's bluff, or whoever it was who telephoned to say they should meet to discuss a delicate matter. He had dismissed as ludicrous the notion that he had been filmed at the country house in England with the pleasant and cultured women who had appeared at the dinner table. But he had been drunk and his recollection of the happenings after the last glass of wine, or was it brandy, had been poured, was limited. Then the tape arrived at the Bank of Japan, suitably transferred to a Japanese frequency. Security had let it through, thankfully, and in the privacy of his home he had watched himself act as the dead meat for his own entrapment and humiliation.

The insulting, deliberately provocative deal from Sternberg Chance at the opening of the foreign exchange market that morning told Koga that Nicholls clearly knew what was going on and the call in the afternoon from Fujimori confirmed that Nicholls had denounced the relationship between the two banks and proposed to make serious and potentially very damaging allegations to his bank's auditors.

Koga packed a briefcase, a visit to make before the dinner with other directors and Sternberg Chance visitors from London. Nicholls's return to London and his departure from Sternberg Chance would not leave his operation secure. He knew the Englishman too well.

His car, driven by the same taciturn broad-shouldered chauffeur who five days earlier had carried the head of Ohyama's treasury and two of his dealers on a journey from which one of them did not return, stopped three blocks short of their goal near Nakano Station. He walked through the covered arcades of shops and restaurants into the area north of the station and stopped opposite a glass-fronted building in a section of older weathered ferro-concrete structures. Local residents had held a week of chanting protests and petitions when the Takagi Economic Research Group had taken the two uppermost floors in the new building but their anger dissipated as generous sweeteners filtered through the citizens' movements and the local bureaucrats.

He was thankful for the fading light and misty rain as he crossed the road, hunching his head into his coat collar, and entered the Tokyo office of the *yakuza*. There he was led by a Korean he knew as Tai Il Kim to a penthouse on the sixth floor and into a bare *tatami* room which opened on to a balcony with a view to the skyscrapers of Shinjuku. Takagi sat on the interwoven reed matting, wearing a *yukata* wrap, and watching a television screen half the size of the wall it was fixed to. He motioned Koga to join him and poured sake from a warmed, ceramic bottle. 'Only the two main bouts remain,' he explained, and complained. 'We really do need another *yokozuna* ranked wrestler.'

'Sumo,' Koga said with an apology. He had little interest in the national sport and had forgotten that when he did not attend the Kokugikan hall personally the *oyabun* Takagi created his own atmosphere for two hours a day during the six fifteen-day tournaments until the senior bouts ended at six in the evening. Koga squatted with the straight-backed *yakuza* leader who talked while the giant wrestlers eye-balled each other and tossed salt in the cleansing ritual and then watched mesmerized as they went at each other with desperately controlled ferocity. Through the opaque *shoji* screen which divided the long recreation room, Koga could see the silhouette of the bodyguard. When the final envelope of prize money from satisfied supporters' clubs had been handed to the last victor, who sat breathless on his haunches, Takagi blanked the screen.

'You've come about the Englishman,' the tall man said, rising to his feet and burying his hands in the sleeves of his kimono. 'I hope he can be persuaded to return to whichever country your friends at *Starnbarg Chansu* decide to send him,' he continued, with derogatory disregard for the proper pronunciation.

Koga lit a cigarette and joined the *oyabun* at the opened panelled glass door shielding them from the balcony.

'He's leaving for London on Thursday and then he'll be gradually eased out of the bank.'

'Good. Very good. That helps you.'

Koga cocked his head. 'Not necessarily,' he said. 'He moved the market against me this morning. He made me quote and dealt against the market forecasts and the charts because he'd started a rumour he knew would hurt me.'

'Disgraceful,' Takagi said with hardly a change of expression.

'He told people in Sternberg that he knows about the put-through dealing they've been doing with Ohyama and he hinted at the special information I have access to.'

Takagi turned abruptly. 'But it won't matter once he's gone, will it?'

'I'm afraid it will. He's going to report it to the bank's auditors.'

'Does he know about Moore?'

Koga drew deeply on his cigarette. 'He believes he's alive.'

Takagi resumed his seat on a cushion by the lacquered tray of drinks and refilled the sake cups. He spoke slowly, his icy, narrow eyes alive with fury. 'On Saturday that journalist Araki took photographs of our meeting at Michiko san's house. The film was missing from the camera he hit my boy with. He may have photographed us. He's probably got you talking to me and Michiko san with Shimizu. We might all be in the next edition of whatever weekly scandal rag he works for. He spent the complete weekend with Nicholls and that American woman. They are not stupid people and you didn't discover what Hirata was doing before he was able to send the tape, and probably a lot of documents as well, to Collier. No doubt these have been taken apart by Araki with the help of his English friend. There was nothing in the house when we burned it down on Saturday. They were out there somewhere listening to you talking to a hundred million dollars worth of future income in the Bank of Japan.' He slapped a fist into a palm and his voice was loud enough to bring Tai Il Kim through a gap in the *shoji* door. He raised a placatory hand. 'Araki knows everything,' he hissed. 'And so does your British dealer.'

Koga's conscience had never been moved sympathetically by the mental and physical suffering of the people who worked for him. He was, after all, Japanese and compassion had its limits. The ultimate penalty of death had not been among the sanctions he had considered until Hiroyuki Hirata had risen in his misguided, vindictive innocence to threaten the strategy he had been planning for five years. His stupid spite could have undermined a grand scheme which the arrival in his life of Michiko Momoyama with her vision and organization, and her web of contacts like Osamu Takagi, was helping to bring to reality.

After all, Japan was changing, he rationalized, and so was he. He had repaid the Ohyama Bank for its twenty-five years of job security with years of high earnings from his treasury. He could stay another five, ten years and pick up another three hundred million yen. He would need them. He had invested his years of high personal earnings in land, which he had mortgaged to buy securities. The bursting of the economic bubble had reduced the value of his land by half and the ensuing stock market crash in 1989 decimated his portfolio of liquid assets. His cash resources were now negligible; his sons had graduated and had secure jobs in Ohyama group companies; and his wife had moved to Kyoto to be near a Buddhist sect's temple where her only interests were spiritual. What had twenty-five years of sixteen hour days gifted him for the last years of his life?

He was taking stock of his life when he met Michiko Momoyama. When she persuaded the Ohyama Bank to lend her ever greater amounts of money against the security of forged certificates of deposit he determined to know her better. He was beguiled by her beauty and fascinated by her total selfishness and ruthless ambition. It was her interest in his work, and the hundreds of billions of dollars which flowed around the world every day, that joined them in conspiracy. She was quick to see the potential rewards waiting to be taken, they seemed to challenge her, and it was her idea to target the vulnerability of the men who were in positions to influence the factors which shaped the foreign exchange market.

Koga expected to take personally twenty million dollars from his share of the Hong Kong operation over the next two years, which was the lifespan he had estimated for the network of informants in the central banks, and then leave Japan with Michiko Momoyama and devote himself entirely to impact trading from bases in Hong Kong, New York and Sydney.

He had been amazed at how easily senior middle managers surrendered their business honesty and their personal morality, although the Bank of Japan official had needed reminding that as a graduate of the elite Tokyo University his downfall would reflect on everyone, including his father-in-law, a bureau chief in the Ministry of Finance and the connection that ensured him a dream career-path through the ministries. Avoiding his suicide was imperative, and Koga had sweetened the man's mental imprisonment by promising to free him from his obligations after four years. The video tape would not, of course, be released to him. Then the fool made the unforgivable mistake of calling him on an unsecure line and by one of those stupid quirks of coincidence it was seized on by a malcontent and troublemaker. He was surprised how easily he had agreed to Takagi's offer to carry out the ultimate sanction. Hirata was a nobody: he had nothing to offer and would not be missed.

Now the entire plan, as complex as it was audacious, was threatened by a trash magazine journalist and two stubborn, unco-operative *gaijin*. It could not be permitted, so he was again with the *yakuza* head he had only wanted as a source of funds for the Hong Kong operation.

Osamu Takagi drew himself to his feet and lifted a *kimono* sleeve back over his watch. 'Violence brings us unwanted attention. It must be avoided by all means, but when it becomes necessary it must be quick and absolute. That tiresome journalist went to the home of

Hirata's widow today. I asked my team to give him a severe warning and I expect by this time his enthusiasm will be diminished.'

Koga approached the *yakuza* chief gingerly, his chin level with the other's shoulder. 'The *gaijin* can destroy the operation, either from Tokyo, Hong Kong or London. He must not be allowed to leave Japan alive.'

Takagi's sigh was followed by a grimace. He returned his hands to his sleeves. 'Dead and missing *gaijins* scattered all over Tokyo like rice. I wanted to avoid violence so badly.' He stepped on to the balcony and stared across the city under lights. Then he turned with a grudging nod.

'Right. It will be done. But the threat won't disappear with the Englishman. We have to take some precautions. Get your precious dealing man out of Japan as soon as possible and when we've obtained what you need from the American on Wednesday we'll clean up the location and move the cameras. I will also instruct Imaizumi to disperse the file information away from Tokyo. Araki may have taken Emi chan's photo in the garden, and remember he found her through Imaizumi's records. If the Englishman has watched the last tape from England, and has found the important business part, it's imaginable that Araki has now seen it as well, and one of them may have been able to identify Emi. It's a very serious moment for our operation.'

The *yakuza* leader twisted the ache from his neck and spoke to the banker as he stared wistfully over the rooftops of Tokyo. 'I hope there is no lack of resolve in your team. It will not be tolerated.'

50

The second body had to be cut from the car after the fire had been doused. The fierce heat had welded it to what remained of the steering column and it was a charred black form, its limbs still grotesquely frozen in time when the firemen had prised it away and set it behind a police cordon near the burnt out wreck. The other occupant, a man, was extremely lucky to be thrown clear from the front passenger seat on impact with the ground and was taken to hospital suffering from unspecified external injuries and minor burns from the fuel which erupted from the car in a fine, dazzling spray. The driver of the high-fronted concrete transporter was tossed around his cab but apart from bruises and a mild concussion his main problem was severe shock.

There were witnesses in a stream of vehicles the car had overtaken earlier at frightening speeds and they were horrified at the recklessness. A driver said he braked hard, barely able to keep control of his Nissan as it slewed all over the road when the offending car raced to overtake him. It misjudged the speed of the oncoming truck and hit its huge fender as it tried to veer with desperate hopelessness at the last moment. The impact tore away the driver's side of the car and propelled the stricken vehicle across the road where it turned on end against the crash barrier and fell down the steep, four-metre grassy embankment on to the open land which bordered the Edogawa River.

A witness on a cycle said there was a moment of silence as the car settled in a cloud of dust before exploding. A jogger came forward to say that he thought there were two cars having a race of some kind but could not remember the colour or make of the other vehicle. Joyriding, a police spokesman told the reporters later, was not unknown on this relatively quiet and open stretch of road.

51

Billy Soh's face was flushed to a bright crimson. When Nicholls arrived, he was in the centre of a group which dominated the bar inside the entrance to Mama Gimbasha's, with the Telerate screen flashing the London afternoon foreign exchange prices busily above it. Billy bought the first drink for his well-wishers but the brokers as usual had left their credit cards behind the bar in the interests of business promotion among the mixed group of Japanese and foreign dealers.

'All the best Billy,' Nicholls said, raising his beer glass.

'You too,' the American's voice rose above the noise and then his face disappeared into the pack.

Nicholls looked at his watch anxiously and then walked through the long bar, where Emi Mori had found him drinking off his losses, to the expansive room of tables, still mostly unoccupied. They were not there. Araki had got through to him at the bank around three on a line barely audible through a background of traffic noise and said he and Jenny would be at Mama G's around six, six thirty. It was now almost seven thirty. Hugh Carter approached from the toilets, still hitching his reluctant trousers over his full girth, and gave Nicholls a solid slap on the shoulders.

'I hear you're leaving this week,' he said.

'Word travels fast. You're right. Back to London.'

'London? I thought you came from Hong Kong.'

They moved to let a Japanese woman with high, shiny cheekbones in a tight red lycra dress slither by. Nicholls fobbed him off with an explanation of changing strategies in his bank and the need to redefine priorities and this process included his redeployment. Hugh Carter's mouth was squeezed in his flabby skin and his lips seemed to erupt when he spoke. 'I hear you pissed a few people off,' he chuckled.

'Did Billy tell you that?'

'You know what the market's like in the Orient. No secrecy at all.'

Nicholls ordered beers in the relative privacy of the long bar while Carter hauled himself on to a stool. 'What does the market tell you about Katsuro Koga, the Ohyama Bank treasurer?' he asked.

'We all know who he is,' Carter said, dragging a bare arm across his mouth. 'Tough bank to deal with. Koga brings in a fortune for his bank, and presumably for himself, but he doesn't make friends doing it.'

'Does it matter?' Nicholls threw out.

'You know as well as I do Kevin, you can't keep taking from your market counterparties without giving something back. When things got tough for the Jap banks last year, when the shares they valued as capital crapped out, and some of them got dragged close to the edge, the friendly ones got the same support as ever from the foreign banks but one or two like Ohyama found out they had few friends.'

'We cut back our trading limits,' Nicholls said unconvincingly. Carter grinned. 'Somebody forgot to tell Tony. He'd quote for anything. Foreign exchange, options, interest rate swaps, cash loans.'

Nicholls gave a nod of silent resignation before speaking. 'I assumed the brokers knew what was going on.'

'Not very difficult,' Carter said. 'As you know, everything goes through us eventually.'

'I've stopped trading with Ohyama,' Nicholls said blandly.

Again, the overweight broker's face stretched into a grin. He ran the podgy fingers of a hand under Nicholls's lapel. 'And in doing so you've fucked yourself,' he said, dropping off the stool.

Nicholls made to return to the front bar.

'Interesting about Anton Landau,' the broker remarked, following him.

Nicholls turned. 'What's that?' he said, his interest aroused.

'I hear he's left the First Consol Fund and he's heading east.'

'Where did you hear that?'

'A broker in New York heard it from one of the banks Landau uses.' Carter paused to finish the foamy beer in one drag. 'He was a close friend of Tony's, wasn't he?'

'Very close. They'd known each other since school in Canada.'

Canada again, Nicholls remembered. Anton Landau was a passionate Québecois and a lone-wolf dealer whose brand of icy calm, technical skill and uncanny foresight was recognized early by the proprietary trading arm of a California bank. He became one of a dozen noted and feared market movers in the 1980s. Already a millionaire, he followed others likewise gifted who knew intuitively how markets behaved and wanted to participate as an individual and not a corporate pawn. He resigned and set up the First Consul Fund –

with two friends, operating from a detached house in New Jersey. Insurance companies with their pension funds, and legal vehicles several tiers removed from their ultimate owners, let Landau manage their money in the volatile but lucrative foreign exchange markets. He geared it up on a margin basis with contracted banks and moved it in and out of different currencies, averaging a quiet twenty-five per cent annual return in the five years of the operation.

Nicholls said, 'What makes you think he's coming east?'

'There's a lot of Cayman, Nassau, Curaçao money sloshing around. Anton wanted to manage this money more than the institutional on-shore funds but he thought the authorities were starting to get interested in his clients.'

'He can't operate freely from Japan,' Nicholls said. 'But Hong Kong's wide open for a few more years.'

'It looks like it,' Carter concluded as they returned to Soh's farewell party.

It was almost eight thirty. Mama Gimbasha's was filling with a thirsty crowd of mostly *gaijins*. The weekend Japanese groupies had gone but there were enough thinly clad disco Filipinas and eager, hard-drinking Australian money market women to engage the dealers and brokers after their unexpectedly hectic pre-G-Seven Monday. There were at least thirty market people drinking in Billy Soh's farewell party, including several Sternberg Chance dealers, but Jenny Collier and Araki were not among the crowd that swelled to the throb of the deep black rhythms pounding from hidden speakers. He had another beer on the fringes and then heard his name being called. It was Pat Regan, the skeletal forex broker who knew Tony Moore as well as Nicholls. He was pointing to the edge of the bar where a tuxedoed barman waited with a telephone in his hand.

'Call for you Kevin,' Regan called. 'Your position's out of court three big figures and you're down half a million bucks. London wants to know if they should double it up for you.'

Nicholls elbowed through the group who laughed at the joke and gave Regan a playful shove on the shoulder, encouraged by the belief that only Araki and Jenny knew he would be in Mama Gimbasha's that evening. He cupped his free ear against the noise and said optimistically: 'Nicholls'. He did not place the owner of the lightly accented voice immediately and she had to identify herself.

'I want to speak to you soon,' she said. 'I know it is difficult for you to believe me but you must.'

Nicholls wanted to slam the telephone on to its rest but something restrained him. Were his friends trapped in a rat-infested cellar somewhere? Was he needed to complete the set?

'How did you know where to find me?' he asked with deepening suspicion.

'It's not important,' she replied.

Nicholls could barely hear her. 'I have to go,' he said. 'I don't think we have anything to discuss.'

'You have to listen to me,' the voice pleaded. 'You realized what I was doing and you have punished me. Now I know too much and my position is very difficult. Please meet me tonight.'

'Talk to me now,' he demanded. He cupped the telephone against the deafening guffaws and loud drink-fuelled badgering but there was silence on the line, as if she was talking to someone else about his counter proposal. Finally, the tense voice said: 'I have to leave my apartment right now and move to another home. I will be near the main entrance of the Olympic swimming pool in Harajuku in thirty minutes.' There was a definitive click on the line. Nicholls thumbed his temples against his fatigue and irritation then found Billy Soh among his guests. 'Do you remember that blonde woman I was with on Saturday at the Capitol Tokyu?' he shouted.

'Gorgeous,' Soh managed in his alcoholic euphoria.

Nicholls eyeballed him. 'Listen Billy. One last favour. If she comes in here tonight tell her to meet me at my apartment. I have to leave and meet someone now.'

'She won't get out of here alive,' the Korean–American slurred.

52

He had seen the impressive swimming pool in photographs of the 1964 Olympics, standing alone in Tokyo's inner city clean grey drabness. The elegant Tange building, with its drooping, concave roof became a symbol of a Japan in the ascendant but in the stagnant dampness of a late May evening, as he surveyed the poorly lit surroundings from the foot of a pedestrian bridge, it had a kind of ghostly menace.

Tokyo, Eastern Capital, the safe-haven urban paradise, would stay in his memory as a dangerous myth. He knew he had been drawn to this meeting place out of anger and frustration. In two weeks he had been exposed to people he knew were ready to resort to violence to protect a brilliant, multi-billion dollar conspiracy to blackmail their way into the heart of the world's vast body of free-flowing money. He was sucked in irresistibly and still unable, in spite of Araki's persistence, to convince the prosecutors that the conspirators and their victims came from the highest, most sensitive levels of their businesses and the lowest strata of their underworld: there was no hard evidence, they protested.

Now his own life, and those of his two friends, was definitely on the line, and if he was walking into a trap in agreeing to meet the woman he knew to be working for Katsuro Koga he was doing it with his eyes open.

He felt strangely unafraid; all of his forebodings, his awful, growing anxieties now strangely gravitating towards Jenny Collier and Araki, who should have made contact by the time he left the bar. He crossed a broad gravel yard and climbed to a walkway which overlooked a covered outdoor pool. With only a couple clinging together under an umbrella in sight, Nicholls felt the unusual sensation of being alone in Tokyo. On one side he saw darkness which he assumed was Yoyogi Park, otherwise it was buildings all around and the moving threads of light from the Yamanote loop line railway. There was a broad, concrete balcony in front of the pool's main entrance, accessed to ground level at either end by a stairway. He drew his damp jacket around him, shook the rain from his hair and withdrew to a corner beneath a roof overlap by a row of vending machines. A security guard on a long patrol smiled weakly towards him before being enveloped in the gloom.

She must have been watching him from one of a dozen dark corners because she suddenly appeared beside him, her crimped hair tucked under the raised collar of a light, black raincoat, her hands hidden inside the pockets. The lenses of her glasses were beaded with mist.

'Thank you for coming here,' Naomi Honda said, her face free of make-up and dreadfully pale.

'Are you alone?' he asked. She nodded, but her head then turned instinctively and she seemed grateful to see the broad balcony, deserted but for a pair of teenagers in a far corner, oblivious to the wetness.

'Come with me,' she said, taking his arm. 'Please pretend we're friends.' Her head barely reached his shoulders but she was half dragging him towards the steps which swept down two flights to the parking lots and thinly planted gardens. At the foot of the stairway, she drew him into a recess beneath the steps. In front, a meshed fence across a narrow access path separated them from the car park.

'How did you know where to find me?' Nicholls wanted to know.

She released her damp hair and shook it loose. 'I heard Billy Soh was having a party in Roppongi at the usual place. I guessed you would join him to say goodbye. I knew you liked him as soon as you arrived in the Tokyo dealing room.'

Nicholls scoffed. 'After your friends at the Ohyama Bank screwed me last week he seemed to be the only one it bothered. But let's not waste time. If this is a trap and you've got a pair of them *ya-kooza* waiting behind a tree over there you'd better think it over carefully before you get yourself into this mess any deeper.' The clichéd words were emerging as he had heard them in a hundred forgotten films since he was a child and felt oddly distanced even as he spoke them. His instinct to survive was concentrated on the behaviour of the woman who he knew was capable of leading her supposed boyfriend into a death trap and had easily lured Nicholls himself to this dark, secluded little spot with nothing more than a plea. He continued, even as her head retreated into the folds of her coat and her lips parted to speak.

'I know from the holiday records you were away from the bank for two weeks at the same time as Sam Collier was supposed to be missing and then you appeared with him at the Capitol Tokyu Hotel and made sure he got drunk enough to get shoved senseless down those steps. That photograph of you with Collier and Hirata wasn't just a casual souvenir picture. Hirata's widow told Collier's sister today how close you two were, at least for the purposes of your plan.'

He jabbed the woman's lapel. 'I'm going to find Tony Moore and you're both going to prison for your part in Collier's murder.'

Naomi Honda looked up, the familiar confident veneer now pierced with fear, which Nicholls took for the effects of his bitter outburst. She retreated until almost hidden by the darkness. 'You were very clever, Nicholls san, to discover what we were doing in Sternberg Chance,' she said, almost with admiration. 'You guessed right that I was trying to remove information showing how close we were to the Ohyama Bank when you made me run out of the office and leave my glasses accidently. But I had to call you tonight. I want to help you.'

Nicholls tossed his head back and scoffed loudly. 'I suggest you ask Mr Koga to give you something to do to use up your limited time at liberty.'

Naomi Honda looked up at him anxiously. 'You don't understand Katsuro Koga. When you dismissed me you cut out the dealing link with the Ohyama Bank and I will be blamed for it.'

'You're one of the gang,' Nicholls said. 'Koga will give you a job. Surely.'

'People don't *leave* Koga san,' Honda insisted, shaking her head. 'You don't know Koga san and the people he knows.'

Images of Jenny Collier's bruised face and Araki's swollen jaw and the smouldering ruin of his house flashed across Nicholls's eyes. 'I think I do,' he said.

A clash of metal somewhere along the fence jolted the frightened woman and she gripped his jacket, not noticing his own spasm of fear. Then there was silence again, apart from the distant rumble of the loop train and a steady drip of rain water from a ledge into their sanctuary. She continued: 'I'm of no use to them anymore. I am blamed for being careless.' There was a catch in her voice. 'I know many things and they will not trust me to keep them secret. Do you understand me?'

Of course he did, but he could find no great depth of sympathy. Then slowly he began to realize that she really was asking for his help, that it was not a trap. For an instant he found the situation funny. He wondered if she was in as much danger as he was.

'I understand you,' he said. 'What are you proposing?'

'If I give this information to you, if I tell you everything I know about what Koga san has been doing, will you help me to stay away from prison and go to a safe place?'

'Why don't you go straight to the police?'

'In Japan, there must be a go-between in such relationships and you are the only person who understands what has happened. You're the only one who can explain how valuable my information is. I need you to speak on my behalf.'

Nicholls moved apart, as if about to leave. Then he said: 'If I helped you avoid a murder charge, Sam

Collier's sister would get one after she killed me. Sorry Naomi, you're on your own and up to your neck in this one.' She looked pitiful, but at the same time he saw in the streaked face and frightened voice that same burning confidence and resilience that had made her a tough dealer in a man's profession in Japan. 'How did you get involved with a rat like Koga?' he needed to ask.

'Is it important?'

'You might have to explain it to the police.'

Naomi Honda rested submissively against a concrete column. 'It was during the months I was sent to the Ohyama Bank for training. There were no women dealers there at all and I was treated very well by the Ohyama staff. At first I was a toy for them and they took me drinking almost every night. But Koga san realized I was better at the work than most of his own dealers and I thought he was going to offer me a job with Ohyama. I was a little disappointed when he didn't. I supposed he didn't want to upset the close relationship Ohyama had with Sternberg Chance.'

'But he recruited you in a different way and you became his plant in Sternberg,' Nicholls finished the explanation. 'A few fat envelopes of ten thousand yen notes gave you the incentive.' She did not have time to deny it before he continued. 'Did you know about Tony Moore's connections with Koga at that stage?'

She shook her head. 'Not until they trusted me and used me in their plans.'

'Which included seducing Sam Collier and setting him up for his death?'

'I didn't know they planned to kill him,' she pleaded. 'I left him outside the hotel because he was completely drunk and the men I was told to introduce him to said they would take him home.'

'I don't believe you,' he declared, his voice dry with anger. 'Jenny won't either. Or the police.'

A car door thumped shut in the darkness. He thought the parking lot had been empty when they descended the stairs.

'I've got to go,' he said, thinking of Jenny Collier.

'I can help you obtain all the information you need,' she offered, following him into the exposed night.

Nicholls was tempted for an instant. 'No deal. Good luck Naomi. You're going to need it.'

They were an arm's length apart and he was moving away when she said, 'Don't you want to know the names of the people in the central banks who give Koga san the inside information?'

His feet crunched on the loose gravel when he turned his dark features towards her again. He approached her, a forefinger extending from a tightly clenched fist. 'I want to see you, Koga, Fujimori, those bloody gangsters, Moore and any other Sternberg people involved in the deaths of Collier and Hirata, locked up for a long time,' he said grimacing. Naomi Honda thought he would hit her and retreated, but she persisted with an argument which was holding him.

'You won't be able to implicate Koga san in anything. Not in Japan. We have political and financial scandals all the time. They're soon forgotten. We seek and pay for favours at all levels and part of the obligation of everyone is to cover for each other. Someone low in the chain, like me, will suffer but the top people won't. *Gaijin* don't understand that this is the way of life in Japan. And you are stupid if you think that Sternberg's favoured dealing with the Ohyama group was important. Yes, it was profitable for us all but it is nothing compared with what Koga san is planning with Tony Moore and other organizations.'

Nicholls bridled at being called stupid by the woman he had fired and even more at the realization that she was right. He now knew from experience that the Japanese police would be passive until the evidence was overwhelming. The only way to break Koga would be to identify the corrupted official in the Bank of Japan, and in the other central banks of the world's principal financial powers, he was sure had been lured into supplying Koga with timely information by a trained sex squad. He knew he could use international exposure to break the brilliant scheme at its core. He took her arm and squeezed it until she had to draw breath deeply and he had to apologize for the outburst of violence that surprised him.

'Koga wouldn't confide that information on his insider contacts to you,' he said dismissively.

'He didn't,' she confessed, 'but I know where it is.'

'Tell me.'

'I must have your help. I'm sorry for what I've done but if you won't give it to me I will disappear, perhaps to a foreign country.'

A torch flared and she flinched, turning her head away. Nicholls raised an elbow across his face. There was a click, and when the light died they saw the embarrassed face of a young policeman. He spoke to Naomi Honda and when they had finished she said in English, 'He is sorry for disturbing us but the area is regularly patrolled and he has to check everyone in it.'

They walked towards Shibuya. A desperate need to know the names of the money market cheats swelled inside him, almost overcoming the common sense course he knew he should take.

'I don't know what I can offer you, if anything,' he said honestly. 'I have to talk it over with these friends

389

of mine. You know who they are,' he said. 'Where can I contact you tonight or tomorrow?'

'I'll call you,' the frightened woman said and accepted a business card with Nicholls's home telephone number on it. 'Think it over very quickly and carefully. There's not much time left.' Her lips parted and her voice softened. 'Please,' she said quietly, before the automatic taxi door enclosed her.

Not much time, Nicholls repeated as he sought his own transport. Why? What's happening this week to bring things to a conclusion? The only big event was G-Seven. Nicholls's mind raced.

53

Not long in Tokyo, the young driver from Akita criss-crossed the unnamed streets murmuring apologies until Nicholls recognized a television studio three blocks from his apartment. A silhouette moved behind the net curtain on the third floor as he left the taxi and he hesitated before turning the key of the outer door. The meeting with a nervous Naomi Honda, and the relief that she was not the bait in the trap, had left him eager to turn her fear to his use and take the ultimate evidence from her. But Araki had called him earlier from a telephone near a noisy road and the intensity of his high pitched voice gave his warning message about Naomi Honda an added edge of terror. And now he and Jenny were hours overdue and someone was in his flat.

He withdrew the key and scanned the windows again. Seeing nothing in the dim light he opted to look for a telephone and call ahead. No response would tell him an unfriendly reception awaited him. He walked to the side of the building and stopped abruptly. A smile formed easily and quickly turned into a loud whoop. An old, unmistakable Toyota stood flush with the wall between an electricity pole and a heap of black bags of rubbish.

Jenny Collier almost knocked him backwards and Araki was only a touch less enthusiastic at seeing him. They held shoulders and stomped a silly jig of relief in the lounge.

'Where were you?' Nicholls said when the euphoria abated.

They spoke in turn, describing the sadness of Hirata's widow and the awful truth that emerged that Naomi Honda had been with Sam Collier in the weeks before his death. Nicholls said he had confirmed this from the holiday roster but he left the story of his meeting with Honda until later. Then Jenny recounted how a white BMW got too close for her comfort and she scooped Araki on the run. Araki, who was wearing what were clearly Sam Collier's tucked-up trousers and sweater, embellished the story with a mixture of admiration and delayed relief at their escape from an unknown but eminently predictable fate. At best a warning, probably more. He forgot to mention that for the last minute of the hairy ride his driver carried a loaded semi-automatic pistol easy to hand between her legs. A curve prevented them from seeing the pursuing car hit the cement carrier and when it failed to appear in the Toyota's mirror again they stopped and ran back to see it on its roof in flames with one of the passengers still inside.

'The other one got out,' Araki said.

'Strange, wasn't it?' she said to Araki. 'His face was

already pretty heavily bandaged when he came out of the car.'

Nicholls raised an eyebrow. 'The guy from Momoyama's place who you clouted with your camera.'

'Right. I guess he's just not lucky.' Araki chuckled, and then turned serious. 'I was trying to tell you on the phone,' he said, helping himself to a generous measure from the last bottle of Tony Moore's whisky. 'The muscle in Koga's operation definitely comes from organized *yakuza* and a particularly vicious bunch. I showed the photograph of Koga and the other guy from Momoyama's garden to my friend in Kanda whose weekly's got the best database on the underworld. The man with Koga is Osamu Takagi. He inherited the gang from his father when it was a small local gang with traditional interests on loan sharking, extortion and prostitution. Takagi the younger had the foresight and intelligence to maintain his independence from the big three syndicates and move into white-collar crime. He operates under something called the Takagi Economic Research Group but he's got a strong-arm division in case he needs to use the traditional skills of the business.'

'You talk about these *yakuza* gangs as if they're in a league table of big companies,' Jenny said with a puzzled look.

'They almost are,' Araki said. 'They have a sort of establishment respectability. I told you the other night in Shinjuku that there are about four thousand gangs but about half their hundred thousand troops belong to the top three syndicates and these operate nationwide. I can see what Takagi's doing. He's been linked to stock pumping and shareholder intimidation. He'd take a big stake in a small company, hype it with the help of legitimate securities firms and then demand the board buy their shares back. Or he buys one share in a company and then demands money to keep order at the annual shareholders' meeting. But I suspect he's probably the first *yakuza* to look at your business Kevin, probably because it was too complex until he had the luck to find an equally clever crook like Koga working inside it. Momoyama was the common factor, of course. She introduced them.'

'And he would order his men to kill,' Jenny said, incredulously. It was not a question. She had the fading bruises to prove their violence and still felt the tension in her body from the afternoon's encounter with the *yakuza*. Her second.

'There's another reason we were late getting to your bar in Roppongi,' Araki remarked. 'I had to see the editor at my magazine and persuade him to print the new story. It's the only way we have to get the worms to the surface for the birds to eat.'

'Will he do it?' Nicholls asked.

Araki said, 'I'll write it tonight and get it to Hirosawa by lunch. He's the editor of *One Point Finance* and they published my article about Tony Moore last week. "Dead Dealer Alive" will be the headline. Think about that for a retraction.'

They all smiled, and Jenny patted his knee. In the five days she had known Araki she had seen him snooze but never sleep. She wondered what drove him, apart from cigarettes and whisky.

Nicholls stood up and wandered to the window. 'What's bothering you, Kevin?' she said, joining him and running her fingers along his arm. He turned to Araki. 'We three here know you're right. But it's only speculation to the police and anyone reading about it. Jenny's brother might have been the body cremated in place of Tony Moore who might be alive. That *geisha* woman Momoyama might now be plotting with a director of the Ohyama Bank and an underworld mob to manipulate the foreign exchange markets. They might have a worldwide network of contacts supplying timely insider information which lets them make a fortune just ahead of the market participants. All speculation. Hard to prove.'

Araki rubbed his thinning hairline and snubbed out his cigarette in submission. He said, 'The Japanese language is ninety per cent abstraction, meaningless expressions of respect, courtesy and dismissal. The tenses fade into vagaries and everyone nods as if they comprehend. I can hide our accusations among this kind of rubbish.'

Nicholls interrupted him. 'But we can't put anyone in prison until the police are convinced there's hard evidence. And we don't have any. We need Tony Moore and the names of the people Koga's blackmailing. Otherwise your story will fade and your system here in Japan will cover the whole thing up as if it never happened,' he said, recalling Naomi Honda's forecast.

'You know a lot about Japan all of a sudden,' Araki scoffed pleasantly and refilled his glass. 'What can we do about Moore? He's hidden in Momoyama's pleasure house and we can't get to him.'

'Maybe not here,' Nicholls agreed, 'but I know how he's going to get out of Japan. Or how he got out if he's gone.'

He retrieved Tony Moore's blackthorn walking stick which he had left propped against the drinks trolley and bounced it on the carpet, spinning on his heels in a triumphant twist and waving the piece of wood towards his companions. 'Canada came up in

394

a couple of conversations this weekend,' he said, 'and it reminded me that Tony was brought up there. I should have remembered. He had a Canadian passport. He didn't use it much, only when he went to Canada or somewhere where he thought it was easier to get in and out of a country. That's how he got out of the States after his drunk driving arrest. He wouldn't have been able to get away with his British passport but he crossed the border with his Canadian identity. Easy. I expect he left Japan for a quick trip recently, using his British passport and holding the required re-entry permit, but came back showing his Canadian passport and was given a short-stay visa, which was enough for his purpose. He got the usual immigration forms stuck into it and he can leave the country whenever he wants. He left the British passport to be found by me.'

'Do you think he's left the country already?' Jenny asked.

Nicholls frowned. 'I don't know. It depends how well the project he's planning with Koga and Fujimori and these *yakuza* characters is going. I heard tonight an old friend of Tony's is heading for Hong Kong to set up some kind of dealing operation. Might be Tony's bag too. A few people, hidden away, taking foreign exchange positions with laundered and legitimate money. Sounds plausible. Maybe that's why my boss is not letting me go back to Hong Kong. In case I come across Moore.'

'Very interesting,' the Japanese said. He fixed Nicholls with his shadowed, tired eyes. 'That could explain Tony Moore's escape route,' he said. 'What about the central bank insiders?'

Nicholls held a short pause. 'Naomi Honda wants us to help her.'

Jenny Collier stiffened.

'I fired her today,' he told his companions. 'But she called me at Mama Gimbasha's while I was waiting for you. She asked me to meet her straight away.'

'Just like that,' Jenny said, welling with anger, which she directed at Nicholls. 'Is that where you were tonight? With her?'

'That's right, Jenny. Just listen to me, please.' She was pacing between the two men. Araki remembered her fearless aggressiveness in the afternoon and retired to the folds of the couch, leaving Nicholls in her firing line.

'After what you told us just now about the coincidence of the vacation,' she was saying. 'She's a murderess, and you actually went to see her.'

'Hold on a second, Jenny,' Nicholls said, raising his palms outwards. But she would not be stopped. Heaving with rage, she said, 'You obeyed her call and off you went. I suppose she confessed about her role in Sam's murder.'

'Yes she did, as a matter of fact.'

'What?'

Araki stepped in. He detested the foreigners' appetite for conflict, for point-scoring followed by brooding silences. He said to Nicholls. 'It might have been dangerous for you. She could have been leading you into a trap. Don't forget that her people see you as a major threat to the little goldmine they've got going.'

Nicholls welcomed the change in the temperature and a chance to explain. 'I thought so myself but it seemed to me that if she genuinely wanted to open up to us she'd be the first crack in their camp, and if we're going to get this mob we need some hard evidence.'

'I don't understand why she's worried about us,' Araki responded. 'It'd be impossible for the police to make a case against her for luring Jenny's brother, especially when they still believe he's only missing. And she's not personally committed a crime against your bank, Kevin.'

Jenny let Nicholls steer her to an armchair and then sit on the edge of the couch, his eyes flaring with intensity. 'That's the whole point,' he said. 'She's not scared of being arrested. She's scared of what Koga will do to her because out of my dealing room she's no use to him. She's let them all down and now she's a threat. She might decide the police are getting too close and run to talk to them or us. It won't comfort you Jenny, but Naomi Honda claims she did not know what was planned for your brother.'

Jenny had calmed herself and was now fascinated by the options facing her antagonist. She summarized. 'So she's willing to risk imprisonment, or whatever, by coming to us and so avoid getting whacked by her former friends. But why come to us? Why not go straight to the police?'

'Because we, especially Kevin, know what questions to ask her.' Araki answered. 'What information to extract which will put Koga and the *yakuza* away. And we can determine the value of that information and be her go-between with the police, help her to plead with the prosecutors. We don't have trial by jury in Japan exactly like the legal systems in your countries. The police here like to arrest the guilty party at the first attempt. Then they pressure hard, a shade too hard for Western people to tolerate, for a confession. If the confession is signed quickly and the criminal expresses sincere regret and contrition he or she will have rehabilitation training in the prison system. Even *yakuza*. Naomi Honda knows where she has a better chance of survival. She might even escape without a sentence if the prosecutor believes she did not know what would happen to Jenny's brother even though she was with him on the night he died.'

'Can we bring her in?' Jenny asked. 'Like a spy.'

Araki said, 'We have to try. If we have the names of those characters in the central banks we can get Koga, Fujimori and the others.'

'We ought to do it quickly,' Nicholls observed.

'She should be safe for the moment,' Araki thought. 'They might not find out she's left your bank for a few days.'

'They will,' Nicholls said with concern. 'Fujimori will tell them. He was in my office this afternoon and I told him what I'd done about her and the Ohyama connection.' The others were not impressed by his timing but they nodded sympathetically. He continued. 'She also intimated that time's getting close for the next big move to happen but she didn't say what it was. Probably doesn't know.'

'That makes sense.' It was Araki, slumping in the soft fabric of the couch with his cigarette. 'It's the big week for you and your foreign exchange people, with the G-Seven conference. We saw some of the delegates arriving on the news while we waited for you.'

Nicholls did not respond: he held his chin pensively.

'Anyway,' Araki said, 'how can we contact Naomi Honda?'

'She'll call me when she can, probably tomorrow,' Nicholls said, looking up.

'OK. Let me work out how we can meet her safely,' the Japanese said, at which point they realized it was close to midnight and the tension and fear had suppressed their appetites until now.

Nicholls put the fries in the lower section of the oven and slid a tray of fillet steaks under the grill. Jenny was

398

making a dressing for the salad when she turned and called over at his back.

'Forty fifty,' she said loudly.

'Yours!' Nicholls said, turning instinctively, and then grinning. He moved across and held her from behind while she mixed the salad.

'What does it mean?' she smiled.

'Where did you hear it? That's my business talk.'

'I know. You said it last night in your sleep. Twice. Different numbers, I think. Know something else?' she said, filling his face with the fragrance of her hair.

'What?'

'You've been back over an hour and you haven't once looked at that goddamn screen in the bedroom.' She felt the moisture of his shoulder kiss through her blouse and then sensed the movement of his hand at his side. It appeared in front of her, clutching the miniaturized version of the Reuters screen she had seen when she met him for the first time in the Press Club. She shook her head with mock irritation and laughed. Then she turned without separating from his body and faced him.

'Sorry I lost it back there,' she murmured.

'I would've been surprised if you hadn't,' Nicholls said, kissing her forehead.

The smell of grilling meat drew Araki to the kitchen. 'That reminds me,' he said to Nicholls. 'Did you find out where the crematorium is?'

54

Nicholls laid the telephone on its rest, rocked on the pivot of his chair and chewed a finger pensively. Naomi Honda called at eight thirty, waking Araki who had just telephoned to let him know. The journalist had been writing until four in the morning when he fell asleep, slumped on Nicholls's couch and unaware of the Englishman's departure at seven. Jenny Collier had sat on a stool by Araki when he spoke to Naomi Honda, nudging him impatiently, hoping for a scrap of detail as the conversation in Japanese stretched.

'She's very frightened,' Araki said sideways at one point. When he put the telephone down his face twitched with tension. 'She's been ordered to meet Koga at one o'clock tomorrow.'

'Isn't that good for her?' Jenny suggested. 'A job offer with Ohyama maybe.'

'It might be,' he said. 'But he's sending a car to pick her up.'

'Jesus!'

'I've told her what we want before we can help her and she's only got a day to think of a way to get it,' he said, bundling on his jacket. 'She's going to call here at twelve and I'll be back by then.'

'Where are you going?'

'To solve the riddle of the ring.'

What Araki had told him was really going to stir things up, Nicholls thought as Yamamoto came in to see him, bringing news of a crashing Hong Kong stock market as Beijing rejected another British request for talks on post-handover democracy. It reminded him to make a call.

'Piss-poor market, Kevin san.'. The thick, Swiss–German voice of Morgan Trinkel boomed through the amplifier from Nicholls's old office in Sternberg Chance, Hong Kong. 'There'll be nothing anywhere till the statement from G-Seven on Saturday. Have they all arrived?'

A weekend joint communiqué annoyed the currency dealers but the participating governments preferred to announce major policy changes when the world's money markets were closed, to postpone the chaos they often unleashed by their intemperate decisions. 'The Treasury Secretary and the Fed Chairman are due in tomorrow,' Nicholls said. 'The Buba's* already in residence, including the President. I don't know where the rest are. I've been a little tied up.'

'I hear you're not coming back to Hong Kong,' Trinkel said carefully. 'Everything all right?'

'Could be better, Morgan. I'll tell you when I can. Can I ask you a favour?'

'If you want a price in Aussie Singapore in the hundred million Aussie, the answer is no.'

He heard Nicholls's friendly but brief laugh, then the question. 'Do you remember Anton Landau?'

After a short silence Trinkel replied. 'Ya, ya. That smart little crooked Canuck arbitrageur. He's got a foreign exchange fund out of New Jersey or somewhere. Manages some big money, I hear.'

'That's him. I heard through the brokers that he may be coming out east, possibly your way. He was an old mate of Tony Moore when Tony worked in our branch in New York. Could I ask you to keep an eye out for him? If you hear his name in the market please let me know. But don't tell him I'm asking about him.'

* Buba – The Bundesbank, Germany's Central Bank

Nicholls gave him his apartment's number, although the time he had left in office or home was down to three days.

'Oh, Morgan. Can you ask Herman Cheung to call me on a private line, please.'

'No problem Kev. Keep me in touch with the G-Seven buzz. *Ciao*.'

'See you Morgan. Say hello to Maria and the boys for me.'

Nicholls sipped the bitter, thick coffee, wondering whether he could trust Morgan Trinkel. He personally faxed eight pages of hand-written Japanese script to the magazine Araki hoped would publish it, subject to receipt of as yet unwritten finale, then patrolled the quiet desks, where the atmosphere was heavy. The dealers' faces met him with empty smiles, the older ones reading in the dead market and making no effort to pretend otherwise when Nicholls greeted them.

Christ! I'm the villain, he thought as he slipped on his jacket and made for the lifts through the rows of desks and computer terminals.

A cute receptionist with an iridescent mother-of-pearl complexion tried to delay his passage to the executive suite but he pushed through the panelled doors into the corridor with a dismissive wave of a wrist. No sign of Warron Hanlon or Gervase Prideaux, but the senior adviser's door was open and Masaaki Fujimori's back was turned away from his desk as he spoke on the telephone. The Japanese was not aware of his visitor's entrance and when he turned his expression betrayed only a split second flash of surprise before it broke into a desultory smile which faded quickly.

'Hi Masa,' Nicholls said in an amiably contemptuous way.

Fujimori stood and reached beneath his desk. The

402

movement tensed Nicholls and he restrained a compelling wish to reach across and seize by the throat the man who had identified Sam Collier's body as Tony Moore's and completed the perfect cover-up by signing the papers which satisfied the Japanese and British authorities. The Japanese's hand emerged with a cigarette which he lit ostentatiously. 'I suppose this is goodbye,' he said.

'I guess it is,' Nicholls said with an ironic shrug. He thought he saw Fujimori's chest betray a slight heave of relief.

'Your brief stay here certainly has made us look at our operation with a little more circumspection. There are improvements to make in our dealing methods and systems. I would say that Sternberg Chance has benefitted from your very helpful stay.'

'Bullshit, Masa,' Nicholls said matter-of-factly. 'This operation's a sham. It deceived me at first. I thought the cosy relationship with Koga and the Ohyama group was the end of it.'

Fujimori shifted in his chair and straightened his broad, silk tie as if he was not listening. Nicholls continued: 'But then you crossed the line. You, Koga, Tony Moore. I don't know where the idea came from first. The foreign exchange market's driven by personal and corporate greed and the opportunities to make fortunes are there every day. Brokers entertain dealers and tout for business. They'll fly you abroad for a big horse-race or a rugby match and they might pay your brothel charges. In Paris the brown envelope stuffed with money is part of the dealing culture. In Hong Kong they'll fill your house with jade if that'll bring your bank's business to them. But most of us are honest. We'll take a drink from them in Mama Gimbasha's but that's about it.'

Was it anxiety, a touch of trepidation cracking Fujimori's smooth facade? Nicholls paused to enjoy it. Then he said, 'But you boys wanted more so you went for the jugular. You went to the heart of our industry, to the central banks where world's currencies are managed but not controlled. You're blackmailing a key person in the Bank of Japan and I assume there are others in the main money centres. Not content with that, Koga's got a bunch of top corporate treasury people in Japan by the balls. Since staff move around all the time I expect the blackmailing operation's an on-going process. The beautiful Miss Mori will no doubt furnish the investigators with the details when she makes her confession.'

He waited while Masaaki Fujimori stood up and strolled to the window. The Japanese was listening unprotestingly, barely noticing the calming view of the Imperial Palace moat and outer wall. Nicholls continued, 'Then I asked myself why you should take these incredible risks in order to earn a fortune for your institutions. Of course, the answer was obvious. You aren't working for Ohyama and Sternberg Chance. You're working for yourselves. I was trying to figure out how you were creaming off a worthwhile personal return while working for your banks. I know Koga and Moore are getting good performance-related percentages and bonuses but it wouldn't be enough to reward the risk of being imprisoned for undermining the country's banking system. From what I've been told your political system is corrupt but it works because the bloody great mountain of bribes and donations gets circulated and everyone benefits. I suspect the financial system's much the same but there are foreign exchange rules on overseas remittances and I know they are monitored. You can't ship money out indefinitely without getting called to account. The only way you're all going to make the fortune you're after is by going off-shore, get away from annoying regulations to somewhere open and friendly. Continue to milk the poor bastards you've trapped but keep all the profits for yourselves. Tony Moore's one of the best dealers in the world. He'll appear with his alternative nationality in a place that doesn't bother too much about people's pasts and run it for you. I haven't figured where this new operation's going to be based but I'm working on it.'

Fujimori turned to Nicholls, his head bobbing as if in submission. 'It's not too late for you,' he said. Nicholls felt uneasy at the words. 'I might still be able to help you.'

Nicholls had had enough. The urge to injure was growing to a dangerous level. He rose to leave and was at the door when he asked: 'What did you do with the ring you found in the ashes at the crematorium?'

Fujimori's face was flushed with anger. 'There was no ring on Tony Moore's hands.'

Nicholls produced a sardonic grin and made a violent, stabbing motion with his forefinger towards the Japanese. 'You're right and you're wrong,' he said. 'You're correct that Tony Moore never wore a ring while I knew him and his secretary and all the others I've asked have not seen him with one in Tokyo.' Fujimori was trying to stop his body rocking with rage and spite. 'But there was a large, American college ring on the body you had cremated so quickly. I don't suppose you kept it as a souvenir but it belonged to Sam Collier, the guy you and your friends murdered so that Tony can appear in another life. No. You can't help me Masa and I can't help you.' And finally, in a more subdued voice he added, 'Don't be too hard on Naomi Honda. She's really not much more than another victim.'

405

55

Nicholls fastened his jacket as he left Fujimori's office and wandered into an open-plan expanse of screens and battery-line workers in the securities operation which shared the executive floor with the corporate finance department and Warron Hanlon's management team. He stopped by a row of equity sales staff and seeing familiar faces he joshed with a pair of warrant dealers whose swept-back hair, fresh faces and laid-back arrogance contrasted with the tense and harassed foreign exchange traders on the lower floor. Then he saw Warron Hanlon, talking with Gervase Prideaux and a woman he had seen in Hong Kong on a business trip, who he thought was a corporate finance director. They saw him and Prideaux smiled weakly.

Approaching them, he raised his arms in surrender. 'I've got some loose ends to tie up today,' he said. 'So I'll say goodbye now.' He extended a hand. 'Warron. You've got a fine dealing operation down there. I'm sorry I lost you a couple of million bucks but I suggest you apply for a refund from one Katsuro Koga of the Ohyama Bank. But do it soon,' he added, a point not missed by Gervase Prideaux.

He turned to his London chief, the Sternberg Chance head of global treasury and capital markets. 'Gervase. I'll see you in London and look forward to discussing my future, if there is one, in a week or so. I've just said my farewells to Masa. What an asset for the bank!'

His sarcasm was so subdued that Hanlon and the woman in the business suit missed it, but their mouths fell open when he said to them as an aside, 'Be gentle with him. He could be in jail by the weekend.'

And before any one could react he left them, each with an impression or a fear, and returned to the dealing room.

'What do you make of it all?' he said abstractly to Tomoko Ueda as Tony Moore's secretary helped him clear his desk and the shelves. She had an uncomfortable body and an expressionless, flat face.

'I'm sorry you are leaving,' she professed. 'I don't understand what this bank is doing in Japan but you have changed many things.'

For no special reason he asked: 'What did you do when you heard Moore san was dead?'

She gave him a genuine smile. 'Nothing,' she said. 'I could not believe it.'

Peter Stark was philosophical about the interim chief dealer's departure after less than two weeks in Tokyo. He was reaching the end of a five-year appointment to Tokyo and he had seen foreign staff dismissed, repatriated, bailed from police stations and even pursued violently by deceived Japanese office women. One was admitted to a mental institution.

Nicholls wanted to tell Chance's helpful office manager that he might be a witness to reincarnation if he kept his eyes open but he resisted it and left him with thanks and a shake of the hand. He invited Mabuchi and Hashida to a farewell lunch and they both felt more comfortable with *sushi* at the counter in Kanpachi in the Shin-Marunouchi building than a sit-down lunch in the Palace Hotel. It helped him because there was much to do if Araki's scheme to obtain Naomi Honda's evidence without a confrontation with the heavy side of Koga's organization was to succeed.

Leaving them in a coffee shop, he made the short hop on the underground to meet a nervous Jenny Collier at ground level in Sony's Ginza showroom.

407

'She hadn't called when I left,' she said, as they walked through the underground passage, with a perilously low ceiling in places, towards Hibiya, where many of the offices at street level were occupied by airlines. 'I hope this works . . .' She gripped his hand, sensing in his touch the pent up tension and wariness as he scanned the broad streets several times with suspicious eyes.

'It will if Naomi Honda can stay healthy. She's got until noon tomorrow before the goons come for her. She sounded scared enough to want to try and get the information we need. I've told her through Araki that there's no deal if the stuff she brings isn't enough to prosecute Koga and unwind the chain. Otherwise I'll give her to you before throwing her back to Koga and his bandits.'

There was no humour in his words. From what Araki had said about the car chase she was ice-cold under pressure, but would she keep cool while watching her brother's murderess-by-association plea bargain her way out of jail or the gallows? The option of leaving her in the car, or meeting her somewhere else when the interview with Honda was finished, skimmed across his mind but the image of the psychopathic *yakuza* removed it just as quickly.

Their final stop was the International Arcade, under bullet train overhead railway tracks and close to the hotel where Jenny Collier had spent her first three weeks in Japan. Nicholls bought a compact cassette recorder and an extra tape while Jenny strolled between the souvenir shops and fingered the cultured pearls.

56

She knew Tomio Imaizumi as well as Katsuro Koga allowed her to know anyone in the different parts of the organization. A young model with a foreign name had been assigned to help her overcome her distaste for foreign men who, like Sam Collier, always seemed to sweat a sickening odour of stale meat. The model had said she worked at Imaizumi's talent agency but took instructions from a woman called Emi Mori. She met her, and a group of people she guessed all belonged to the mysterious syndicate, at a cherry blossom party and among them were Imaizumi and a younger man who was the technical expert. His name was Koizumi and she had dated him several times before Koga instructed her to concentrate on the American. He was secretive about his role and this led her to believe it was important and he knew more about the overall operation than he had divulged.

Imaizumi was deeply involved under a high intensity light, arranging with vigorous manual intervention the pose of a teenage talent hopeful with an inane, embarrassed smile fixed on her childlike features. He broke away reluctantly to unlock the private door behind the desk in his office and give her entry to Koizumi's data control room. Headphones clamped to his ears as he transcribed a bilingual dialogue from a tape on to a word-processor, Koizumi did not hear Naomi Honda's stealthy entrance. She walked up softly behind him and tugged his pigtail. He jerked in surprise, but his pale face lit up when he saw the intelligent, attractive woman with a lovely playful sense of humour who now appeared to be free to resume their friendship.

Stopping the tape, he reciprocated a nodded bow with a limp handshake. She let him talk, filling the necessary time gap before she could reasonably ask for the impossible. Finally she said with controlled urgency, 'I have our senior's authority to ask you for access to the black files.'

Koizumi rocked in his chair, pondered the implications of such a request and reached for the telephone. She spread a delicate hand over his, bringing her small face and perfumed hair close to his. 'Please confirm it with him later,' she pleaded.

57

'You're late,' Araki admonished when the two *gaijin* returned to the fortress apartment in Kojimachi. 'I'm seeing Fujii in an hour.' His agitation was uncharacteristic and his annoyance barely below the surface. They had never seen him expose quite so much emotion. An undulating bank of cigarette smoke hugged the ceiling of Nicholls's living room but the curtains, like the windows, were closed.

'I'm going to gag if I don't get some air,' Jenny said, gripping the drapes.

Araki was beside her in two strides. 'That's not a great idea,' he said sharply. Carefully, he spread the dark, frilled curtain just enough for their faces to fill the gap.

Jenny squinted as she peered through the net blind. 'They've been out there all day,' he said. 'Watch. A skinny one with the moustache is due round the front any second.'

She exchanged a glance with Nicholls, who joined them, placing his hands on their shoulders. As they watched the blurred images in the street through the mesh a figure came into view riding a delivery bicycle fitted with a spring contraption on the back for carrying noodles without spillage. He stopped, took out a road map and studied it, looking around for a bearing.

Araki drew them back so their silhouettes would not be visible from the outside.

'What's the problem?' Jenny scoffed. 'Those guys on the funny bikes are everywhere.'

'The same person in the same place for the sixth time today?' Araki said. 'And he's never got any dishes on the back. Please believe me. It's one of Takagi's men.'

'Do you think he'd take a pot shot at us?' Jenny asked.

'No. He could have got you when you came back. I think that after their failure yesterday they'll try and take us all together because we can damage them just as much as individuals on the loose and would be a lot harder for them to catch us. At the moment they don't know what we're planning so they have to watch us, especially you Kevin. They'll know from Fujimori that you have to leave Japan in two days and once you're outside Japan you'll be more difficult to get. But just as dangerous. If we're planning to hurt them in some way they know it's going to be in the next forty-eight hours. I assume you made Fujimori completely aware that you know about Tony Moore and his false identification of the body. I hope you made it clear that the matter is still to be resolved. Did you tell him about the ring?'

Nicholls affirmed each point.

'Good,' he said, contented. 'The crematorium attendant was quite certain the body was wearing a large ring, and it was taken by one of the two mourners.'

Naomi Honda had not telephoned Araki while Nicholls had been in his Tokyo office to take his leave and poison Fujimori's golden rice bowl. And the afternoon was fading quickly, making Araki even more irritable. She would obviously go into hiding during the dangerous night hours. The desperate woman was less than a day away from being delivered to her appointment with Katsuro Koga, a meeting which she was convinced would never take place because she would be the victim of yet another sad death, like Hiroyuki Hirata.

Shame suicide of dismissed foreign bank dealer, Araki guessed the newspaper headline would read.

'I have to go,' he declared. 'If she calls in the next couple of hours you'll have to explain to her in English where we're going to meet tomorrow.' The others gathered at the dining table where he had spread Tony Moore's map of Tokyo in its romanized English version. 'It's a place I know well. Fairly quiet but our friends will be watching us while we talk to Honda. It's there.' He fingered a pinhead piece of greenery. 'We'll leave separately and confuse our watchdogs.

'Jenny. You'll turn right outside Kevin's apartment block and walk very carefully to the end of this street and right again until you come to Yotsuya Station. Wait there, with people around you, for Kevin.

'Kevin. You drive left and work your way back to the Sotobori-dori Avenue and left at Ichigaya and you're at Yotsuya in a couple of minutes. Pick Jenny up and make your way there.'

He pointed to Meguro, on a south-west heading. 'See the station, Kevin? It's about twenty, twenty-five minutes' drive from here. I'll meet you there and we'll take your car to this small park in Denencho-fu. It's really a thick wood on a steep slope with paths and

412

a carp pond and a kid's playground. We tell Naomi Honda to meet us on the hill which passes the park on the main road from the station to the Tama river.'

He saw their puzzled looks and said, 'I've written the directions here in English for you to explain to her. The only thing you have to tell her is the actual meeting place. Don't scare her by telling her there'll be unmarked police cars watching from the crossroads at the top of the hill and on the road at the bottom. There'll also be couples strolling in the park itself and they'll be armed police.' He looked at his watch, asked them to study the map carefully and left with his usual warnings about answering the door.

Araki had been gone long enough for them to drink a cup of coffee before the removal company arrived. Everything was ready. The apartment was bare except for what Nicholls guessed belonged to Sternberg Chance, like the furniture and the cutlery. Jenny's inventory of the cellar revealed that a few bottles of wine remained but Araki had just about finished the spirits. Nicholls addressed the packing chests to his private home, intending to hold Tony Moore's goods as evidence and deny him the pleasure of returning to his Tokyo flat to repossess the pieces he had deliberately left behind to deceive his successor who came to grieve for him. Jenny packed her possessions in one case, holding back only a change of clothes and her cosmestics, and Nicholls would sign for it to be sent to Chicago courtesy of his bank. She choked when Nicholls placed the white urn amongst the clothes.

When the packers had left, he opened a chilled bottle of wine and they ate the contents of the refrigerator in an improvised casserole.

'One more day in these goddamn jeans,' Jenny said afterwards, breathing in and unzipping the tight trousers as Nicholls checked the bedroom Reuters monitor. 'I can tell you're bored with me already,' she said, lifting an endless leg on to the bed next to him.

'You pushy bloody Yanks,' he protested, his eyes on the screen. He moved his fingertips around the soft flesh behind her thighs and into the mound of warmth between her legs. She caught her breath. They were stepping into the shower when the telephone on the bedside table rang.

58

Araki rolled out of the spare bed, looking confused and worse than ever, woken from a shallow sleep by a ringing sound beyond the walls, through his open door. 'Is that Naomi?' he said excitedly stumbling into the living room and flinching at the light pouring through the open drapes. He found Jenny in the dining alcove pouring coffee and Nicholls looking serious as he talked into the portable telephone.

'No it's not,' Jenny whispered. 'She called last night. We're on for one this afternoon.' They carried their cups into the lounge. 'She won't wait for the driver Koga's sending for her and if she's not at the agreed place it might distract them for a time while they wait or go and look for her. When we're convinced that she's told us what we want to know she'll put herself in the hands of the police for protection and, she hopes, lenient treatment.'

'My friend Superintendant Fujii promises that she

will receive all the assistance she needs.' Araki declared. 'He's cleared it up the line.'

Jenny smiled. 'I'm glad. In spite of what she did to Sam, I believe Kevin when he says she genuinely wants to make amends. Will he be there?'

'It's not his case but he is seen as the go-between and in Japan . . .'

Jenny cut him short. 'I know. I know. In Japan you have to have a go-between.'

They shared the moment with a grin when Nicholls joined them, telephone in hand, a rueful smile on his face. 'Thanks Herman, and pass the same on to your brother,' he was saying. 'I'll drop in and buy you both a drink some time.'

'Good news?' Araki asked thickly.

'Could be,' he said. 'A guy in the dealing room in Hong Kong. His brother's in the immigration service.' He depressed the antenna. 'You look like death,' he complained to Araki, 'and we needed you sharp today. I didn't hear you come back last night.'

'Very late,' the Japanese confessed like an errant child. 'Putting some finishing touches to the plan with Fujii san.'

'Shinjuku? The Roman?' Jenny suggested frivolously.

Araki's shirt was creased and stained on the collar and the top buttons of his trousers were undone. He nodded painfully. 'Are you both ready?'

They indicated a pair of shoulder bags holding a change of clothes and their personal documents.

'What are you going to do next week when the lease runs out at Jenny's brother's place?' Nicholls asked Araki.

'I'll go back there tonight, if that's all right with you Jenny, and work through the evidence we get today. I think the police will want me to do that. Afterwards,

I don't know. I'm not very good at planning beyond the next bowl of noodles.'

They each made their final preparations. Araki showered and scavenged for clothes, finding items of Tony Moore's underwear and socks in a bag Nicholls had assigned to the garbage pile. Nicholls looked ready for travel in a blazer and slacks and an open, patterned shirt. Jenny wore what Araki called her 'business outfit' again: a last clean sweatshirt, one with a Chicago Cubs motif she resorted to when homesick, over body-moulded jeans and flat comfortable shoes. She wore her loose, collarless cotton jacket open and turned the sleeves back above her wrists.

'Naomi said we should arrive in Tony Moore's car because she'd been in it and knew what it looked like,' Nicholls said as they leaned over the map and went through the plan again.

'That's what I'd propose anyway,' retorted Araki, writing the key Chinese letters that Nicholls might see on the road and then throwing Jenny a mock expression of rebuke.

'I'm sorry about your car,' she said. 'I really had to push it, but I was impressed by the punch it had when I got the hang of the shifts.'

Araki became serious again. 'When we've got her statement on the tape, and all the facts we need to convict these people, and you're completely happy with them Kevin, we'll bring her back ourselves into Tokyo and take her to the metropolitan police headquarters in Kasumigaseki.'

'Her condition for putting her life at risk is that the information comes to the three of us first so that we can speak for her when it gets to the courts,' Jenny reminded them.

'Right,' Araki said. 'She doesn't know that the police

are going to be around the park today and they won't do anything unless there's trouble.' He stubbed out his last cigarette and checked his watch. 'Should we go?' he said.

Jenny tossed the small green sports bag to Araki. After the car chase two days earlier she had thrown out the shoe box and left the gun swaddled in her brother's clothes. 'With all the firepower round the park today, I don't suppose we're going to use the piece now,' she said. 'It served its purpose.'

'You first, Jenny,' Araki said and the two men watched from the window as she looked indecisively in both directions before moving off to the right. They waited but no one seemed to be following her. Then Araki was gone, giving the tall Englishman a curious shake of the hand as if it was a final farewell. Nicholls took a last look at the scene of so much drama over nine days and left the keys to the apartment with the caretaker who had been confused but not surprised by the strange movements in the *gaijin's* apartment.

Dazzling sunshine caused him to flinch as he turned the Mitsubishi Diamante out of the cellar garage into the road. It seemed to Nicholls that the weather tended to be fine during the day, warm with spells of intense heat, but as evening fell the cooling rain came, sometimes violently. The start of the *tsuyu*, Araki had explained.

Tall, sun reflecting off trails of blonde hair, Jenny attracted friendly attention she did not seek. Waiting at the intersection, Yotsuya Station and the grey, prison-like buildings of Sophia University behind her, she looked lost, and when she saw the low-slung outline of the metallic grey car slowing towards her she sighed with relief.

The map on her lap, they set off towards the Akasaka

417

crossroads and, as Araki had directed, turned right at Azabudai, where Tokyo's imitation of the Eiffel Tower loomed over the office blocks and St Alban's church stood incongruously on the corner. Meguro, 'black eyes', Araki had translated needlessly, was well signposted in roman script and when they had passed under the overhead expressway for the second time they found themselves on a wide road which split into the one-way system around Meguro Station and its urban shopping centre.

Nicholls drew up near a queue of taxis and was relieved when Araki stepped through the endless flow of people.

'Take the front seat,' Jenny said, sliding out of the Diamante's passenger seat into the street.

'No problems?' he asked as Nicholls took off. 'Piece of cake,' the Englishman said.

Straight on was the only directive necessary. The route along Meguro-dori twisted for another five or six kilometres before it reached the spot where Araki had marked a left turn to Jiyugaoka, a few minutes' drive from the site he had picked for the meeting. Jenny sat in the back with the cassette deck primed to record and the small but dangerous sports bag. The less important luggage was stashed in the trunk. Araki motioned towards Otori Shrine as they crossed Yamate Road but his companions were not interested. As they crossed the Kan-nana intersection, descending towards Toritsu-daigaku, the car telephone purred. Nicholls threw a glance towards Araki and pressed the connection. A woman's voice they recognized came through the voice box, clear but hesitant.

'Hello,' Nicholls ventured.

'This is Naomi,' it said. 'Naomi Honda. I'm so glad I had the number of Mr Moore's car phone.'

'We'll be at the spot in fifteen minutes,' Araki said in Japanese.

Her reply was in English. 'I've got a big problem. They've found me. There's a man following me.'

'Shit!' Nicholls said from the corner of his mouth.

Araki leaned towards the speaker. 'Are you sure? You're not just getting nervous, are you?'

There was a grainy hiss on the line.

'Are you there?' Nicholls asked urgently.

'Yes, I am. But I'm scared. I can see him now.'

'Where are you?' Araki barked.

'I'm calling from outside Denencho-fu station. He's watching me from the other side of the pond, by a coffee shop.'

'How do you know he's following you?'

'Because I've seen him before. When I worked at the Ohyama Bank. He took messages around, or something, drove for Koga san. It can't be a coincidence. What should I do?'

'We've got to help her,' Jenny insisted from the back of the car.

'Let me think,' Araki said, a hand over his mouth. Then he pointed. 'Left at the next light, Kevin. Naomi san.' he called.

'*Hai.*'

'We're approaching Jiyugaoka from Meguro-dori. We can be in front of Denencho-fu station in ten minutes. Be ready to get in the car quickly.' There was another, more dangerous lapse on the line. Then her voice came back, high-pitched and afraid.

'It's too late. He's started to move. I've got to go. There's a train coming in. Listen. I'll try and lose him and make for Gotanda. Please go there and wait for my call.' And the line went dead.

'Where's Gotanda?' Nicholls asked. The disappointment had drained him.

Araki knew it was a matter of two left turns on to main roads: The Kan-pachi, just ahead and then the number two Tokyo–Yokohama road. It would take about twenty minutes at the weekend but they were in Wednesday traffic, crawling between obstinate lights. He told Nicholls.

'She can get there by train direct from where she is,' he told the others.

'Won't he get to her while she's waiting for the train?' Jenny thought.

'She said there was a train coming. And anyway trains run every five minutes inside Tokyo. Three in the rush-hour.'

'Excuse me,' Jenny apologized. 'Another thing. Wasn't it strange the way she had the telephone number of this car?'

Araki agreed, but Nicholls shook his head as they caught the tail-end of yet another stream of vehicles.

'Dealers always keep each other's private phone numbers. They're going to need them some time. In dealing crises. If I'm in bed when the Bank of England's intervening, I want to know about it right away.'

Araki shuffled in his pocket unsuccessfully for a piece of paper with a contact number. He had not considered the possibility that the plan could collapse even before the meeting with the informant took place. Fujii and the other plain-clothes policemen would be in place around the Horai park, probably holding radio silence until the woman was brought in. He slapped the dashboard in frustration and then dialled one, one, zero, the police emergency number and asked to be put through to the metropolitan police headquarters.

'Is this a real emergency?' a woman's voice asked suspiciously.

'Yes. Very serious.' She made a note of his name and connected him.

'Senior Police Superintendent Fujii's department, please.'

After a silence a man's voice said, 'Is that Akiyoshi Fujii or Daisuke Fujii?'

Araki was shaking. 'Daisuke. This is an emergency. Could you hurry please.' It seemed a long time before a man admitted his chief was on a mission and could not be contacted for security reasons. 'My name's Araki and I have to talk about the same mission. As soon as you can reach him, tell him I'm in Gotanda. There's been a major problem.' The policeman on the line tediously repeated the message and thanked him. 'Give me a direct telephone number,' Araki demanded, and wrote it on his cigarette packet. 'I'll try and contact him later.'

There was a parking lot on a vacant site awaiting development where the road entered the vast ring system around Gotanda station. Araki instructed Nicholls to pull in and they waited in silence with only a mesh fence to watch. It was warm and growing muggy and they could see rain clouds in the distance, rising far over Tokyo Bay. Nicholls lowered the electric windows.

Jenny was lounging against the car when she heard the telephone and quickly resumed her seat.

'It's me,' Naomi Honda said, less tense, they thought, than before.

'You sound OK,' Nicholls said.

'Better. I think I've lost him but we must hurry. I've thought about how we can meet, but we must be careful.'

'We'll pick you up,' Araki said. 'Where exactly are you?'

She sounded exasperated to the point of anger. 'But what if you're being followed? They've been watching you all for days. Can't you understand that? They're waiting for a chance to eliminate you. And now me.'

'I understand,' Araki said, his own nerves stretched. 'What do you suggest? We're listening.'

'I know somewhere absolutely safe but you'll have to be careful. I'm near the station,' she told them, and they could hear the rumble of trains on the telephone link. 'Take the Yamanote Line direction for Tokyo Station. I'll be watching for you on the platform, the two *gaijin* san will be easy to see, but I won't talk to you until I'm sure we're not being followed and it's time to get off. Travel in the first carriage and wait for me to contact you. When you see me leave the train, follow a good distance behind until I reach the place I think will be free to receive us. If I see any of their people again I must run away.'

'Agreed,' Araki said, but she had already severed the connection. 'Let's go.'

Jenny unzipped the sports bag, delved among the clothes and then placed the cassette recorder on top of them. Outside the car she gave the bag to Araki and smoothed the line of her jacket.

On the platform Araki said, 'It's a loop line. Goes around Tokyo in about an hour, hour and a quarter. She told us to take the anti-clockwise route.'

'I can't see her,' Nicholls said, surveying the groups of people, mostly students and the middle-aged, waiting on the platform. With its stairways, rising to station exits or descending to an access tunnel to other lines, newpapers stands and other stalls, there were abundant places for Naomi to conceal herself.

'She's being very smart,' Araki declared, as the light green, square-fronted train slipped quietly alongside the platform, 'let's do what she says.' He guided them to the front carriage where passengers occupied most of the lateral seats, dozing in the heavy air or reading weekly magazines and comics.

Five stations passed and there was no sign of her. Araki walked the length of the carriage and peered into the next. A man with a scowl and a permanent wave who they had watched since he swaggered on to the train at Tamachi and leered at Jenny, left it at Kanda. Nicholls took Jenny's wrists.

'I've never seen a woman without a handbag of some sort before.'

She gave him a thin smile, but the lines of concern broke through the facade. 'I hope you remember where the car is,' she half-joked. 'My passport, papers and my security make-up. It's all in my purse.' The train shuddered as another passed in the opposite direction. 'My brother must have felt like this,' she said sadly. 'You know, stripped of his identity, ready to be killed.' She fixed him with her ice-blue eyes. 'One moment I feel sorry for that goddamn woman Honda. The next I want to kill her.'

'She won't get away free.' Nicholls said, reassuringly. 'Whatever she tells us, she'll still have to pay for what she's done. She'll get her punishment and so will the people who used her.' But inside him, where she could not see, a nagging virus of uncertainty was on the move.

He flicked at the sleeve of his sports jacket. It was almost two thirty. The original meeting with Naomi Honda was ninety minutes overdue.

At Okachimachi a young woman in baggy trousers and a zipped jacket had trotted along the platform and entered their carriage three doors away. She turned her back to them, lost in a group of plump, giggling high school girls in severe dark blue uniforms. Her hair was tucked under a beret and the brief view of her face was distracted behind sunglasses.

The tracks multiplied as the train pulled into a major station, splitting the bleak, grey landscape of packed buildings, signs and power poles. Araki pointed out the spreading greenery of Ueno Park to their left, with the zoo and lake. When the train slowed, the woman in the sunglasses sidled down the carriage and without speaking smiled harmlessly towards Araki and his friends. They exchanged looks and followed her from the carriage. The terminus for trains to Japan's cold northern frontiers, Ueno Station, and its approaches showed unusual neglect in their ageing low ceilings, peeling walls and general run-down appearance. They stepped around slumbering vagrants in rags and savoured the odorous mixture of fumes from the toilets and fried noodle stalls.

Naomi ignored Araki's group, even when they came close at the crossing to the Ameyoko-cho market, an area of packed food and general goods shops, most of them under cover in the claustrophic maze between two main streets. Passing a man selling terrapins and a shop whose seafood stall spilled across the street, Araki said, 'It was the big black market after the war. Now it's just a great cheap place to shop.'

The foreigners did not hear him. Their attention was on the woman who was the key to bringing Jenny Collier's dreadful nightmare to an end and restoring credibility to Nicholls's foreign exchange career. She had stopped to talk to a shopkeeper, and check quickly among the crowd for any unwelcome and dangerously familiar face. She seemed contented and continued to sidestep her way along the street. Araki dropped back as Jenny, attached by the hand to Nicholls, walked ahead. When they realized he was not with them they turned and saw him slot a cigarette into his mouth and then squeeze the empty Seven Star packet. Naomi Honda was also looking in their direction, her hat like a beacon on the sea of black hair.

Araki lit the last cigarette and with a look of disgust tossed the crushed packet towards a wiry shopkeeper with a head-band who glared as the scruffy, unshaven man passed on. Naomi bore left at a shop selling military paraphernalia and passed under the Number One Metropolitan expressway and into an entertainment district of restaurants and bars, with love hotels located between high walls in the darker alleys. She seemed relieved when the trio joined her outside a building, its exterior tiled in white, between the overhead expressway and the multiple tracks of the Yamanote loop railway and other urban lines. An unlit neon sign outside told them it was a 'sauna', a health club in name but really the modern version of the old public bath. It would have a small gym, television relaxing rooms, hot and cold baths for soaking and a sauna hot room, and probably a blind person to give an expert massage.

What was Naomi Honda's connection with this place, Araki asked himself? They descended a flight of steps into a reception area. A bored man with a creased dark face, rough unbrushed hair and showing a thin vest of summer underwear protested that they were closed. He lifted his thin frame and looked suspiciously at the two foreigners, the first he had ever seen so close to him. There was a short conversation with Naomi Honda, whom he appeared to recognize. His eyes followed Jenny Collier through a set of swing doors before he returned gratefully to his pornographic comic.

'There's a women's section,' Naomi said. 'I used to stop here after I finished the night shift at Sternberg Chance at two in the morning. It was beautiful. They open at five and stay in business all night. There are private rooms for working or resting and we can use one of them for a while.' She appeared relaxed, safe from the dangers in the street, and when they entered a staff room with a table, some chairs and a stand with a hot water boiler for green tea she had regained the confidence Nicholls recalled from his week in the dealing room. The next room held a large sunken bath and the steam from it was permeating through the sliding door, filling the room with humidity. Naomi slipped her jacket from her shoulders and the men followed her example. Jenny declined, folding her arms across her chest.

'I'm sorry about the meeting earlier,' Naomi Honda said. 'I was so frightened. They must have put someone on to me very soon after you fired me,' she remarked to Nicholls.

'I didn't know you'd become expendable,' the Englishman half apologized.

'You managed to lose him easily though,' Araki said.

Their informant smiled weakly. 'I'm quite fit. It wasn't difficult to jump on and off the trains and pile my hair under my hat and put sunglasses on.'

Nicholls opened the holdall and removed the cassette recorder, checking the tape and the microphone. Araki and Jenny sipped green tea as Nicholls began his debriefing. Turning on the machine, he gave the date and time of the meeting and those present and then verified the informant's name and recent employment, including the secondment to the Ohyama Bank earlier that year.

'At one point in February, Katsuro Koga asked you to work secretly for him, even though you were employed by Sternberg Chance.'

'Correct,' she said.

'What incentive does he give you?'

'I receive three hundred thousand yen a month in cash.'

'Is that a lot of money compared with your salary?'

'It's about a half of my Sternberg Chance monthly salary. It's very useful.'

'What did he want for his money?'

'I had to work with Moore san, who appointed me as account dealer for all the companies in the Ohyama group. I had to look after their interests, make sure they got the best prices at all times.'

He made her record the companies which, guided by Koga, put their foreign exchange business through Sternberg Chance. Then he asked: 'What was your relationship with Samuel Collier?'

She tapped her knuckles together and looked at the dead man's sister uneasily. 'He was a research student from an American university attached to the Ohyama Bank. He wrote some articles for certain American magazines which Koga san did not like. He also had made friends in the bank who Koga san suspected of giving confidential information to Sam Collier.'

'Hiroyuki Hirata was one of these?'

'Yes, he was. It was obvious Hirata san and the American were very good friends.'

'OK. Sorry. Continue about you and Sam Collier.'

'In March, around the middle I think, Koga san asked, I should say ordered, me to befriend Samuel Collier and gain his confidence.'

'And you became lovers,' Nicholls said.

Another glance at Jenny. 'Yes.'

The American woman was shaking her head in disgust. 'Did you have any feelings for him at all? Or did you just do it to set him up?'

'Jenny, please. We don't have much time. Just let me get to the facts.' It was Nicholls, and he put a soothing hand over hers. He returned to the Japanese.

'On Thursday night, two weeks ago, you were drinking with Sam Collier and two other men. Who were they?'

'I don't know their names. I was told by Koga that they would meet us for dinner and drink on from there. We were to pretend we were friends. They gave silly common names like Suzuki and Tanaka.'

'What were you supposed to do?'

She looked at the table dismally. 'We had to make him very drunk.'

'Was it easy?'

'He had a lot of sake with dinner, then beer. We went to a club and then to the Capitol Tokyu Hotel. He drank a lot of whisky in those places. We pretended to drink with him but we didn't.'

'When you left the hotel Sam Collier could hardly stand up. Is that correct?'

'Yes,' she said softly.

'Louder, please,' Nicholls said, indicating the recorder.

'Yes, the men had to support him.'

'Did you go with them through the Hie Shrine.'

'No.'

'Did you know what your new friends intended to do with Sam?'

'No.'

'Weren't you surprised when Sam didn't call you again?'

'Yes. I telephoned him but there was no reply.'

Nicholls sipped the tea to loosen his dry throat. 'When Tony Moore's body was supposedly found in the Hie Shrine the next day, weren't you a little surprised at the coincidence?'

'Of course I was. I realized it was strange but I was told not to discuss Sam Collier or Tony Moore with anyone, not even casually with my colleagues.'

'Who told you? Who ordered you to keep quiet?'

The room was desperately silent. The three were close to the truth. They hung on her reply, and none of them picked up a dull metallic echo as a door closed somewhere in the building.

'It was Fujimori san. The senior adviser.'

Nicholls continued. 'Did he say what would happen if you talked about Sam or Tony Moore?'

Naomi shrugged. 'No. He just said the subject was forbidden.'

'OK. Tell me. Is anyone else in Sternberg Chance's Tokyo office involved with Koga?'

'I don't know.'

'What about Sternberg London?'

'I believe there is somebody but I don't know his name.'

Nicholls paused and looked at his colleagues. When he spoke it was to know the ultimate. 'Did you know that Koga and a *yakuza* organization run by a man called Takagi were blackmailing dealers in the central banks, including the Bank of Japan?'

'I knew that Koga san was making a lot of money just before important interventions or interest rate changes and Moore san always seemed to know when to take big positions. But nobody ever talked about it to me.'

Nicholls leaned forward, piercing her with the look in his intense, deep eyes. 'But you've been able to get me the names of the people being blackmailed in the central banks?' The cassette tape turned with a faint hiss in the silence as Noami Honda searched in her handbag. Araki motioned for Nicholls to stop the recorder.

'Is this place empty?' he asked Honda. She looked up, a disc and a folded piece of paper in her hands. 'I suppose the staff are preparing for the opening,' she said.

Araki stood up. 'I think I'll get some exercise while you finish here,' he declared, and hoisting the green sports bag on to a shoulder left the room.

The recorder turned again. Naomi Honda handed him the paper where names had been written in roman script.

'The spellings might not be correct,' she admitted. 'I took them from the Japanese on this floppy,' and she pushed a stolen computer disc towards Nicholls.

There were sixteen names on the stiffish paper, eleven of them Japanese, each written precisely with their business positions and companies or banks. The vital contact in the Bank of Japan was called Kodaira. Nicholls had met him years ago. When he saw the name with Bank of England written against it his head dropped with disappointment. He had lunched with the man during a trip to England in March and when Nicholls worked in London he would often talk to him at night when both were doing the night watch for their banks. He was a pleasant man amongst arrogant stuffed shirts in the British central bank. Tipped for greater things, he had somehow succumbed to the Ohyama honey trap and would now be dismissed in disgrace and probably prosecuted. Nicholls did not recognize the Bundesbank official but assumed he would also call his nearest Ohyama branch at crucial moments and betray his country into giving millions to the Japanese bank. Fools, Nicholls thought. Poor sad fools.

He read the names into the tape and then said, puzzled, to Naomi Honda who had crossed her legs and looked around as if bored by the proceedings. 'Isn't there someone in the Federal Reserve in Washington?'

The Japanese woman shrugged. 'It doesn't seem so.'

Nicholls pocketed the disc and the piece of paper.

'Have you heard of Michiko Momoyama?' he said to Honda.

After a lapse she replied. 'She was in the newspapers years ago. Some financial scandal or other.'

'What about Emi Mori?'

She nodded.

'So you know her,' Nicholls said to the microphone. 'Where did you get the information on the blackmail operation?'

'There's a talent company. Excell Image Agency. It's run by a man called Imaizumi. It's what you call a front for the women Emi Mori controlled for Koga san.'

There were muffled voices outside the room. Jenny Collier stiffened. When the door opened Araki stood in the space, a curiously baffled expression on his face and the barrel of an automatic pistol behind an ear. The sliding doors to the baths were rammed apart and three men, one with row of a fresh, inflamed stitches below an eye, stepped into the room. Two of them held Japanese short-swords in tight grips while the other carried a silver revolver at his side and a briefcase in the other hand. Caught like animals in a spotlight, the three stood instinctively, rigid with fear and bewilderment, and were joined by Araki, shoved forward by the fourth man, with the automatic.

Shock blurred their perception of reality. It couldn't be happening.

Nicholls took Jenny Collier's arm protectively; Araki stared at Naomi Honda, who lowered her head with dejection. The shorter, heavy man in the business suit was the leader, speaking calmly, the revolver used as an indicator. The other gunman was a tense outcast Korean, Tai Il Kim. Elbows brushing his sides, hands outstretched and cupped together, his grip was firm on the Russian Tokarev automatic as he covered the four captives in a slow sweep. The muscles in his cheek twitched with fierce concentration. The other two babbled with excitement at their success, speaking with the gutteral, slurred arrogance of their calling as street punk *yakuza*. Shimizu approached the table, stopped the cassette recorder and extracted the tape. He made a sour face at the Englishman and pointed his gun towards the bank of steam along the opening in the wall. He spoke to Araki who translated for his colleagues. He was struggling to control his shaking body, which made his voice quiver and distort.

'We're being taken to talk to their *oyabun*, the head of the syndicate,' Araki managed. 'I suppose it's Takagi.'

'And then what?' Nicholls growled uselessly at Shimizu. 'We're going to end up like Hirata.' Picking out the name of the Ohyama trader they had beaten up and killed provoked Koike, the young and volatile trooper. His face creased in a ugly scowl as he put the razor-edged blade below the Englishman's jaw and with his free hand spun him and shoved him towards the bathing hall, followed unprotestingly by Jenny and Araki, who still carried the sports bag.

Plastic stools and rinsing bowls were arranged neatly in front of a long row of taps and shower hoses protruding at knee height along one wall, each set provided with soap, shampoo and shaving equipment. Steam rose from the huge, sunken soaking bath and condensed in trails on the tiled walls. There was also a smaller bath, filled with cold water near the foot of the steps which led to the customers' changing room. The Korean led the group, moving sideways, his gun looser in his hand. The injured Yokoi was last, his short-sword held outwards. Their goal was a private door beyond the cold bath which gave access to the machine room and an underground garage where a high-sided enclosed van awaited them.

'Where's Naomi?' It was Jenny who had turned. 'Where is she? If you bastards hurt her . . .'

The captives looked round. Naomi Honda stood with Shimizu in the room where she had disclosed so much. She was laughing: a rich outburst of cheery relief. Shimizu opened the briefcase and Naomi peered into it. She lifted a wrapped bundle of new bank notes, flicked them and then pressed the case shut as the smile on her face broadened again. A fearsome anger welled inside the American. Her head jutted forward as the venom exploded into a scream which resonated in a deafening echo in the chamber.

'Bitch! Murdering bitch!'

Shimizu slid the door shut against the interruption. Yokoi leapt forward, his feet slipping on the wet floor. He grasped the front of her shirt and pushed her against the wall, the knife raised in his right hand. Nicholls and Araki both moved towards her.

'*Tomare*!' the Korean shrieked, the gun aimed at Nicholls.

'*Gaijin one*. Japanese two,' he said, the English rough, the meaning unmistakable.

'Don't move Kevin,' Araki ordered.

433

Yokoi loosened his hold on Jenny, slowly, deliberately, the back of his hand kneading her breasts. He smirked. The heat had beaded his face with sweat and the wound throbbed around the recent suture. He was a head shorter than his victim and he had to lift his chin as he snarled into her face. After a short, vicious staccato speech he pointed the knife towards Araki.

'*Eigo de*,' he commanded. 'In English.'

Araki breathed deeply. 'Don't react Jenny, please,' he pleaded. 'He says that you killed his friend on Monday in the car. The other guy's badly injured. He says that I almost blinded him with the camera. We are going to be punished for our crimes.'

'Tell him he won't be so lucky next time,' she said. 'We'll take his goddamn head off.'

'More, more,' Yokoi bawled in English.

Araki's insides were loose and his chest thumped in his shirt. Sweat oozed in the steam and stung his eyes. He moved a hand agonizingly slowly across his chest to the bag which hung on his left side. His trembling fingers, hidden below his armpit searched for the zip. He fought with himself not to look at it as he spoke to Jenny with a voice that cracked. 'He says that your punishment will be doubly enjoyable.' The sliver of metal was between his thumb and forefinger. He tugged, feeling it give easily. Yokoi turned again to Jenny. Araki's basic animal impulse urged him to survive, to attack and destroy the obscene evil threatening them. He had not translated everything, like Yokoi's boasts about the suffering he would inflict on Jenny's body and his hints at the length of Kevin's remaining time of earth. He had to try, to raise a last alarm. The gun was the only way. Jenny's instructions tumbled uselessly through his mind. His hand was in the bag, among the smothering clothes.

'Freeze!' Kim screamed, and levelled the gun at Araki's chest. 'Throw the bag over here. Now!'

The command ripped through him. It was almost a relief. He lowered the bag and swung it towards the end of the row of taps. Kim ignored it, his gun again scanning the prisoners.

Back against the wall, arms spread, Jenny flexed the fingers of both hands. Sweat stung her eyes and her shirt was clammy beneath the open jacket. She breathed deeply, teeth clenched, and transferred her weight to her left side. Yokoi's fist tightened on her shirt, his face creased in a malicious smirk.

'Show her what you've got planned. A little demonstration,' Koike drawled. He looked towards the room where Shimizu was still talking to Naomi Honda behind the frosted glass door. 'While we wait for the boss.'

Kim bellowed his approval from across the massive, steaming bath, the grip on his pistol relaxing, his arm falling to his side.

What the hell was their leader doing with that woman apart from paying her off? Nicholls agonized, urging him to appear and take control. Yokoi's blade, ridged and hilted like a shortened *samurai* sword, cut easily through Jenny's thin, damp shirt which Yokoi stretched in a firm clasp. Jenny flinched as it grazed the swell of her breasts. A string of blood oozed through the tear. She breathed again and held it. There was no time to warn her friends; and the *yakuza* had missed the signals, the positioning of her weight, the breathing and the utter desperation of someone who would not go quietly to her absolutely clear fate.

There was little space between her attacker for her to raise a foot and bring her leg upwards and so the force in the knee that hit Yokoi's groin came from the strength in her thigh. It was a cruel, merciless and unrestrained strike. Yokoi's eyes popped and there was a moment when he seemed to be suspended in silence as the others watched. The screams came as he hit the tiles, clutching his testicles which were crushed half into his body, and rolling in agony. It was an immeasurable moment: the surprise, the participants frozen in the steam. Except for Jenny Collier.

Before Yokoi's body had hit the floor she had pivoted towards Tai Il Kim, whipped her jacket aside and reached behind for the handle of the Beretta which protruded from her jeans. The sights of the automatic were lined on his chest. It was not impulsive. She had been mentally contemplating it for minutes, frightened by her own callousness. She couldn't give him an option. How could he understand her demand for him to drop the weapon? Through a translator? The Korean had lowered his gun when he was urging Yokoi to assault her. Now he could drop or raise it. His eyes flared and he chose. A flash, a violent explosion and Kim's look of surprise as the bullet took away his control, hitting him in the chest, near his right armpit and lodging in his shoulder blade, splitting it. The empty shell case spun in the air and fell into the bath with a hiss. Kim thumped helplessly against the wall, his knees slowly buckling beneath him. He slipped to the floor and watched his blood dilute into the drainage gutter as the pain began to surface.

Jenny had turned on Koike almost before Kim realized he had been hit and screamed an order, unequivocal in any language. He raised his knife but his face said surrender. Araki picked up a plastic stool and brought it down on Koike's wrist. The knife was held limply and it fell easily. Araki retrieved it.

'Now get the gun,' Jenny hollered. Her own weapon

and concentration had swung to the closed, glass-panelled door. 'Kevin. Get out the way, for Chrissake!' In all of his depraved fantasies Shimizu could never have been prepared for a tall, blonde American woman, bathed in sweat but inwardly cool, breath expelled, one eye closed, the other sighting the barrel of an automatic at his heart. He had assumed Kim had stupidly shot one of the captives and when he flung the door back his silver Smith and Wesson was still bulging the pocket of his suit.

'*Nan da kore?*' he shouted, his eyes raging. Two of his men lay moaning on the floor, one of them swilling it with his own blood. The other was cowering in front of Araki, who wielded a gun and a short sword. The air was hot with steam and reeked of burnt cordite, and Yokoi's vomit. His hand went for his pocket, and it was the Englishman, hard against the tiled wall and unseen, who saved his life. His teeth clenched and his body taut, he seized Shimizu by the collar and swung him into the room. The Japanese tripped on the door runners and collapsed under Nicholls's weight, his teeth smashing against the rim of the bath. Jenny ran to them, splayed Shimizu's arm and legs on the tiles and put the automatic to his ear.

'Get that woman!' she ordered Nicholls, extracting the pistol from her captive's pocket. And the cassette tape. Nicholls returned with Naomi Honda. She had tried to leave when she saw Shimizu's legs take off but the clasps on the briefcase of money were stiff and she had only managed to reach the door of the small room.

Jenny was in total command. 'Keep the tape and the notes dry, Kevin.' She walked around Tai Il Kim, sniffed and then checked Yokoi. 'Leave them alone,' she said. 'They'll be OK when they've had some treatment.'

Araki wanted to go and find a telephone, though they all guessed the commotion would bring the police eventually. 'Not yet, please,' Jenny said. 'There's one more thing to do.'

Nicholls exchanged glances with Araki. Their smiles of relief vanished. Gun at her side, she ordered Shimizu, Koike and Naomi Honda to sit facing the hot water on the raised rim around the bath. 'Sit on your hands,' she commanded. 'The two men stayed motionless, uncomprehending. She put her mouth close to Naomi Honda's ear and through gritted teeth said, 'Tell your friends to sit on their fucking hands and dangle their legs in the water. You too.' They obeyed, deathly afraid of the mad *gaijin* woman.

'What are you going to do?' Araki asked. 'You can't shoot them.'

Naomi Honda began to cry and beg.

'Shut up!' Jenny bawled, seizing her hair. 'You might survive.' She tapped Koike's backside with her toe. 'I saw it on a film. Keeps their hands out of mischief.' She moved to Shimizu and placed the barrel of her gun behind his head. 'Translate for your friend, Naomi. I want to know, within ten seconds, who killed my brother Sam Collier.' She nudged Shimizu with the muzzle of the Beretta. He looked at Naomi Honda, who was snivelling and struggling to speak.

'*Ichi*,' Jenny remembered.

'What's she saying?' Shimizu demanded.

'*Ni*.'

The Japanese woman managed a translation.

'*San*,' Jenny said.

'*Shi*.'

Shimizu turned his head towards Kim who lay pale and curled, unmoving.

'Five.' She had forgotten the Japanese.

'Six.'

Shimizu spoke to Honda. Araki raised his arms and smiled with relief.

Honda said, 'The two men in the hotel with your brother were a man called Maeda from the Ohyama Bank and Koike who is here. Maeda left after me, but Koike and your brother walked through the shrine. Yokoi and Kim were waiting. Those three killed him.'

Jenny's body slackened.

'And Hirata? Who tied him in his car and pushed him into the ocean?'

There was another exchange of Japanese before Naomi Honda replied, her head bowed. 'Yokoi, Kim and the man who died in the car crash. His name was Kubokawa.'

Was there an instant, Araki would debate with Nicholls much later, when they believed Jenny Collier would execute Yokoi, Koike and Kim. She stood over her prisoners, the gun resting on a shoulder, lost in thought for a moment. Finally she turned to her colleagues.

Araki embraced her. 'You must go,' he said, taking the gun. 'I'll handle the police. I can hear the sirens.' She was heaving against his body. 'Thank you. I love you like a brother.'

'I'll call you tomorrow,' Nicholls said, his own voice breaking. 'We'll have to come back to testify, I suppose.'

They left quickly. Araki surveyed the scene of the mayhem as the sirens grew louder. He stood behind the three uninjured prisoners.

'Get in the bath. All three of you,' he commanded, helping Koike in with a firm shove.

59

The driver of the yellow and green chequered taxi might have refused the tall *gaijin* couple a ride as he idled outside Ueno Station. They had no bags, looked soaked although it was not raining yet and the woman's sweat shirt was torn. The man, nerves on edge, rapped the top of the taxi when he delayed opening the automatic rear door. But it was a good ride to Gotanda, although the train would probably have been quicker for them, given the rush-hour traffic.

Delayed shock was causing Jenny to shiver. She wrapped herself in Nicholls's coat and held him across his chest, letting his hands roam and warm her. They did not speak until the lights and familiar buildings of the Ginza cast their own feeling of security.

Nicholls said, 'Thank God the gun wasn't in the bag. Araki couldn't have fired it. Neither could I.' His ears were still ringing, pummelled by a sharp rolling pain.

'I've never fired a gun before without headphones. That goddamn bathhouse echo chamber didn't help.'

'One helluva shot,' he admitted.

'You reckon?' she said, lifting his shirt, needing the warmth, the feel of his skin.

'You've done it before.'

'About a thousand times,' she said casually, without boasting. 'I told you. At the range in Chicago.' Her words drifted away, her face brushed lightly with sadness. The design on her shirt, the little Chicago cub bear swinging a baseball bat, was shorn neatly through the animal's head. A pink stain spread on either side of the cut. Nicholls produced a handkerchief and slipped it through the gap on to the graze.

'Steady on big guy,' Jenny quipped, catching the driver's eyes in the rear-view mirror. 'It's not bad. My bra took most of the knife.' And suddenly the situation overtook them. They broke into demented laughter of relief, an explosive outburst of gratitude for their deliverance. Their hands fought, their faces clashed and their legs shifted restlessly. The driver hissed and pretended to ignore them. When the moment subsided they sat speechless, their heads slumped on the headrests as the lights of Tokyo slipped by. Nicholls recognized the Gotanda roundabout.

'When did you hide the gun in your jeans?' he asked, suddenly recalling how he had been as surprised as the *yakuza* gunman when Jenny produced the Beretta. She laughed. 'It was over there,' she said, as they approached the vacant lot with its parking spaces.

'What made you do it?'

She shrugged. 'I was coming unstuck after Naomi called. I don't know why. It was too much of a coincidence. The call to the car, just when we were about to see her; the complicated plan to meet. I could tell Araki wasn't convinced either but he was so fired up to get to her his judgement was clouded. I couldn't cope with that stuff. When we reached the parking lot and I was putting the cassette recorder in the bag I just decided on impulse to remove the gun and stick it in my jeans.'

'You didn't trust us with it, did you?' Nicholls groaned, with exaggerated outrage.

She reached and kissed him. 'Of course I did,' she lied.

'Plot the route quickly,' Nicholls urged when he brought the Diamante into the evening traffic. 'The flight's at seven.'

'How come we can leave Japan from the middle of

Tokyo?' she asked as they crept up the ramp towards the highway toll booth.

'It's an old businessman's trick,' Nicholls said, easing the car into the southbound lanes of the bay expressway. 'Haneda's Tokyo's domestic airport. It's only fifteen minutes from downtown Tokyo. It used to be the international airport until they built that bloody horror-story forty miles away at Narita. It'd take us at least three hours to get to Narita, no chance of making the last flight to Hong Kong. So we're booked on China Airlines to Taipei from Haneda. We should make the last connection of the night from there. It's only an hour to Kai Tak.'

'Why can the Taiwanese use Haneda?' Jenny was puzzled.

'The Beijing Chinese refuse to land at the same airport as the Taiwan Chinese. So the brilliant Japanese compromise is to have the People's Republic land at Narita, in the middle of the paddy fields, with all the other airlines, and let China Airlines land at Haneda, the domestic airport right on Tokyo Bay. If you're on a business trip through Asia you can route yourself through Taipei and avoid a three hour transit from Narita.

'Come on,' Nicholls urged the trail of traffic crawling from the perimeter underpass.

'Another job for Stark,' he said, when they were in the car park. 'I'll post him the keys.' He was hauling their meagre luggage out of the boot when he saw it again. The sturdy piece of blackthorn. 'Hope they'll let me take it on board,' he said, slotting it through the straps of the two shoulder bags.

They wanted to change into dry clothes but the flight was already being called for boarding. The check-in clerk questioned their suitability for business class with a swift visual body scan and hastened them to the departure gates. They changed in the tight lavatories on the seven four seven.

'What are we going to do if your hunch is wrong?' Jenny said sceptically, when she returned in loose slacks and a sweater.

Nicholls rubbed a coarse jaw and stared into a distant orange sunset over the East China Sea.

'My whole case collapses. I'll be on the street, unemployed.'

She set the seat at an angle and dozed until a steward served a much needed cocktail.

'Kevin,' she said, a tired slur in her voice. 'Was Naomi Honda ever on our side? I mean, did she genuinely intend to give herself up to the police when she got you to meet her at the swimming pool?'

Nicholls gulped the well-watered whisky and completed the implication. 'And had her mind changed for her between seeing me and her no-show at the park.'

'Right. She got picked up, threatened and had to set us up or suffer some fate or other.'

'No. I don't think she ever left the Koga camp, although she had me completely fooled. And Araki.'

'You're too soft,' Jenny chided. 'You even let me take you over.' They clinked glasses and waved for a refill. 'And why did they have to give her a case of money like that?' she asked. 'Right in front of us.'

Mellowed by the drink and creeping fatigue, Nicholls moulded himself in the bucket seat, a hand drooped across the handrest into Jenny's lap. He closed his eyes and saw the poised figure of Naomi Honda, immaculately dressed, dominating the dealing room with confident flicks of her jewelled wrist and sharing long conversations with her Ohyama group customers.

'She never left Koga,' he said coldly, without opening

his eyes. 'She was totally and utterly committed to the good life he was giving her. It wasn't hard for him to corrupt her when Tony sent her for a training secondment to the Ohyama Bank in March. Tony had no doubt picked her out as the dealer most likely to succumb to Koga's bribes and be his Japanese ears and eyes in the Sternberg Chance dealing room. He was right. She's been living in a two-bedroom apartment which Hirata claimed in his notes to your brother was for Koga's exclusive use. She was paid a secret salary by him and probably got a cut of the money they all made from insider trading. She wouldn't give up those goodies easily.'

Prompted by a stewardess, he straightened his seat and unfolded the table for dinner. Looking at Jenny he said, 'When we let her know we'd found out she'd helped set up your brother's murder she had the option of helping us expose them or helping them plug the hole by wiping us out. Hardly a choice in hindsight. The call to me, the plea for leniency in return for her evidence. It was all a sham. She knew that I wouldn't deal with her unless she gave me the names of the central bank insiders and I wouldn't bargain for her with the police unless I questioned her directly and was convinced of the authenticity of the list and the information. So she planned with Koga and the *yakuza* to sell us the story about being followed and then set up the substitute meeting. Which seemed plausible to me and Araki at the time but fortunately not to you. And then she was able to get us to sit like a bunch of stuffed ducks, holding our attention until Takagi's heavies moved in.'

'And the money?' Jenny asked, probing with chopsticks in a bed of tempura fish and rice.

'The way I see it, she was finished in the dealing market in Japan. Even if she stayed out of prison she would be unemployable, even in Ohyama Bank. The foreign exchange market in Tokyo's a small, incestuous little world. No. She had to get out of Japan after delivering us to the *yakuza* for extermination. She'd take the cash that guy had readied for her and head for the airport. It wouldn't have surprised me if she turned up abroad with this new outfit Koga's been planning.'

'The reason why we'll be in Hong Kong tonight?' Jenny added.

'Right. It's just a hunch. I hope it works out.'

The aeroplane banked and the pilot announced an earlier than scheduled arrival at Chiang Kai-shek airport.

Levelling her seat, Jenny took Nicholls's arm. 'Are you regretting not playing along with Koga and Prideaux?' she said seriously.

Nicholls tried to force a smile but failed.

'There were millions in it, weren't there?' she persisted.

'You can make millions honestly,' Nicholls said drily. 'And I'm working on it. What the market doesn't need are the crooks and manipulators. Even if they're friends.'

Jenny Collier took in the reply but was still bothered. 'I'm going to have to watch you in Hong Kong,' she said.

60

Takagi paced the basement machine room, with its massive rumbling boiler, returning after each circuit to the empty staff rest area with its crude table, kettle and a noisome toilet behind a chipboarded door, to catch the latest score in the televised baseball game between Tokyo's Giants and their arch rival, the Tigers from Osaka. He willed the Kansai team from the south to victory, safe and dry under the roof of the Tokyo Dome on a wet, miserable night, and wished he were there. A week earlier he had watched the breaking of the wretched traitor Hirata in this safe warehouse by the bay. He looked at his watch for the tenth time, concerned at the delay in the arrival of his people with the misguided trio who regrettably had to be disciplined and sent away in three different directions.

British-made raincoat over his shoulders, he was pouring from a pot of warmed sake when he heard a door clash in the building. He relaxed, the operation at last back on course. The young former-biker Shimamura, with his sleek, brushed-back greased hair and reckless enthusiasm, stood in the doorway, framed by a trail of pipes. He had been assigned against his wishes to the passive role of driver and bodyguard to his *oyabun*, having begged to be allowed to participate in the Ueno mission.

'What's the matter?' Takagi barked, jolting the youngster.

Shimamura was shaking his head in disbelief. 'The police, *oyabun*.'

Takagi's eyes narrowed, his head lowering. 'Speak clearly man! What police?'

'They're here,' Shimamura said, drawing a short-sword uselessly. 'They're surrounding the warehouse.'

They both reacted to the sound of rasping metal and heavy feet on concrete floors and soon they heard the bellowed warnings, cautions and orders in the warehouse above. Takagi sank onto a chair.

'Give me your sword,' he said calmly to his follower.

'*Oyabun*! No,' Shimamura protested, the muscles in his face flaring. 'I'll go instead.'

'Give me the blade,' Takagi said, slowly and menacingly. 'And give yourself up to the police. Delay them for a while if you can.'

'*Oyabun*, I refuse.'

Takagi rose, the coat falling from his shoulders. 'You cannot refuse,' he said, moving in on the boy and holding out his palm for the sword.

'*Hai*.' The young *yakuza* jerked his head forward and handed over the sword.

'Now go and meet the police and buy me a few minutes.'

When his loyal follower had left, Takagi locked the door and turned off the weak light above the table, leaving him alone with the flickering images from the television and the baseball commentary. Top of the eighth innings, the superimposed line-score told him. The game tied at one run apiece. Black and gold Tiger uniforms on first and third, one out, top of the batting order, the Giants' pitcher behind the slugger three balls to one strike. He hung his tailored suit jacket carefully around the horns of a chair, unbuttoned his shirt and pulled his undershirt out of his trousers. He thought of his father, who would have chosen this way to go if he had not been shot in the short gangland war three years ago.

'Strike!' the pro-Giants commentator shouted glee-fully. Full count. The payoff pitch to come. Like my next move, Takagi thought. One more strike and I'm out. He wiped the blade with a handkerchief, savouring the sensual, perfect smoothness, and held it in a two handed grip, the razor tip against his abdomen.

'Ball!' The camera panned to the packed, hysterical ranks of the Tigers supporters behind third base, waving banners, banging drums and chanting in uni-son. The batter slung his bat aside and trotted to first. Bases loaded, one out. The *yakuza* heard muted voices beyond the door, in the machinery room.

The Giants manager was on the mound and the infield players had gathered to hear his wisdom, obey his commands. The pitcher looked miserable but the manager left him in to find that inspirational pitch. 'Hurry up,' Takagi urged. 'I have to kill myself.'

Now the voices were at the door, ordering him to open: unseen hands twisting the handle, then fists banging against the panels. The Tigers batter watched a curve ball bend in on him. Strike! The voices outside were more insistent. A gun was drawn. Takagi's grip on the hilt loosened. 'I apologize Father,' he intoned, tossing the short-sword on to the table. 'Times are different.' He approached the door, opening it gently, a hand raised to indicate his willingness to surrender without fuss. The police moved in, seized his arm and spun him towards the television while they searched him. The Tigers batter, a lean, long-legged left-handed youngster, connected on a fastball and sent it screaming over the Giants second baseman who had drawn in for the double play. '*Banzai!*' Takagi hollered, arms aloft, wrists already in handcuffs.

61

The young hood in the charcoal-grey suit, sheltering from the rain in a doorway, had time only to press the first two digits on his mobile telephone before he was seized by the detectives who left their saloon car dressed like four businessmen on the prowl and then pounced as they reached his shelter. They were followed by black and white patrol cars, their sirens stilled. Others approached from the river side, their officers taking up positions around the walls of the old-fashioned residence and in the alleys between the two weathered ferro-concrete blocks.

Gervase Prideaux had embarked on a conversation with T. Michael Schweiker, number two in the US delegation to the Secretary of the Treasury at the G-seven meeting, about the rivalry between the Ministry of Finance and the Bank of Japan and ways to exploit the differences. Move slowly and cautiously, Emi Mori had said when they planned the entrapment. The American was the most important prize in the central bank network. Let the girls lean on him gently during dinner, weaken his defences a little with a dropped comment, a subtle compliment and then you bring him back to reality in the annexe with some business talk. Make him anxious. Notice how he looks at the girls. See if he wants to take it to another stage. When you're sure about his intentions make a move.

Prideaux asked if he might watch the CNN news beamed into the English language television station. 'Sure,' the American had said, relieved to be free of business talk, his head swimming pleasantly. Lisa Hamazaki filled his glass.

'Are you having one?' Schweiker said cordially. 'You girls have worked hard tonight.'

Lisa looked around timidly. 'Why not?' she ventured, and found a glass close to hand. She sat demurely on the edge of the couch, and touched his glass with hers. He pretended to find the television interesting. When he rolled his tired head from side to side Lisa Hamazaki said: 'The muscles in your neck must be very tight.'

'How do you know that?' he said admiringly.

'It's part of our training. We don't want our foreign guests to suffer while they are on important business in Japan. Let me see.' She stood behind the couch and kneaded his shoulders, then his neck. 'Very tight,' she confided. 'It was the long flight and the tension you are feeling before your meetings. She eased the pressure until it was her fingertips which brushed the hairs on the back of his neck and the skin behind his ears. He was conscious of the tingling contact and her intoxicating scent which filled his nostrils. His head lolled, his eyes closed.

'I have to call the States,' Prideaux said nonchalantly, getting to his feet. 'They'll let me do it from here. I may be a few moments but I hope we can continue this most interesting chat when I get back.'

'Sure, sure,' the American said.

When Prideaux had left, Lisa said, 'Are you feeling refreshed, Mr Schweiker. I'd really like you to stay longer.'

The police found the camera room first. A task force had scaled the outer wall, descending at the side of the smallest, most brightly lit of the three classical buildings. They arrested three people: a foreigner called Prideaux, who had to be restrained, a Japanese woman in a kimono whose name was Michiko Momoyama and a man named later as Koizumi who was operating a video camera from a tripod behind a two-way mirror. The police crowded into the room to watch the object of the surveillance: a large, ghostly-white *gaijin* on a massive, low bed. He was fondling a slim short-haired woman in black lace full-body underwear. Another, a woman with light brown skin and large, firm breasts, who wore only string panties, rubbed his body with oil. At the foot of the bed sat a third woman, long haired, wearing a short leather skirt and nothing else. She seemed to be keeping her face deliberately turned away from the mirror behind her, at least until Michiko Momoyama, with a desperate scream, lunged at the camera and carried it though the mirror. She fell with a thunderous crash at the feet of her daughter, bleeding and weeping.

62

Clouds hung around the Peak, their rolling edges of cold mist engulfing the trees and the higher houses on Magazine Gap Road. The emerald green saloon drew alongside two new Japanese turbo-charged models on the semi-circle of gravel, leaving the two navy blue Hong Kong police cars on the road in the shade of the tall, panel fencing which hid the bungalow.

Brushing aside the old Chinese woman who opened the door reluctantly, they took stock of the lavishly furnished living room and the deceptive size of the hillside hideaway. Through the French windows they saw how the L-shaped extension stretched around a tiled quadrangle centred with a weathered stone fountain. They followed the woman's directions to the door with the coded entry box fixed to the wall. The occupants were obviously not expecting visitors: the door was open the width of a foot. With the head of Detective Inspector Stuart Jefferson of the Hong Kong police at his shoulder, Nicholls splayed his fingers on the door and gave it a gentle push. A low, rasping buzz from a news service printer shrouded any sound the newcomers made.

A short, slender man with thin, straw blond hair was standing next to a thick-necked stocky figure who sat hunched in front of a row of television-sized screens and built-in telephones. The two were too engrossed in the rows of numbers and multi-coloured graphs on a Knight-Ridder display to sense the arrival of the two men and a tall woman. The man in the seat was tracing the dips and peaks on the charts with a stubby finger.

Nicholls raised the blackthorn stick and rapped it violently on the door.

'Got a price in dollar-yen Tony? Not large.'

He cursed himself for not having a camera to record the expressions before him, frozen in their own milliseconds of surprise. Anton Landau was the less bothered, and the first to react. 'Who the hell are you?' he said angrily. 'We don't have a visitors' gallery here.' His expression showed genuine annoyance at the interruption. Tony Moore's was a blend of anger and fear.

Anton Landau was unaware how his Japanese paymasters had put Pacific Impact Trader together and cared even less. Welcoming sweeteners of a million Canadian dollars and two hundred million Japanese yen had been paid into his accounts in Switzerland and Grand Cayman and were enough to guarantee his loyalty. He would never see a rent demand for the quiet, split level apartment leased for him. He had never met

Nicholls, knowing him only by reputation, and he was inclined to return to the shifting lines on the dollar-yen chart projections they had been studying. But seeing the badge and listening incredulously to the monotone, practised words of caution from the detective, he began to sense they were in trouble. He looked towards Moore for an explanation.

The English dealer's reincarnation was to be short-lived. His face almost broke into a thin, ironic smile while his sharp mind assessed the alternatives, or lack of them. 'For Chrissake Kevin,' he said finally, slapping the desk. 'You're supposed to be out of this.'

'We almost were,' Nicholls scowled. 'Thanks to you.'

The shock had worn off as they flew south to Taipei, the in-flight drinks loosening them, awakening the fears and horrors they had tried to suppress. He and Jenny knew it had been close. Too close. In the end they had saved themselves but they also paid tribute to the Japanese police.

Badgered by Araki, Fujii had persuaded, cajoled, put his reputation on the line to convince his superiors to approve a raid on the Asakusa *ryotei* pleasure house at the same time as Araki and his foreign friends were receiving the incriminating evidence from Naomi Honda. The plan looked doomed when the informant and her confessors failed to appear at the Horai Park rendezvous. But an hour later Fujii's headquarters received a call from a puzzled store-holder in the Ameyoko-cho market in Ueno to say that an agitated man had thrown him an empty cigarette packet stuffed with a five thousand yen note on which he had scribbled the policeman's telephone number.

Fujii's team rushed to Ueno, drawn finally by the gunshot to a scene he would relive with Araki for a decade. It was late evening before the police waiting to move on Momoyama's private retreat received confirmation that the evidence had been secured from the informant and it was an unexpected bonus to find the honey trap in progress when they scaled the walls. A confession from the edge of the hot bath took the police to the Chiba side of Tokyo Bay and the basement of a cold produce warehouse where they found the head of a major *yakuza* syndicate waiting for Araki and the two foreign victims.

'What's going on?' Anton Landau snapped. 'Somebody tell me for fuckssake.'

Nicholls carried the gnarled stick before him like a weapon. Jenny followed him to the dealing desks. 'Latest gear,' he said admiringly, tapping a keyboard, and then to Landau. 'You're working for a phoney funds management outfit set up by Katsuro Koga, a big Japanese crime figure called Takagi and my cheating boss in Sternberg Chance. It was to be a front to launder bad money from the Japanese *yakuza* and good, recycled money from Koga's bank and other Ohyama group companies. You'd be acting on real-time inside information from blackmailed sources in the Bank of Japan and other central banks, maybe even the Fed. Well, I should say you *were* working for Pacific Impact Trader. Your career was the shortest on record. You're busted.'

Laudau spun on Moore, his wire-framed glasses jumping off the bridge of his nose. 'What's he talking about?'

Jefferson took the Canadian's elbow. 'Let's go outside and talk about voluntary statements.' He lifted a jacket off the back of a chair, slipped a hand inside and removed a passport then handed the coat to Landau.

'I want to talk to the boss,' Landau protested.

'You'll get the chance,' Jefferson proclaimed, steering his charge through the door and motioning the others to follow.

Moore positioned his elbows to raise his heavy and crippled body aloft. Two weeks of voluntary confinement in the Tokyo *geisha* house had left him heavier and palid. On his feet he reached for the substitute walking stick, a smooth, walnut-covered staff with a curved handle.

'I suggest you come clean, Tony,' Nicholls said. 'You're off back to Japan and the police there like confessions.'

Tony limped to the refrigerator cabinet and removed a tin of tonic water. 'The air-conditioning makes my hip stiffer,' he complained. 'It's going to be hard to make a run for it,' he chortled.

'This is Jenny Collier,' Nicholls said. 'You knew her brother. Sam.'

Moore rested his weight on the dealing desk and pulled the tab off his drink with a hiss. He swivelled towards the American woman whose eyes spiked him with hatred. Neither spoke.

'Koga wasn't caught in the roundup in Tokyo yesterday so we assumed he's on his way to be with you and Landau. He arrived in Kai Tak last night and spent the evening with his subordinates in Ohyama Bank's local operations. The others are under arrest. Fujimori, Prideaux, Naomi Honda, your good-looking corporate dealer, a driver at the Ohyama Bank and mister big and his boys in the *yakuza*. A bunch of central bank officials around the world will be questioned today. And we also got a tough little number called Emi Mori.'

'Emi too?' Moore looked disappointed. She was due to join him in Hong Kong at the weekend. Then he looked at Jenny. 'I never met your brother,' he said.

'But will it help if I say I'm sorry for what happened to him?'

'Not at all,' she replied, her head moving slowly from side to side. 'Nothing you or the other murderers say will help.' He'd always had it, but Nicholls realized he hadn't noticed it in Moore's voice before. The rough edges of his south London accent trimmed to a mild mid-Atlantic drawl by his Canadian experience. His grip on the strong piece of wood tightened as he probed for the truth. 'Why the hell did you get in bed with Koga? You could have worked something out with the Americans.'

Tony Moore smirked. 'You're kidding. You must have seen the letters I left in the flat. It was either the US bloody justice department who'd lock me away or her avaricious, blood-sucking parents who wanted everything I owned and another ten years of my earnings on top. Or both. Some choice. I've known Koga a long time, like you, and he knew I was good. He also found out about my problems in the States, probably through Prideaux.' He swallowed the remains of the tonic water. 'We started to do more business together, I saw more of him, his team, and finally, I suppose it was inevitable, he told me about his plans for an off-shore fund and his search for someone trustworthy and controllable to run it.'

'And you brought in Landau?' Nicholls said.

'Yeah. But he doesn't know everything about the Japanese side. He's not interested. Only wants to deal. The Fed investigators were getting too interested in the origins of the funds he was managing, especially the Cayman stuff, so he pulled out of the States.' He pushed himself away from the desk.

Jenny came in close to Moore as he stopped to collect a bag of things from a room off the central corridor. 'So my brother was perfectly placed to solve your problem and Koga's.'

Moore shouldered the bag. 'He was getting close to what we were doing,' he said coldly.

'So you killed him!' Jenny screamed, spitting venom through her hatred.

'Let's get going,' Moore said.

They heard the babble of protesting voices penetrating the bungalow before they reached the door.

'Your boss's arrived,' Nicholls suggested. Jenny clenched a raised a fist in triumph and led them into the sunlight. Moore stopped on the step and slapped a thigh with his free hand.

'I've left my briefcase. I assume I can take it with me,' he said. 'It's got the few personal papers I kept.'

'Get whatever you need,' Nicholls responded. 'And bring some dealing slips. You and Koga can play pretend dealing. You'll have sacks of time for it.'

Katsuro Koga stood between a Caucasian in a suit and a uniformed Chinese policeman. He had arrived with two Japanese in a Mercedes and they were protesting vigorously to the Hong Kong police. Two more officers were questioning Anton Landau while another pair patrolled near the gate. The Scottish detective patrolled the scene, gesturing, ordering and finally waving away the protests of Koga's local staff.

Koga had exploded in an incoherent babble of frenzied English, the veins in his face bulging, his anger swelling and clouding his reason as the fortune and the future he had planned with Michiko Momoyama evaporated with the appearance of a cabal of Hong Kong police. His driver sat impassively behind the wheel of the Mercedes. Helpless, unarmed, desperate, Koga advanced on Nicholls, directing his anger at the living-dead Englishman who had destroyed his life.

Nicholls's grip on the strong piece of wood tightened as the Japanese snarled at him. To smash it between the eyes of this crook, this conspirator to corruption, fraud and murder would be a small return for the suffering the Japanese had unleashed and give him a sensation rarely achieved outside the bedroom. Jenny sensed his intentions and took his arm, easing the Englishman out of the way as the police steered Koga to their cars.

'He's a bonus for us,' Jefferson said, joining them. 'I'm impressed by the way your friends in Tokyo kept the roundup under wraps until we cleaned up here. Koga had no idea what happened in Tokyo yesterday. Guess they forgot to call in the *fung shui* man before they arranged the desks,' the detective chuckled as they walked to the cars.

Jenny took Nicholls's arm. 'You almost lost it back there. Almost broke the promise,' she admonished. 'You were about ready to drill Koga with that stick. You noticed I only killed Moore with my laser gun eyes?'

'You're right. I nearly gave it to him.'

'How did you know these guys would be here?' Jenny asked, with Jefferson listening.

'Lots of clues,' Nicholls said modestly. 'There aren't many financial centres where Tony can operate relatively anonymously with his Canadian identity. Hong Kong's the only one, realistically. Then I heard about Landau's move to the Orient. Tony and Landau were very close friends when they both worked out of New York. I knew I was right when my old dealer here, Herman Cheung, asked his brother in the immigration department to check the entry records for the last two weeks. Sure enough, Landau came into the colony two days ago on Tuesday.'

Jenny sighed at the magnificence of the view across

Victoria Harbour. 'Is it true about this place being a twenty-four hour shopping mall?' she said, brushing her creased shirt and trousers.

Nicholls grinned, his gaze towards the high-rise apartments stacked around the Happy Valley race-cource in the distance. Then he looked at the lively, eager face of his companion, with the exciting, ice-blue eyes and ready, rich smile. 'Let's find out,' he said. 'Via the hotel.'

'Let's get these characters to headquarters,' Stuart Jefferson said, after a discreet cough. Then he snapped his head towards the police cars.

'Hey. Where's Moore. I thought he was in the car.'

'He went back to get his briefcase,' Nicholls said.

'Why didn't you tell me?' the Scot said, reeling away and trotting to the bungalow's porched entrance. 'Peng,' he bawled to the officer following him. 'Get men around the back and into the road. You're looking for a fat *guailo*.

'I hope he hasn't legged it,' he said as they followed the passage to the rear of the house. There's an old stairway from the garden to the road.'

'He can't get far with a limp like that,' Nicholls said hopefully, shoving open the dealing room door.

In five minutes, Tony Moore had vanished. The man who had plotted his own death and was staring at a long prison sentence in any one of three countries had nothing to lose from a desperate dash for freedom. Jefferson slammed the door, cursing his own stupidity and carelessness.

Officers swept the bungalow and the grounds but Moore had left through the fire door, making his final escape through the security gate hidden behind the hanging outgrowths from the perimeter fence. It was open, and creaked on rusty hinges.

Jefferson led Nicholls and Jenny down the crude stairway of logs buried into the steep hillside and through a high latticed gate which gave onto Magazine Gap Road across a culvert. One way the road curved upwards past the gate where the police had their cordon; to the left it dropped sharply towards the zoo and the teeming warrens of shops and houses on the stepped levels of Sheung Wan. The officer Jefferson had rushed to the escape route stood with hands on hips looking puzzled, the magnificent harbour sparkling below him. He shrugged his shoulders at his superior. Drivers were slowing to rubberneck.

'Get me my car,' Jefferson commanded, his eyes raking the road in both directions, his mind evaluating Moore's limited options.

'He wouldn't have risked going uphill, past the bungalow. Has to be that way,' he said, pointing to the city. A green Rover squealed to a stop.

'Get in,' he ordered Nicholls and Jenny, stabbing a portable siren to the roof. 'You know what he looks like. I only had a five-minute view, mostly of the side of his head.'

'He must have got a ride,' Jenny said. 'He couldn't have got more than a hundred yards with a limp like that.'

Jefferson spoke into the radio, ordering motorcycles to peel off and check May Road and Tregunter Path and when his car had negotiated the tricky hairpin bends ahead of the botanical gardens he sent a police car into Garden Road and Cotton Tree Drive.

'Or the bus,' Nicholls said, as a crowded doubledecker drew alongside them on an overpass.

'Could be,' Jefferson agreed. 'There was a stop twenty yards or so from the gate. Pull the bus over,' he said to his Chinese driver.

They watched the rough, oily face of the bus driver relax when he realized he was not in trouble from the young officer who had leapt from the saloon. Then their driver was back and they were once again in the traffic, their eyes searching the pavements and sidestreets as they passed.

The driver said, 'Only one bus on this route. Takes Robinson road and finishes in Bonham. No *guailo* on his bus. The bus in front is ten minutes ahead. Just reaching terminus.'

'Go for it,' Jefferson said drily, activating the siren.

Trees and landscaped greenery gave way quickly to the upper levels of the living city state with weathered tenements, cramped workshops and a thousand shops and restaurants lodged on steep inclines divided by flights of steps. Crowds were thickening.

'Slow down,' Jenny said irritably where the road widened. She'd been an arm's length from the man who had destroyed her brother's life and now he'd escaped. A final, stupid mistake and she blamed herself for not hearing Kevin agree to Moore's return to the house. 'We can't see him at this speed.'

The driver indicated a bus drawn into a layby in the busy road. A truck with a high-sided cargo obscured the upper deck but the head of a male foreigner rose above the passengers who milled around the rear entrance. The police driver braked and pointed enthusiastically.

'It's not him. Moore's fatter in the face, darker hair,' Nicholls said.

They crawled forward, creating an impatient, protesting chain behind them.

'Hold it a second,' Nicholls said looking back. 'That bus is emptying.' He leaned over the seat rest and spoke to the driver. 'You said the bus terminates along here somewhere. Was that it back there? The last stop.'

'Suppose so,' the driver said. 'People walk to Central. Go shopping.'

'Go back,' Jefferson ordered brusquely, and he clung to the seat-belt hinge as the car swung and lurched on its suspension, the tyres screeching as they struggled for a grip. Three blue patrol cars and a swarm of motorcycles returning from the secret dealing room gathered around the bus. He ordered the officers to disperse, to search for and detain a limping *guailo* with a walking stick. He couldn't tell them it was a long shot. The man could have found a taxi, be in an airport check-in by now. The detective had put out an alert at the obvious exits but more than likely Moore had gone to ground until he could organize a safe departure.

'Find the crew that brought this bus in,' he ordered his driver when it became clear they had left the area for a break.

Carved into the hillside which rises from Victoria Harbour to the Peak, the streets of Sai Ying Pun buzzed with the relentless life of Hong Kong as shoppers struggled for space among the traders and their stalls which packed the streets and breathtakingly steep steps. Jenny followed Nicholls down a flight, stopping where an alley joined on a broad landing and, back to back, swept the crowds with long, urgent gazes.

'He must have been on that bus,' he concluded. 'He would have been caught if he'd walked.'

'Or a taxi,' Jenny said.

He nodded. 'In which case he's long gone. But taxi's don't cruise the quiet roads up around the bungalow. Let's imagine he was lucky when the bus came.'

'And unlucky when it reached the end of its route after a couple of miles.' Jenny commented.

Tony Moore's left side throbbed with pain, from the hip

along the line of his leg, as the tension, fear and anxiety welled inside his heavy frame. His good fortune had held when he made the desperate dash from the cover of the hidden gateway to the bus heaving to a stop on the quiet hillside. He relaxed as it rolled towards the city and then cursed when it ended its route less then ten minutes from the bungalow. But it was in central Hong Kong, and he knew the swamp of humanity would suck him in and hide him.

He missed the sturdy blackthorn walking stick Nicholls had bought him. It had been a mistake not to leave it with the body of Sam Collier. Finally he had to sacrifice it, give his disappearance credibility by having a Koga contact put it in Moore's car when Nicholls persisted in sniffing for it. The bog standard stick with the metal tip he had bought to replace it slipped in his grip as he struggled on the inclines.

The merchants and the shoppers ignored the sweating *guailo* resting in the musty darkness of a doorway behind the street stalls. He heard a police siren somewhere above him, where the steps reached a wide plateau, and forced his dealer's mind to line up the alternatives in the seconds that remained before the price changed against him. A thirty-minute taxi ride would take him to Kai Tak airport but he knew his name was already flashing on the immigration officers' screens. To hide in a cheap Kowloon hotel would buy him a few days until his face, screaming from every tacky tabloid and television screen, tempted a local to turn in a detested foreigner for a small wedge of dollars. He needed to stretch his luck one last time and opted to make for the Macao hydrofoil, or one of the conventional ferries. If it held, the luck that had protected him in Japan, swelled his bank acccounts, given him Emi Mori and kept the legal vultures in the

States away from him, had only to help him drag his aching body undetected to the ferry landing. He could make it in twenty minutes. It was just possible the police might overlook this little outlet to the old Portuguese colony. Downhill all the way, he thought, managing a smile as he contemplated the hurdle spreading below him in the shape of a hundred steps.

'He's taken a cab,' Jenny concluded morosely, hands on hips as Chinese sidled past her at shoulder height.

'Maybe,' Nicholls agreed reluctantly. 'When he got off the bus.'

'Does he know Hong Kong?'

'He's been here often on business so he's got a reasonable feel for the place.'

They walked through a crowded alley, narrowed by opened store fronts and stalls, down a flight of steps and along a short passage to the next parallel set of steps. Holding Jenny's hand, Nicholls checked his footing on the worn stairs before raking the crowds for a head bobbing above the others. Then he felt her grip tighten painfully and her body tense against his.

'Look over there,' she breathed urgently.

He followed her arm. They had reached a broad landing where alleys crossed and she was pointing into one of them, towards the back of a head half hidden behind racks of bags and other leather goods. Jenny's voice was drowned by the babble and the cries of the hawkers. The man, if it was one, disappeared in the swell of the crowd.

'Let's check it anyway,' she urged, tugging him forcefully towards the passage.

His hip had locked, causing his left foot to drag lifelessly behind him. Excruciating pain seared through his limbs each time he took the full weight of his body and levered himself further towards safety. The deep cascade of steps at the end of the alley would take him close to sea level he guessed as he rested again in a doorway haven. His mind and complete concentration were fixed on his laboured propulsion and when he lurched carelessly into a gap in the trail of people crossing the passage he gave Nicholls and the American woman a clear flash of his retreating figure.

'Tony!' Nicholls bellowed instinctively and stupidly. Tony Moore turned once and let the crowds swallow him. His pursuers danced and weaved in frustration, unable to reach the man they wanted for their own desperate reasons.

With Emi Mori Moore's body strength had responded to the pleasure and the release but now it was ebbing rapidly, protesting at the racking excesses of the getaway as he poised himself to take the steps, somehow in twos. On the rise, where the last short flight topped, a uniformed policeman had seen the disturbance in the pattern of the crowd movement before he too saw what looked like the foreigner they were seeking. He shouted to a colleague in gunfire Cantonese who passed the word along the sweep of the search line. Jefferson elbowed a way through the people when he heard the call. He reached a corner at the head of the steps as outbursts of shouting and high pitched panicky women's voices rose above the normal easy rumble of the crowd. Then a frenzied scream froze him.

Tony Moore was using his stick like a short pole-vault, to support him and carry his weight as he lowered himself down the steps in long, ambitious drops. Sweat stung his eyes and his heart thumped in protest at the effort. On the third set of steps he failed.

The steps were uneven and slick from wear, and when he stabbed the ground with the stick, his concentration ruffled by the police whistles and the idea of Nicholls somewhere close behind him, it shot away from him as if kicked maliciously. With his bodyweight committed forward, Moore's last conscious image was of suspension in air, his final mortal thought disbelief.

Nicholls heard the sharp crack as the back of Moore's head split on the splintered concrete edge and he watched in horrified fascination as his bulk rolled in a mass of disjointed limbs, falling an entire flight, scattering pedestrians and spraying blood, before settling on a landing, broken and bleeding from the gash in his skull and from his nose and ears.

Jenny saw the ironic scene evolve like a dream sequence, her mind numbed, her senses oblivious to the noise and the chaos and the crowd which, quickly swelling, consumed the broken body of Tony Moore.

Moore was kept alive for several hours but he never regained consciousness. The damage to his brain was irreparable; the life-support machine was quietly disconnected.

Nicholls was an arm's length away when Moore fell, and he would later reflect and be grateful that he did not give cause for doubt on the manner of his death. Witnesses said that Tony Moore was alone and untouched when he missed his footing. Nicholls was glad neither he nor Jenny had had the choice of holding on to him or shoving him down.

EPILOGUE

Investigators in eight countries worked for two years, piecing together the components of the blackmail and money laundering enterprise Katsuro Koga and Osamu Takagi had built across the boundaries of what the world knew as the foreign exchange market. Legitimate Ohyama Bank subsidiaries in Hong Kong, Panama and Zurich were unwittingly implicated in the establishment of paper companies in tropical safe havens and cooler European climes on behalf of Takagi's underworld syndicate and Pacific Impact Trader, the funds management vehicle to be run by Tony Moore which had been crushed at birth.

It was impossible to track and trace all the money the conspirators had quietly remitted from Japan in the years before they employed Tony Moore and Anton Landau to manage it. Prospective investors with money accumulated outside the range of any regulatory authority quickly severed any connection with *Pacific Impact Trader* and diverted their sensitive wealth to other discreet hedge fund managers.

Japanese prosecutors were slow to proceed as the defendants produced the usual obstacles to justice. There were quiet calls from political friends of the president of the Ohyama Bank; Fujimori went into hospital with a mystery illness which kept him from interrogation for four months; a newspaper whose shareholders included eleven Ohyama group companies suggested a deliberate attempt by foreign sources to destabilize Japan's currency and profit from its vulnerability.

Beyond the obstructions, the prosecutors found some vaguely familiar patterns in the complex and twisted financial labyrinth. Money from criminal activities in Japan had been washed into the Tokyo stock market through real estate and other dubious fronts and then as second generation legitimate funds used to invest in US government stocks, Hawaiian condominiums and Australian real estate. Illicit arrangements in several top Japanese securities brokers ensured that Takagi's investments received special treatment which insured them against losses if the stock market plunged. Other funds were channelled abroad through the Ohyama Bank and its compliant group companies. The legitimacy of these remittances was easily justified and approved. The plan was that every time an overseas asset was sold the cash proceeds would be channelled to an offshore account in the Cayman Islands, and other discreet locations, and managed through the foreign exchange markets from Hong Kong by Tony Moore and Anton Landau. Occasional, but very timely, inside information from Koga's network of blackmailed officials in the key central banks would ensure that the profits on funds employed would be spectacular.

When the offshore operation was fully established, and the missing Federal Reserve link in place, the principal conspirators, Katsuro Koga, Masaaki Fujimori, Michiko Momoyama and her daughter, known as Emi Mori, planned to move overseas before the inevitable mistake occurred and their liberty was threatened at home. Momoyama, the Peach Lady, would follow Koga: her daughter would live with Tony Moore while their intense mutual physical attraction survived. Gervase Prideaux had already bought a house in Sydney with his share of profits earned so far but was reluctant to leave his country house and golf course in Britain just yet. The same for Osamu Takagi. He needed more time to nurture a successor before he could betray his father's memory and move abroad, although he could always justify moving by saying he had to supervise the syndicate's offshoots in

Honolulu, Los Angeles and New York. Naomi Honda, probably the most devious of the conspirators according to one prosecutor, may have thought of swinging in more than one direction once she realized the operation was in jeopardy. But if she had debated the options in her mind, in the end she chose wrongly. Cash in hand was the only stimulus she needed and she had tried to sell Kevin Nicholls and his friends for a briefcase full of yen.

Kevin Nicholls returned to Japan to give evidence and when Sternberg Chance re-organized its worldwide dealing activities he was appointed head of treasury for the Far East, based in Tokyo.

Jenny Collier went from Hong Kong to Chicago to bury her brother's ashes. Returning to Tokyo to give evidence, she quickly became a minor celebrity in a country obsessed with blonde Caucasian women and accepted an offer to work for a local newspaper. She progressed to television and later became a media personality, picking up a working knowledge of the language with unusual alacrity.

Araki documented the events, stretching them over six articles in *One Point Finance* and later a book. There was some debate as to who had fired the gun which immobilized the *yakuza* killer. The comrades from three countries said it was Araki, who modestly took the credit; the criminals said it was the *gaijin* woman but nobody believed them.

Araki led the campaign for compensation on behalf of the relatives of the two victims. The Ohyama Bank agreed to a quiet settlement of three hundred million yen with the widow of Hiroyuki Hirata and the entire board of directors took a ten per cent salary cut for six months as a gesture of remorse and responsibility. This was expected in Japan.

POCKET
B O O K S

CONTENTS UNDER PRESSURE
Edna Buchanan

'Buchanan is a skilled writer and builds a terrific pace' *Sunday Telegraph*

When a black football star dies suspiciously following a police car chase, tough crime reporter Britt Montero suspects a cover-up and is determined to dig for the truth – despite warnings to stay away.

From the high intensity of the newsroom Montero's investigations soon lead her to danger – riding the deadly midnight beat with the cops, entering the outraged black community which threatens to erupt into violence, and taking a forbidden lover, a man she cannot trust.

POCKET BOOKS
Fiction
ISBN: 0 671 85097 0
£4.99

POCKET
B O O K S

THE CHESHIRE MOON
ROBERT FERRIGNO

'A gripping new novel' *The New York Times*

When Quinn, a hot journalist, still running from the
killing that nearly ended his career, and Jake Takamura,
a photographer who snaps war crimes for breakfast,
team up in the heat of Los Angeles, the trouble comes
looking, faster than flies. It begins with a gruesome
killing, and before long the news hounds are running
out of control, chasing the long-dead trail of a film
star's evil past, a chat show hostesses grimy present and
the terrifying future of a semi-crippled monster pumped
full of steroids and hate. They might even be related –
but first t hey have to be stopped…

**'Ferrigno is a skilled narrator and introduces the
twists and turns in a way that makes the story
utterly compulsive'** *For Him*

POCKET BOOKS
Fiction
ISBN: 0 671 85084 9
£4.99

POCKET
B O O K S

FLAMES OF HEAVEN
RALPH PETERS

A vivid, richly textured novel of the disintegration of
the Soviet Union, from the fall of the Berlin Wall to the
coup of August 1991.

The liaison between Sasha Leskov, an artist, and Shirin
Talala, the beautiful and mysterious daughter of Ali
Talala, an Uzbek mafia chieftain, is doomed from the
start by their uncontrollable passions which blind them
to reason, and by their tragically crossed affiliations:
Shirin's father is wanted by the KGB for his bloody,
merciless crimes, and Sasha's brother Pavel Leskov is
the KGB colonel assigned to get him – and his family.

With an epic novel as vast and turbulent as Russia
itself, New York Times bestseller, soldier and writer
Ralph Peters, takes us into the heart of a violent people
swept into the vortex of history.

'A master storyteller' *Washington Post*

POCKET BOOKS
FICTION
ISBN: 0 671 85090 3
PRICE: £4.99

POCKET
B O O K S

THE HORSE LATITUDES
ROBERT FERRIGNO

'Rivals Carl Hiaasen at full tilt' *The Sunday Times*

Danny DiMedici's ex-wife Laura is missing, there's a
corpse in her blood-splattered beach house, and Danny
is prime suspect. Desperate to get to Laura before the
cops, Danny returns to the underworld he had known as
a drug-dealer, a world of fast sex and hard drugs, casual
violence and sudden death. From rich beauties with a
taste for perversion to body builders high on
testosterone kicks, Danny walks the knife-edge between
law and order and dark dealings, but as the line begins
to blur he must decide, once and for all, where he
stands.

**'An illuminating novel that never fails to entertain
but also, surprisingly, makes us feel'** *Time*

POCKET BOOKS
FICTION
ISBN: 0 671 85241 8
PRICE: £4.99